samuel r. delany

babel-17

Samuel R. Delany was born in 1942 and grew up in New York City's Harlem. His first novel appeared when he was twenty. His sixth, *Babel-17*, completed when he was twenty-three, won him the first of his four Nebula Awards, as best science fiction novel of its year. More recently he was the author of the bestselling nonfiction study, *Times Square Red, Times Square Blue* (1999) as well as the essay collections *Longer Views* (1996) and *Shorter Views* (1999). Currently he is a professor of English and creative writing at Temple University in Philadelphia.

Also by Samuel R. Delany

babel-17

babel-17

samuel r. delany

Vintage Books
A Division of Random House, Inc.
New York

FIRST VINTAGE BOOKS EDITION, DECEMBER 2001

All epigraphs in *Babel-17* are from poems by Marilyn Hacker. Most of those excerpted were later included in her collections *Presentation Piece* (Viking Press, New York, 1974) and *Separations* (Alfred A. Knopf, New York, 1976). A few lines are earlier versions of those to be found in the volume collections.

Library of Congress Cataloging-in-Publication Data
Delany, Samuel R.
Babel-17 / Samuel R. Delany.
p. cm.
ISBN 0-375-70669-0 (pbk.)
1. Language and languages—Fiction.   2. Women linguists—Fiction.
3. Women poets—Fiction.   I. Title: Babel-seventeen.   II. Title.
PS3554.E437 B33 2001
813'.54—dc21   2001025844

Author photograph by James Hamilton
Book design by Robert Bull Design

www.vintagebooks.com

Printed in the United States of America
10 9 8 7 6 5 4 3 2 1

*—this one, now, is
for Bob Folsom,
to explain just a little of
the past year—*

NOTE

All epigraphs in *Babel-17* are from the poems of Marilyn Hacker. Most were excerpted from poems later included in *Presentation Piece* (by Marilyn Hacker, Viking Press: New York, 1974) and *Separations* (by Marilyn Hacker, Alfred A. Knopf: New York, 1976). A few lines here are earlier versions of those to be found in the volume collections.

—S.R.D.

part one

rydra wong

. . . Here is the hub of ambiguity.
Electric spectra splash across the street.
Equivocation knots the shadowed features
of boys who are not boys; a quirk of darkness
shrivels a full mouth to senility
or pares it to a razor-edge, pours acid
across an amber cheek, fingers
a crotch, or smashes in the pelvic arch
and wells a dark clot oozing in a chest
dispelled with motion or a flare of light
that swells the lips and dribbles them with blood.
They say the hustlers paint their lips with blood.
They say the same crowd surges up the street
and surges down again, like driftwood borne
tidewise ashore and sucked away with backwash,
only to slap into the sand again,
only to be jerked out and spun away.
Driftwood; the narrow hips, the liquid eyes,
the wideflung shoulders and the rough-cast hands,
the gray-faced jackals kneeling to their prey.
The colors disappear at break of day
when stragglers toward the west riverdocks meet
young sailors ambling shipward on the street . . .
—from *Prism and Lens*

1

It's a port city.

Here fumes rust the sky, the General thought. Industrial gases flushed the evening with oranges, salmons, purples with too much red. West, ascending and descending transports, shuttling cargoes to stellarcenters and satellites, lacerated the clouds. It's a rotten poor city too, thought the General, turning the corner by the garbage-strewn curb.

Since the Invasion six ruinous embargoes for months apiece had strangled this city whose lifeline must pulse with interstellar commerce to survive. Sequestered, how could this city exist? Six times in twenty years he'd asked himself that. Answer? It couldn't.

Panics, riots, burnings, twice cannibalism—

The General looked from the silhouetted loading-towers that jutted behind the rickety monorail to the grimy buildings. The streets were smaller here, cluttered with Transport workers, loaders, a few stellarmen in green uniforms, and the horde of pale, proper men and women who managed the intricate sprawl of customs operations. They are quiet now, intent on home or work, the General thought. Yet all these people have lived for two decades under the Invasion. They've starved during the embargoes, broken windows, looted, run screaming before fire-hoses, torn flesh from a corpse's arm with decalcified teeth.

Who is this animal man? He asked himself the abstract question to blur the lines of memory. It was easier, being a general, to ask about the "animal man" than about the woman who had sat in the middle of the sidewalk during the last embargo holding her skeletal baby by one leg, or the three scrawny teenage girls who had attacked him on the street with razors (—she had hissed through brown teeth, the bar of metal glistening toward his chest, "Come here, Beefsteak! Come get me, Lunch meat . . ." He had used karate—) or the blind man who had walked up the avenue, screaming.

Pale and proper men and women now, who spoke softly, who always hesitated before they let an expression fix their faces, with pale, proper, patriotic ideas: work for victory over the Invaders; Alona Star and Kip Rhyak were great in "Stellar Holliday" but Ronald Quar was the best serious actor around. They listened to Hi Lite's music (or did they listen, wondered the General, during those slow dances where no one touched). A position in Customs was a good secure job.

Working directly in Transport was probably more exciting and fun to watch in the movies; but really, such strange people—

Those with more intelligence and sophistication discussed Rydra Wong's poetry.

They spoke of the Invasion often, with some hundred phrases consecrated by twenty years' repetition on newscasts and in the papers. They referred to the embargoes seldom, and only by the one word.

Take any of them, take any million. Who are they? What do they want? What would they say if given a chance to say anything?

Rydra Wong has become this age's voice. The General recalled the glib line from a hyperbolic review. Paradoxical: a military leader with a military goal, he was going to meet Rydra Wong now.

The streetlights came on and his image glazed on the plate glass window of the bar. That's right, I'm not wearing my uniform this evening. He saw a tall, muscular man with the authority of half a century in his craggy face. He was uncomfortable in the gray civilian suit. Till age thirty, the physical impression he had left with people was "big and bumbling." Afterwards—the change had coincided with the Invasion—it was "massive and authoritarian."

Had Rydra Wong come to see him at Administrative Alliance Headquarters, he would have felt secure. But he was in civvies, not in stellarman-green. The bar was new to him. And she was the most famous poet in five explored galaxies. For the first time in a long while he felt bumbling again.

He went inside.

And whispered, "My God, she's beautiful," without even having to pick her from among the other women. "I didn't know she was so beautiful, not from the pictures . . ."

She turned to him (as the figure in the mirror behind the counter caught sight of him and turned away), stood up from the stool, smiled.

He walked forward, took her hand, the words *Good evening, Miss Wong,* tumbling on his tongue till he swallowed them unspoken. And now she was about to speak.

She wore copper lipstick, and the pupils of her eyes were beaten disks of copper—

"Babel-17," she said. "I haven't solved it yet, General Forester."

A knitted indigo dress, and her hair like fast water at night spilling one shoulder; he said, "That doesn't really surprise us, Miss Wong."

Surprise, he thought. She puts her hand on the bar, she leans back on the stool, hip moving in knitted blue, and with each movement, I am amazed, surprised, bewildered. Can I be this off guard, or can she really be that—

"But I've gotten further than you people at Military have been able to." The gentle line of her mouth bowed with gentler laughter.

"From what I've been led to expect of you, Miss Wong, that doesn't surprise me either." Who is she? he thought. He had asked the question of the abstract population. He had asked it of his own reflected image. He asked it of her now, thinking, No one else matters, but I must know about her. That's important. I have to know.

"First of all, General," she was saying, "Babel-17 isn't a code."

His mind skidded back to the subject and arrived teetering. "Not a code? But I thought Cryptography had at least established—" He stopped, because he wasn't sure what Cryptography had established, and because he needed another moment to haul himself down from the ledges of her high cheekbones, to retreat from the caves of her eyes. Tightening the muscles of his face, he marshaled his thoughts to Babel-17. The Invasion: Babel-17 might be one key to ending this twenty-year scourge. "You mean we've just been trying to decipher a lot of nonsense?"

"It's not a code," she repeated. "It's a language."

The General frowned. "Well, whatever you call it, code or language, we still have to figure out what it says. As long as we don't understand it, we're a hell of a way from where we should be." The exhaustion and pressure of the last months homed in his belly, a secret beast to strike the back of his tongue, harshening his words.

Her smile had left, and both hands were on the counter. He wanted to retract the harshness. She said, "You're not directly connected with the Cryptography Department." The voice was even, calming.

He shook his head.

"Then let me tell you this. Basically, General Forester, there are two types of codes, ciphers, and true codes. In the first, letters, or symbols that stand for letters, are shuffled and juggled according to a pattern. In the second, letters, words, or groups of words are replaced by other letters, symbols, or words. A code can be one type or the other, or a combination. But both have this in common: once you find the key, you just plug it in and out come logical sentences. A language, however, has its own internal logic, its own grammar, its own way of putting thoughts together with words that span various spectra of meaning. There is no key you can plug in to unlock the exact meaning. At best you can get a close approximation."

"Do you mean that Babel-17 decodes into some other language?"

"Not at all. That's the first thing I checked. We can take a probability scan on various elements and see if they are congruent with other language patterns, even if these elements are in the wrong order. No. Babel-17 is a language itself which we do not understand."

"I think—" General Forester tried to smile—"what you're trying to tell me is that because it isn't a code, but rather an alien language, we might as well give up." If this were defeat, receiving it from her was almost relief.

But she shook her head. "I'm afraid that's not what I'm saying at all. Unknown languages have been deciphered without translations, Linear B and Hittite for example. But if I'm to get further with Babel-17, I'll have to know a great deal more."

The General raised his eyebrows. "What more do you need to know? We've given you all our samples. When we get more, we'll certainly—"

"General, I have to know everything you know about Babel-17; where you got it, when, under what circumstances, anything that might give me a clue to the subject matter."

"We've released all the information that we—"

"You gave me ten pages of double-spaced typewritten garble with the code name Babel-17 and asked me what it meant. With just that I can't tell you. With more, I might. It's that simple."

He thought: If it were that simple, if it were only that simple, we would never have called you in about it, Rydra Wong.

She said: "If it were that simple, if it were only that simple, you would never have called me in about it, General Forester."

He started, for one absurd moment convinced she had read his mind. But of course, she would know that. Wouldn't she?

"General Forester, has your Cryptography Department even discovered it's a language?"

"If they have, they haven't told me."

"I'm fairly sure they don't know. I've made a few structural inroads on the grammar. Have they done that?"

"No."

"General, although they know a hell of a lot about codes, they know nothing of the nature of language. That sort of idiotic specialization is one of the reasons I haven't worked with them for the past six years."

Who is she? he thought again. A security dossier had been handed him that morning, but he had passed it to his aide and merely noted, later, that it had been marked "approved." He heard himself say, "Perhaps if you could tell me a little about yourself, Miss Wong, I could speak more freely with you." Illogical, yet he'd spoken it with measured calm and surety. Was her expression quizzical?

"What do you want to know?"

"What I already know is only this: your name, and that some time ago you worked for Military Cryptography. I know that even though you left when very young, you had enough of a reputation so that, six years later, the people who remembered you said unanimously—after they had struggled with Babel-17 for a month—'Send it to Rydra Wong.'" He paused. "And you tell me you have gotten someplace with it. So they were right."

"Let's have drinks," she said.

The bartender drifted forward, drifted back, leaving two small glasses of smoky green. She sipped, watching him. Her eyes, he thought, slant like astounded wings.

"I'm not from Earth," she said. "My father was a Communications engineer at Stellarcenter X-11-B just beyond Uranus. My mother was a translator for the Court of Outer Worlds. Until I was seven I was the spoiled brat of the Stellarcenter. There weren't many children. We moved rockside to Uranus-XXVII in '52. By the time I was twelve, I knew seven Earth languages and could make myself understood in five extraterrestrial tongues. I pick up languages like most people pick up the lyrics to popular songs. I lost both parents during the second embargo."

"You were on Uranus during the embargo?"

"You know what happened?"

"I know the Outer Planets were hit a lot harder than the Inner."

"Then you don't know. But, yes, they were." She drew a breath as memory surprised her. "One drink isn't enough to make me talk about it, though. When I came out of the hospital, there was a chance I may have had brain damage."

"Brain damage—?"

"Malnutrition you know about. Add neurosciatic plague."

"I know about plague, too."

"Anyway, I came to Earth to stay with an aunt and uncle here and receive neurotherapy. Only I didn't need it. And I don't know whether it was psychological or physiological, but I came out of the whole business with total verbal recall. I'd been bordering on it all my life so it wasn't too odd. But I also had perfect pitch."

"Doesn't that usually go along with lightning calculation and eidetic memory? I can see how all of them would be of use to a cryptographer."

"I'm a good mathematician, but no lightning calculator. I test high on visual conception and special relations—dream in technicolor and all that—but the total recall is strictly verbal. I had already begun writing. During the summer I got a job translating with the government and began to bone up on codes. In a little while I discovered that I had a certain knack. I'm not a good cryptographer. I don't have the patience to work that hard on anything written down that I didn't write myself. Neurotic as hell; that's another reason I gave it up for poetry. But the 'knack' was sort of frightening. Somehow, when I had too much work to do, and somewhere else I really wanted to be, and was scared my supervisor would start getting on my neck, suddenly everything I knew about communication would come together in my head, and it was easier to read the thing in front of me and say what it said than to be that scared and tired and miserable."

She glanced at her drink.

"Eventually the knack almost got to where I could control it. By then I was nineteen and had a reputation as the little girl who could crack anything. I guess it was knowing something about language that did it, being more facile at recognizing patterns—like distinguishing grammatical order from random rearrangement by feel, which is what I did with Babel-17."

"Why did you leave?"

"I've given you two reasons. A third is simply that when I mastered the knack, I wanted to use it for my own purposes. At nineteen, I quit the Military and, well, got . . . married, and started writing seriously. Three years later my first book came out." She shrugged, smiled. "For anything after that, read the poems. It's all there."

"And on the worlds of five galaxies, now, people delve your imagery and meaning for the answers to the riddles of language, love, and isolation." The three words jumped his sentence like vagabonds on a boxcar. She was before him, and was talking; here, divorced from the military, he felt desperately isolated; and he was desperately in . . . No!

That was impossible and ridiculous and too simple to explain what coursed and pulsed behind his eyes, inside his hands.

"Another drink?" Automatic defense. But she will take it for automatic politeness. Will she? The bartender came, left.

"The worlds of five galaxies," she repeated. "That's so strange. I'm only twenty-six." Her eyes fixed somewhere behind the mirror. She was only half-through her first drink.

"By the time Keats was your age, he was dead."

She shrugged. "This is an odd epoch. It takes heroes very suddenly, very young, then drops them just as quickly."

He nodded, recalling half a dozen singers, actors, even writers in their late teens or early twenties who had been named genius for a year, two, three, only to disappear. Her reputation was only a phenomenon of three years' duration.

"I'm part of my times," she said. "I'd like to transcend my times, but the times themselves have a good deal to do with who I am." Her hand retreated across the mahogany from her glass. "You in Military, it must be much the same." She raised her head. "Have I given you what you want?"

He nodded. It was easier to lie with a gesture than a word.

"Good. Now, General Forester, what's Babel-17?"

He looked around for the bartender, but a glow brought his eyes back to her face: the glow was simply her smile, but from the corner of his eye he had actually mistaken it for a light. "Here," she said, pushing her second drink, untouched, to him. "I won't finish this."

He took it, sipped. "The Invasion, Miss Wong . . . it's got to be involved with the Invasion."

She leaned on one arm, listening with narrowing eyes.

"It started with a series of accidents—well, at first they seemed like accidents. Now we're sure it's sabotage. They've occurred all over the Alliance regularly since December '68. Some on warships, some in Space Navy Yards, usually involving the failure of some important equipment. Twice, explosions have caused the death of important officials. Several times these 'accidents' have happened in industrial plants producing essential war products."

"What connects all these 'accidents,' other than that they touched on the war? With our economy working this way, it would be difficult for any major industrial accident not to affect the war."

"The thing that connects them all, Miss Wong, is Babel-17."

He watched her finish her drink and set the glass precisely on the wet circle.

"Just before, during, and immediately after each accident, the area is flooded with radio exchanges back and forth from indefinite sources; most of them only have a carrying power of a couple of hundred yards. But there are occasional bursts through hyperstatic channels that blanket a few light-years. We have transcribed the stuff during the last three 'accidents' and given it the working title Babel-17. Now. Does that tell you anything you can use?"

"Yes. There's a good chance you're receiving radio instructions for the sabotage back and forth between whatever is directing the 'accidents'—"

"But we can't find a *thing*!" Exasperation struck. "There's nothing but that blasted gobbledygook, piping away at double speed! Finally someone noticed certain repetitions in the pattern that suggested a code. Cryptography seemed to think it was a good lead but couldn't crack it for a month; so they called you."

As he talked, he watched her think. Now she said, "General Forester, I'd like the original monitors of these radio exchanges, plus a thorough report, second by second if it's available, of those accidents timed to the tapes."

"I don't know if—"

"If you don't have such a report, make one during the next 'accident' that occurs. If this radio garbage is a conversation, I have to be able to follow what's being talked about. You may not have noticed, but, in the copy Cryptography gave me, there was no distinction as to which voice was which. In short, what I'm working with now is a transcription of a highly technical exchange run together without punctuation, or even word breaks."

"I can probably get you everything you want except the original recordings—"

"You have to. I must make my own transcription, carefully, and on my own equipment."

"We'll make a new one to your specifications."

She shook her head. "I have to do it myself, or I can't promise a thing. There's the whole problem of phonemic and allophonic distinctions. Your people didn't even realize it was a language, so it didn't occur to them—"

Now he interrupted her. "*What* sort of distinctions?"

"You know the way some Orientals confuse the sounds of R and L when they speak a Western language? That's because R and L in many Eastern languages are allophones, that is, considered the same sound, written and even heard the same—just like the *th* at the beginning of *they* and at the beginning of *theater*."

"What's different about the sound of *th*eater and *th*ey?"

"Say them again and listen. One's voiced and the other's unvoiced, they're as distinct as V and F; only they're allophones—at least in British English; so Britishers are used to hearing them as though they were the same phoneme. Now Americans, of course, have the minimal pair 'ether/either,' where the voicing alone marks the semantic difference—"

"Oh . . . !"

"But you see the problem a 'foreigner' has transcribing a language he doesn't speak; he may come out with too many distinctions of sound, or not enough."

"How do you propose to do it?"

"By what I know about the sound systems of a lot of other languages and by feel."

"The 'knack' again?"

She smiled. "I suppose."

She waited for him to grant approval. What wouldn't he have granted her? For a moment he had been distracted by her voice through subtleties of sound. "Of course, Miss Wong," he said, "you're our expert. Come to Cryptography tomorrow and you can have access to whatever you need."

"Thank you, General Forester. I'll bring my official report in then."

He stood in the static beam of her smile. I must go now, he thought desperately. Oh, let me say something more—"Fine, Miss Wong. I'll speak to you then." Something more, something—

He wrenched his body away. (I must turn from her.) Say one thing more, thank you, be you, love you. He walked to the door, his thoughts quieting: Who *is* she? Oh, the things that should have been said. I have been brusque, military, efficient. But the luxuriance of thought and word I would have given her. The door swung open and evening brushed blue fingers on his eyes.

My god, he thought, as coolness struck his face, all that inside me and she doesn't know! I didn't communicate a thing! Somewhere in the depths the words, *not a thing, you're still safe*. But stronger on the surface was the outrage at his own silence. Didn't communicate a thing at all—

Rydra stood up, her hands on the edge of the counter, looking at the mirror. The bartender came to remove the glasses at her fingertips. As he reached for them, he frowned.

"Miss Wong?"

Her face was fixed.

"Miss Wong, are you—"

Her knuckles were white, as the bartender watched, the whiteness crept along her hands till they looked like shaking wax.

"Is there something wrong, Miss Wong?"

She snapped her face toward him. "You noticed?" Her voice was a hoarse whisper, harsh, sarcastic, strained. She whirled from the bar and started toward the door, stopped once to cough, then hurried on.

---

2   "Mocky, help me!"

"Rydra?" Dr. Marksu T'mwarba pushed himself from the pillow in the darkness. Her face sprung in smoky light above the bed. "Where are you?"

"Downstairs, Mocky. Please. I've g-got to talk to you." Her agitated features moved right, left, trying to avoid his look. He squinched his eyes against the glare, then opened them slowly. "Come on up."

Her face disappeared.

He waved his hand across the control board, and soft light filled the sumptuous bedroom. He shoved back the gold quilt, stood on the fur rug, took a black silk robe from a gnarled bronze column, and as he swung it across his back the automatic contour wires wrapped the panels across his chest and straightened the shoulders. He brushed the induction bank in the rococo frame again, and aluminum flaps fell back on the sideboard. A steaming carafe and liquor decanters rolled forward.

Another gesture started bubble chairs inflating from the floor. As Dr. T'mwarba turned to the entrance cabinet, it creaked, mica wings slid out, and Rydra caught her breath.

"Coffee?" He pushed the carafe and the force-field caught it and carried it gently toward her. "What've you been doing?"

"Mocky, it . . . I . . . ?"

"Drink your coffee."

She poured a cup, lifted it halfway to her mouth. "No sedatives?"

"Crème de cacao or crème de café?" He held up two small glasses. "Unless you think alcohol is cheating, too. Oh, and there're some some franks and beans left over from dinner. I had company."

She shook her head. "Just cacao."

The tiny glass followed the coffee across the beam. "I've had a perfectly dreadful day." He folded his hands. "No work all afternoon, dinner guests who wanted to argue, and then deluged with calls from the moment they left. Just got to sleep ten minutes ago." He smiled. "How was your evening?"

"Mocky, it . . . it was terrible."

Dr. T'mwarba sipped his liqueur. "Good. Otherwise I'd never forgive you for waking me up."

In spite of herself she smiled. "I can . . . can always c-c-count on you for s-sympathy, Mocky."

"You can count on me for good sense and cogent psychiatric advice. Sympathy? I'm sorry, not after eleven-thirty. Sit down. What happened?" A final sweep of his hand brought a chair up behind her. The edge tapped the back of her knees and she sat. "Now stop stuttering and talk to me. You got over that when you were fifteen." His voice had become very gentle and very sure.

She took another sip of coffee. "The code, you remember the c-code I was working on?"

Dr. T'mwarba lowered himself to a wide leather hammock and brushed back his white hair, still awry from sleep. "I remember you were asked to work on something for the government. You were rather scornful of the business."

"Yes. And . . . well, it's not the code—which is a language, by the way—but just this evening. I t-talked to the General in charge, General Forester, and it happened . . . I mean again, it happened, and I *knew*!"

"Knew what?"

"Just like last time, knew what he was thinking!"

"You read his mind?"

"No. No, it was just like last time! I could tell, from what he was doing, what he was saying . . ."

"You've tried to explain this to me before, but I still don't understand, unless you're talking about some sort of telepathy."

She shook her head, shook it again.

Dr. T'mwarba locked his fingers and leaned back. Suddenly Rydra said in an even voice: *"Now I do have some idea of what you're trying to say, dear, but you'll have to put it in words yourself.* That's what you were about to say, Mocky, wasn't it?"

T'mwarba raised the white hedges of his eyebrows. "Yes. It was. You say you didn't read my mind? You've demonstrated this to me a dozen times—"

"I know what *you're* trying to say; and you don't know what *I'm* trying to say. It's not fair!" She nearly rose from her seat.

They said in unison: "That's why you're such a fine poet." Rydra went on, "I know, Mocky. I have to work things out carefully in my head and put them in my poems so people will understand. But that's not what I've been doing for the past ten years. You know what I do? I listen to other people, stumbling about with their half thoughts and half sentences and their clumsy feelings that they can't express—and it hurts me. So I go home and burnish it and polish it and weld it to a rhythmic frame, make the dull colors gleam, mute the garish artificiality to pastels, so it doesn't hurt anymore: that's my poem. I know what they want to say, and I say it for them."

"The voice of your age," said T'mwarba.

She said something unprintable. When she finished there were tears starting on her lower lids. "What *I* want to say, what I want to express, *I* just . . ." Again she shook her head. "I can't say it."

"If you want to keep growing as a poet, you'll have to."

She nodded. "Mocky, up till a year ago, I didn't even realize I was just saying other people's ideas. I thought they were my own."

"Every young writer who's worth anything goes through that. That's when you learn your craft."

"And now I have things to say that are all my own. They're not what other people have said before, put in an original way. And they're not just violent contradictions of what other people have said, which amounts to the same thing. They're new—and I'm scared to death."

"Every young writer who becomes a mature writer has to go through that."

"It's easy to repeat; it's hard to speak, Mocky."

"Good, if you're learning that now. Why don't you start by telling me exactly how this . . . this business of your understanding works?"

She was silent for five, stretching to ten, seconds. "All right. I'll try again. Just before I left the bar, I was standing there, looking in the mirror, and the bartender came up and asked me what was wrong."

"Could he sense you were upset?"

"He didn't 'sense' anything. He looked at my hands. They were clenched on the edge of the bar and they were turning white. He didn't have to be a genius to figure out something odd was going on in my head."

"Bartenders are pretty sensitive to that sort of signal. It's part of their job." He finished his coffee. "Your fingers were turning white? All right, what was this General saying to you, or not saying to you, that he wanted to say?"

A muscle in her cheek jumped twice, and Dr. T'mwarba thought, Should I be able to interpret that more specifically than just her nervousness?

"He was a brisk, ramrod efficient man," she explained, "probably unmarried, with a military career, and all the insecurity that implies. He was in his fifties, and feeling odd about it. He walked into the bar where we were supposed to meet; his eyes narrowed, then opened, his hand was resting against his leg, and the fingers suddenly curled, then straightened. His pace slowed as he came in, but quickened by the time he was three steps toward me—and he shook my hand like he was afraid it would break."

T'mwarba's smile turned into laughter. "He fell in love with you!"

She nodded.

"But why in the world should that upset you? I think you should be flattered."

"Oh, I was!" She leaned forward. "I *was* flattered. And I could follow the whole thing through his head. Once, when he was trying to get his mind back on the code, Babel-17, I said exactly what he was thinking, just to let him know I was so close to him. I watched the thought go by that perhaps I was reading his mind—"

"Wait a minute. This is the part I don't understand. How did you know *exactly* what he was thinking?"

She raised her hand to her jaw. "He told me, here. I said something about needing more information to crack the language. He didn't want to give it to me. I said I had to have it or I couldn't get any further, it was that simple. He raised his head just a fraction— to avoid shaking it. If he had shaken his head, with a slight pursing of the lips, what do you think he would have been saying?"

Dr. T'mwarba shrugged. "That it wasn't as simple as you thought?"

"Yes. Now he made one gesture to avoid making that one. What does that mean?"

T'mwarba shook his head.

"He avoided the gesture because he connected its not being that simple with my being there. So he raised his head instead."

"Something like: If it were that simple, we wouldn't need you," T'mwarba suggested.

"Exactly. Now, while he raised his head, there was a slight pause halfway up. Don't you see what that adds?"

"No."

"If it were that simple—now the pause—if *only* it were that simple, we wouldn't have called you in about it." She turned her hands up in her lap. "And I said it back to him; then his jaw clenched—"

"In surprise?"

"—Yes. That's when he wondered for a second if I could read his mind."

Dr. T'mwarba shook his head. "It's too exact, Rydra. What you're describing is muscle-reading, which can be pretty accurate, especially if you know the logical area the person's thoughts are centered on. But it's still too exact. Get back to why you were upset by the business. Your modesty was offended by the attention of this . . . uncouth stellarman?"

She came back with something neither modest nor couth.

Dr. T'mwarba bit the inside of his lip and wondered if she saw.

"I'm not a little girl," she said. "Besides, he wasn't thinking anything uncouth. As I said, I was flattered by the whole thing. When I pulled my little joke, I was just trying to let him know how much in key we were. I thought he was charming. And if he had been able to see as clearly as I could he would have known I had nothing but good feeling for him. Only when he left—"

Dr. T'mwarba heard roughness work back into her voice.

"—when he left, the last thing he thought was, 'She doesn't know; I haven't communicated a thing to her.'"

Her eyes darkened—no, she bent slightly forward and half-dropped her upper lids so that her eyes looked darker. He had watched that happen thousands of times since the scrawny near-autistic twelve-year-old girl had been sent to him for neurotherapy, which had developed into psychotherapy, and then into friendship. This was the first time he'd understood the mechanics of the effect. Her precision of observation had inspired him before to look more closely at others. Only since therapy had officially ended had it come full circle and made him look more closely at her. What did the darkening signify other than change? He knew there were myriad marks of personality about him that she read with a microscope. Wealthy, worldly, he had known many people equal to her in reputation. The reputation did not awe him. Often, however, she did.

"He thought I didn't understand. He thought nothing had been communicated. And I was angry. I was hurt. All the misunderstandings that tie the world up and keep people apart were quivering before me at once, waiting for me to untangle them, explain them, and I couldn't. I didn't know the words, the grammar, the syntax. And—"

Something else was happening in her Oriental face, and he strained to catch it. "Yes?"

"—Babel-17."

"The language?"

"Yes. You know what I used to call my 'knack'?"

"You mean you suddenly understood the language?"

"Well, General Forester had just told me what I had was not a monologue, but a dialogue, which I hadn't known before. That fitted in with some other things I had in the back of my mind. I realized I could tell where the voices changed myself. And then—"

"Do you understand it?"

"I understand some of it better than I did this afternoon. There's something about the language itself that scares me even more than General Forester."

Puzzlement fixed itself to T'mwarba's face. "About the language itself?"

She nodded.

"What?"

The muscle in her cheek jumped again. "For one thing, I think I know where the next accident is going to be."

"Accident?"

"Yes. The next sabotage that the Invaders are planning, if it is the Invaders, which I'm not sure of. But the language itself— it's . . . it's strange."

"How?"

"Small," she said. "Tight. Close together—That doesn't mean anything to you, does it? In a language, I mean?"

"Compactness?" asked Dr. T'mwarba. "I would think it's a good quality in a spoken language."

"Yes," and the sibilant became a breath. "Mocky, I *am* scared!"

"Why?"

"Because I'm going to try to do something, and I don't know if I can or not."

"If it's worth trying, you should be a little afraid. What is it?"

"I decided it back in the bar, and I figured out I'd better talk to somebody first. That usually means you."

"Give."

"I'm going to solve this whole Babel-17 business myself."

T'mwarba leaned his head to the right.

"Because I have to find out who speaks this language, where it comes from, and what it's trying to say."

His head went left.

"Why? Well, most textbooks say language is a mechanism for expressing thought, Mocky. But language *is* thought. Thought is information given form. The form is language. The form of this language is . . . amazing."

"What amazes you?"

"Mocky, when you learn another tongue, you learn the way another people see the world, the universe."

He nodded.

"And as I see into this language, I begin to see . . . too much."

"It sounds very poetical."

She laughed. "You always say that to me to bring me back to earth."

"Which I don't have to do too often. Good poets tend to be practical and abhor mysticism."

"Something about trying to hit reality; you figure it out," she said. "Only, as poetry tries to touch something real, maybe this *is* poetical."

"All right. I still don't understand. But how do you propose to solve the Babel-17 mystery?"

"You really want to know?" Her hands fell to her knees. "I'm going to get a spaceship, get a crew together, and get to the scene of the next accident."

"That's right, you do have Interstellar Captain's papers. Can you afford it?"

"The government's going to subsidize it."

"Oh, fine. But why?"

"I'm familiar with a half dozen languages of the Invaders. Babel-17 isn't one of them. It isn't a language of the Alliance. I want to find out who speaks this language—because I want to find out who, or what, in the Universe thinks that way. Do you think I can, Mocky?"

"Have another cup of coffee." He reached back over his shoulder and sailed the carafe across to her again. "That's a good question. There's a lot to consider. You're not the most stable person in the world. Managing a spaceship crew takes a special sort of psychology which—you have. Your papers, if I remember, were the result of that odd—eh, marriage of yours, a couple of years ago. But you only used an automatic crew. For a trip this length, won't you be managing Transport people?"

She nodded.

"Most of my dealings have been with Customs persons. You're more or less Customs."

"Both parents were Transport. I was Transport up till the time of the Embargo."

"That's true. Suppose I say, 'yes, I think you can'?"

"I'd say, 'thanks,' and leave tomorrow."

"Suppose I said I'd like a week to check over your psyche-indices with a microscope, while you took a vacation at my place, taught no classes, gave no public readings, avoided cocktail parties?"

"I'd say, 'thanks.' And leave tomorrow."

He grinned. "Then why are you bothering me?"

"Because—" She shrugged. "Because tomorrow I'm going to be busy as the devil . . . and I won't have time to say good-bye."

"Oh." The wryness of his grin relaxed into a smile.

And he thought about the myna bird again.

Rydra, thin, thirteen, and gawky, had broken through the triple doors of the conservatory with the new thing called laughter she had just discovered how to make in her mouth. And he was parental proud that the near-corpse, who had been given into his charge six months ago, was now a girl again, with boy-cropped hair and sulks and tantrums and questions and caresses for the two guinea pigs she had named Lump and Lumpkin. The air-conditioning pressed back the shrubbery to the glass wall and sun struck through the transparent roof. She had said, "What's that, Mocky?"

And he, smiling at her, sun-spotted in white shorts and superfluous halter, said, "It's a myna bird. It'll talk to you. Say hello."

The black eye was dead as a raisin with a pinhead of live light jammed in the corner. The feathers glistened and the needle beak lazed over a thick tongue. She cocked her head as the bird head cocked, and whispered, "Hello?"

Dr. T'mwarba had trained it for two weeks with fresh-dug earthworms to surprise her. The bird looked over its left shoulder and droned, *"Hello, Rydra, it's a fine day out and I'm happy."*

Screaming.

As unexpected as that.

He'd thought she'd started to laugh. But her face was contorted, she began to beat at something with her arms, stagger backwards, fall. The scream rasped in near-collapsed lungs, choked, rasped again. He ran to gather up her flailing, hysterical figure, while the drone of the bird's voice undercut her wailing: *"It's a fine day out and I'm happy."*

He'd seen acute anxiety attacks before. But this had shaken him. When she could talk about it later, she simply said—tensely, with white lips, "It frightened me!"

Which would have been it, had the damned bird not gotten loose three days later and flown up into the antenna net he and

Rydra had put up together for her amateur radio stasiscrafter, with which she could listen to the hyperstatic communications of the transport ships in this arm of the galaxy. A wing and a leg got caught, and it began to beat against one of the hot lines so that you could see the sparks even in the sunlight. "We've got to get him out of there!" Rydra had cried. Her fingertips were over her mouth, but as she looked at the bird, he could see the color draining from under her tan. "I'll take care of it, honey," he said. "You just forget about him."

"If he hits that wire a couple of more times he'll be dead!"

But he had already started inside for the ladder. When he came out, he stopped. She had shinnied four-fifths up the guy wire on the leaning catalpa tree that shaded the corner of the house. Fifteen seconds later he was watching her reach out, draw back, reach out again toward the wild feathers. He knew she wasn't afraid of the hot line, either; she'd strung it up herself. Sparks again. So she made up her mind and grabbed. A minute later she was coming across the yard, holding the rumpled bird at arm's length. Her face looked as if it had been blown across with powdered lime.

"Take it, Mocky," she said, with no voice behind her trembling lips, "before it says something and I start hollering again."

So now, thirteen years later, something else was speaking to her, and she said she was scared. He knew how scared she could be; he also knew with what bravery she could face down her fears.

He said, "Good-bye. I'm glad you woke me up. I'd be mad as a damp rooster if you hadn't come. Thank you."

"The thanks goes to you, Mocky," she said. "I'm still frightened."

3 Danil D. Appleby, who seldom thought of himself by his name—he was a Customs Officer—stared at the order through wire-framed glasses and rubbed his hand across his crew-cut red hair. "Well, it says you can, if you want to."

"And—?"

"And it is signed by General Forester."

"Then I expect you to cooperate."

"But I have to approve—"

"Then you'll come along and approve on the spot. I don't have time to send the reports in and wait for processing."

"But there's no way—"

"Yes, there is. Come with me."

"But Miss Wong, I don't walk around Transport Town at night."

"I enjoy it. Scared?"

"Not exactly. But—"

"I have to get a ship and a crew by the morning. And it's General Forester's signature. All right?"

"I suppose so . . ."

"Then come on. I have to get my crew approved."

Insistent and hesitant respectively, Rydra and the officer left the bronze and glass building.

They waited for the monorail nearly six minutes.

When they came down, the streets were narrower, and a continuous whine of transport ships fell across the sky. Warehouses and repair- and supply-shops sandwiched rickety apartments and rooming houses. A larger street cut past, rumbling with traffic, busy loaders, stellarmen. They passed neon enter-

tainments, restaurants of many worlds, bars, and brothels. In
the crush the Customs Officer pulled his shoulders in, walked
more quickly to keep up with Rydra's long-legged stride.

"Where do you intend to find—?"

"My pilot? That's who I want to pick up first." She stopped
on the corner, shoved her hands into the pockets of her leather
pants, and looked around.

"Do you have someone in mind?"

"I'm thinking of several people. This way." They turned on a
narrower street, more cluttered, more brightly lit.

"Where are we going? Do you know this section?"

But she laughed, slipped her arm through his, and, like a
dancer leading without pressure, she turned him toward an iron
stairway.

"In here?"

"Have you ever been to this place before?" she asked with an
innocent eagerness that made him feel for a moment he was
escorting her.

He shook his head.

Up from the basement café, black burst: a man, ebony-
skinned, with red and green jewels set into his chest, face, arms,
and thighs. Moist membranes, also jeweled, fell from his arms,
billowing on slender tines as he hurried up the steps.

Rydra caught his shoulder. "Hey, Lome!"

"Captain Wong!" The voice was high, the white teeth needle-
filed. He whirled to her with extending sails. Pointed ears shifted
forward. "What you here for?"

"Lome, Brass is wrestling tonight?"

"You want to see him? Aye, Skipper, with the Silver Dragon,
and it's an even match. Hey, I look for you on Deneb. I buy your
book too. Can't read much, but I buy. And I no find you. Where
you been a' six months?"

"Earthside, teaching at the University. But I'm going out again."

"You ask Brass for pilot? You heading out Specelli way?"

"That's right."

Lome dropped his black arm around her shoulder and the sail cloaked her, shimmering. "You go out Caesar, you call Lome for pilot, ever you do. Know Caesar—" He screwed his face and shook his head. "Nobody know it better."

"When I do, I will. But now it's Specelli."

"Then you do good with Brass. Work with him before?"

"We got drunk together when we were both quarantined for a week on one of the Cygnet planetoids. He seemed to know what he was talking about."

"Talk, talk, talk," Lome derided. "Yeah, I remember you, Captain who talk. You go watch that son of a dog wrestle; then you know what sort of pilot he make."

"That's what I came to do." Rydra turned to the Customs Officer, who shrank against the iron banister. (God, he thought, she's going to introduce me!) But she cocked her head with a half-smile and turned back. "I'll see you again, Lome, when I get home."

"Yeah, yeah, you say that and say that twice. But I no in six months see you." He laughed. "But I like you, lady Captain. Take me to Caesar some day, I show you."

"When I go, you go, Lome."

A needle leer. "Go, go, you say. I got go now. Bye-bye, lady Captain—" he bowed and touched his head in salute—"Captain Wong." And was gone.

"You shouldn't be afraid of him," Rydra told the Officer.

"But he's—" During his search for a word, he wondered, How did she know? "Where in five hells did he come from?"

"He's an Earthman. Though I believe he was born en route

from Arcturus to one of the Centauris. His mother was a Slug, I think, if he wasn't lying about that too. Lome tells tall tales."

"You mean all that getup is cosmetisurgery?"

"Um-hm." Rydra started down the stairs.

"But why the devil do they do that to themselves? They're all so weird. That's why decent people won't have anything to do with them."

"Sailors used to get tattoos. Besides, Lome has nothing else to do. I doubt he's had a pilot's job in forty years."

"He's not a good pilot? What was all that about the Caesar Nebula?"

"I'm sure he knows it. But he's at least a hundred and twenty years old. After eighty, your reflexes start to go, and that's the end of a pilot's career. He just shuttle-bums from port city to port city, knows everything that happens to everybody, stays good for gossip—and advice."

They entered the café on a ramp that swerved above the heads of the customers drinking at bar and table thirty feet below. Above and to the side of them, a fifty-foot sphere hovered like smoke, under spotlights. Rydra looked from the globe to the Customs Officer. "They haven't started the games yet."

"Is this where they hold those . . . *fights?*"

"That's right."

"But that's supposed to be illegal!"

"Never passed the bill. After they debated, it got shelved."

"Oh . . ."

As they descended among the jovial Transport workers, the Customs Officer blinked. Most were ordinary men and women, but the results of cosmetisurgery were numerous enough to keep his eyes leaping. "I've never *been* in a place like this before!" he whispered. Amphibian or reptilian creatures argued and laughed with griffins and metallic-skinned sphinxes.

"Leave your clothing here?" smiled the check girl. Her naked skin was candy green, her immense coif piled like pink cotton. Her breasts, navel, and lips flashed.

"I don't believe so," the Customs Officer said quickly.

"At least take your shoes and shirt off," Rydra said, slipping off her blouse. "People will think you're strange." She bent, rose and handed her sandals over the counter. She had begun to unbuckle her waist cinch when she caught his desperate look, smiled, and fastened the buckle again.

Carefully he removed jacket, vest, shirt, and undershirt. He was about to untie his shoes when someone grabbed his arm. "Hey, Customs!"

He stood up before a huge, naked man with a frown on his pocked face like a burst in rotten rind. His only ornaments were mechanical beetle lights that swarmed in patterns over his chest, shoulders, legs, and arms.

"*Eh* . . . pardon me?"

"What you doing here, Customs?"

"Sir, I am not bothering you."

"And I'm not bothering you. Have a drink, Customs. I'm being friendly."

"Thank you very much, but I'd rather—"

"I'm being friendly. You're not. If you're not gonna be friendly, Customs, I'm not gonna be friendly either."

"Well, I'm with some—" He looked helplessly at Rydra.

"Come on. Then you both have a drink. On me. Real friendly, damn it." His other hand fell toward Rydra's shoulder, but she caught his wrist. The fingers opened from the many-scaled stellarimeter grafted onto his palm. "Navigator?"

He nodded, and she let the hand go, which landed.

"Why *are* you so 'friendly' tonight?"

The intoxicated man shook his head. His hair was knotted in a stubby black braid over his left ear. "I'm just friendly with Customs here. I like *you*."

"Thanks. Buy us that drink and I'll buy you one back."

As he nodded heavily, his green eyes narrowed. He reached between her breasts and fingered up the gold disk that hung from the chain around her neck. "*Captain* Wong?"

She nodded.

"Better not mess with you, then." He laughed. "Come on, Captain, and I'll buy you and Customs here something to make you happy." They pushed their way to the bar.

What was green and came in small glasses at more respectable establishments, here was served in mugs.

"Who you betting on in the Dragon/Brass skirmish, and if you say the Dragon, I'll throw this in your face. Joking, of course, Captain."

"I'm not betting," Rydra said. "I'm hiring. You know Brass?"

"Was a navigator on his last trip. Got in a week ago."

"You're friendly for the same reason he's wrestling?"

"You might say that."

The Customs Officer scratched his collarbone and looked puzzled.

"Last trip Brass made went bust," Rydra explained to him. "The crew is out of work. Brass is on exhibit tonight." She turned again to the Navigator. "Will there be many captains bidding for him?"

He put his tongue under his upper lip, squinted one eye and dropped his head. He shrugged.

"I'm the only one you've run into?"

A nod, a large swallow of liquor.

"What's your name?"

"Calli, Navigator Two."

"Where are your One and Three?"

"Three's over there somewhere getting drunk. One was a sweet girl named Cathy O'Higgins. She's dead." He finished the drink and reached over for another one.

"My treat," Rydra said. "Why's she dead?"

"Ran into Invaders. Only people who ain't dead, Brass, me, and Three; and our Eye. Lost the whole platoon, our Slug. Damned good Slug too. Captain, that was a bad trip. The Eye, he cracked up without his Ear and Nose. They'd been discorporate for ten years together. Ron, Cathy, and me, we'd only been tripled for a couple of months. But even so . . ." He shook his head. "It was bad."

"Call your Three over," Rydra said.

"Why?"

"I'm looking for a full crew."

Calli wrinkled his forehead. "We don't got no One anymore."

"You're going to mope around here forever? Go to the Morgue."

Calli *humphed*. "You wanna see my Three, you come on."

Rydra shrugged in acquiescence, and the Customs Officer followed behind them.

"Hey, stupid, swing around."

The kid who turned on the bar stool was maybe nineteen. The Customs Officer thought of a snarl of metal bands. Calli was a large, comfortable man—

"Captain Wong, this is Ron—best Three to come out of this Solar System."

—but Ron was small, thin, with uncannily sharp muscular definition: pectorals like scored metal plates beneath drawn wax skin; stomach like ridged hosing, arms like braided cables. Even the facial muscles stood at the back of the jaw and jammed against the separate columns of his neck. He was unkempt and towheaded and sapphire-eyed, but the only cosmetisurgery evident was the bright rose growing on his shoulder. He flung out a quick smile and touched his forehead with a forefinger in salute. His nails were nub-gnawed on fingers like knotted lengths of white rope.

"Captain Wong is looking for a crew."

Ron shifted on the stool, raising his head a little; every other muscle in his body moved too, like snakes under milk.

The Customs Officer saw Rydra's eyes widen. Not understanding her reaction, he ignored it.

"Don't got no One," Ron said. His smile was quick and sad again.

"Suppose I found a One for you?"

The Navigators looked at each other.

Calli turned to Rydra and rubbed the side of his nose with his thumb. "You know the thing about a triple like us—"

Rydra's left hand caught her right. "Like this, you have to be. My choice is subject to your approval, of course."

"Well, it's pretty difficult for someone else—"

"It's impossible. But it's your choice. I just make suggestions. But my suggestions are damned good ones. What do you say?"

Calli's thumb moved from his nose to his earlobe. He shrugged. "You can't make an offer much better than that."

Rydra looked at Ron.

The kid put one foot up on the stool, hugged his knee, and peered across his patella. "I say, let's see who you suggest."

She nodded. "Fair."

"You know, jobs for broken triples aren't that easy to come by." Calli put his hand on Ron's shoulder.

"Yeah, but—"

Rydra looked up. "Let's watch the wrestling."

Along the counter, people raised their heads. At the tables, patrons released the catch in their chair arms so that the backs swung to half-recline.

Calli's mug clinked on the counter, and Ron raised both feet to the stool and leaned back against the bar.

"What are they looking at?" the Customs Officer asked. "Where's everybody—" Rydra put her hand on the back of his neck and did something so that he laughed and swung his head up. Then he sucked a great breath and let it out slowly.

The smoky, null-grav globe, hung in the vault, was shot with colored light. The room had gone dim. Thousands of watts of floodlights struck the plastic surface and gleamed on the faces below as smoke in the bright sphere faded.

"What's going to happen?" the Customs Officer asked. "Is that where they wrestle . . . ?"

Rydra brushed her hand over his mouth and he nearly swallowed his tongue, but was quiet.

And the Silver Dragon came, wings working in the smoke, silver feathers like clashed blades, scales on the grand haunches shaking. She rippled her ten-foot body and squirmed in the anti-gravity field, green lips leering, silver lids batting over green. "It's a woman!" breathed the Customs Officer.

An appreciative tattoo of finger snapping scattered through the audience.

Smoke rolled in the globe—

"That's our Brass!" whispered Calli.

—and Brass yawned and shook his head, ivory saber teeth glistening with spittle, muscles humped on shoulders and arms; brass claws unsheathed six inches from yellow plush paws. Bunched bands on his belly bent above them. The barbed tail beat on the globe's wall. His mane, sheared to prevent hand-holds, ran like water.

Calli grabbed the Customs Officer's shoulder. "Snap your fingers, man! That's *our* Brass!"

The Customs Officer, who had never been able to, nearly broke his hand trying.

The globe flared red. The two pilots turned to one another across the sphere's diameter. Voices quieted. The Customs Officer glanced from the ceiling to the people around him. Every other face was up. The Navigator Three was hunched in a fetal knot on the bar stool. Copper shifting; Rydra too dropped her eyes to glance at the lean bunched arms and straited thighs of the rose-shouldered boy.

Above, the opponents flexed and stretched, drifting. A sudden movement from the Dragon, and Brass drew back, then launched from the wall.

The Customs Officer grabbed something.

The two forms struck, grappled, spun against a wall and ricocheted. People began to stamp. Arm reached over arm, leg wrapped around leg, till Brass whirled loose from her and was hurled to the upper wall of the arena. Shaking his head, he righted. Below, alert, the Dragon twisted and writhed; anticipation jerked her wings. Brass leapt from the ceiling, reversed suddenly, and caught the Dragon with his hind feet. She staggered back, flailing. Saber teeth came together and missed.

"What are they trying to do?" the Customs Officer whispered. "How can you tell who's winning?" He looked down again: what he'd grabbed was Calli's shoulder.

"When one can throw the other against the wall and only touch the far wall himself with one limb on the ricochet," Calli explained, not looking down, "that's a fall."

The Silver Dragon snapped her body like bent metal released, and Brass shot away and spread-eagled against the globe. But as she floated back to take the shock on one hind leg, she lost her balance and the second leg touched too.

An anticipatory breath loosed in the audience. Encouraging snapping; Brass recovered, leaped, pushed her to the wall, but his rebound was too sharp and he, too, staggered on three limbs.

A twist in the center again. The Dragon snarled, stretched, shook her scales. Brass glowered, peered with eyes like gold coins hooded, spun back quaking, then leapt forward.

Silver whirled beneath his shoulder blow, hit the globe. She looked for the world as if she were trying to climb the wall.

Brass rebounded lightly, caught himself on one paw, then pushed away.

The globe flashed green, and Calli pounded the bar. "Look at him show that tinsel bitch!"

Grappling limbs braided one another, and claw caught claw till the stifled arms shook, broke apart. Two more falls that went to neither side; then the Silver Dragon came headfirst into Brass's chest, knocked him back, and recovered on tail alone. Below the crowd stamped.

"That's a foul!" Calli exclaimed, shaking the Customs Officer away. "Damn it, that's a foul!" But the globe flashed green again. Officially the second fall was hers.

Warily now they swam in the sphere. Twice the Dragon feinted, and Brass jerked aside his claws or sucked in his belly to avoid hers.

"Why don't she lay off him?" Calli demanded of the roof. "She's nagging him to death. Grapple and fight!"

As if in answer, Brass sprang, swiping her shoulder; what would have been a perfect fall got messed up because the Dragon caught his arm and he swerved off, smashing clumsily against the plastic.

"She can't do that!" This time it was the Customs Officer. He grabbed Calli again. "Can she do that? I don't think they should allow—" And he bit his tongue because Brass swung back, hauled her from the wall, flipped her between his legs, and, as she scrambled off the plastic, he bounced on his forearm and hovered centrally, flexing for the crowd.

"That's it!" cried Calli. "Two out of three!"

The globe flashed green again. Snapping broke into applause. "Did he win?" demanded the Customs Officer. "Did he win?"

"Listen! Of course he won! Hey, let's go see him. Come on, Captain!"

Rydra had already started through the crush. Ron sprang

behind her, and Calli, dragging the Customs Officer, came after. A flight of black tile steps took them into a room with couches where a few groups of men and women stood around Condor, a great gold and crimson creature, who was being made ready to fight Ebony who waited alone in the corner. The arena exit opened and Brass came in sweating.

"Hey," Calli called. "Hey, that was great, boy. And the Captain here wants to talk to you."

Brass stretched, then dropped to all fours, a low rumble in his chest. He shook his mane, then his gold eyes widened in recognition. "Ca'tain Wong!" The mouth, distended through cosmetisurgically implanted fangs, could not deal with a plosive labial unless it was voiced. "How you'd like me tonight?"

"Well enough to want you to pilot me through the Specelli." She roughed a tuft of yellow behind his ear. "You said sometime ago you'd like to show me what you could do."

"Yeah," Brass nodded. "I just think I'm dreaming." He pulled away his loin rag and swabbed his neck and arms with the bunched cloth, then caught the Customs Officer's amazed expression. "Just cosmetisurgery." He kept on swabbing.

"Hand him your psyche-rating," Rydra said, "and he'll approve you."

"That means we leave tomorrow, Ca'tain?"

"At dawn."

From his belt pouch Brass drew a thin metal card. "Here you go, Customs."

The Customs Officer scanned the runic marking. On a metal tracing plate from his back pocket, he noted the shift in stability index, but decided to integrate for the exact summation later on. Practice told him it was well above acceptable. "Miss Wong, I mean Captain Wong, what about their cards?" He turned to Calli and Ron.

Ron reached behind his neck and rubbed his scapula. "You

don't worry about us till you get a Navigator One." The hard, adolescent face held an engaging belligerence.

"We'll check them later," Rydra said. "We've got more people to find first."

"You're looking for a full crew?" asked Brass.

Rydra nodded. "What about the Eye that came back with you?"

Brass shook his head. "Lost his Ear and Nose. They were a real close tri'le, Ca'tain. He hung around maybe six hours before he went back to the Morgue."

"I see. Can you recommend anyone?"

"No one in 'articular. Just hang around the Discor'orate Sector and see what turns u'."

"If you want a crew by morning, we better start now," said Calli.

"Let's go," said Rydra.

As they walked to the ramp's foot, the Customs Officer asked, "The Discorporate Sector?"

"What about it?" Rydra was at the rear of the group.

"That's so—well, I don't like the idea."

Rydra laughed. "Because of the dead men? They won't hurt you."

"And I know *that's* illegal, for bodily persons to be in the Discorporate Sector."

"In certain parts," Rydra corrected, and the other men laughed now. "We'll stay out of the illegal sections—if we can."

"Would you like your clothes back?" the check-girl asked.

People had been stopping to congratulate Brass, pounding at his hip with appreciative fists and snapping their fingers. Now he swung his contour cape over his head. It fell to his shoulders, clasped his neck, draped under his arms and around his thick hams. Brass waved to the crowd and started up the ramp.

"You can really judge a pilot by watching him wrestle?" the officer inquired of Rydra.

She nodded. "In the ship, the pilot's nervous system is connected directly with the controls. The whole hyperstasis transit consists of him literally wrestling the stasis shifts. You judge by his reflexes, his ability to control his artificial body. An experienced Transporter can tell exactly how he'll work with hyperstasis currents."

"I'd heard about it, of course. But this was the first time I've seen it. I mean in person. It was . . . exciting."

"Yes," Rydra said, "isn't it?"

As they reached the ramp's head, lights again pierced the globe. Ebony and Condor circled in the fighting sphere.

On the sidewalk Brass dropped back, loping on all fours, to Rydra's side. "What about a Slug and a 'latoon?"

The platoon was a group of twelve who did all the mechanical jobs on the ship. Such simple work was done by the very young, so they usually needed a nursemaid: that was the Slug.

"I'd like to get a one-trip platoon if I can."

"Why so green?"

"I want to train them my way. The older groups tend to be too set."

"A one-tri' grou' can be a hell of a 'roblem to disci'line. And inefficient as 'iss, so I've heard. Never been with one myself."

"As long as there're no out-and-out nuts, I don't care. Besides, if I want one now, I can be surer of getting one by morning if I put my order in at Navy."

Brass nodded. "Your request in yet?"

"I wanted to check with my pilot first and see if you had any preferences."

They were passing a street phone on the corner lamppost.

Rydra ducked beneath the plastic hood. A minute later she was saying, "—a platoon for a run toward Specelli scheduled at dawn tomorrow. I know that it's short notice, but I don't need a particularly seasoned group. Even a one-trip will do." She looked from under the hood and winked at them. "Fine. I'll call later to get their psyche-indices for Customs approval. Yes, I have an Officer with me. Thank you."

She came from under the hood. "Closest way to the Discorporate Sector is through there."

The streets narrowed about them, twisting through one another, deserted. Then a stretch of concrete where metal turrets rose. Crossed and recrossed, wires webbed them. Pylons of bluish light dropped half shadows.

"Is this . . . ?" the Customs Officer began. Then he was quiet. Walking out, they slowed their steps. Against the darkness red light shot between towers.

"What . . . ?"

"Just a transfer. They go on all night," Calli explained. Green lightning crackled to their left.

"Transfer?"

"It's a quick exchange of energies resulting from the relocation of discorporate states," the Navigator Two volunteered glibly.

"But I still don't . . ."

They had moved between the pylons now, when a flickering coalesced. Silver latticed with red fire glimmered through industrial smog. Three figures formed: the women's sequined skeletons glittered toward them, casting hollow eyes.

Kittens clawed the Customs Officer's back, for strut work pylons gleamed behind the apparitional bellies.

"The faces," he whispered. "As soon as you look away, you can't remember what they look like. When you look at them, they look like people, but when you look away—" He caught his breath as another passed. "You can't remember . . . !" He stared after them. "Dead?" He shook his head. "You know I've been approving psyche-indices on Transport workers corporate and discorporate for ten years. And I've never been close enough to speak to a discorporate soul. Oh, I've seen pictures and occasionally passed one of the less fantastic on the street. But this . . ."

"There're some jobs—" Calli's voice was as heavy with alcohol as his shoulders with muscle—"some jobs on a transport ship you just can't give to a live human being."

"I know, I know," said the Customs Officer. "So you use dead ones."

"That's right." Calli nodded. "Like the Eye, Ear, and Nose. A live human scanning all that goes on in those hyperstasis frequencies would—well, die first and go crazy second."

"I do know the theory," the Customs Officer stated sharply.

Calli suddenly hooked the Officer's neck with his hand and pulled him close to his own pocked face. "You don't know anything, Customs." The tone was of their first exchange in the café. "Aw, you hide in your Customs cage, cage hid in the safe gravity of Earth, Earth held firm by the sun, sun fixed headlong toward Vega, all in the predicted tide of this spiral arm—" He gestured across night where the Milky Way would run over a less bright city. "And you never break free!" Suddenly he pushed the little spectacled red head away. "Ehhh! You have nothing to say to me!"

The bereaved navigator caught a guy cable slanting from support to concrete. It *twanged*. The low note set something loose in the Officer's throat which reached his mouth with the metal taste of outrage.

He would have spat it, but Rydra's copper eyes were now as close to his face as the hostile, pitted visage had been.

She said: "He was part," the words lean, calm, her eyes intent on not losing his, "of a triple, a close, precarious, emotional, and sexual relation with two other people. And one of them has just died."

The edge of her tone hued away the bulk of the Officer's anger; but a sliver escaped him: "Perverts!"

Ron put his head to the side, his musculature showing clear the double of hurt and bewilderment. "There're some jobs," he echoed Calli's syntax, "some jobs on a transport ship you just can't give to two people alone. The jobs are too complicated."

"I *know*." Then he thought, I've hurt the boy, too. Calli leaned on a girder. Something else was working in the Officer's mouth.

"*You* have something to say," Rydra said.

Surprise that she knew prized his lips. He looked from Calli to Ron, back. "I'm sorry for you."

Calli's brows raised, then returned, his expression settling. "I'm sorry for you too."

Brass reared. "There's a transfer conclave about a quarter of a mile down in the medium energy states. That would attract the sort of Eye, Ear, and Nose you want for Specelli." He grinned at the Officer through his fangs. "That's one of your illegal sections. The hallucination count goes way u', and some cor'orate egos can't handle it. But most sane 'eo'le don't have any 'roblem."

"If it's illegal, I'd just as soon wait here," the Customs Officer said. "You can just come back and pick me up. I'll approve their indices then."

Rydra nodded. Calli threw one arm around the waist of the ten-foot pilot, the other around Ron's shoulder. "Come on, Captain, if you want to get your crew by morning."

"If we don't find what we want in an hour, we'll be back anyway," she said.

The Customs Officer watched them move away between the slim towers.

4 —recall from broken banks and color of earth breaking into clear pool water her eyes; the figure blinking her eyes
and speaking.

He said: "An Officer, ma'am. A Customs Officer."

Surprise at her witty return, at first hurt, then amusement
following. He answered: "About ten years. How long have you
been discorporate?"

And she moved closer to him, her hair holding the recalled
odor of. And the sharp transparent features reminding him of.
More words from her, now, making him laugh.

"Yes, this is all very new to me. Doesn't the whole vagueness
with which everything seems to happen get you, too?"

Again her answer, both coaxing and witty.

"Well, yes," he smiled. "For you I guess it wouldn't be."

Her ease infected him; and either she reached playfully to take
his hand or he amazed himself by taking hers, and the appari-
tion was real beneath his fingers with skin as smooth as.

"You're so forward. I mean I'm not used to young women
just coming up and . . . behaving like this."

Her charming logic again explained it away, making him feel
her near, nearer, nearing, and her banter made music, a phrase
from.

"Well, yes, you're discorporate, so it doesn't matter. But—"

And her interruption was a word or a kiss or a frown or a
smile, sending not humor through him now, but luminous
amazement, fear, excitement; and the feel of her shape against
his completely new. He fought to retain it, pattern of pressure

and pressure, fading as the pressure itself faded. She was going away. She was laughing like, as though, as if. He stood, losing her laughter, replaced by whirled bewilderment in the tides of his consciousness fading—

---

5 When they returned, Brass called, "Good news! We got who we wanted."

"Crew's coming along," commented Calli.

Rydra handed him the three index cards. "They'll report to the ship discorporate two hours before—what's wrong?"

Danil D. Appleby reached to take the cards. "I . . . she . . ." and couldn't say anything else.

"Who?" Rydra asked. The concern on her face was driving away even his remaining memories, and he resented it, memories of, of.

Calli laughed. "A succubus! While we were gone, he got hustled by a succubus!"

"Yeah!" from Brass. "Look at him!" Ron laughed, too.

"It was a woman . . . I think. I can remember what *I* said—"

"How much did she take you for?" Brass asked.

"Take me?"

Ron said, "I don't think he knows."

Calli grinned at the Navigator-Three and then at the Officer. "Take a look in your billfold."

"Huh?"

"Take a look."

Incredulously he reached in his pocket. The metallic envelope flipped apart in his hands. "Ten . . . twenty . . . But I had *fifty* in here when I left the café!"

Calli slapped his thighs laughing. He loped over and encircled the Customs Officer's shoulder. "You'll end up a Transport man after that happens a couple of more times."

"But she . . . I . . ." The emptiness of his thefted recollections was real as any love loss. The rifled wallet seemed trivial. Tears banked his eyes. "But she was—" Confusion snarled the sentence's end.

"What was she, friend?" Calli asked.

"She . . . was." That was the sad entirety.

"Since discor'oration, you *can* take it with you," said Brass. "They try for it with some 'retty shady methods, too. I'd be embarrassed to tell you how many times that's ha''ened to me."

"She left you enough to get home with," Rydra said. "I'll reimburse you."

"No, I . . ."

"Come on, Captain. He paid for it, and he got his money's worth, aye, Customs?"

Choking on the embarrassment, he nodded.

"Then . . . check these ratings," Rydra said. "We still have a Slug to pick up, and a Navigator-One."

At a public phone, Rydra called back to Navy. Yes, a platoon had turned up. A Slug had been recommended along with them. "Fine," Rydra said, and handed the phone to the officer. He took the psyche-indices from the clerk and incorporated them for final integration with the Eye, Ear, and Nose cards that Rydra had given him. The Slug looked particularly favorable. "Seems to be a talented coordinator," he ventured.

"Can't have too good a Slug. Es'ecially with a new 'latoon." Brass shook his mane. "He's got to keep those kids in line."

"This one should do it. Highest compatibility index I've seen in a long while."

"What's the hostility on him?" asked Calli. "Compatibility, hell! Can he give your butt a good kick when you need it?"

The Officer shrugged. "He weighs two hundred and seventy pounds and he's only five nine. Have you met a fat person yet who wasn't mean as a rat underneath it all?"

"There you go!" Calli laughed.

"Where do we go to fix the wound?" Brass asked Rydra.

She raised her brows questioningly.

"To get a first navigator," he explained.

"To the Morgue."

Ron frowned. Calli looked puzzled. The flashing bugs collared his neck, then spilled his chest, scattering. "You know our first navigator's got to be a girl who will—"

"She will be," Rydra said.

They left the Discorporate Sector and took the monorail through the tortuous remains of Transport Town, then along the edge of the space-field. Blackness beyond the windows was flung across with blue signal lights. Ships rose on white flares, blued through distance, and became bloody stars in the rusted sky.

They joked for the first twenty minutes over the humming runners. The fluorescent ceiling dropped greenish light on their faces, in their laps. One by one, the Customs Officer watched them go silent while the side-to-side inertia became a headlong drive. He had not spoken at all, still trying to regain her face, her words, her shape. But it stayed away, frustrating as the imperative comment that leaves your mind as speech begins, and the mouth is left empty, a lost referent to love.

When they stepped onto the open platform at Thule Station, warm wind flushed from the east. The clouds had shattered under an ivory moon. Gravel and granite silvered the broken edges. Behind was the city's red mist. Before, on broken night, rose the black Morgue.

They went down the steps and walked quietly through the stone park. The garden of water and rock was eerie and empty. Nothing grew here.

At the door slabbed metal without external light blotted the darkness. "How do you get in?" the Officer asked, as they climbed the shallow steps.

Rydra lifted the Captain's pendant from her neck and placed it against a small disk. Something hummed, and light divided the entrance as the doors slid back. Rydra stepped through; the rest followed.

Calli stared at the metallic vaults overhead. "You know there's enough transport meat deep-frozen in this place to service a hundred stars and all their planets."

"And Customs people too," said the Officer.

"Does anybody ever bother to call back a Customs who decided to take a rest?" Ron asked with candid ingenuousness.

"Don't know what for," said Calli.

"It's been known to happen," responded the Officer dryly. "Occasionally."

"More rarely than with Transport," Rydra said. "As of yet, the Customs work involved in getting ships from star to star is a science. The Transport work maneuvering through hyperstasis levels is an art. In a hundred years they may both be sciences. Fine. But today a person who learns the rules of art well is a little rarer than the person who learns the rules of science. Also, there's a tradition involved. Transport people are used to dying and getting called back, working with dead men or live. This is still a little hard for Customs to take. Over here to the Suicides."

They left the main lobby for the labeled corridor that sloped up through the storage chambers. It emptied them onto a plat-form in an indirectly lighted room, racked up its hundred-foot height with glass cases, catwalked and laddered like a spider's den. In the coffins, dark shapes were rigid beneath frost-shot glass.

"What I don't understand about this whole business," the Officer whispered, "is the calling back. Can anybody who dies be made corporate again? You're right, Captain Wong, in Customs it's almost impolite to talk about things like . . . this."

"Any suicide who discorporates through regular Morgue channels can be called back. But a violent death where the Morgue just retrieves the body afterward, or the run-of-the-mill senile ending that most of us hit at a hundred and fifty or so, then you're dead forever; although there, if you pass through regular channels, your brain pattern is recorded and your thinking ability can be tapped if anyone wants it, though your consciousness is gone wherever consciousness goes."

Beside them, a twelve-foot filing crystal glowed like pink quartz. "Ron," said Rydra. "No, Ron and Calli too."

The Navigators stepped up, puzzled.

"You know some first navigator who suicided recently that you think we might—"

Rydra shook her head. She passed her hand before the filing crystal. In the concaved screen at the base, words flashed. She stilled her fingers. "Navigator Two . . ." She turned her hand. "Navigator One . . ." She paused and ran her hand in a different direction. ". . . male, male, male, female. Now, you talk to me, Calli, Ron."

"Huh? About what?"

"About yourselves, about what you want."

Rydra's eyes moved back and forth between the screen and the man and boy beside her.

"Well, huh . . . ?" Calli scratched his head.

"Pretty," said Ron. "I want her to be pretty." He leaned forward, an intense light in his blue eyes.

"Oh, yes," said Calli, "but she can't be a sweet, plump Irish girl with black hair and agate eyes and freckles that come out after four days of sun. She can't have the slightest lisp that makes you tingle even when she reels off her calculations quicker and more accurate than a computer voice, yet still lisping, or makes you tingle when she holds your head in her lap and tells you about how much she needs to feel—"

"Calli!" from Ron.

And the big man stopped with his fist against his stomach, breathing hard.

Rydra watched, her hand drifting through centimeters over the crystal's face. The names on the screen flashed back and forth.

"But pretty," Ron repeated. "And likes sports, to wrestle, I think, when we're planetside. Cathy wasn't very athletic. I always thought it would have been better, for me, if she was, see. I can talk better to people I can wrestle with. Serious though, I mean about working. And quick like Cathy could think. Only . . ."

Rydra's hand drifted down, then made a jerk motion to the left.

"Only," said Calli, his hand falling from his belly, his breath more easy, "she's got to be a whole person, a new person, not somebody who is half what we remember about somebody else."

"Yes," said Ron. "I mean if she's a good navigator, and she loves us."

". . . could love us," said Calli.

"If she was all you wanted and herself besides," asked Rydra, her head shaking between two names on the screen, "could you love her?"

The hesitation, the nod slow from the big man, quick from the boy.

Rydra's hand came down on the crystal face, and the name glowed on the screen. "Mollya Twa, Navigator One." Her coordinate numbers followed. Rydra dialed them at the desk.

Seventy-five feet overhead something glittered. One among hundreds of thousands of glass coffins was tracking from the wall above them on an inductor beam.

The recall-stage jutted up a pattern of lugs, the tips glowing. The coffin dropped, its contents obscured by streaks and hexagonal bursts of frost inside the glass. The lugs caught the template on the coffin's base. It rocked a moment, settled, clicked.

The frost melted all of a sudden, and the inside surface fogged, then ran with droplets. They stepped forward to see.

Dark band on dark. A movement beneath the glaring glass; then the glass parted, melting back from her dark, warm skin and beating, terrified eyes.

"It's all right," Calli said, touching her shoulder. She raised her head to look at his hand, then dropped back to the pillow. Ron crowded the Navigator-Two. "Hello?"

"*Eh* . . . Miss Twa?" Calli said. "You're alive now. Will you love us?"

"*Ninyi ni nani?*" Her face was puzzled. "*Nino wapi hapa?*"

Ron looked up amazed. "I don't think she speaks English."

"Yes. I know," Rydra grinned. "But other than that she's perfect. This way you'll have to get to know each other before you can say anything really foolish. She likes to wrestle, Ron."

Ron looked at the young woman in the case. Her graphite-colored hair was natural, her dark lips purpled with chill. "You wrestle?"

"*Ninyi ni nani?*" she asked again.

Calli lifted his hand from her shoulder and stepped back. Ron scratched his head and frowned.

"Well?" said Rydra.

Calli shrugged. "Well, we don't know."

"Navigation Instruments are standard gear. There won't be any trouble communicating there."

"She is pretty," Ron said. "You are pretty. Don't be frightened. You're alive now."

"*Ninaogapa!*" She seized Calli's hand. "*Jee, ni usiku au mchana?*" Her eyes were wide.

"Please don't be frightened!" Ron took the wrist of the hand that had seized Calli's.

"*Sielewi lugha yenu.*" She shook her head, a gesture containing no negation, only bewilderment. "*Sikujuweni ninyi nani. Ninaogapa.*"

And with bereavement-born urgency, both Ron and Calli nodded in affirmative reassurance.

Rydra stepped between them and spoke.

After a long silence, the woman nodded slowly.

"She says she'll go with you. She lost two-thirds of her triple seven years ago, also killed through the Invasion. That's why she came to the Morgue and killed herself. She says she will go with you. Will you take her?"

"She's still afraid," Ron said. "Please don't be. I won't hurt you. Calli won't hurt."

"If she'll come with us," Calli said, "we'll take her."

The Customs Officer coughed. "Where do I get her psyche rating?"

"Right on the screen under the filing crystal. That's how they're arranged within the larger categories."

The Officer walked back to the crystal. "Well—" He took out his pad and began to record the indices. "It's taken a while but you've got just about everybody."

"Integrate," Rydra said.

He did, and looked up, surprised in spite of himself. "Captain Wong, I think you've got your crew!"

6 *Dear Mocky,*

When you get this I'll have taken off two hours ago. It's a half hour before dawn and I want to talk to you, but I won't wake you up again.

I am, nostalgically enough, taking out Fobo's old ship, the Rimbaud *(the name was Muels' idea, remember). At least, I'm familiar with it; lots of good memories here. I leave in twenty minutes.*

Present location: I'm sitting in a folding chair in the freight lock looking over the field. The sky is star speckled to the west, and gray to the east. Black needles of ships pattern around me. Lines of blue signal lights fade toward the south. It's calm now. Subject of my thinking: a hectic night of crew hunting that took me all over Transport Town and out to the Morgue, through dives and glittering byways, etc. Loud and noisy at the beginning, calming to this at the end.

To get a good pilot you watch him wrestle. A trained captain can tell exactly what sort of a pilot a person will make by observing his reflexes in the arena. Only I am not that well trained.

Remember what you said about muscle-reading? Maybe you were righter than you thought. Last night I ran into a kid, a Navigator, who looks like Brancusi's graduation offering, or maybe what Michelangelo wished the human body was. He was born in Transport and knows pilot wrestling inside out, apparently. So I watched him watch my pilot wrestle, and just looking at his quivers and jerks I got a complete analysis of what was going on over my head.

You know De Faure's theory that psychic indices have their corresponding muscular tensions (a restatement of the old Wilhelm Reich hypothesis of muscular armature): I was thinking about it last night. The kid I was telling you about was part of a broken triple, two guys and a girl and the girl got it from the Invaders. The boys made me want to cry. But I didn't. Instead I took them to the Morgue and found them a replacement. Weird business. I'm sure they'll think it was magic for the rest of their lives. The basic requirements, however, were all on file: a female Navigator-One who lacks two men. How to adjust the indices? I read Ron's and Calli's from watching them move while they talked. The corpses are filed under psyche-indices so I just had to feel out when they were congruent. The final choice was a stroke of genius, if I do say so. I had it down to six young ladies who would do. But it needed to be more precise than that, and I couldn't play it more precise, at least not by ear. One young lady was from N'gonda Province in Pan Africa. She'd suicided seven years ago. Lost two husbands in an Invasion attack, and returned to earth in the middle of an embargo. You remember what the politics were like then between Pan Africa and Americasia; I was sure she didn't speak English. We woke her, and she didn't. Now, at this point, their indices may be a mite jarring. But, by the time they fight through learning to understand each other—and they will, because they need to—they'll graph out congruent a foot down the logarithmic grid. Clever?

And Babel-17, the real reason for this letter. Told you I had deciphered it enough to know where the next attack will be. The Alliance War Yards at Armsedge. Wanted to let you know that's where I'm going, just in case. Talk and talk and talk: what sort of mind can talk like that language talks? And why? Still scared—like a kid at a spelling bee—but having fun. My platoon reported an hour ago. Crazy, lazy lovable kids all. In just a few minutes I'll be going to see my Slug (fat galoof with black eyes, hair, beard; moves slow and thinks fast). You know, Mocky, getting this crew together I was interested in one thing (above competency, and they are all competent): they had to be people I could talk to. And I can.

Love,

Rydra.

7 Light but no shadow. The General stood up on the saucer-sled, looking at the black ship, the paling sky. At the base he stepped from the gliding two-foot diameter disk, climbed onto the lift, and rose a hundred feet toward the lock. She wasn't in the captain's cabin. He ran into a fat bearded man who directed him up the corridor to the freight lock. He climbed to the top of the ladder and took hold of his breath because it was about to run away.

She dropped her feet from the wall, sat up in the canvas chair and smiled. "General Forester, I thought I might see you this morning." She folded a piece of message tissue and sealed the edge.

"I wanted to see you . . ." and his breath was gone and had to be caught once more, "before you left."

"I wanted to see you, too."

"You told me if I gave you the license to conduct this expedition, you would inform me where you—"

"My report, which you should find satisfactory, was mailed last night and is on your desk at Administrative Alliance Headquarters—or will be in an hour."

"Oh, I see."

She smiled. "You'll have to go shortly. We take off in a few minutes."

'Yes. Actually, I'm taking off for Administrative Alliance Headquarters myself this morning, so I was here at the field, and I'd already gotten a synopsis of your report by stellarphone a few minutes ago, and I just wanted to say . . ." and he said nothing.

"General Forester, once I wrote a poem I'm reminded of. It was called 'Advice to Those Who Would Love Poets.'"

The General opened his teeth without separating his lips.

"It started something like:

> Young man, she will gnaw out your tongue.
> Lady, he will steal your hands . . .

You can read the rest. It's in my second book. If you're not willing to lose a poet seven times a day, it's frustrating as hell."

He said simply: "You knew I . . ."

"I knew and I know. And I'm glad."

The lost breath returned and an unfamiliar thing was happening to his face: he smiled. "When I was a private, Miss Wong, and we'd be confined to barracks, we'd talk about girls and girls and girls. And somebody would say about one: she was so pretty she didn't have to give me any, just promise me some." He let the stiffness leave his shoulders a moment, and though they actually fell half an inch, the effect was that they seemed broader by two. "That's what I was feeling."

"Thank you for telling me," she said. "I like you, General. And I promise I'll still like you the next time I see you."

"I . . . thank you. I guess that's all. Just thank you . . . for know-ing and promising." Then he said, "I have to go now, don't I?"

"We'll be taking off in ten minutes."

"Your letter," he said, "I'll mail it for you."

"Thanks." She handed it to him, he took her hand, and for the slightest moment with the slightest pressure, held her. Then he turned, left. Minutes later she watched his saucer-sled glide across the concrete, its sun-side flaring suddenly as light blis-tered the east.

part two

_____

ver dorco

If words are paramount I am afraid
that words are all my hands have ever seen . . .
—from *Quartet*

1 The retranscribed material passed on the sorting screen. By the computer console lay the four pages of definitions she had amassed and a *cuaderno* full of grammatical speculations. Chewing her lower lip, she ran through the frequency tabulation of depressed diphthongs. On the wall she had tacked three charts labeled:

Possible Phonemic Structure . . .

Possible Phonetic Structure . . .

Semiotic, Semantic, and Syntactic Ambiguities . . .

The last contained the problems to be solved. The questions, formulated and answered, were transferred as certainties to the first two.

"Captain?"

She turned on the bubble seat.

Hanging from the entrance hatch by his knees was Diavalo.

"Yes?"

"What you want for dinner?" The little platoon cook was a boy of seventeen. Two cosmetisurgical horns jutted from shocked albino hair. He was scratching one ear with the tip of his tail.

Rydra shrugged. "No preferences. Check around with the rest of the platoon."

"Those guys'll eat liquified organic waste if I give it to them. No imagination, Captain. What about pheasant under glass, or maybe rock Cornish game hen?"

"You're in the mood for poultry?"

"Well . . ." He released the bar with one knee and kicked the wall so he swung back and forth. "I could go for something birdy."

"If nobody objects, try coq au vin, baked Idahos, and broiled beefsteak tomatoes."

"Now you're cookin'!"

"Strawberry shortcake for dessert?"

Diavalo snapped his fingers and swung toward the hatch. Rydra laughed and turned back to the console.

"Macon on the coq, May wine with the meal!" The pink-eyed face was gone.

Rydra had discovered the third example of what might have been syncope when the bubble chair sagged back. The cuaderno slammed against the edge of the desk. Her shoulders wrenched. Behind her the skin of the bubble chair split and showered suspended silicon.

The cabin stilled and she turned to see Diavalo spin through the hatch and crack his hip as he grabbed at the transparent wall.

Jerk—!

She slipped on the wet, deflated skin of the bubble chair. The Slug's face jounced on the intercom. "Captain!"

"What the hell . . . !" she demanded.

The blinker from Drive Maintenance was flashing. Something jarred the ship again.

"Are we still breathing?"

"Just a . . ." The Slug's face, heavy and rimmed with a thin black beard, got an unpleasant expression. "Yes. Air: all right. Drive Maintenance has the problem."

"If those damned kids have . . ." She clicked them on.

Flip, the platoon Maintenance Foreman, said, "Jesus, Captain, something blew."

"What?"

"I don't know." Flop's face appeared over his shoulder.

"A and B shifters are all right. C's glittering like a Fourth of July sparkler. Where the hell are we, anyway?"

"On the first hour shift between Earth and Luna. We haven't even got free of Stellarcenter-9. Navigation?" Another click.

Mollya's dark face popped up.

"*Wie gehts?*" demanded Rydra.

The First Navigator reeled off their probability curve and located them between two vague logarithmic spirals. "We're orbiting Earth so far," Ron's voice cut over. "Something knocked us way off course. We don't have any drive power and we're just drifting."

"How high up and how fast?"

"Calli's trying to find out now."

"I'm going to take a look around outside." She called down to the Sensory Detail: "Nose, what does it smell like out there?"

"It stinks. Nothing in this range. We've hit soup."

"Can you hear anything, Ear?"

"Not a peep, Captain. All the stasis currents in this area are at a standstill. We're too near a large gravitational mass. There's a faint ethric undertow about fifty spectres K-ward. But I don't think it will take us anywhere except around in a circle. We're riding in momentum from the last stiff wind from Earth's magnosphere."

"What's it look like, Eyes?"

"Inside of a coal shuttle. Whatever happened to us, we picked a dead spot to have it happen in. In my range that undertow is a little stronger and might move us into a good tide."

Brass cut in. "But I'd like to know where it's going before I went jum'ing off into it. That means I gotta know where we are, first."

"Navigation?"

Silence for a moment. Then the three faces appeared. Calli said, "We don't know, Captain."

The gravity field had stabilized a few degrees off. The silicon suspension from the ruptured chair collected in one corner. Little

Diavalo shook his head and blinked. Through the contortion of pain on his face he whispered, "What happened, Captain?"

"Damned if I know," Rydra said. "But I'm going to find out."

Dinner was eaten silently. The platoon, all kids under twenty-one, made as little noise as possible. At the officers' table the Navigators sat across from the apparitional figures of the discorporate Sensory Observers. The hefty Slug at the table's head poured wine for the silent crew. Rydra dined with Brass.

"I don't know." He shook his maned head, turning his glass in gleaming claws. "It was smooth sailing with nothing in the way. Whatever ha''ened, ha''ened inside the shi'."

Diavalo, hip in a pressure bandage, dourfully brought in the shortcake, served Rydra and Brass, then retired to his seat at the platoon table.

"So," Rydra said, "we're orbiting Earth with all our instruments knocked out and can't even tell where we are."

"The hy'erstasis instruments are good," he reminded her. "We just don't know where we are on this side of the jum'."

"And we can't jump if we don't know where we're jumping from." She looked over the dining room. "Do you think they're expecting to get out of this, Brass?"

"They're ho'ing you can get them out, Ca'tain."

She touched the rim of her glass to her lower lip.

"If somebody doesn't, we'll sit here eating Diavalo's good food for six months, then suffocate. We can't even get a signal out until after we lea' for hy'erstasis with the regular communicator shorted. I asked the Navigators to see if they could im'rovise something, but no go. They just had time to see that we were launched in a great circle."

"We should have windows," Rydra said. "At least we could

look out at the stars and time our orbit. It can't be more than a couple of hours."

Brass nodded. "Shows you what modern conveniences mean. A 'orthole and an old-fashioned sextant could set us right, but we're electronicized to the gills, and here we sit, with a neatly insoluble 'roblem."

"Circling—" Rydra put down her wine.

"What is it?"

"*Der Kreis,*" said Rydra. She frowned.

"What's that?" asked Brass.

"*Ratas, orbis, il cerchio.*" She put her palms flat on the table-top and pressed. "Circles," she said. "Circles in different languages!"

Brass's confusion was terrifying through his fangs. The glinting fleece above his eyes bristled.

"Sphere," she said, "*il globo, gumlas.*" She stood up. "*Kule, kuglet, kring!*"

"Does it matter what language it's in? A circle is a cir—"

But she was laughing, running from the dining room.

In her cabin she grabbed up her translation. Her eyes fled down the pages. She banged the button for the Navigators. Ron, wiping whipped cream from his mouth, said, "Yes, Captain? What do you want?"

"A watch," said Rydra, "and a—bag of marbles!"

"Huh?" asked Calli.

"You can finish your shortcake later. Meet me in G-center, right now."

"Mar-bles?" articulated Mollya wonderingly. "Marbles?"

"One of the kids in the platoon must have brought along a bag of marbles. Get it and meet me in G-center."

She jumped over the ruined skin of the bubble seat and leapt up the hatchway, turned off at the radial shaft seven, and launched down the cylindrical corridor toward the hollow spherical chamber of G-center. The calculated center of gravity of the ship, it was a chamber thirty feet in diameter in constant free fall where certain acceleration-sensitive instruments took their readings. A moment later the three Navigators appeared through triametric entrances. Ron held up a mesh bag of glass balls. "Lizzy asks you to try and get these back to her by tomorrow afternoon because she's been challenged by the kids in Drive and she wants to keep her championship."

"If this works she can probably have them back tonight."

"Work?" Mollya wanted to know. "Idea you?"

"I do. Only it's not really my idea."

"Whose is it, and what is it?" Ron asked.

"I suppose it belongs to somebody who speaks another language. What we've got to do is arrange the marbles around the wall of the room in a perfect sphere, and then sit back with the clock and keep tabs on the second hand."

"What for?" asked Calli.

"To see where they go and how long it takes them to get there."

"I don't get it," said Ron.

"Our orbit tends toward a great circle about the Earth, right? That means everything in the ship is also tending to orbit in a great circle, and, if left free of influence, will automatically seek out such a path."

"Right. So what?"

"Help me get these marbles in place," Rydra said. "These things have iron cores. Magnetize the walls, will you, to hold them in place, so they can all be released at once." (Ron, confused, went to power the metal walls of the spherical chamber.) "You still don't see? You're mathematicians, tell me about great circles."

Calli took a handful of marbles and started to space them—tiny click after click—over the wall. "A great circle is the largest circle you can cut through a sphere."

"The diameter of the great circle equals the diameter of the sphere," from Ron, as he came back from the power switch.

"The summation of the angles of intersection of any three great circles within one topologically contained shape approaches five-hundred-and-forty degrees. The summation of the angles of N great circles approaches N times one hundred and eighty degrees." Mollya intoned the definitions, which she had begun memorizing in English with the help of a personafix that morning, in her musically inflected voice. "Marble here, yes?"

"All over, yes. Evenly as you can space them, but they don't have to be exact. Tell me some more about the intersections."

"Well," said Ron, "on any given sphere all great circles intersect each other—or lie congruent."

Rydra laughed. "Just like that, hey? Are there any other circles on a sphere that have to intersect no matter how you maneuver them?"

"I think you can push around any other circles so that they're equidistant at all points and don't touch. But all great circles have to have at *least* two points in common."

"Think about that for a minute and look at these marbles, all being pulled along great circles."

Mollya suddenly floated back from the wall with an expression of recognition and brought her hands together. She blurted something in Kiswahili, and Rydra laughed. "That's right," she said. To Ron's and Calli's bewilderment she translated: "They'll move toward each other and their paths'll intersect."

Calli's eyes widened. "That's right, at exactly a quarter of the way around our orbit, they should have flattened out to a circular plane."

"Lying along the plane of our orbit," Ron finished.

Mollya frowned and made a stretching motion with her hands. "Yeah," Ron said, "a distorted circular plane with a tail at each end, from which we can compute which way the earth lies."

"Clever, huh?" Rydra moved back into the corridor opening. "I figure we can do this once, then fire our rockets enough to blast us maybe seventy or eighty miles either up or down without hurting anything. From that we can get the length of our orbits, as well as our speed. That'll be all the information we need to locate ourselves in relation to the nearest major gravitational influence. From there we can jump stasis. All our communications instruments for stasis are in working order. We can signal for help and pull in some replacements from a stasis station."

The amazed Navigators joined her in the corridor. "Count down," Rydra said.

At zero Ron released the magnetic walls. Slowly the marbles began to drift, lining up slowly.

"Guess you learn something every day," Calli said. "If you'd asked me, I would have said we were stuck here forever. And knowing things like this is supposed to be my job. Where did you get the idea?"

"From the word for 'great circle' in . . . another language."

"Language speaking tongue?" Mollya asked. "You mean?"

"Well," Rydra took out a metal tracing plate and a stylus. "I'm simplifying it a little, but let me show you." She marked the plate. "Let's say the word for circle is: O. This language has a melody system to illustrate comparatives. We'll represent this by the diacritical marks: ˇ, ¯, and ^, respectively, means smallest, ordinary, and biggest. So what would Ǒ mean?"

"Smallest possible circle?" said Calli. "That's a single point."

Rydra nodded. "Now, when referring to a circle on a sphere, suppose the word for just an ordinary circle is Ō followed by either of two symbols, one of which means not touching anything else, the other of which means crossing—11 or X. What would ŌX mean?"

"Ordinary circle that intersects," said Ron.

"And because all great circles intersect, in this language the word for great circle is always ÔX. It carries the information right in the word. Just like *bus stop* or *foxhole* carry information in English that *la gare* or *le terrier*—comparable words in French—lack. 'Great Circle' carries *some* information with it, but not the right information to get us out of the jam we're in. We have to go to another language in order to think about the problem clearly without going through all sorts of roundabout paths for the proper aspects of what we want to deal with."

"What language is this?" asked Calli.

"I don't know its real name. For now it's called Babel-17. From what little I know about it already, most of its words carry more information about the things they refer to than any four or five languages I know put together—and in less space." She gave a brief translation for Mollya.

"Who speak?" Mollya asked, determined to stick to her minimal English.

Rydra bit the inside of her lip. When she'd asked herself that question, her stomach would tighten, her hands start toward something and the yearning for an answer grow nearly to pain in the back of her throat. It happened now; it faded. "I don't know. But I wish I did. That's what the main reason for this trip is, to find out."

"Babel-17," Ron repeated.

One of the platoon tube-boys coughed behind them.

"What is it, Carlos?"

Squat, taurine, with a lot of curly black hair, Carlos had big, loose muscles, and a slight lisp. "Captain, could I show you something?" He shifted from side to side in adolescent awkwardness, scuffing his bare soles, heat-callused from climbing over the drive tubes, against the door sill. "Something down in the tubes. I think you should take a look at it yourself."

"Did Slug tell you to get me?"

Carlos prodded behind his ear with a gnawed thumbnail. "Um-hm."

"You three can take care of this business, can't you?"

"Sure, Captain." Calli looked at the closing marbles.

Rydra ducked after Carlos. They rode down the ladderlift and hunched through the low-ceilinged causeway.

"Down here," Carlos said, hesitantly taking the lead beneath arched bus bars. At a mesh platform he stopped and opened a component cabinet in the wall. "See." He removed a board of printed circuits. "There." A thin crack ran across the plastic surface. "It's been broken."

"How?" Rydra asked.

"Like this." He took the plate in both hands and made a bending gesture.

"Sure it didn't crack by itself?"

"It can't," Carlos said. "When it's in place, it's supported too well. You couldn't crack it with a sledge hammer. This panel carries all the communication circuits."

Rydra nodded.

"The gyroscopic field deflectors for all our regular space maneuvering . . ." He opened another door and took out another panel. "Here."

Rydra ran her fingernail along the crack in the second plate. "Someone in the ship broke these," she said. "Take them to the shop. Tell Lizzy when she finishes reprinting them to bring them to me and I'll put them in. I'll give her the marbles back then."

2 Drop a gem in thick oil. The brilliance yellows slowly, ambers, goes red at last, dies. That was the leap into hyperstatic space.

At the computer console, Rydra pondered the charts. The dictionary had doubled since the trip began. Satisfaction filled one side of her mind like a good meal. Words, and their easy patterning, facile always on her tongue, in her fingers, ordered themselves for her, revealing, defining, and revealing.

And there was a traitor. The question, a vacuum where no information would come to answer who or what or why, made an emptiness on the other side of her brain, agonizing to collapse. Someone had deliberately broken those plates. Lizzy said so, too. What words for this? The names of the entire crew, and by each, a question mark.

Fling a jewel into a glut of jewels. This was the leap from hyperstasis into the area of the Alliance War Yards at Armsedge.

At the communication board, she put on the Sensory Helmet. "Do you want to translate for me?"

The indicator light blinked acceptance. Each discorporate observer perceived the details of the gravitational and electromagnetic flux of the stasis currents for a certain frequency with all his senses, each in his separate range. Those details were myriad, and the pilot sailed the ship through those currents as sailing ships winded the liquid ocean. But the helmet made a condensation that the captain could view for a general survey of the matrix, reduced to terms that would leave the corporate viewer sane.

She opened the helmet, covering her eyes, ears, and nose.

Flung through loops of blue and wrung with indigo, drifted the complex of stations and planetoids making up the War Yards. A musical hum punctured with bursts of static sounded over the earphones. The olfactory emitters gave a confused odor of perfumes and hot oil charged with the bitter smell of burning citrus peel. With three of her senses filled, she was loosed from the reality of the cabin to drift through sensory abstractions. It took nearly a minute to collect her sensations, to begin their interpretation.

"All right. What am I looking at?"

"The lights are the various planetoids and ring stations that make up the War Yards," the Eye explained to her. "That bluish color to the left is a radar net they have spread out toward Stellarcenter Forty-two. Those red flashes in the upper right-hand corner are just a reflection of Bellatrix from a half-glazed solar-disk rotating four degrees outside your field of vision."

"What's that low humming?" Rydra asked.

"The ship's drive," the Ear explained. "Just ignore it. I'll block it out if you want."

Rydra nodded, and the hum ceased.

"That clicking—" the Ear began.

"—is morse code," Rydra finished. "I recognize that. It must be two radio amateurs that want to keep off the visual circuits."

"That's right," the Ear confirmed.

"What stinks like that?"

"The overall smell is just Bellatrix's gravitational field. You can't receive the olfactory sensations in stereo, but the burnt lemon peel is the power plant that's located in that green glare right ahead of you."

"Where do we dock?"

"In the sound of the E-minor triad."

"In the hot oil you can smell bubbling to your left."

"Home in on that white circle."

Rydra switched to the pilot. "Okay, Brass, take her in."

The saucer-disk slid down the ramp as she balanced easily in the four-fifths gravity. A breeze through the artificial twilight pushed her hair back from her shoulders. Around her stretched the major arsenal of the Alliance. Momentarily she pondered the accident of birth that had seated her firmly inside the Alliance's realm. Born a galaxy away, she might as easily have been an Invader. Her poems were popular on both sides. That was upsetting. She put the thought away. Here, gliding the Alliance War Yards, it was not clever to be upset over that.

"Captain Wong, you come under the auspices of General Forester."

She nodded as her saucer stopped.

"He forwarded us information that you are at present the expert on Babel-17."

She nodded once more. Now the other saucer paused before hers.

"I'm very happy then, to meet you, and for any assistance I can offer, please ask."

She extended her hand. "Thank you, Baron Ver Dorco."

Black eyebrows raised and the slash of mouth curved in the dark face. "You read heraldry?" He raised long fingers to the shield on his chest.

"I do."

"An accomplishment, Captain. We live in a world of isolated communities, each hardly touching its neighbor, each speaking, as it were, a different language."

"I speak many."

The Baron nodded. "Sometimes I believe, Captain Wong, that without the Invasion, something for the Alliance to focus its energies upon, our society would disintegrate. Captain Wong—" He stopped, and the fine lines of his face shifted, contracted to concentration, then a sudden opening. "*Rydra* Wong . . . ?"

She nodded, smiling at his smile, yet wary before what the recognition would mean.

"I didn't realize—" He extended his hand as though he were meeting her all over again. "But, of course—" The surface of his manner shaled away, and had she never seen this transformation before she would have warmed to his warmth. "Your books, I want you to know—" The sentence trailed in a slight shaking of the head. Dark eyes too wide; lips, in their humor, too close to a leer; hands seeking one another: it all spoke to her of a disquieting appetite for her presence, a hunger for something she was or might be, a ravenous—"Dinner at my house is served at seven." He interrupted her thought with unsettling appropriateness. "You will dine with the Baroness and myself this evening."

"Thank you. But I wanted to discuss with my crew—"

"I extend the invitation to your entire entourage. We have a spacious house, conference rooms at your disposal, as well as entertainment, certainly less confined than your ship." The tongue, purplish and flickering behind white, white teeth; the brown lines of his lips, she thought, form words as languidly as the slow mandibles of the cannibal mantis.

"Please come a little early so we can prepare you—"

She caught her breath, then felt foolish; a faint narrowing of his eyes told her he had registered, though not understood, her start.

"—for your tour through the Yards. General Forester has suggested you be made privy to all our efforts against the Invaders. This is quite an honor, Madam. There are many well-seasoned officers at the Yards who have not seen some of the things you will be shown. A good deal of it will probably be tedious, I dare say. In my opinion, it's stuffing you with a lot of trivial tidbits. But some of our attempts have been rather ingenious. We keep our imaginations simmering."

This man brings out the paranoid in me, she thought. I don't like him. "I'd prefer not to impose on you, Baron. There are some matters on my ship that I must—"

"Do come. Your work here will be much facilitated if you accept my hospitality, I assure you. A woman of your talent and accomplishment would be an honor to my house. And recently I have been starved—" dark lips slid together over gleaming teeth— "for intelligent conversation."

She felt her jaw clamp involuntarily on a third ceremonious refusal. But the Baron was saying: "I will expect you, and your crew, leisurely, before seven."

The saucer-disk slid away over the concourse. Rydra looked back at the ramp where her ship waited, silhouetted against the false evening. Her disk began to negotiate the slope back to the *Rimbaud*.

"**W**ell," she said to the little albino cook who had just come out of his pressure bandage the day before, "you're off tonight. Slug, the crew's going out to dinner. See if you can brush the kids up on their table manners—make sure everyone knows which knife to eat his peas with, and all that."

"The salad fork is the little one on the outside," the Slug announced suavely, turning to the platoon.

"And what about the little one outside that?" Allegra asked.

"That's for oysters."

"But suppose they don't serve oysters?"

Flop rubbed his underlip with the knuckle of his thumb. "I guess you could pick your teeth with it."

Brass dropped a paw on Rydra's shoulder. "How you feel, Ca'tain?"

"Like a pig over a barbecue pit."

"You look sort of done—" Calli began.

"Done?" she asked.

"—in," he finished, quizzically.

"Maybe I've been working too hard. We're guests at the Baron Ver Dorco's this evening. I suppose we can all relax a bit there."

"Ver Dorco?" asked Mollya.

"He's in charge of coordinating the various research projects against the Invaders."

"This is where they make all the bigger and better secret weapons?" Ron asked.

"They also make smaller, more deadly ones. I imagine it should be an education."

"These sabotage attem'ts," Brass said. She had given them a rough idea of what was going on. "A successful one here at the War Yards could be 'retty bad to our efforts against the Invaders."

"It's about as central a hit as they could try, next to planting a bomb in Administrative Alliance Headquarters itself."

"Will you be able to stop it?" Slug asked.

Rydra shrugged, turning to the simmering absences of the discorporate crew. "I've got a couple of ideas. Look, I'm going to ask you guys to be sort of unhospitable this evening and do some spying. Eyes, I want you to stay on the ship and make sure you're the only one here. Ears, once we leave for the Baron's, go invisible and from then on, don't get more than six feet away from me until we're all back to the ship. Nose, you run messages back and forth. There's something going on that I don't like. I don't know whether it's my imagination or what."

The Eye spoke something ominous. Ordinarily the corporate

could only converse with the discorporate—and remember the conversation—over special equipment. Rydra solved the problem by immediately translating whatever they spoke to her into Basque before the weak synapses broke. Though the original words were lost, the translation remained: Those broken circuit plates weren't your imagination, was the gist of the Basque she retained.

She looked over the crew with gnawing discomfort. If one of the kids or officers was merely psychotically destructive, it would show up on his psyche index. There was, among them, a consciously destructive one. It hurt, like an unlocatable splinter in the sole of her foot that jabbed occasionally with the pressure of walking. She remembered how she had searched them from the night. Pride. Warm pride in the way their functions meshed as they moved her ship through the stars. The warmth was the relieved anticipation for all that could go wrong with the machine-called-the-ship, if the machine-called-the-crew were not interlocked and precise. Cool pride in another part of her mind, at the ease with which they moved by one another: the kids, inexperienced both in living and working; the adults, so near pressure situations that might have scarred their polished efficiency and made psychic burrs to snag one another. But she had chosen them; and the ship, her world, was a beautiful place to walk, work, live, for a journey's length.

But there was a traitor.

That shorted something. *Somewhere in Eden, now* . . . she recalled, again looking over the crew. *Somewhere in Eden, now, a worm, a worm.* Those cracked plates told her: the worm wanted to destroy not just her, but the ship, its crew, and contents, slowly. No blades plunged in the night, no shots from around a corner, no cord looped on the throat as she entered a dark cabin. Babel-17, how good a language would it be to argue with for your life?

"Slug, the Baron wants me to come over first to see some of his latest methods of slaughter. Have the kids there decently early, will you? I'm leaving now. Eye and Ear, hop aboard."

"Righto, Captain," from Slug.

The discorporate crew deperceptualized.

She leaned her sled over the ramp again and slid away from the milling youngsters and officers, curious at the source of her apprehension.

---

3 "Gross, uncivilized weapons." The Baron gestured toward the row of plastic cylinders increasing in size along the rack. "It's a shame to waste time on such clumsy contraptions. The little one there can demolish an area of about fifty square miles. The big ones leave a crater twenty-seven miles deep and a hundred and fifty across. Barbaric. I frown on their use. That one on the left is more subtle: it explodes once with enough force to demolish a good size building, but the bomb casing itself is hidden and unhurt under the rubble. Six hours later it explodes again and does the damage of a fair-sized atomic bomb. This leaves the victims enough time to concentrate their reclamation forces, all sorts of reconstruction workers, Red Cross nurses, or whatever the Invaders call them, lots of experts determining the size of the damage. Then *poof*. A delayed hydrogen explosion, and a good thirty or forty miles crater. It doesn't do as much physical damage as even the smallest of these others, but it gets rid of a lot of equipment and busybody do-gooders. Still, a schoolboy's weapon. I keep them in my own personal collection just to show them we have standard fare."

She followed him through the archway into the next hall. There were filing cabinets along the wall and a single display case in the center of the room.

"Now here is one I'm justly proud of." The Baron walked to the case and the transparent walls fell apart.

"What," Rydra asked, "exactly is it?"

"What does it look like?"

"A . . . piece of rock."

"A chunk of metal," corrected the Baron.

"Is it explosive—or particularly hard?"

"It won't go bang," he assured her. "Its tensile strength is a bit over titanium steel, but we have much harder plastics."

Rydra started to extend her hand, then thought to ask, "May I pick it up and examine it?"

"I doubt it," the Baron said. "Try."

"What will happen?"

"See for yourself."

She reached out to take the dull chunk. Her hand closed on air two inches above the surface. She moved her fingers down to touch it, but they came together inches to the side. Rydra frowned.

She moved her hand to the left, but it was on the other side of the strange shard.

"Just a moment." The Baron smiled, picked up the fragment. "Now if you saw this just lying on the ground, you wouldn't look twice, would you?"

"Poisonous?" Rydra suggested. "Is it a component of something else?"

"No." The Baron turned the shape about thoughtfully. "Just highly selective. And obliging." He raised his hand. "Suppose you needed a gun"—in the Baron's hand now was a sleek vibra-gun of a model later than she had ever seen—"or a crescent wrench." Now he held a foot-long wrench. He adjusted the opening. "Or a machete." The blade glistened as he waved his arm back. "Or a small crossbow." It had a pistol grip and a bow length of not quite ten inches. The spring, however, was doubled back on itself and held with quarter-inch bolts. The Baron pulled the trigger—there was no arrow—and the *thump* of the release, followed by the continuous *pinnnng* of the vibrating tensile bar, set her teeth against one another.

"It's some sort of illusion," Rydra said. "That's why I couldn't touch it."

"A metal punch," said the Baron. It appeared in his hand, a hammer with a particularly thick head. He swung it against the floor of the case that held the "weapon" with a strident clang. "There."

Rydra saw the circular indentation left by the hammerhead. Raised in the middle was the faint shape of the Ver Dorco shield. She moved the tips of her fingers over the bossed metal, still warm from impact.

"No illusion," said the Baron. "That crossbow will put a six-inch shaft completely through three inches of oak at forty yards. And the vibra-gun—I'm sure you know what *it* can do."

He held the—it was a chunk of metal again—above its stand in the case. "Put it back for me."

She stretched her hand beneath his, and he dropped the chunk. Her fingers closed to grab it. But it was on the stand again.

"No hocus-pocus. Merely selective and . . . obliging."

He touched the edge of the case and the plastic sides closed over the display. "A clever plaything. Let's look at something else."

"But how does it work?"

Ver Dorco smiled. "We've managed to polarize alloys of the

heavier elements so that they exist only on certain perceptual matrices. Otherwise, they deflect. That means that, besides visually—and we can blank that out as well—it's undetectable. No weight, no volume; all it has is inertia. Which means simply by carrying it aboard any hyperstasis craft, you'll put its drive controls out of commission. Two or three grams of this anywhere near the inertia-stasis system will create all sorts of unaccounted-for strain. That's its major function right there. Smuggle that on board the Invaders' ships and we can stop worrying about them. The rest—that's child's play. An unexpected property of polarized matter is tensile-memory." They moved toward an archway into the next room. "Annealed in any shape for a time, and codified, the structure of that shape is retained down to the molecules. At any angle to the direction that the matter has been polarized in, each molecule has completely free movement. Just jar it, and it falls into that structure like a rubber figure returning to shape." The Baron glanced back at the case. "Simple, really. There—" he motioned toward the filing cabinets along the wall—"is the real weapon: approximately three thousand individual plans incorporating that little polarized chunk. The 'weapon' is the knowledge of what to do with what you have. In hand-to-hand combat, a six-inch length of vanadium wire can be deadly. Inserted directly into the inner corner of the eye, piercing diagonally across the frontal lobes, then brought quickly down, it punctures the cerebellum, causing general paralysis; thrust completely in, and it will mangle the joint of spinal cord and the medulla: death. You can use the same piece of wire to short out a Type 27-QX communications unit, which is the sort currently employed in the Invaders' stasis systems."

Rydra felt the muscles along her spine tighten. The repulsion which she had quelled till now came flooding back.

"This next display is from the Borgia. The Borgia—" he laughed—"my nickname for our toxicology department. Again, some terribly gross products." He picked a sealed glass phial from a wall rack. "Pure diphtheria toxin. Enough here to make the reservoir of a good-sized city fatal."

"But standard vaccination procedure—" Rydra began.

"Diphtheria toxin, my dear. Toxin! Back when contagious diseases were a problem, you know, they would examine the corpses of diphtheria victims and discover nothing but a few hundred thousand baccilli, all in the victim's throat. Nowhere else. With any sort of bacillis, that's enough of an infection to cause a minor cough. It took years to discover what was going on. That tiny number of bacilli produced an even tinier bit of a substance that is still the most deadly natural organic compound we know of. The amount required to kill a man—oh, I'd even say thirty or forty men—is, for all practical purposes, undetectable. Up till now, even with all our advances, the only way you could obtain it was from an obliging diphtheria bacillus. The Borgia has changed that." He pointed to another bottle. "Cyanide, the old war horse! But then, the telltale smell of almonds—are you hungry? We can go up for cocktails anytime you wish."

She shook her head, quickly and firmly.

"Now these are delicious. Catalytics." He moved his hand from one phial to the next. "Color blindness, total blindness, tone deafness, complete deafness, ataxia, amnesia, and on and on." He dropped his hand and smiled like a hungry rodent. "And they're all controlled by this. You see, the problem with anything of such a specific effect is that you have to introduce comparatively huge amounts of it. All these require at least a tenth of a gram or more. So, catalytics. None of what I've shown you would have any effect at all even if you swallowed the whole phial." He lifted the last container he had pointed to and pressed a stud at the end and there was a faint hiss of escaping gas. "Until now. A perfectly harmless atomized steroid."

"Only it activates the poisons here to produce ... these effects?"

"Exactly," smiled the Baron. "And the catalyst can be in doses nearly as microscopic as the diphtheria toxin. The contents of that blue jar will give you a mild stomach ache and minor head pains for half an hour. Nothing more. The green one beside it: total cerebral atrophy over a period of a week. The victim becomes a living vegetable the rest of his life. The purple one: death." He raised his hands, palms up, and laughed. "I'm famished." The hands dropped. "Shall we go up to dinner?"

Ask him what's in that room over there, she said to herself, and would have dismissed the passing curiosity, but she was thinking in Basque: it was a message from her discorporate bodyguard, invisible beside her.

"When I was a child, Baron—" she moved toward the door— "soon after I came to Earth, I was taken to the circus. It was the first time I had ever seen so many things so close together that were so fascinating. I wouldn't go home till almost an hour after they had intended to leave. What do you have in this room?"

Surprise in the little movement in the muscles of his forehead.

"Show me."

He bowed his head in mocking, semi-formal aquiescence. "Modern warfare can be fought on so many delightfully different levels," he continued, walking back to her side as if no interruption of the tour had been suggested. "One wins a battle by making sure one's troops have enough blunderbusses and battle axes like the ones you saw in the first room; or by the well-placed six-inch length of vanadium wire in a Type 27-QX communications unit. With the proper orders delayed, the encounter never takes place. Hand-to-hand weapons, survival kit, plus training, room, and board: three thousand credits per enlisted stellarman over a period of two years active duty. For a garrison of fifteen hundred men that's an outlay of four million, five hundred credits. That same garrison will live in and fight from three hyperstasis battleships which, fully equipped, run about a million and a half credits apiece—a total outlay of nine million credits. We have spent, on occasion, perhaps as much as a million on the preparation of a single spy or saboteur. That is rather higher than usual. And I can't believe a six-inch length of vanadium wire costs a third of a cent. War is costly. And although it has taken some time, Administrative Alliance Head-quarters is beginning to realize subtlety pays. This way, Miss— Captain Wong."

Again they were in a room with only a single display case, but it was seven feet high.

A statue, Rydra thought. No, real flesh, with detail of muscle and joint; no, it must be a statue because a human body, dead or in suspended animation, doesn't look that . . . alive. Only art could produce that vibrancy.

"So you see, the proper spy is very important." Though the door had opened automatically, the Baron held it with his hand in vestigial politeness. "This is one of our more expensive models. Still well under a million credits, but one of my favorites—though in practice he has his faults. With a few minor alterations I would like to make him a permanent part of our arsenal."

"A model of a spy?" Rydra asked. "Some sort of robot or android?"

"Not at all." They approached the display case. "We made half a dozen TW-55's. It took the most exacting genetic search. Medical science has progressed so that all sorts of hopeless human refuse lives and reproduces at a frightening rate—infe-rior creatures that would have been too weak to survive a hand-ful of centuries ago. We chose our parents carefully, and then with artificial insemination we got our half dozen zygotes, three male, three female. We raised them in, oh, such a carefully controlled nutrient environment, speeding the growth rate by hormones and other things. But the beauty of it was the experiential imprinting. Gorgeously healthy creatures; you have no idea how much care they received."

"I once spent a summer on a cattle farm," Rydra said shortly.

The Baron's nod was brisk. "We'd used the experiential imprints before, so we knew what we were doing. But never to synthesize completely the life situation of, say, a sixteen-year-old human. Sixteen was the physiological age we brought them to in six months. Look for yourself what a splendid specimen it is. The reflexes are fifty percent above those of a human aged normally. Human musculature is beautifully engineered: a three-day-starved, six-month-atrophied myasthenia gravis case, can, with the proper stimulant drugs, overturn a ton-and-a-half automobile. It will kill him—but that's still remarkable efficiency. Think what the biologically perfect body, operating at all times at point nine-nine efficiency, could accomplish in physical strength alone."

"I thought hormone growth incentive had been outlawed. Doesn't it reduce the life span some drastic amount?"

"To the extent we used it, the life span reduction is seventy-five percent and over." He might have smiled the same way watching some odd animal at its incomprehensible antics. "But, Madam, we are making weapons. If TW-55 can function twenty years at peak efficiency, then it will have outlasted the average battle cruiser by five years. But the experiential imprinting! To find among ordinary men someone who can function as a spy, is *willing* to function as a spy, you must search the fringes of neurosis, often psychosis. Though such deviations might mean strength in a particular area, it always means an overall weakness in the personality. Functioning in any but that particular area, a spy may be dangerously inefficient. And the Invaders have psyche-indices too, which will keep the average spy out of anyplace we might want to put him. Captured, a good spy is a dozen times as dangerous as a bad one. Post-hypnotic suicide suggestions and the like are easily gotten around with drugs; and are wasteful. TW-55 here will register perfectly normal on a psyche integration. He has about six hours of social conversation, plot synopses of the latest novels, political situations, music, and art criticism—I believe in the course of an evening he is programmed to drop your name twice, an honor you share only with Ronald Quar. He has one subject on which he can expound with scholarly acumen for an hour and a half—this one, I believe, is 'haptoglobin groupings among the marsupials.' Put him in formal wear and he will be perfectly at home at an ambassadorial ball or a coffee break at a high-level government conference. He is a crack assassin, expert with all the weapons you have seen up till now, and more. TW-55 has twelve hours' worth of episodes in fourteen different dialects, accents, or jargons concerning sexual conquests, gambling experiences, fisticuff encounters, and humorous anecdotes of semi-illegal enterprises, all of which failed miserably. Tear his shirt, smear grease on his face and slip a pair of overalls on him, and he could be a service mechanic on any one of a hundred spaceyards or stellarcenters on the other side of the Snap. He can disable any space drive system, communications components, radar works, or alarm system used by the Invaders in the past twenty years with little more than—"

"Six inches of vanadium wire?"

The Baron smiled. "His fingerprints and retina pattern, he can alter at will. A little neural surgery has made all the muscles of his face voluntary, which means he can alter his facial structure drastically. Chemical dyes and hormone banks beneath the scalp enable him to color his hair in seconds, or, if necessary, shed it completely and grow a new batch in half an hour. He's a past master in the psychology and physiology of coercion."

"Torture?"

"If you will. He is totally obedient to the people whom he has been conditioned to regard as his superiors; totally destructive toward what he has been ordered to destroy. There is nothing in that beautiful head even akin to a superego."

"He is . . ." and she wondered at herself speaking, "beautiful." The dark-lashed eyes with lids about to quiver open, the broad hands hung at the naked thighs, fingers half-curled, about to straighten or become a fist. The display light was misty on the tanned, yet near-translucent skin. "You say this isn't a model, but really alive?"

"Oh, more or less. But it's rather firmly fixed in something like a yoga trance, or a lizard's hibernation. I could activate it for you—but it's ten to seven. We don't want to keep the others waiting at the table now, do we?"

She looked away from the figure in glass to the dull, taut skin of the Baron's face. His jaw, beneath his faintly concave cheek, was involuntarily working on its hinge.

"Like the circus," Rydra said. "But, I'm older now. Come." It was an act of will to offer her arm. His hand was paper dry, and so light she had to strain to keep from flinching.

---

4   "Captain Wong! I *am* delighted."

The Baroness extended her plump hand, of a pink and gray hue suggesting something parboiled. Her puffy freckled shoulders heaved beneath the straps of an evening dress tasteful enough over her distended figure, still grotesque.

"We have so little excitement here at the Yards that when someone as distinguished as yourself pays us a visit . . ." She let the sentence end in what would have been an ecstatic smile, but the weight of her doughy cheeks distorted it into a porcine pastiche of itself.

Rydra held the soft, malleable fingers as short a time as politeness allowed and returned the smile. She remembered, as a little girl, being obliged not to cry through punishment. Having to smile was worse. The Baroness seemed a muffled, vast, vacuous silence. The small muscle shifts, those counter communications that she was used to in direct conversation, were blunted in the Baroness under the fat. Even though the voice came from the heavy lips in strident little screeches, it was as though they talked through blankets.

"But your crew! We intended them all to be present—twenty-one, now that's what a full crew consists of." She shook her finger in patronizing disapproval. "I read up on these things, you know. And there are only eighteen of you here."

"I thought the discorporate members might remain on the ship," Rydra explained. "You need special equipment to talk with them and I thought they might upset your other guests. They're really more content with themselves for company, and they don't eat."

They're having barbecued lamb for dinner and you'll go to hell for lying, she commented to herself—in Basque.

"Discorporate?" The Baroness patted the lacquered intricacies of her high-coifed hair. "You mean dead? Oh, of course. Now I hadn't thought of that at all. You see how cut off we are from one another in this world? I'll have their places removed." Rydra wondered whether the Baron had discorporate detecting equipment operating, as the Baroness leaned toward her and whispered confidentially, "Your crew has enchanted everybody! Shall we go in?"

With the Baron on her left—his palm a parchment sling for her forearm—and the Baroness leaning on her right—breathy and damp—they walked from the white stone foyer into the hall.

"Hey, Captain!" Calli bellowed, striding toward them from a quarter of the way across the room. "This is a pretty neat place, huh?" With his elbows he gestured around at the crowded hall, then held up his glass to show the size of his drink. He pursed his lips and nodded approvingly. "Let me get you some of these, Captain." Now he raised a handful of tiny sandwiches, olives stuffed with liver, and bacon-wrapped prunes. "There's a guy with a whole tray full running around over there." He pointed again with his elbow. "Ma'am, sir—" he looked from the Baroness to the Baron—"can I get you some, too?" He put one of the sandwiches in his mouth and followed it with a gulp from his glass. "*Uhmpmnle.*"

"I'll wait till he brings them over here," the Baroness said.

Amused, Rydra glanced at her hostess, but there was a smile, much more the proper size, winding through her fleshy features. "I hope you like them."

Calli swallowed. "I do." Then he screwed up his face, set his teeth, opened his lips, and shook his head. "*Except* those really salty ones with the fish. I didn't like those at all, ma'am. But the rest are okay."

"I'll tell you—" the Baroness leaned forward, the smile crumbling into a chesty chuckle—"I never really liked the salty ones either!"

She looked from Rydra to the Baron with a shrug of mock surrender. "But one is so tyrannized by one's caterer nowadays, what can one do?"

"If I didn't like them," Calli said, jerking his head aside in determination, "I'd tell him don't bring none!"

The Baroness looked back with raised eyebrows. "You know,

you're perfectly right! That's exactly what I'm going to do!" She peered across Rydra to her husband. "That's just what I'm going to do, Felix, next time."

A waiter with a tray of glasses said, "Would you care for a drink?"

"She don't want one of them little tiny ones," Calli said, gesturing toward Rydra. "Get her a big one like I got."

Rydra laughed. "I'm afraid I have to be a lady tonight, Calli."

"Nonsense!" cried the Baroness. "I want a big one, too. Now let's see, I put the bar somewhere over there, didn't I?"

"That's where it was when I saw it last," Calli said.

"We're here to have fun this evening, and nobody is going to have fun with one of *those*." She seized Rydra's arm and called back to her husband, "Felix, be sociable," and led Rydra away. "That's Dr. Keebling. The woman with the bleached hair is Dr. Crane, and that's my brother-in-law, Albert. I'll introduce you on the way back. They're all my husband's colleagues. They work with him on those dreadful things he was showing you in the cellar. I wish he wouldn't keep his private collection in the house. It's gruesome. I'm always afraid one of them will crawl up here in the middle of the night and chop our heads off. I think he's trying to make up for his son. You know we lost our little boy, Nyles—I think it's been eight years. Felix has thrown himself totally into his work since. But that's a terribly glib explanation, isn't it? Captain Wong, do you find us dreadfully provincial?"

"Not at all."

"You should. But then, you don't know any of us well, do you. Oh, the bright young people who come here, with their bright, lively imaginations. They do nothing all day long but think of ways to kill. It's a terribly placid society, really. But, why shouldn't it be? All its aggressions are vented from nine to five.

Still, I think it does something to our minds. Imagination should be used for something other than pondering murder, don't you think?"

"I do." Concern grew for the weighty woman.

Just then they were stopped by clotted guests.

"What's going on here?" demanded the Baroness. "Sam, what are they doing in there?"

Sam smiled, stepped back, and the Baroness wedged herself into the space, still clutching Rydra's arm.

"Hold 'em back some!"

Rydra recognized Lizzy's voice. Someone else moved and she could see. The kids from Drive had cleared a space ten feet across, and were guarding it like junior police. Lizzy crouched with three boys, who, from their dress, were local gentry of Armsedge. "What you have to understand," she was saying, "is that it's all in the wrist." She flipped a marble with her thumbnail: it struck first one, then another, and one of the struck ones struck a third.

"Hey, do that again!"

Lizzy picked up another marble. "Only one knuckle on the floor, now, so you can pivot. But it's mostly from the wrist."

The marble darted out, struck, struck, and struck. Five or six people applauded. Rydra was one.

The Baroness touched her breast. "Lovely shot! Perfectly lovely!" She remembered herself and glanced back. "Oh, you must want to watch this, Sam. You're the ballistics expert, anyway." With polite embarrassment she relinquished her place and turned to Rydra as they continued across the floor. "There. There, that is why I'm so glad you and your crew came to us this evening. You bring something so cool and pleasing, so fresh, so crisp."

"You speak about us as though we were a salad." Rydra laughed. In the Baroness the "appetite" was not so menacing.

"I dare say if you stayed here long enough we would devour you, if you let us. What you bring we are very hungry for."

"What is it?"

They arrived at the bar, then turned with their drinks. The Baroness's face strained toward hardness. "Well, you . . . you come to us and immediately we start to learn things, things about you, and ultimately about ourselves."

"I don't understand."

"Take your Navigator. He likes his drinks big and all the *hors d'oeuvres* except the anchovies. That's more than I know about the likes and dislikes of anyone else in the room. You offer Scotch, they drink Scotch. You offer tequila, tequila they then down by the gallon. And just a moment ago I discovered—" she shook her supine hand—"that it's all in the wrist. I never knew *that* before."

"We're used to talking to each other."

"Yes, but you tell the important things. What you like, what you don't like, how you do things. Do you really want to be introduced to all those stuffy men and women who kill people?"

"Not really."

"Didn't think so. And I don't want to bother, myself. Oh, there are three or four here whom I think you would like. But I'll see that you meet them before you leave." She barreled into the crowd.

Tides, Rydra thought. Oceans. Hyperstasis currents. Or the movement of people in a large room. She drifted along the least resistant ways that pulsed open, then closed as someone moved to meet someone, to get a drink, to leave a conversation.

Then there was a corner, a spiral stair. She climbed, pausing as she came around the second turn to watch the crowd beneath. There was a double door ajar at the top, a breeze. She stepped outside.

Violet had been replaced by artful, cloud-streaked purple.

Soon the planetoid's chromadome would simulate night. Moist vegetation lipped the railing. At one end, the vines had completely covered the white stone.

"Captain?"

Ron, shadowed and brushed with leaves, sat in the corner of the balcony, hugging his knees. Skin is not silver, she thought, yet whenever I see him that way, curled up in himself, I picture a knot of white metal. He lifted his chin from his kneecaps and put his back against the verdant hedge so there were leaves in his corn-silk hair.

"What're you doing?"

"Too many people."

She nodded, watching him press his shoulders downward, watching his triceps leap on the bone, then still. With each breath in the young gnarled body, the tiny movements sang to her. She listened to the singing for nearly half a minute while he watched her, sitting still, yet always the tiny entrancements. The rose on his shoulder whispered against the leaves. When she had listened to the muscular music awhile, she asked:

"Trouble between you, Mollya, and Calli?"

"No. I mean . . . just . . ."

"Just what?" She smiled and leaned on the balcony edge.

He leaned his chin to his knees again. "I guess they're fine. But, I'm the youngest . . . and . . ." Suddenly the shoulders raised. "How the hell would you understand! Sure, you know about things like this, but you don't *really* know. You write what you see. Not what you do." It came out in little explosions of half-whispered sound. She heard the words and watched the jaw muscle jerk and beat and pop, a small beast inside his cheek. "Perverts," he said. "That's what you Customs all really think. The Baron and the Baroness, all those people in there staring at us, who can't understand why you could want more than one lover. And you can't understand either."

"Ron?"

He snapped his teeth on a leaf and yanked it from the stem.

"Five years ago, Ron, I was . . . tripled."

The face turned to her as if pulling against a spring, then yanked back. He spit the leaf. "You're Customs, Captain. You circle Transport, but just the way you let them eat you up with their eyes, the way you turn and watch to see who you are when you walk by: you're a Queen, yeah. But a Queen in Customs. You're not Transport."

"Ron, I'm public. That's why they look. I write books. Customs people read them, yes, but they look because they want to know who the hell wrote them. Customs didn't write them. I talk to Customs and Customs looks at me and says: 'You're Transport.'" She shrugged. "I'm neither. But even so, I was tripled. I know about that."

"Customs don't triple," he said.

"Two guys and myself. If I ever do it again it'll be with a girl and a guy. For me that would be easier, I think. But I was tripled for three years. That's over twice as long as you've been."

"Yours didn't stick, then. Ours did. At least it was sticking together with Cathy."

"One was killed," Rydra said. "One is in suspended animation at Hippocrates General waiting for them to discover a cure for Caulder's disease. I don't think it will be in my lifetime, but if it is . . ." In the silence he turned to her. "What is it?" she asked.

"Who were they?"

"Customs or Transport?" She shrugged. "Like me, neither really. Fobo Lombs, he was captain of an interstellar transport; he was the one who made me go through and get my Captain's papers. Also he worked planetside doing hydroponics research, working on storage methods for hyperstatic hauls. Who was he? He was slim and blond and wonderfully affectionate and drank too much sometimes, and would come back from a trip and get drunk and in a fight and in jail, and we'd have to bail him out— really it only happened twice. But we teased him about it for a year. And he didn't like to sleep in the middle of the bed because he always wanted to let one arm hang over."

Ron laughed, and his hands, grasping high on his forearms, slid to his wrists.

"He was killed in a cave-in exploring the Ganymede Catacombs during the second summer that the three of us worked together on the Jovian Geological Survey."

"Like Cathy," Ron said, after a moment.

"Muels Aranlyde was—"

"*Empire Star* . . . ?" Ron said, his eyes widening. "And the rest of the 'Comet Jo' books! You were tripled with Muels Aranlyde?"

She nodded. "Those books were a lot of fun, weren't they?"

"Hell, I must've read all of them," Ron said. His knees came apart. "What sort of a guy was he? Was he anything like Comet?"

"As a matter of fact, Comet Jo started out to be Fobo. Fobo would get involved in something or other, I'd get upset, and Muels would start another novel."

"You mean they're like . . . *true* stories?"

She shook her head. "Most of the books are just all the fantastic things that could have happened, or that we worried might have happened. Muels himself? In the books he always disguises himself as a computer. He was dark, and withdrawn, and incredibly patient and incredibly kind. He showed me all about sentences and paragraphs—did you know the emotion unit in writing is the paragraph?—and how to separate what you can say from what you can imply, and when to do one or the other—" She stopped. "Then he'd give me a manuscript and say, 'Now you tell me what's wrong with the words.' The only thing I could ever find was that there were too many of them. It was just after Fobo was killed that I really got down to my poetry. Muels used to tell me if I ever would, I'd be great because I knew so much about its elements to start. I had to get down something then, because Fobo was . . . but you know about that, though. Muels caught Caulder's disease about four months later. Neither one of them saw my first book, though they'd seen most of the poems. Maybe someday Muels will read them. He might even write some more of Comet's adventures—and maybe even go to the Morgue and call back my thinking pattern and ask, 'Now tell me what's wrong with the words'; and I'll be able to tell him so much more, so much. But there won't be any consciousness left . . ." She felt herself drift toward the dangerous emotions, let them get as close as they would. Dangerous or not, it had been three years since her emotions had scared her too much to watch them. ". . . so much more."

Ron sat cross-legged now, forearms on his knees, hands hanging.

"*Empire Star* and Comet Jo; we had so much fun with those stories, whether it was arguing about them all night over coffee, or correcting galleys, or sneaking into bookshops and pulling them out from behind the other books."

"I used to do that, too," Ron said. "But just 'cause I liked them."

"We even had fun arguing about who was going to sleep in the middle."

It was like a cue. Ron began to pull back together, knees rising, arms locking around them, chin down. "I got both of mine, at least," he said. "I guess I should be pretty happy."

"Maybe you should. Maybe you shouldn't. Do they love you?"

"They said so."

"Do you love them?"

"Christ, yes. I talk to Mollya and she's trying to explain

something to me and she still don't talk so good yet, but suddenly I figure out what she means, and . . ." He straightened his body and looked up as though the word he was searching for was someplace high.

"It's wonderful," she supplied.

"Yeah, it's . . ." He looked at her. "It's wonderful."

"You and Calli?"

"Hell, Calli's just a big old bear and I can tumble him around and play with him. But it's him and Mollya. He still can't understand her so well. And because I'm the youngest he thinks he should learn quicker than me. And he doesn't, so he keeps away from both of us. Now like I say, when he gets in a mood, I can always handle him. But she's new, and thinks he's mad at her."

"Want to know what to do?" Rydra asked, after a moment.

"Do you know?"

She nodded. "It hurts more when there's something wrong between them because there doesn't seem to be anything you can do. But it's easier to fix."

"Why?"

"Because they love you."

He was waiting now.

"Calli gets into one of his moods, and Mollya doesn't know how to get through to him."

Ron nodded.

"Mollya speaks another language, and Calli can't get through that."

He nodded again.

"Now you can communicate with both of them. You can't act as a go-between; that never works. But you can teach each of them how to do what you know already."

"Teach . . . ?"

"What do you do with Calli when he gets moody?"

"I pull his ears," Ron said. "He tells me to cut it out until he starts laughing, and then I roll him around on the floor."

Rydra made a face. "It's unorthodox, but if it works, fine. Now show Mollya how. She's athletic. Let her practice on you till she gets it right, if you have to."

"I don't like to get *my* ears pulled," Ron said.

"Sometimes you have to make sacrifices." She tried not to smile; and smiled anyway.

Ron rubbed his left earlobe with the ham of his thumb. "I guess so."

"And you have to teach Calli the words to get through to Mollya."

"But I don't know the words myself, sometimes. I can just guess better than he can."

"If he knew the words, would it help?"

"Sure."

"I've got Kiswahili grammar books in my cabin. Pick them up when we get back to the ship."

"Hey, that would be fine—" He stopped, withdrawing just a bit into the leaves. "Only Calli don't read much of anything."

"You'll help him."

"Teach him?" Ron asked.

"That's right."

"Do you think he'll do it?"

"To get closer to Mollya?" asked Rydra. "Do you think so?"

"He will." Like metal unbending, Ron suddenly stood. "He will."

"Are you going inside now?" she asked. "We'll be eating in a few minutes."

Ron turned to the rail and looked at the vivid sky. "They keep a beautiful shield up here."

"To keep from being burned up by Bellatrix," Rydra said.

"So they don't have to think about what they're doing."

Rydra raised her eyebrows. Still the concern over right and wrong, even amidst domestic confusion. "That, too," she said and wondered about the war.

His tensing back told her he would come later, wanted to think some more. She went through the double doors and started down the staircase.

"I saw you go out, and I thought I'd wait for you to come back in."

Déjà vu, she thought. But she couldn't have seen him before in her life. Blue-black hair over a face craggy but in its late twenties. He stepped back to make way for her on the stairway with an incredible economy of movement. She looked from hands to face for a gesture revealing something. He watched her back, giving nothing; then he turned and nodded toward the people below. He indicated the Baron, who stood alone toward the middle of the room. "Yon Cassius has a lean and hungry look."

"I wonder how hungry he is?" Rydra said, and felt strange again.

The Baroness was churning toward her husband through the crowd, to ask advice about whether to begin dinner or wait another five minutes, or some other equally desperate decision.

"What must a marriage between two people like that be?" the stranger asked with austerely patronizing amusement.

"Comparatively simple, I suppose," Rydra said. "They've just got each other to worry about."

A polite look of inquiry. When she offered no elucidation, the stranger turned back to the crowd. "They make such odd faces when they glance up here to see if it's you, Miss Wong."

"They leer," she said, shortly.

"Bandicoots. That's what they look like. A pack of them."

"I wonder if their artificial sky makes them seem so sickly?" She felt herself leaking a controlled hostility.

He laughed. "Bandicoots with thalassanemia!"

"I guess so. You're not from the Yards?" His complexion had a life that would have faded under the artificial sky.

"As a matter of fact, I am."

Surprised, she would have asked him more, but the loud-speakers suddenly announced: "Ladies and Gentlemen, dinner is served."

He accompanied her down the stairs, but two or three steps into the crowd she discovered he had disappeared. She continued toward the dining room alone.

Under the arch the Baron and Baroness waited for her. As the Baroness took her arm, the chamber orchestra on the dais fell to their instruments.

"Come, we're down this way."

She kept near the puffy matron through the people milling about the serpentine table that curved and twisted back on itself.

"We're over there."

And the Basque message: Captain, on your transcriber, something's coming over back on the ship. The small explosion in her mind stopped her.

"Babel-17—!"

The Baron turned to her. "Yes, Captain Wong?" She watched uncertainty score tense lines on his face.

"Is there anyplace in the Yards with particularly important materials or research going on that might be unguarded now?"

"That's all done automatically. Why?"

"Baron, there's a sabotage attack about to take place, or taking place right now."

"But how do you—"

"I can't explain now, but you'd better make sure everything is all right."

And the tension turned.

The Baroness touched her husband's arm, and said with sudden coolness, "Felix, there's your seat."

The Baron pulled out his chair, sat down, and unceremoniously pushed aside his place setting. There was a control panel beneath the doily. As people seated themselves, Rydra saw Brass, twenty feet away, lower himself on the special hammock that had been set up for his glittering, gigantic bulk.

"You sit here, my dear. We'll simply go on with the party as if nothing was happening. I think that's best."

Rydra seated herself next to the Baron, and the Baroness lowered herself carefully to the chair on her left. The Baron was whispering into a throat microphone. Pictures, which she was at the wrong angle to see clearly, flashed on the eight-inch screen. He looked up long enough to say, "Nothing yet, Captain Wong."

"Ignore what he's doing," the Baroness said. "This is much more interesting over here."

Into her lap she swung out a small console from where it had hung beneath the table edge.

"Ingenious little thing," the Baroness continued, looking around. "I think we're ready. There!" Her pudgy forefinger struck at one of the buttons, and lights about the room began to lower. "I control the whole meal just by pressing the right one at the right time. Watch!" She struck at another one.

Along the center of the table now, under the gentled light, panels opened and great platters of fruit, candied apples and sugared grapes, halved melons filled with honeyed nuts, rose up before the guests.

"And wine!" said the Baroness, reaching down again.

Along the hundreds of feet of table, basins rose. Sparkling froth foamed the brim as the fountain mechanism began. Spurting liquid streamed.

"Fill your glass, dear. Drink up," prompted the Baroness, raising her own beneath a jet; the crystal splashed with purple.

On her right the Baron said: "The Arsenal seems to be all right. I'm alerting all the special projects. You're sure this sabotage attack is going on right now?"

"Either right now," she told him, "or within the next two or three minutes. It might be an explosion, or some major piece of equipment may fail."

"That doesn't leave me much to go on. Though communications has picked up your Babel-17. I've been alerted to how these attempts run."

"Try one of these, Captain Wong." The Baroness handed her a quartered mango which Rydra discovered, when she tasted it, had been marinated in Kirsch.

Nearly all the guests were seated now. She watched a platoon kid, named Mike, searching for his name-card halfway across the hall. And down the table length she saw the stranger who had stopped her on the spiral stair hurrying toward them behind the seated guests.

"The wine is not grape, but plum," the Baroness said. "A little heavy to start with, but so good with fruit. I'm particularly proud of the strawberries. The legumes are a hydroponicist's nightmare, you know, but this year we were able to get such lovely ones."

Mike found his seat and reached both hands into the fruit bowl. The stranger rounded the last loop of table. Calli was holding a goblet of wine in each hand, looking from one to the other—trying to determine the larger . . . ?

"I could be a tease," the Baroness said, "and bring out the sherbets first. Or do you think I ought best go on to the caldo verde? The way I prepare it, it's very light. I can never decide—"

The stranger reached the Baron, leaned over his shoulder to watch the screen, and whispered something. The Baron turned to him, turned back slowly with both hands on the table—and fell forward! A trickle of blood wormed from beneath his face.

Rydra jerked back in her chair. Murder. A mosaic came together in her head, and when it was together, it said: murder. She leapt up.

The Baroness exhaled hoarse breath and rose, overturning her chair. She flapped her hands hysterically toward her husband and shook her head.

Rydra whirled to see the stranger snatch a vibra-gun from beneath his jacket. She yanked the Baroness out of the way. The shot was low and struck the console.

Once moved, the Baroness staggered to her husband and grasped him. Her breathy moan took voice and became a wail. The hulking form, like a blimp deflating, sank and pulled Felix Ver Dorco's body from the table, till she was kneeling on the floor, holding him in her arms, rocking him gently, screaming.

Guests had risen now; talking became roaring.

With the console smashed, along the table the fruit platters were pushed aside by emerging peacocks, cooked, dressed, and reassembled with sugared heads, tail feathers swaying. None of the clearing mechanisms were operating. Tureens of caldo verde crowded the wine basins till both overturned, flooding the table. Fruit rolled over the edge.

Through the voices, the vibra-gun hissed on her left, left again, then right. People ran from their chairs, blocked her view. She heard the gun once more and saw Dr. Crane double over, to be caught by a surprised neighbor as her bleached hair came undone and tumbled her face.

Spitted lambs rose to upset the peacocks. Feathers swept the floor. Wine fountains spurted the glistening amber skins which hissed and steamed. Food fell back into the opening and struck red heating coils. Rydra smelled burning.

She darted forward, caught the arm of the fat, black-bearded man. "Slug, get the kids out of here!"

"What do you think I'm doing, Captain?"

She darted away, came up against a length of table, and vaulted the steaming pit. The intricate, oriental dessert—sizzling bananas dipped first in honey then rolled to the plate over a ramp of crushed ice—was emerging as she sprang. The sparkling confections shot across the ramp and dropped to the floor, honey crystallized to glittering thorns. They rolled among the guests, cracked underfoot. People slipped and flailed and fell.

"Snazzy way to slide on a banana, huh, Captain?" commented Calli. "What's going on?"

"Get Mollya and Ron back to the ship!"

Urns rose now, struck the rotisserie arrangement, overturned, and grounds and boiling coffee splattered. A woman shrieked, clutching her scalded arm.

"This ain't no fun anymore," Calli said. "I'll round them up."

He started away as Slug hurried back the other way. "Slug, what's a bandicoot?" She caught his arm again.

"Vicious little animal. Marsupial, I think. Why?"

"That's right. I remember now. And thalassanemia?"

"Funny time to ask. Some sort of anemia."

"I know that. *What* sort? You're the medic on the ship."

"Let me see." He closed his eyes a moment. "I got all this once in a hypno-course. Yeah, I remember. It's hereditary, the Caucasian equivalent of sickle cell anemia, where the red blood cells collapse because the haptoglobins break down—"

"—and allow the hemoglobins to leak out and the cell gets crushed by osmotic pressure. I've figured it out. Get the hell out of here."

Puzzled, the Slug started toward the arch.

Rydra started after him, slipped in wine sherbet, and grabbed Brass, who now gleamed above her. "Take it easy, Ca'tain!"

"Out of here, baby," she demanded. "And fast."

"Ho' a ride?" Grinning, he hooked his arms at his hip, and she climbed to his back, clutching his sides with her knees and holding his shoulders. The great muscles that had defeated the Silver Dragon bunched beneath her, and he leapt, clearing the table and landing on all fours. Before the fanged, golden beast, guests scattered. They made for the arched door.

---

5 Hysterical exhaustion frothed.

She smashed through it, into the *Rimbaud*'s cabin, and punched the intercom. "Slug, is every—"

"All present and accounted for, Captain."

"The discorporate—"

"Safe aboard, all three."

Panting, Brass filled the entrance hatch behind her.

She switched to another channel, and a near-musical sound filled the room. "Good. It's still going."

"That's it?" asked Brass.

She nodded. "Babel-17. It's being automatically transcribed so I can study it later. Anyway, here goes nothing." She threw a switch.

"What you doing?"

"I prerecorded some messages and I'm sending them out now. Maybe they'll get through." She stopped the first tape and started a second. "I don't know it well, yet. I know a little, but not enough. I feel like someone at a performance of Shakespeare shouting catcalls in pidgin English."

An outside line signaled for her attention. "Captain Wong, this is Albert Ver Dorco." The voice was perturbed. "We've had a terrible catastrophe, and we're in total confusion here. I could not find you at my brother's, but flight clearance just told me you had requested immediate takeoff for hyperstasis jump."

"I requested nothing of the kind. I just wanted to get my crew out of there. Have you found out what's going on?"

"But, Captain, they said you were in the process of clearing for flight. You have top priority, so I can't very well countermand your order. But I called to request that you please stay until this matter is cleared up, unless you are acting on some information that—"

"We're *not* taking off!" Rydra said.

"We better not be," interjected Brass. "I'm not wired into the ship yet."

"Apparently your automatic James Bond ran berserk," Rydra told Ver Dorco.

" . . . Bond?"

"A mythological reference. Forgive me. TW-55 flipped."

"Oh, yes. I know. It assassinated my brother, and four extremely important officials. It couldn't have picked out four more key figures if it had been planned."

"It was. TW-55 was sabotaged. And no, I don't know how. I suggest you contact General Forester back at—"

"Captain, flight clearance says you're still signaling for take-off! I have no official authority here, but you must—"

"Slug! Are we taking off?"

"Why, yes. Didn't you just issue orders down here for emergency hyperstasis exit?"

"Brass isn't even at his station yet, you idiot!"

"But I just received clearance from you thirty seconds ago. Of course he's hooked in. I just spoke—"

Brass lumbered across the floor and bellowed into the microphone. "I'm standing right behind her, numbskull! What are you gonna do, dive into the middle of Bellatrix? Or maybe come out inside some nova? These things head for the biggest mass around when they drift!"

"But you just—"

A grinding started somewhere below them. And a sudden surge.

Over the loudspeaker from Albert Ver Dorco: "Captain Wong . . . !"

Rydra shouted again, "Idiot, cut the stasis gen—"

But the generators were already whistling over the roar.

A surge again; she jerked against her hands holding the desk edge, saw Brass flail one claw in the air. And—

part three

Jebel Tarik

Real, grimy, and exiled, he
eludes us.
I would show him books and bridges.
I would make a language we could all speak.
No blond fantasy
Mother has sent to plague us in the Spring,
he has his own bad dreams, needs work, gets drunk,
maybe would not have chosen to be beautiful.
   —from *The Navigators*

You have imposed upon me a treaty of silence.
   —from *The Song of Liadan*

1 Abstract thoughts in a blue room: Nominative, genitive, elative, accusative one, accusative two, ablative, partitive, illative, instructive, abessive, adessive, inessive, essive, allative, translative, comitative. Sixteen cases to the Finnish noun. Odd, some languages get by with only singular and plural. The North American Indian languages even failed to distinguish number. Except Sioux, in which there was a plural only for animate objects. The blue room was round and warm and smooth. No way to say *warm* in French. There was only *hot* and *tepid*. If there's no word for it, how do you think about it? And, if there isn't the proper form, you don't have the how even if you have the words. Imagine, in Spanish, having to assign a gender to every object: dog, table, tree, can opener. Imagine, in Hungarian, not being able to assign a gender to anything: *he, she, it* all the same word. Thou art my friend, but you are my king; thus the distinctions of Elizabeth the First's English. But with some oriental languages, which all but dispense with gender and number, you are my friend, *you* are my parent, and YOU are my priest, and *YOU* are my king, and **You** are my servant, and *You* are my servant whom I'm going to fire tomorrow if *You* don't watch it, and **YOU** are my king whose policies I totally disagree with and have sawdust in **YOUR** head instead of brains, **YOUR** highness, and *YOU* may be my friend, but I'm still gonna smack *YOU* up side the head if *YOU* ever say that to me again: and who the hell are you anyway . . . ?

What's your name? she thought in a round warm blue room.

Thoughts without a name in a blue room: Ursula, Priscilla, Barbara, Mary, Mona, and Natica: respectively, Bear, Old Lady,

Chatterbox, Bitter, Monkey, and Buttock. Name. Names?
What's in a name? What name am I in? In my father's father's
land, his name would come first, Wong Rydra. In Mollya's
home, I would not bear my father's name at all, but my
mother's. Words are names for things. In Plato's time things
were names for ideas—what better description of the Platonic
Ideal? But were words names for things, or was that just a bit of
semantic confusion? Words were symbols for *whole* categories
of things, where a name was put to a single object: a name on
something that requires a symbol jars, making humor. A symbol
on something that takes a name jars, too: a memory that
contained a torn window shade, his liquored breath, her
outrage, and crumpled clothing wedged behind a chipped, cheap
night table, "All right, *woman,* come here!" and she had whispered, with her hands achingly tight on the brass bar, "My *name*
is *Rydra!*" An individual, a thing apart from its environment,
and apart from all things in that environment; an individual was
a type of thing for which symbols were inadequate, and so
names were invented. I am invented. I am not a round warm
blue room. I am someone in that room; I am—

Her lids had been half-closed on her eyeballs. She opened
them and came up suddenly against a restraining web. It
knocked her breath out, and she fell back, turning about to look
at the room.

No.

She didn't "look at the room."

She "*something*ed at the *something*." The first something was
a tiny vocable that implied an immediate, but passive, perception that could be aural or olfactory as well as visual. The
second something was three equally tiny phonemes that blended
at different musical pitches: one, an indicator that fixed the size
of the chamber at roughly twenty-five feet cubical, the second
identifying the color and probable substance of the walls—some

blue metal—while the third was at once a placeholder for parti-
cles that should denote the room's function when she discovered
it, and a sort of grammatical tag by which she could refer to the
whole experience with only the one symbol for as long as she
needed. All four sounds took less time on her tongue and in her
mind than the one clumsy diphthong in "room." Babel-17; she
had felt it before with other languages, the opening, the widening, the mind forced to sudden growth. But this, this was like the
sudden focusing of a lens blurry for years.

She sat up again. Function?

What was the room used for? She rose slowly, and the web
caught her around the chest. Some sort of infirmary. She looked
down at the . . . not "webbing," but rather a three-particle
vowel differential, each particle of which defined one stress of
the three-way tie, so that the weakest points in the mesh were
identified when the total sound of the differential reached its
lowest point. By breaking the threads at these points, she realized, the whole web would unravel. Had she flailed at it, and not
named it in this new language, it would have been more than
secure enough to hold her. The transition from "memorized" to
"known" had taken place while she had been—

Where had she been? Anticipation, excitement, fear! She
pulled her mind back into English. Thinking in Babel-17 was
like suddenly seeing all the way down through water to the
bottom of a well that a moment ago you'd thought was only a
few feet deep. She reeled with vertigo.

It took her a blink to register the others. Brass hung in the
large hammock at the far wall—she saw the tines of one yellow
claw over the rim. The two smaller hammocks on the other side
must have been platoon kids. Above one edge she saw shiny
black hair as a head turned in sleep: Carlos. She couldn't see the
third. Curiosity made a small, unfriendly fist on something
important in her lower abdomen.

Then the wall faded.

She had been about to try and fix herself, if not in place and hour, at least in some set of possibilities. With the fading wall, the attempt stopped. She watched.

It happened in the upper part of the wall to her left. It glowed, grew transparent, and a tongue of metal formed in the air, sloping gently toward her.

Three men:

The closest, at the ramp's head, had a face like brown rock cut roughly and put together fast. He wore an outdated garment, the sort that had preceded contour capes. It automatically formed to the body, but was made of porous plastic and looked rather like armor. A black, deep-piled material cloaked one shoulder and arm. His worn sandals were laced high on his calves. Tufts of fur beneath the thongs prevented chafing. His only cosmetisurgery was false silver hair and upswept metallic eyebrows. From one distended earlobe hung a thick silver ring. He touched his vibra-gun holster resting on his stomach as he looked from hammock to hammock.

The second man stepped in front. He was a slim, fantastic concoction of cosmetisurgical invention, sort of a griffin, sort of a monkey, sort of a sea horse: scales, feathers, claws, and beak had been grafted to a body she was sure had originally resembled a cat's. He crouched at the first man's side, squatting on surgically distended haunches, brushing his knuckles on the metal flooring. He glanced up as the first man absently reached down to scratch his head.

Rydra waited for them to speak. A word would release identification: Alliance or Invader. Her mind was ready to spring on whatever tongue they spoke, to extract what she knew of its thinking habits, tendencies toward logical ambiguities, absence of presence of verbal rigor, in whatever areas she might take advantage of—

The second man moved back and she saw the third who still stood at the rear. Taller, and more powerfully built than the others, he wore only a breech, was mildly round-shouldered. Grafted onto his wrists and heels were cock spurs—they were sometimes sported by the lower elements of the Transport underworld, and bore the same significance as brass knuckles or blackjacks of centuries past. His head had been recently shaved and the hair had started back in a dark, static-electric brush. Around one knotty bicep was a band of red flesh, like a blood bruise or inflamed scar. The brand had become so common on characters in mystery novels five years back that now it had been nearly dropped as a hopeless cliché. It was a convict's mark from the penal caves of Titin. Something about him was brutal enough to make her glance away. Something was graceful enough to make her look back.

The two on the head of the ramp turned to the third. She waited for words, to define, fix, identify. They looked at her, then walked into the wall. The ramp began to retract.

She pushed herself up. "Please," she called out. "Where are we?"

The silver-haired man said, "Jebel Tarik." The wall solidified.

Rydra looked down at the web (which was something else in another language) popped one cord, popped another. The tension gave, till it unraveled and she jumped to the floor. As she stood she saw the other platoon kid was Kile, who worked with Lizzy in Repair. Brass had started struggling. "Keep still a second." She began to pop cords.

"What did he say to you?" Brass wanted to know. "Was that his name, or was he telling you to lie down and shut u'?"

She shrugged and broke another. "Jebel, that's *mountain* in Old Moorish. Tarik's Mountain, maybe."

Brass sat up as the frayed string fell. "How do you do that?" he asked. "*I* pushed against the thing for ten minutes and it wouldn't give."

"Tell you some other time. Tarik could be somebody's name."

Brass looked back at the broken web, clawed behind one tufted ear, then shook his puzzled head and reared.

"At least they're not Invaders," Rydra said.

"Who says?"

"I doubt that many humans on the other side of the axis have even heard of Old Moorish. The Earthmen who migrated there all came from North and South America before Americasia was formed and Pan Africa swallowed up Europe. Besides, the Titin penal caves are inside Caesar."

"Oh, yeah," Brass said. "Him. But that don't mean one of its alumni has to be."

She looked at where the wall had opened. Grasping their situation seemed as futile as grasping that blue metal.

"What the hell ha''ened anyway?"

"We took off without a pilot," Rydra said. "I guess whoever broadcast in Babel-17 can also broadcast English."

"I don't think we took off without a 'ilot. Who did Slug talk to just before we shot? If we didn't have a 'ilot, we wouldn't be here. We'd be a grease s'ot on the nearest, biggest sun."

"Probably whoever cracked those circuit boards." Rydra cast her mind into the past as the plaster of unconsciousness crumbled. "I guess the saboteur doesn't want to kill me. TW-55 could have picked me off as easily as he picked off the Baron."

"I wonder if the s'y on the shi' s'eaks Babel-17 too?"

Rydra nodded. "So do I."

Brass looked around. "Is this all there is? Where's the rest of the crew?"

"Sir, Ma'am . . . ?"

They turned.

Another opening in the wall. A skinny girl, with a green scarf binding back brown hair, held out a bowl.

"The master said you were about, so I brought this." Her eyes were dark and large, and the lids beat like bird wings. She gestured with the bowl.

Rydra responded to her openness, yet also detected a fear of strangers. But the thin fingers grasped surely on the bowl's edge. "You're kind to bring this."

The girl bowed slightly and smiled.

"You're frightened of us, I know," Rydra said. "You shouldn't be."

The fear was leaving; bony shoulders relaxed.

"What's your master's name?" Rydra asked.

"Tarik."

Rydra looked back and nodded to Brass.

"And we're in Tarik's Mountain?" She took the bowl from the girl. "How did we get here?"

"He hooked your ship up from the center of the Cygnus-42 nova just before your stasis generators failed this side of the jump."

Brass hissed, his substitute for a whistle. "No wonder we went unconscious. We did some fast drifting."

The thought pulled the plug from Rydra's stomach. "Then we did drift into a nova area. Maybe we didn't have a pilot after all."

Brass removed the white napkin from the bowl. "Have some chicken, Ca'tain." It was roasted and still hot.

"In a minute," she said. "I have to think about that one some more." She turned back to the girl. "Tarik's Mountain is a ship, then. And we're on it?"

The girl put her hands behind her back and nodded. "And it's a good ship, too."

"I'm sure you don't take passengers. What cargo do you haul?"

She had asked the wrong question. Fear again; not a personal distrust of strangers, something formal and pervasive. "We carry no cargo, ma'am." Then she blurted, "I'm not supposed to talk to you none. You have to speak with Tarik." She backed into the wall.

"Brass," Rydra said, turning and scratching her head, "there're no space-pirates anymore, are there?"

"There haven't been any hijacks on transport ships for seventy years."

"That's what I thought. So what sort of ship are we on?"

"Beats me." Then the burnished planes of his cheeks shifted in the blue light. Silken brows pulled down over the deep disks of his eyes. "*Hooked* the *Rimbaud* out of the Cygnus-42? I guess I know why they call it Tarik's Mountain. This thing must be big as a damned battleshi'."

"If it is a warship, Tarik doesn't look like any stellarman I ever saw."

"And they don't allow ex-convicts in the army, anyway. What do you think we've stumbled on, Ca'tain?"

She took a drumstick from the bowl. "I guess we wait till we speak to Tarik." There was a movement in the other hammocks. "I hope the kids are all right. Why didn't I ask that girl if the rest of the crew was aboard?" She strode to Carlos' hammock. "How do *you* feel this morning?" she asked brightly. For the first time she saw the snaps that held the webbing to the underside of the sling.

"My head," Carlos said, grinning. "I got a hangover, I think."

"Not with that leer on your face. What do you know about hangovers, anyway?" The snaps took three times as long to undo as breaking the net.

"The wine," Carlos said, "at the party. I had a lot. Hey, what happened?"

"Tell you when I find out. Upsy-daisy." She tipped the hammock and he rolled to his feet.

Carlos pushed the hair out of his eyes. "Where's everybody else?"

"Kile's over there. That's all of us in this room."

Brass had freed Kile, who sat on the hammock edge now, trying to put his knuckles up his nose.

"Hey, baby," Carlos said. "You all right?"

Kile ran his toes up and down his Achilles tendon, yawned, and said something unintelligible at the same time.

"You did not," Carlos said, "because I checked it just as soon as I got in."

Oh well, she thought, there were still languages left at which she might gain more fluency.

Kile was scratching his elbow now. Suddenly he stuck his tongue in the corner of his mouth and looked up.

So did Rydra.

The ramp was extending from the wall again. This time it joined the floor.

"Will you come with me, Rydra Wong?"

Tarik, holstered and silver-haired, stood in the dark opening.

"The rest of my crew," Rydra said, "are they all right?"

"They are all in other wards. If you wish to see them—"

"Are they all right?"

Tarik nodded.

Rydra thumped Carlos on his head. "I'll see you later," she whispered.

The commons was arched and balconied, its walls dull as rock. The expanses were hung with green and crimson zodiac signs or representations of battles. And the stars—at first, she thought the light-flecked void beyond the gallery columns was an actual view-port; but it was only a great hundred-foot-long projection of the night beyond their ship.

Men and women sat and talked around wooden tables, or lounged by the walls. Down a broad set of steps was a wide counter filled with food and pitchers. The opening hung with pots, pans, and platters, and behind it she saw the aluminum and white recess of the galley where aproned men and women prepared dinner.

The company turned when they entered. Those nearest touched their foreheads in salute. She followed Tarik to the raised steps and walked to the cushioned benches at the top.

The griffin man came scurrying up. "Master, this is she?" Tarik turned to Rydra, his rocky face softening. "This is my amusement, my distraction, my ease of ire, Captain Wong. In him I keep the sense of humor that all around will tell you I lack. Hey, Klik, leap up and straighten the seats for conference."

The feathered head ducked brightly, black eye winking, and Klik whacked the cushions puffy. A moment later Tarik and Rydra sank into them.

"Tarik," asked Rydra, "what route does your ship run?"

"We stay in the Specelli Snap." He pushed his cape back from his three-knobbed shoulder. "What was your original position before you were caught up in the noval tide?"

"We . . . took off from the War Yards at Armsedge."

Tarik nodded. "You are fortunate. Most shadow-ships would have left you to emerge in the nova when your generators gave out. It would have been a rather final discorporation."

"I guess so." Rydra felt her stomach sink at the memory. Then she asked, "Shadow-ships . . . ?"

"Yes. That's Jebel Tarik."

"I'm afraid I don't know what a shadow-ship is."

Tarik laughed, a soft, rough sound in the back of his throat. "Perhaps it's just as well. I hope you never have occasion to wish I had not told you."

"Go ahead," Rydra said. "I'm listening."

"The Specelli Snap is radio-dense. A ship, even a mountain like Tarik, over any long-range is undetectable. It also runs across the stasis side of Cancer."

"That galaxy lies under the Invaders," Rydra said, with conditioned apprehension.

"The Snap is the boundary along Cancer's edge. We . . . patrol the area and keep the Invader ships . . . in their place."

Rydra watched the hesitation in his face. "But not officially?"

Again he laughed. "How could we, Captain Wong?" He stroked a ruff of feathers between Klik's shoulder blades. The jester arched his back. "Even official warships cannot receive their orders and directions in the Snap because of the radio-density. So Administrative Alliance Headquarters is lenient with us. We do our job well; they look the other way. They cannot give us orders; neither can they supply us with weapons or provisions. Therefore we ignore certain salvage conventions and capture regulations. Stellarmen call us looters." He searched her for a reaction. "We are staunch defenders of the Alliance, Captain Wong, but . . ." He raised his hand, made a fist, and brought the fist against his belly. "But if we are hungry, and no Invader ship has come by—well, we take what comes past."

"I see," Rydra said. "Do I understand I am taken?" She recalled the Baron, the rapaciousness implicit in the lean figure.

Tarik's fingers opened on his stomach. "Do I look hungry?"

Rydra grinned. "You look very well fed."

He nodded. "This has been a prosperous month. Were it not, we would not be sitting together so amiably. You are our guests for now."

"Then you will help us repair the burned-out generators?"

Tarik raised his hand again, signaling her to halt. ". . . for now," he repeated.

Rydra had moved forward on her seat; she sat back again.

Tarik spoke to Klik: "Bring the books." The jester stepped quickly away and delved into a stand beside the couches. "We live dangerously," Tarik went on. "Perhaps that is why we live well. We are civilized—when we have time. The name of your ship convinced me to heed the Butcher's suggestion to hook you out. Here on the *rim* we are seldom visited by a *Bard*." Rydra smiled as politely as she could at the pun.

Klik returned with three volumes. The covers were black with silver edging. Tarik held them up. "My favorite is the second. I was particularly struck with the long narrative 'Exiles in Mist.' You tell me you have never heard of shadow-ships, yet you do know the feelings 'that loop night to bind you'—that is the line, isn't it? I confess, your third book I do not understand. But there are many references and humorous allusions to current events. We here are out of the mainstream." He shrugged. "We . . . salvaged the first from the collection of the captain of an Invader Transport tramp that had wandered off course. The second— well, it came from an Alliance destroyer. I believe there's an inscription on the inside cover." He opened it and read: " 'For Joey on the first flight; she says so well what I have always wanted to say so much. With so much, much love, Lenia.' " He closed the cover. "Touching. The third I only acquired a month ago. I will read it several times more before I speak of it to you again. I am astounded at the coincidence that brings us together." He placed the books in his lap. "How long has the third one been out?"

"A little under a year."

"There is a fourth?"

She shook her head.

"May I inquire what literary work you are engaged in now?"

"Now, nothing. I've done some short poems that my publisher wants to put out in a collection, but I want to wait until I have another large, sustained work to balance them."

Tarik nodded. "I see. But your reticence deprives us of great pleasure. Should you be moved to write, I will be honored. At meals we have music, some dramatic or comic entertainment, directed by clever Klik. If you would give us prologue or epilogue with what fancy you choose, you will have an appreciative audience." He extended his brown, hard hand. Appreciation is not a warm feeling, Rydra realized, but cool, and makes your back relax at the same time that you smile. She took his hand.

"Thank you, Tarik," she said.

"I thank you," Tarik returned. "Having your good will, I shall release your crew. They are free to wander Jebel as my own men are." His brown gaze shifted and she released his hand. "The Butcher." He nodded, and she turned.

The convict who had been with him on the ramp now stood on the step below.

"What was that blot that lay toward Rigel?" Tarik asked.

"Alliance running, Invader tracking."

Tarik's face furrowed, then relaxed. "No, let them both pass. We eat well enough this month. Why upset our guests with violence? This is Rydra—"

The Butcher brought his right fist cracking into his left palm. People below turned. She jumped at the sound, and with her eyes she tried to strip meaning from the faintly quivering muscles, the fixed, full-lipped face: lancing but inarticulate hostility; an outrage at stillness, a fear of motion halted, safety in silence furious with movement—

Now Tarik spoke again, voice lower, slower, harsh. "You're right. But what whole man is not of two minds on any matter of moment, eh, Captain Wong?" He rose. "Butcher, pull us closer to their trajectory. Are they an hour out? Good. We will watch awhile, then trounce—" he paused and smiled at Rydra—"the Invaders."

The Butcher's hands came apart, and Rydra saw relief (or release) ease his arms. He breathed again.

"Ready Jebel; and I will escort our guest to where she may watch."

Without response, the Butcher strode to the bottom of the steps. Those nearest had overheard, and the information saturated the room. Men and women rose from their benches. One upset his drinking horn. Rydra saw the girl who had served them in the infirmary run with a towel to sop the drink.

At the head of the gallery stairs she looked over the balcony rail at the commons below, empty now.

"Come." Tarik motioned her through the columns toward the darkness and the stars. "The Alliance ship is coming through there." He pointed to a bluish cloud. "We have equipment that can penetrate a good deal of this mist, but I doubt the Alliance ship even knows it is being tracked by Invaders." He moved to a desk and pressed a raised disk. Two dots of light flashed in the mist. "Red for Invaders," Tarik explained. "Blue for Alliance. Our little spider-boats will be yellow. You can follow the progress of the encounter from here. All our sensory evaluations and sensory perceptors and navigators remain on Jebel and direct the major strategy by remote control, so formations remain consistent. But within a limited range, each spider-boat battles for itself. It's fine sport for the men."

"What sort of ships are these you hunt?" She was amused that the slight archaic tone that perfused Tarik's speech had begun to affect hers.

"The Alliance ship is a military supply ship. The Invader is tracking her with a small destroyer."

"How far apart are they?"

"They should engage each other in about twenty minutes."

"And you are going to wait sixty minutes before you ... trounce the Invaders?"

Tarik smiled. "A supply ship doesn't have much chance against a destroyer."

"I know." She could see him waiting, behind the smile, for her to object. She looked for objection in herself, but it was blocked by a clot of tiny singing sounds on an area of her tongue smaller than a coin: Babel-17. They defined a concept of exactingly necessary expedient curiosity that became in any other language a clumsy string of polysyllables. "I've never watched a stellar skirmish," she said.

"I would have you come in my flagship, but I know that the little danger there is, is danger enough. From here you can follow the whole battle much more clearly."

Excitement caught her up. "I'd like to go with you." She hoped he might change his mind.

"Stay here," Tarik said. "The Butcher rides with me this time. Here's a sensory helmet if you wish to view the stasis currents. Though with combat weapons, there's so much electromagnetic confusion I doubt that even a reduction would mean much." A run of lights flashed across the desktop. "Excuse me. I go to review my men and check my cruiser." He bowed shortly. "Your crew has revived. They will be directed up here and you may explain their status as my guests however you see fit."

As Tarik walked to the steps, she looked back to the glittering view-screen and a few moments later thought: What an amazing graveyard they have on this hulk; it must take fifty discorporate souls to do all the sensory reading for Tarik and its spider-

boats—in Basque again. She looked back and saw the translucent shapes of her Eye, Ear, and Nose across the gallery.

"Am I glad to see you!" she said. "I didn't know whether
Tarik had discorporate facilities!"

"Does it ever!" came the Basque response. "We'll take you on
a trip through the Underworld here, Captain. They treat you like
the lords of Hades."

From the speaker came Tarik's voice: "Hear this: the strategy
is Asylum. Asylum. Repeat a third time, Asylum. Inmates gather
to face Caesar. Psychotics ready at the K-ward gate. Neurotics
gather before the R-ward gate. Criminally insane prepare for
discharge at the T-ward gate. All right, drop your straitjackets."

At the bottom of the hundred-foot screen appeared three
groups of yellow lights—the three groups of spider-boats that
would attack the Invader once it had overtaken the Alliance
supply ship. "Neurotics advance. Maintain contact to avoid
separation anxiety." The middle group began to move slowly
forward. On the under-speakers now, punctuated with static,
Rydra heard lower voices as the men began to report back to the
Navigators on Jebel:

Keep us on course, now, Kippi, and don't get shook.
Sure thing. Hawk, will you get your reports back on time?
Ease up. My caper-unit keeps sticking.
Who told you to leave without getting overhauled?
Come on, ladies, be kind to us for once.
Hey, Pigfoot, you want to be lobbed in high or low?
Low, hard, and fast. Don't hang me up.
You just get your reports in, honeybunch.

Over the main speaker Tarik said: "The Hunter and the
Hunted have engaged—" The red light and the blue light started
blinking on the screen. Calli, Ron, and Mollya came from the
head of the steps.

"What's going . . . ?" Calli started, but silenced at a gesture from Rydra.

"That red light's an Invader ship. We're attacking it in a few moments. We're the yellow lights down here." She left the explanation at that.

"Good luck, us," Mollya said, dryly.

In five minutes there was only the red light left. By now Brass had clanked up the steps to join them. Tarik announced: "The Hunter has become the Hunted. Let the criminally-insane schiz out." The yellow group on the left started forward, spreading apart.

That Invader looks pretty big, there, Hawk.

Don't worry. She'll run us out tough.

Hell. I don't like hard work. Got my reports yet?

Right-o. Pigfoot, stop jamming Ladybird's beam!

Okay, okay, okay. Did anyone check out tractor's nine and ten?

You think of everything at the right time, don't you?

Just curious. Don't the spiral look pretty back there?

"Neurotics proceed with delusions of grandeur. Napoleon Bonaparte take the lead. Jesus Christ bring up the rear." The ships on the right moved forward now in diamond formation. "Stimulate severe depression, noncommunicative, with repressed hostility."

Behind her she heard young voices. The Slug herded the platoon up the steps. Arriving, they quieted before the vast representation of night. The explanation of the battle filtered back among the children in whispers.

"Commence the first psychotic episode." Yellow lights ran forward into the darkness.

The Invader must have spotted them at last, for it began to move away. The gross bulk could not outrun the spiders unless it jumped currents. And there was not enough leeway to check

out. The three groups of yellow lights—formed, unformed, and
dispersed—drew closer. After three minutes, the Invader stopped
running. On the screen there was a sudden shower of red lights.
It had released its own barrage of cruisers which also separated
into the three standard attack groups.

"The life goal has become dispersed," Tarik announced. "Do
not become despondent."

Come on, let them babies try and get us!

Remember, Kippi, low, fast, and hard!

If we scare them into offensive, we got it made!

"Prepare to penetrate hostile defense mechanisms. All right.
Administer medication!"

The formation of the Invader's cruiser, however, was not
offensive. A third of them fanned horizontally across the stars,
the second group combed over their paths at a sixty-degree
angle, and the third group moved through another rotation of
sixty degrees so they made a three-way defensive grid before the
mother ship. The red cruisers doubled back on themselves at the
end of their run and swept out again, netting the space before
the Invader with small ships.

"Take heed. The enemy has tightened its defense mechanisms."

What's with this new formation, anyway?

We'll get through. You worried—

Static chopped out one speaker.

Damn, they strafed Pigfoot!

Pull me back, Kippi. There you go. Pigfoot?

Did you see how they got him? Hey, let's go.

"Administer active therapy to the right. Be as directive as you
can. Let the center enjoy the pleasure principle. And the left go
hang."

Rydra watched, fascinated, as yellow lights engaged the red,
which still swept hypnotically along their grid, net, web—

Webbing! The picture flipped over in her mind and the other side had all the missing lines. The grid was identical to the three-way web she had torn off the hammock hours before, with the added factor of timing, because the strands were the paths of ships, not strings; but it worked the same way. She snatched up a microphone from the desk. "Tarik!" The word took forever to slide from post-dental, to palatal stop, beside the sounds that danced through her brain now. She barked at the Navigators beside her: "Calli, Mollya, Ron, coordinate the battle area for me."

"Huh?" said Calli. "All right." He began to adjust the dial of the stellarimeter in his palm. Slow motion, she thought. They're all moving in slow motion. She knew what should be done, must be done, and watched the situation changing.

"Rydra Wong, Tarik is occupied," came the Butcher's gravelly voice.

Calli said over his shoulder: "Coordinates 3-B, 41-F, and 9-K. Pretty quick, huh?"

It seemed she'd asked for them an hour ago. "Butcher, did you get those coordinates down? Now look in . . . twenty-seven seconds a cruiser will pass through—" She gave a three-number location. "Hit it with your closest neurotics." While she waited for a response, she saw where the next hit must lie. "Forty seconds off, starting—eight, nine, ten, *now,* an Invader cruiser will pass through—" another location—"Get it with whatever's nearest. Is the first ship out of commission?"

"Yes, Captain Wong."

Her amazement and relief took no breath. At least the Butcher was listening; she gave the coordinates of three more ships in the "web." "Now hit them straight on and watch things fall apart!"

As she put the microphone down, Tarik's voice announced: "Advance for group therapy!"

The yellow spider-boats surged into the darkness again. Where there should have been Invaders, there were empty holes; where there should have been reinforcements, there was confusion. First one, then another, red cruiser fled its position.

The yellow lights were through. The flare of a vibra-blast shattered the red glow of the Invader ship.

Ratt jumped up and down, holding on to Carlos' and Flop's shoulder. "Hey, we won!" the midget Reconversion Engineer cried out. "We won!"

The platoon murmured to one another. Rydra felt oddly far away. They talked so slowly, taking such impossible time to say what could be so quickly delineated by a few simple—

"Are you all right, Ca'tain?" Brass put his yellow paw around her shoulder.

She tried to speak, but it came out a grunt. She staggered against his arm.

The Slug had turned now. "You feel well?" he asked.

"Sssssss," and realized that she didn't know how to say it in Babel-17. Her mouth bit into the shape and feel of English. "Sick," she said. "Jesus, I feel . . . sick."

As she said it, the dizziness passed.

"Maybe you better lie down," the Slug suggested.

She shook her head. The tenseness in her shoulders and back, the nausea was leaving. "No. I'm all right. I just got a little too excited, I think."

"Sit down a minute," Brass said, letting her lean against the desk. But she pushed herself upright.

"Really, I'm okay now." She took a deep breath. "See?" She pulled from under Brass's arm. "I'm going to take a walk. I'll feel better then." Still unsteady, she started away. She felt their wariness to let her go, but suddenly she wanted to be somewhere else. She continued across the gallery floor.

Her breath got back to normal when she reached the upper

levels. Then, from six different directions, hallways joined with rolling ramps to descend toward other floors. She stopped, confused over which way to take, then turned at a sound.

A group of Tarik's crew was crossing the corridor. The Butcher, among them, paused to lean against the door frame. He grinned at her, seeing her confusion, and pointed to the right. She didn't feel like speaking, so merely smiled and touched her forehead in salute. As she started toward the right-hand ramp, the meaning behind his grin surprised her. There was the pride of their joint success (which had allowed her to remain silent), yes; and a direct pleasure at offering her his wordless aid. But that was all. The expected amusement over someone who had lost her way was missing. Its presence would not have annoyed her. But its absence charmed. Also it fit the angular brutality she had watched before, as well as the great animal grace of him.

She was still smiling when she reached the commons.

---

2   She leaned on the catwalk railing to watch the activity in the cradle of the loading dock curving below. "Slug, take the kids down to give a hand with those carter-winches. Tarik said they could use some help."

Slug guided the platoon to the chairlift that dropped into Jebel's pit:

". . . all right, when you get down there, go over to that man in the red shirt and ask him to put you to work. Yeah, work. Don't look so surprised, stupid. Kile, strap yourself in, will you. It's two hundred and fifty feet down and a little hard on your head if you fall. Hey, you two, cut it out. I know he started first. Just get down there and be constructive . . ."

Rydra watched machinery and organic supplies—Alliance and Invader—handed in from the dismantling crews that worked over the ruins of the two ships, and their swarm of cruisers. The stacked, sorted crates were piled along the loading area.

"We'll be jettisoning the cruiser ships shortly. I'm afraid the *Rimbaud* will have to go, too. Is there anything you'd like to salvage before we dump it, Captain?" She turned at Tarik's voice.

"There are some important papers and recordings I have to get. I'll leave my platoon here and take my officers with me."

"Very well." Tarik joined her at the railing. "As soon as we finish here, I'll send a work crew with you in case there's anything large you want to bring back."

"That won't be . . ." she begun. "Oh, I see. You need fuel, don't you."

Tarik nodded. "And stasis components; also spare parts for our own spider-boats. We will not touch the *Rimbaud* until you have finished with it."

"I see. I guess that's only fair."

"I'm impressed," Tarik went on to change the subject, "with your method of breaking the Invader's defense net. That particular formation has always given us some trouble. The Butcher tells me you tore it apart in less than five minutes, and we only lost one spider. That's a record. I didn't know you were a master strategist as well as a poet. You have many talents. It is lucky that Butcher took your call, though. *I* would not have had sense enough to follow your instructions just on the spur of the moment. Had the results not been so praiseworthy, I would have been put out with him. But, then, his decisions have never yet brought me less than profit." He looked across the pit.

On a suspended platform in the center, the ex-convict lounged, silent overseer to the operations below.

"He's a curious man," Rydra said. "What was he in prison for?"

"I have never asked," Tarik said, raising his chin. "He has never told me. There are many curious persons on Jebel. And privacy is important in so small a space. Oh, yes. In a month's time you will learn how tiny the Mountain is."

"I forgot myself," Rydra apologized. "I shouldn't have inquired."

An entire foresection of a blasted Invader's cruiser was being dragged through the funnel on a twenty-foot wide, pronged conveyor. Dismantlers swarmed up the side with bolt punches and laser spots. Gig-cranes caught on the smooth hull and began to turn it slowly.

A workman at the port-disk suddenly cried out and swung hastily aside. His tools clattered down the bulkhead. The port-disk swung up and a figure in a silver skin suit dropped the twenty-five feet to the conveyor belt, rolled between two prongs, regained footing, leaped down the next ten-foot drop to the floor, and ran. The hood slipped from her head to release shoulder-length brown hair which swung wildly as she changed her course to avoid a trundling sledge. She moved fast, yet with a certain awkwardness. Then Rydra recognized that what she had taken for paunchiness in the fleeing Invader was at least a seven months' pregnancy. A mechanic flung a wrench at her, but she dodged so that it deflected off her hip. She was running toward an open space between the stacked supplies.

Then the air was cut by a vibrant hiss: the Invader stopped, sat down hard on the floor as the hiss repeated; she pitched to the side, kicked out one leg, kicked again.

On the tower, the Butcher put his vibra-gun back in the holster.

"That was unnecessary," Tarik said, with shocking softness.

"Couldn't we have . . ." and there seemed to be nothing to suggest. On Tarik's face was pain and curiosity. The pain, she realized, was not at the double death on the deck below, but the chagrin of a gentleman caught at something ugly. His curiosity was at her reaction. And it might be worth her life to react to the twisting in her stomach. She watched him preparing to speak: he was going to say—and so she said it for him—: "They *will* use pregnant women as pilots on fighting ships. Their reflexes are faster." She watched for him to relax, saw the relaxation begin.

The Butcher was already stepping from the chairlift onto the catwalk. He came toward them, banging his fist against his corded thigh with impatience. "They should ray everything before they take it on. They won't listen. Second time in two months now." He grunted.

Below, Jebel's men and her platoon mingled over the body.

"They will, next time." Tarik's voice was still soft and cool. "Butcher, you seemed to have pricked Captain Wong's interest. She was wondering what sort of a fellow you were, and I really couldn't tell her. Perhaps you can explain why you had to—"

"Tarik," Rydra said. Her eyes, seeking him, snagged on the Butcher's dark gaze. "I'd like to go to my ship now and see to it before you start salvaging."

Tarik exhaled the rest of the breath he'd held since the hiss of the vibra-gun. "Of course."

"No, not a monster, Brass." She unlocked the door to the captain's cabin of the *Rimbaud* and stepped through. "Just expedient. It's just like . . ." And she said a lot more to him till his fang-distended mouth sneered and he shook his head.

"Talk to me in English, Ca'tain. I don't understand you."

She took the dictionary from the console and placed it on top of the charts. "I'm sorry," she said. "This stuff is wicked. Once you learn it, it makes everything so easy. Get those tapes out of the playback. I want to run through them again."

"What are they?" Brass brought them over.

"Transcriptions of the last Babel-17 dialogues at the War Yards just before we took off." She put them on the spindle and started the first playing.

A melodious torrent rippled through the room, caught her up in ten- and twenty-second bursts she could understand. The plot to undermine TW-55 was delineated with hallucinatory vividness. When she reached a section she could not understand, she was left shaking against the wall of noncommunication. While she listened, while she understood, she moved through psychedelic perceptions. When understanding left, her breath left her lungs with shock, and she had to blink, shake her head, once accidentally bit her tongue, before she was free again to comprehend.

"Captain Wong?"

It was Ron. She turned her head, aching slightly now, to face him.

"Captain Wong, I don't want to disturb you."

"That's all right," she said. "What is it?"

"I found this in the Pilot's Den." He held up a small spool of tape.

Brass was still standing by the door. "What was it doing in my part of the shi'?"

Ron's features fought with each other for an expression. "I just played it back with Slug. It's Captain Wong's—or somebody's—request to Flight Clearance back at the War Yards for takeoff, and the all-clear signal to Slug to get ready to blast."

"I see," Rydra said. She took the spool. Then she frowned.

"This reel is from my cabin. I use the three-lobed spools I brought with me from the University. All the other machines on the ship are supplied with four-lobed ones. That tape came from this machine here."

"So," Brass said, "a''arently somebody snuck in and made it when you were out."

"When I'm out, this place is locked so tight a discorporate flea couldn't crawl under the door." She shook her head. "I don't like this. I don't know where I'll be fouled up next. Well—" she stood up—"at least I know what I have to do about Babel-17 now."

"What's that?" Brass asked. Slug had come to the door and was looking over Ron's flowered shoulder.

Rydra looked over the crew. Discomfort or distrust, which was worst? "I really can't tell you now, can I?" she said. "It's that simple." She walked to the door. "I wish I could. But it would be a little silly after this whole business."

"**B**ut I would rather speak to Tarik!"

Klik ruffled his feathers and shrugged. "Lady, I would honor your desire above all others' on the mountain, save Tarik's. And it is Tarik's desire that you now counter. He wishes not to be disturbed. He is plotting Jebel's destination over the next time-cycle. He must judge the currents carefully, and weigh even the weights of the stars about us. It is an arduous task, and—"

"Then where's the Butcher? I'll ask him, but I would prefer to talk directly with—"

The jester pointed with a green talon. "He is in the biology theater. Go down through the commons and take the first lift to level twelve. It is directly to your left."

"Thank you." She headed toward the gallery steps.

At the top of the lift she found the huge iris door, and pressed the entrance disk. Leaves folded, and she blinked in green light.

His round head and mildly humped shoulders were silhouetted before a bubbling tank in which a tiny figure floated: the spray of bubbles that rose about the form deflated on the feet, caught in the crossed curved hands like sparks, frothed the bent head, and foamed in the brush of birth-hair that swirled up in the miniature currents.

The Butcher turned, saw her, and said, "It died." He nodded with vigorous belligerence. "It was alive until five minutes ago. Seven and a half months. It should have lived. It was strong enough!" His left fist cracked against his right palm, as she had seen him do in the commons. Shaking muscles stilled. He thumbed toward an operating table where the Invader's body lay—sectioned. "Badly hurt before she got out. Internal organs messed up. A lot of abdominal necrosis all the way though." He turned his hand so the thumb now pointed over his shoulder to the drifting homunculus, and the gesture that had seemed rough took on an economical grace. "Still—it should have lived."

He switched off the light in the tank and the bubbles ceased. He stepped from behind the laboratory table. "What the Lady want?"

"Tarik is planning Jebel's route for the next months. Could you ask him . . ." She stopped. Then she asked, "Why?"

Ron's muscles, she thought, were living cords that snapped and sang out their messages. On this man, muscles were shields to hold the world out, the man in. And something inside was leaping up again and again, striking the shield from behind. The scored belly shifted, the chest contracted over a let breath; the brow smoothed, then creased again.

"Why?" she repeated. "Why did you try to save the child?"

He twisted his face for answer, and his left hand circled the convict's mark on his other bicep as though it had started to sting. Then he gave up with disgust. "Died. No good anymore. What the Lady want?"

What leaped and leaped retreated now—and so did she. "I want to know if Tarik will take me to Administrative Alliance Headquarters. I have to deliver some important information concerning the Invasion. My pilot tells me the Specelli Snap runs within ten hyperstatic units, which a spider-boat could make, so Jebel could remain in radio-dense space all the way. If Tarik will escort me to Headquarters, I will guarantee his protection and a safe return to the denser part of the Snap."

He eyed her. "All the way down the Dragon's Tongue?"

"Yes. That's what Brass told me the tip of the Snap was called."

"Protection guaranteed?"

"That's right. I'll show you my credentials from General Forester of the Alliance if you . . ."

But he waved for her silence. "Tarik." He spoke into the wall intercom.

The speaker was directional so she couldn't hear the answer.

"Make Jebel go down the Dragon's Tongue during the first cycle."

There was either questioning or objection—

"Go down the Tongue and it'll be good."

He nodded to the unintelligible whisper, then said, "It died," and switched off. "All right. Tarik will take Jebel to Headquarters."

Amazement undercut her initial disbelief. It was an amazement she would have felt before when he responded so unquestioningly to her plan to destroy the Invader's defense, had not Babel-17 precluded such feelings. "Well, thanks," she began. "but you haven't even asked me . . ." Then she decided to phrase the whole thing another way.

But the Butcher made a fist:

"Knowing what ships to destroy, and ships are destroyed." He banged his fist against his chest. "Now to go down the

Dragon's Tongue, Jebel go down the Dragon's Tongue." He banged his chest again.

She wanted to question, but looked at the dead fetus turning in dark liquid behind him and said instead, "Thank you, Butcher." As she stepped through the iris door, she mulled over what he had said to her, trying to frame some explanation of his actions. Even the rough way in which his words fell—

His *words*—!

It struck her at once, and she hurried down the corridor.

---

3   "Brass, he can't say 'I'!" She leaned across the table, surprised curiosity impelling her excitement.

The pilot locked his claws around his drinking horn. The wooden tables across the commons were being set up for the evening meal.

"Me, my, mine, myself. I don't think he can say any of those either. Or think them. I wonder where the hell he's from."

"You know any language where there's no word for 'I'?"

"I can think of a couple where it isn't used often, but no one that doesn't even have the concept, if only hanging around in a verb ending."

"Which all means what?"

"A strange man with a strange way of thinking. I don't know why, but he's aligned himself with me, sort of my ally on this trip and a go-between with Tarik. I'd like to understand, so I won't hurt him."

She looked around the commons at the bustle of preparation.

The girl who had brought them chicken was glancing at her now, wondering, still afraid, fear melting to curiosity which brought her two tables nearer, then curiosity evaporating to indifference, and she was off for more spoons from the wall drawer.

She wondered what would happen if she translated her perceptions of people's movement and muscle tics into Babel-17. It was not only a language, she understood now, but a flexible matrix of analytical possibilities where the same "word" defined the stresses in a webbing of medical bandage, or a defensive grid of spaceships. What would it do with the tensions and yearnings in a human face? Perhaps the flicker of eyelids and fingers would become mathematics, without meaning. Or perhaps . . . While she thought, her mind changed gears into the headlong compactness of Babel-17. And she swept her eyes around the—voices.

Expanding and defining through one another, not the voices themselves, but the minds making the voices, braiding with one another, so that the man entering the hall now she knew to be the grieving brother of Pigfoot, and the girl who'd served them was in love, so in love with the dead youth from the discorporate sector who tickled her dreams turning about the general hunger, a belly beast with teeth in one man, a lazy pool in another, now the familiar rush of adolescent confusion as the *Rimbaud*'s platoon came pummeling in, driven by the deep concern of Slug, and further over amidst ebullience, hunger, and love, a *fear!* It gonged in the hall, flashed red in the indigo tide, and she searched for Tarik or the Butcher because their names were in the fear, but found neither in the room; instead, a thin

She sat in the great commons while men and women filed in for the evening meal, and was aware of so much more.

They set her place, brought first a flagon, then bread, which she saw and smiled at but was seeing so much else.

man named Geoffry Cord in whose brain crossed wires sparked and sputtered *Make death with the knife I have sheathed to my leg,* and again *With my steel tongue make me a place in an eyrie high on Jebel,* and the minds about him, groping and hungering, mumbling over humor and hurt, loving a little and groping for more, all cross-

Around her people were sitting, relaxing, while the serving people hurried to the food counter where the roasts and fried fruit steamed.

hatched with relaxation one way at the coming meal, and in others anticipation at what clever Klik would present that evening, the minds of the actors of the pantomime keyed to performance while they perused the spectators whom, at an earlier hour, they had worked with and slept with, one elderly navigator with a geometrical head hurrying to give the girl, who was to play in the play at being in love, a silver clasp he had melted and scribed himself to see

if she would play at loving him, yet through all this her mind circled back to the alarm of Geoffry Cord, *I must act this evening as the actors close,* and unable to focus on anything but his urgency, she watched him roil and ravel through his plot-tings, to hurry forward when the pantomime began as if he wanted to get a closer look as many would do, slip beside the table where Tarik would be sitting, then blade between

She saw so much more than the little demonic jester on the stage saying, "Before our evening's entertainment I wish to ask our guest, Captain Wong, if she would speak some few words or perhaps recite for us." And she knew with a very small part of her mind—but it took no more—that she must use this chance to denounce him.

Tarik's ribs with his serpent fang, and the grooved metal ran with paralytic poison, then chomp down on his hollow tooth that was filled with hypnotic drugs so that when he was taken prisoner they would think he was under somebody else's control, and at last he would release a wild story, implanted below the level of the hypnotics by many painful hours under the person-afix, that he was under the Butcher's control; then somehow he would contrive to be alone with the Butcher and bite the Butcher's hand or wrist or leg, injecting the same hypnotic drugs that poisoned his own mouth and rend the hulking convict helpless, and he would control him, and when the Butcher ultimately became Jebel's ruler after the assassination, Geoffry Cord would become the Butcher's lieutenant as the Butcher was now Tarik's, and when Tarik's Jebel was the Butcher's Jebel, Geoffry would control the Butcher the same way he suspected the Butcher controlled Tarik, and there would be a reign of harshness and all strangers expelled from the berg to death by vacuum, and they would fall mightily on all ships, Invader, Alliance, or Shadow in the Snap, and Rydra tore her mind from his and swept the brief surface of Tarik and the Butcher, and saw no hypnotics, but also that they suspected no treachery and her own delayed fear, taking her from what she felt in her slipping and lapping with doubled and halved voice and no yes, she was able, even as she

The realization momentarily blotted everything else, but then returned to its proper size, for she knew she could not let Cord stop her from getting to Headquarters, so she stood up and walked to the stage at the end of the commons, picking from Cord's mind as she walked a deadly blade so quickly to fit into the cracks of Geoffry Cord.

Her fear broke from her vast ship-picture while she felt schismic rages of him and still would survive it and found his fear as porous, porous as a sponge.

walked to pick the words and images that would drive and push him to her betrayal and no yes, once struck by his fear and rebounding, she brought herself back to a single line that scribed through both perception and action, speech and communication, no yes, both one now, picking down sounds that would persuade with the deliberation this lengthened time lent and she reached the platform beside the gorgeous beast, Klik, and mounted, hearing the voices that sang in the hall's silence, and tossed her words now from the sling of her vibrant voice, so that they hung outside her, and she watched them and watched his watching: the rhythm which was barely intricate to most ears in the commons was to him painful because it was timed to the processes of his body, to jar and strike against them . . . and she was surprised he

"All right, Cord,
to be lord of this black barrack,
Tarik's, you need more than jackal lore,
or a belly full of murder and jelly knees.
Open your mouth and your hands. To understand
power, use your wit, please.
Ambition like a liquid ruby stains
your brain, birthed in the cervixed will
to kill, swung in the arc of death's again,
you name yourself victim each time you fill
with swill the skull's cup lipping murder. It
predicts your fingers' movement toward the blade
long laid against the leather sheath cord-fixed
to pick the plan your paling fingers made;
you stayed in safety, missing worlds of wonder,
under the lithe hiss of the personafix
inflicting false memories to make them blunder
while thunder cracks the change of Tarik.
You stick pins in peaches, place your strange
blade, ranged with a grooved tooth, while the long

and strong lines of my meaning make your mind change   had
from fulgent to frangent. Now you hear the wrong   held
cord-song, to instruct you. Assassin,   up
pass in . . ."   this
  long.

She looked directly at Geoffry Cord. Geoffry Cord looked directly at her—and shrieked.

The scream snapped something. She had been thinking in Babel-17 and choosing her English words with it. But now she was thinking in English again.

Geoffry Cord jerked his head sideways, black hair shaking, flung his table over, and ran, raging, toward her. The drugged knife which she had seen only through his mind was out and aimed at her stomach.

She jumped back, kicked at his wrist as he vaulted the platform edge, missed, but struck his face. He fell backwards, rolling on the floor.

Gold, silver, amber: Brass was running from his side of the room. Silver-haired Tarik was coming from the other, his cloak billowing. And the Butcher had already reached her, was between her and the uncoiling Cord.

"What is this?" Tarik demanded.

Cord was on one knee, knife still poised. His black eyes went from vibra-gun muzzle to vibra-gun muzzle, then to Brass's unsheathed claws. He froze.

"I don't appreciate attacks on my guests."

"That knife was meant for you, Tarik," she panted. "Check the records of Jebel's personafix. He was going to kill you and get the Butcher under hypnotic control, and take over Jebel."

"Oh," Tarik said. "One of those." He turned to the Butcher. "It was time for another one, wasn't it? About once every six months. I'm again grateful to you, Captain Wong."

The Butcher stepped forward and took the knife from Cord,

whose body seemed frozen, whose eyes danced. Rydra listened to Cord's breath measure out the silence, while the Butcher, holding the knife by the blade, examined it. The blade itself, in the Butcher's heavy fingers, was printed steel. The handle, a seven-inch length of bone, was ridged, runneled, and stained with walnut dye.

With his free hand, the Butcher caught his fingers in Cord's black hair. Then, not particularly quickly, he pushed the knife to the hilt into Cord's right eye—handle first.

The scream became a gurgle. The flailing hands fell from the Butcher's shoulders. Those sitting close stood.

Rydra's heart banged twice to break her ribs. "But you didn't even check . . . Suppose I was wrong . . . Maybe there was more to it than . . ." Her tongue wagged through meaningless protests. And maybe her heart had stopped.

The Butcher, both hands bloody, looked at her coldly. "He moved with a knife on Jebel toward Tarik or Lady and he dies." Right fist ground on left palm, now soundless with red lubricant.

"Miss Wong," Tarik said, "from what I've seen, there's little doubt in my mind that Cord was certainly dangerous. I'm sure there's not much in yours, either. You are highly useful. I am highly obliged. I hope this trip down the Dragon's Tongue proves propitious. The Butcher just told me that it was at your request that we are going."

"Thank you, but . . ." Her heart was pounding again. She tried to form some clause to hang from the hook of "but" still hesitant in her mouth. Instead she got very sick, and pitched forward, half-blinded. The Butcher caught her on red palms.

The round, warm, blue room again. But alone, and she was at last able to think about what had happened in the commons. It was not what she'd repeatedly tried to describe to Mocky. It was what Mocky had repeatedly insisted to her: telepathy. But, apparently, telepathy was the nexus of old talent and a new way of thinking. It opened worlds of perception, of action. Then why was she sick? She recalled how time slowed when her mind worked under Babel-17, how her mental processes speeded up. If there was a corresponding increase in her physiological functions, her body might not be up to the strain.

The tapes from the *Rimbaud* had told her the next "sabotage" attempt would be at Administrative Alliance Headquarters. She wanted to get there with the language, the vocabulary, and grammar, give it to them, and retire. She was almost ready to hand over the search for this mysterious speaker. But no, not quite; there was still something, something to be heard and spoken . . .

Sick and falling, she snagged on bloody finger, woke starting. The Butcher's egoless brutality, hammered linear by what she could not know, less than primitive, was for all its horror, still human. Though bloody-handed, he was safer than the precision of the world linguistically corrected. What could you say to a man who could not say "I"? What could he say to her? Tarik's cruelties, kindnesses, existed at the articulate limits of civilization. But this red bestiality . . . fascinated her!

---

4   She rose from the hammock, this time unsnapping the bandage. She'd felt better nearly an hour, but she had lain still thinking most of the time. The ramp tilted to her feet.

When the infirmary wall solidified behind her, she paused in the corridor. The airflow pulsed like breath. Her translucent slacks brushed the tops of her bare feet. The neckline of her black silk blouse lay loose on her shoulders.

She had rested well into Jebel's night shift. During a period of high activity, the sleeping time was staggered, but when they merely moved from location to location, there were hours when nearly the whole population slept.

Rather than head toward the commons, she turned down an unfamiliar sloping tunnel. White light diffused from the floor, became amber fifty feet on, then amber became orange—she stopped and looked at her hands in orange light—and forty feet further, the orange light was red. Then . . .

Blue.

The space opened around her, the walls slanting back, the ceiling rising into darkness too high for her to see. The air flickered and blotted with the afterimage from the change in color. Insubstantial mists plus her unsettled eyes made her turn to orient herself.

A man was silhouetted against the red entrance to the hall. "Butcher?"

He walked toward her, blue light fogging his features as he neared. He stopped, nodded.

"I decided to take a walk when I felt better," she explained. "What part of the ship is that?"

"Discorporate quarters."

"I should have known." They fell in step with one another. "Are you just wandering around, too?"

He shook his heavy head. "An alien ship passes close to Jebel and Tarik wants its sensory vectors."

"Alliance or Invader?"

The Butcher shrugged. "Only to know that it is not a human ship."

There were nine species among the five explored galaxies with interstellar travel. Three had allied themselves definitely with the Alliance. Four had sided with the Invaders. Two were not committed.

They had gone so far into the discorporate sector, nothing seemed solid. The walls were blue mist without corners. The echoing crackle of transference energies caused distant lightning, and her eyes were deviled by half-remembered ghosts, who had always passed moments ago, yet were never there.

"How far do we go?" she asked, having decided to walk with him, thinking as she spoke: If he doesn't know the word for "I," how can he understand "we"?

Understanding or not, he answered, "Soon." Then he looked directly at her with dark, heavy browed eyes and asked, "Why?"

The tone of his voice was so different, she knew he was not referring to anything in their exchange during the past few minutes. She cast in her mind for anything she had done that might strike him as perplexing.

He repeated, "Why?"

"Why what, Butcher?"

"Why the saving of Tarik from Cord?"

There was no objection in his question, only ethical curiosity. "Because I like him, and because I need him to get me to Headquarters; and I would feel sort of funny if I'd let him . . ." She stopped. "Do you know who 'I' am?"

He shook his head.

"Where do you come from, Butcher? What planet were you born on?"

He shrugged. "The head," he said, after a moment, "they said there was something wrong with the brain."

"Who?"

"The doctors."

Blue fog drifted between them.

"The doctors on Titin?" she hazarded.

The Butcher nodded.

"Then why didn't they put you in a hospital instead of a prison?"

"The brain is not crazy, they said. This hand"—he held up his left—"kill four people in three days. This hand"—he raised the other—"kill seven. Blow up four buildings with thermite. The foot"—he slapped his left leg—"kicked in the head of the guard at the Telechron Bank. There's a lot of money there, too much to carry. Carry maybe four hundred thousand credits. Not much."

"You robbed the Telechron Bank of four hundred thousand credits!"

"Three days, eleven people, four buildings: all for four hundred thousand credits. But Titin—" his face twisted—"was not fun at all."

"So I'd heard. How long did it take for them to catch you?"

"Six months."

Rydra whistled. "I take my hat off to you, if you could keep out of their hands that long, after a bank robbery. And you know enough biotics to perform a difficult Caesarean section and keep the fetus alive. There's something in that head."

"The doctors say the brain not stupid."

"Look, you and I are going to talk to each other. But first I have to teach—" she stopped—"the brain something."

"What?"

"About *you* and *I*. You must hear the words a hundred times a day. Don't you ever wonder what they mean?"

"Why? Most things make sense without them."

"Hey, speak in whatever language you grew up with."

"No."

"Why not? I want to see if it's one I know anything about."

"The doctors say there's something wrong with the brain."

"All right. What did they say was wrong?"

"Aphasia, alexia, amnesia."

"Then you were pretty messed up." She frowned. "Was that before or after the bank robbery?"

"Before."

She tried to order what she had learned. "Something happened to you that left you with no memory, unable to speak or read, and so the first thing you did was rob the Telechron bank— which Telechron Bank?"

"On Rhea-IV."

"Oh, a small one. But, still—and you stayed free for six months. Any idea what happened to you before you lost your memory?"

The Butcher shrugged.

"I suppose they went through all the possibilities that you were working for somebody else under hypnotics. You don't know what language you spoke before you lost your memory? Well, your speech patterns now must be based on your old language or you would have learned about *I* and *you* just from picking up new words."

"Why must these sounds mean something?"

"Because you asked a question just now that I can't answer if you don't understand them."

"No." Discomfort shadowed his voice. "No. There is an answer. The words of the answer must be simpler, that's all."

"Butcher, there are certain ideas which have words for them. If you don't know the words, you can't know the ideas. And if you don't have the idea, you don't have the answer."

"The word *you* four times, yes? Still nothing unclear, and *you* means nothing."

She sighed. "That's because I was using the word phatically— ritually, without regard for its real meaning . . . as a figure of speech. Look, I asked you a question that you couldn't answer."

The Butcher frowned.

"See, you have to know what they mean to make sense out of what I just said. The best way to learn a language is by listening to it. So listen. When you"—she pointed to him—"said to me," and she pointed to herself, *"Knowing what ships to destroy, and ships are destroyed. Now to go down the Dragon's Tongue, Jebel go down the Dragon's Tongue,* twice the fist—" she touched his left hand—"banged the chest." She raised his hand to his chest. The skin was cool and smooth under her palm. "The fist was trying to tell something. And if you had used the word 'I,' you wouldn't have had to use your fist. What you wanted to say was: 'You knew what ships to destroy, and I destroyed the ships. You want to go down the Dragon's Tongue; I will get Jebel down the Dragon's Tongue.'"

The Butcher frowned. "Yes, the fist to tell something."

"Don't you see? Sometimes you want to say things, and you're missing an idea to make them with, and missing a word to make the idea with. In the beginning was the word. That's how somebody tried to explain it once. Until something is named, it doesn't exist. And it's something the brain needs to have exist, otherwise you wouldn't have to beat your chest, or strike your fist on your palm. The brain wants it to exist. Let me teach it the word."

The frown cut deeper into his face.

Just then mist blew away before them. In star-flecked blackness something drifted, flimsy and flickering. They had reached a sensory port, but it was transmitting over frequencies close to regular light. "There," said the Butcher, "there is the alien ship."

"It's from Çiribia-IV," Rydra said. "They're friendly to the Alliance."

The Butcher was surprised she'd recognized it. "A very odd ship."

"It does look funny to us, doesn't it."

"Tarik did not know where it came from." He shook his head.

"I haven't seen one since I was a kid. We had to entertain delegates from Çiribia to the Court of Outer Worlds. My mother was a translator there." She leaned on the railing and gazed at the ship. "You wouldn't think something that's so flimsy and shakes around like that would fly or make stasis jumps. But it does."

"Do they have this word, *I*?"

"As a matter of fact they have three forms of it: I-below-a-temperature-of-six-degrees-centigrade, I-between-six-and-ninety-three-degrees-centigrade, and I-above-ninety-three."

The Butcher looked confused.

"It has to do with their reproductive process," Rydra explained. "When the temperature is below six degrees they're sterile. They can only conceive when the temperature is between six and ninety-three, but to actually give birth, they have to be above ninety-three."

The Çiribian ship moved like floppy feathers across the screen.

"Maybe I can explain something to you this way; with all nine species of galaxy-hopping life forms, each as widespread as our own, each as technically intelligent, with as complicated an economy, seven of them engaged in the same war we are, still we hardly ever run into them; and they run into us or each other about as frequently: so infrequently, that even when an experienced spaceman like Tarik passes alongside one of their ships, he can't identify it. Wonder why?"

"Why?"

"Because compatibility factors for communication are incredibly low. Take the Çiribians, who have enough knowledge to sail their triple-yolked poached eggs from star to star: they have no word for 'house,' 'home,' or 'dwelling.' 'We must protect our families and our homes.' When we were preparing the treaty between the Çiribians and ourselves at the Court of Outer Worlds,

I remember that sentence took forty-five minutes to say in Çirib-ian. Their whole culture is based on heat and changes in temper-ature. We're just lucky that they do know what a 'family' is, because they're the only ones beside humans who have them. But for 'house' you have to end up describing '. . . an enclosure that creates a temperature discrepancy with the outside environ-ment of so many degrees, capable of keeping comfortable a crea-ture with a uniform body temperature of ninety-eight-point-six, the same enclosure being able to lower the temperature during the months of the warm season and raise it during the cold season, providing a location where organic sustenance can be refrigerated in order to be preserved, or warmed well above the boiling point of water to pamper the taste mechanism, of the indigenous habitants who, through customs that go back through millions of hot and cold seasons, have habitually sought out this temperature changing device . . .' and so forth and so on. At the end you have given them some idea of what a 'home' is and why it is worth protecting. Give them a schematic of the air-conditioning and central heating system, and things begin to get through. Now: there is a huge solar-energy conversion plant that supplies all the electrical energy for the Court. The heat amplifying and reducing components take up an area a little bigger than Jebel. One Çiribian can slither through that plant and then go describe it to another Çiribian who never saw it before so that the second can build an exact duplicate, even to the color the walls are painted—and this actually happened, because they thought we'd done something ingenious with one of the circuits and wanted to try it themselves—where each piece is located, how big it is, in short completely describe the whole business, in nine words. Nine very small words, too."

The Butcher shook his head. "No. A solar-heat conversion system is too complicated. These hands dismantle one, not too long ago. Too big. Not—"

"Yep, Butcher, nine words. In English it would take a couple of books full of schematics and electrical and architectural specifications. They have the proper nine words. We don't."

"Impossible."

"So's that." She pointed toward the Çiribian ship. "But it's there and flying." She watched the brain, both intelligent and injured, thinking. "If you have the right words," she said, "it saves a lot of time and makes things easier."

After a while he asked, "What is *I*?"

She grinned. "First of all it's very important. A good deal more important than anything else. The brain will let any number of things go to pot as long as 'I' stay alive. That's because the brain is part of I. Look. A book *is*, a ship *is*, Tarik *is*, the universe *is*; but, as you must have noticed, I *am*."

The Butcher nodded. "Yes. But I am what?"

Fog closed over the view-port, misting stars, and the Çiribian ship. "That's a question only you can answer."

"You must be important too," the Butcher mused, "because the brain has overheard that you are."

"Good boy!"

Suddenly he put his hand on her cheek. The cock spur rested lightly on her lower lip. "You and I," the Butcher said. He moved his face close to hers. "Nobody else is here. Just you and I. But which is which?"

She nodded, cheek moving on his fingers. "You're getting the idea." His chest had been cool; his hand was warm. She put her hand on top of his. "Sometimes you frightened me."

"I and me," the Butcher said. "Only a morphological distinction, yes? The brain figure that out before. Why does you frighten me sometimes?"

"*Do* frighten. A morphological correction. You frighten me because you rob banks and put knife handles in people's heads, Butcher!"

"You do?" Then his surprise left. "Yes, you do, don't you. You forgot."

"But I didn't," Rydra said.

"Why does that frighten I? . . . correction, me. Overhear that too."

"Because it's something I've never done, never wanted to do, never could do. And I like you, I like your hand on my cheek, so that if you suddenly decided to put a knife handle in *my* eye, well . . ."

"Oh. You never would put a knife handle in my eye," the Butcher said. "I don't have to worry."

"You could change your mind."

"You won't." He looked at her closely. "I don't really think you're going to kill me. You know that. I know that. It's something else. Why don't I tell you something else that frightened me? Maybe you can see some pattern and you will understand then. The brain is not stupid."

His hand slid to her neck, and there was concern in his puzzled eyes. She had seen it before the moment he'd turned from the dead fetus in the biology theater. "Once . . ." she began slowly, ". . . well, there was a bird."

"Birds frighten me?"

"No. But this bird did. I was just a kid. You don't remember being a kid, do you? In most people what you were as a kid has a lot to do with what you are now."

"And what I am too?"

"Yes, me too. My doctor had gotten this bird for me as a present. It was a myna bird, which can talk. But it doesn't know what it's saying. It just repeats like a tape recorder. Only I didn't know that. A lot of times I know what people are trying to say to me, Butcher. I never understood it before, but since I've been on Jebel, I've realized it's got something to do with telepathy. Anyway, this myna bird had been trained to talk by feeding it earthworms when it said the right thing. Do you know how big an earthworm is?"

"Like so?"

"That's right. And some of them even run a few inches longer. And a myna bird is about eight or nine inches long. In other words an earthworm can be about five-sixths as long as a myna bird, which is what's important. The bird had been trained to say: Hello, Rydra, it's a fine day out and I'm happy. But the only thing this meant in the bird's mind was a rough combination of visual and olfactory sensations that translated loosely, *There's another earthworm coming.* So when I walked into the greenhouse and said hello to this myna bird, and it replied, 'Hello, Rydra, it's a fine day and I'm happy,' I knew immediately it was lying. There was another earthworm coming, that I could see and smell, and it was this thick and five-sixths as long as I was tall. And I was supposed to eat it. I got a little hysterical. I never told my doctor, because I never could figure exactly what happened until now. But when I remember, I still get shaky."

The Butcher nodded. "When you left Rhea with the money, you eventually holed up in a cave in the ice-hells of Dis. You were attacked by worms, twelve-foot ones. They burrowed up out of the rocks with acid slime on their skins. You were scared, but you killed them. You rigged up an electric net from your hop-sled power source. You killed them, and when you knew you could beat them, you weren't afraid anymore. The only reason you didn't eat them was because the acid made their flesh toxic. But you hadn't eaten anything for three days."

"I did? I mean . . . you did?"

"You are not frightened of the things I am frightened of. I am not frightened of the things you are frightened of. That's good, isn't it?"

"I guess so."

Gently he leaned his face against hers, then pulled away, and searched her face for a response.

"What is it that you're frightened of?" she asked.

He shook his head, not in negation but in confusion, as she saw him trying to articulate. "The baby, the baby that died," he said. "The brain afraid, afraid for you, that you would be alone."

"How afraid that you would be alone, Butcher?"

He shook his head again.

"Loneliness is not good."

She nodded.

"The brain knows that. For a long time it didn't know, but after a while it learned. Lonely on Rhea, you were, even with all the money. Lonelier on Dis; and in Titin, even with the other prisoners, you were loneliest of all. No one really understood you when you spoke to them. You did not really understand them. Maybe because they said *I* and *you* so much, and you just now are beginning to learn how important you are and I am."

"You wanted to raise the baby yourself so he would grow up and . . . speak the same language you speak? Or at any rate speak English the same way you speak it?"

"Then both not be alone."

"I see."

"It died," Butcher said. He grunted once again. "But now you are not quite so alone. I teach you to understand the others, a little. You're not stupid, and you learn fast." Now he turned fully toward her, rested his fists on her shoulder and spoke gravely. "You like me. Even when I first came on Jebel, there was something about me that you liked. I saw you do things I thought were bad, but you liked me. I told you how to destroy the Invaders' defensive net, and you destroyed it, for me. I told you I wanted to go to the tip of the Dragon's Tongue, and you saw that I get there. You will do anything I ask. It's important that I know that."

"Thank you, Butcher," she said wonderingly.

"If you ever rob another bank, you will give me all the money."

Rydra laughed. "Why, thank you. Nobody ever wanted to do that for me. But I hope you don't have to rob—"

"You will kill anyone that tries to hurt me, kill them a lot worse than you ever killed anyone before."

"But you don't have to—"

"You will kill all of Jebel if it tries to take you and me apart and keep us alone."

"Oh, Butcher—" She turned from him and put her fist against her mouth. "One hell of a teacher I am! You don't understand a thing—I—*I* am talking about."

The voice, astonished and slow: "I don't understand you, you think."

She turned back to him. "But I do, Butcher! I do understand you. Please believe that. But trust me that you have a little more to learn."

"You trust me," he said firmly.

"Then listen. Right now we've met each other halfway. I haven't really taught you about *I* and *you*. We've made up our own language, and that's what we're talking now."

"But—"

"Look, every time you've said *you* in the last ten minutes, you should have said *I*. Every time you've said *I*, you meant *you*."

He dropped his eyes to the floor, then raised them again, still without answer.

"What I talk about as I, you must speak of as you. And the other way around, don't you see?"

"Are they the same word for the same thing, that they are interchangeable?"

"No, just . . . yes! They both mean the same sort of thing. In a way they're the same."

"Then you and I are the same."

Risking confusion, she nodded.

"I suspect it. But you—" he pointed to her—"have taught me." He touched himself.

"And that's why you can't go around killing people. At least you better do a hell of a lot of thinking before you do. When you talk to Tarik, I and you still exist. With anyone you look at on the ship, or even through a view-screen, I and you are still there."

"The brain must think about that."

"You must think about that, with more than your brain."

"If I must then I will. But we are one, more than others." He touched her face again. "Because you taught me. Because with me you do not have to be afraid of anything. I have just learned, and I may make mistakes with other people; for an *I* to kill a *you* without a lot of thought is a mistake, isn't it? Do I use the words correctly now?"

She nodded.

"I will make no mistakes with you. That would be too terrible. I will make as few mistakes as I possibly can. And someday I will learn completely." Then he smiled. "Let's hope nobody tries to make any mistakes with me, though. I am sorry for them if they do, because I will probably make a mistake with them very quickly and with very little thought."

"That's fair enough for now, I guess," Rydra said. She took his arms in her hands. "I'm glad you and I are together, Butcher." Then his arms came up and caught her against his body, and she pressed her face on his shoulder.

"I thank you," he whispered. "I thank you and thank you."

"You're warm," she said into his shoulder. "Don't let go for a little while."

When he did, she blinked up at his face through blue mist and turned all cold. "What *is* it, Butcher!"

He took her face between his hands and bent his head till amber hair brushed her forehead.

"Butcher, remember I told you I can tell what people are thinking? Well, I can tell something's wrong—now. You said I didn't have to be afraid of you, but you're scaring me now."

She raised his face. There were tears on it.

"Look, just the way something wrong with me would scare you, one thing that's going to scare hell out of me for a long time is something wrong with you. Tell me what it is."

"I can't," he said hoarsely. "*I* can't. *I* can't tell *you*." And the one thing she understood immediately was that it was the most horrible thing he could conceive with his new knowledge.

She watched him fight, and fought herself: "Maybe I can help, Butcher! There's a way I can go into the brain and find out what it is."

He backed away and shook his head. "*You* mustn't do that to *me*. Please."

"Butcher, I w-won't." She was confused. "Th-then I . . . I won't." Confusion hurt. "Butcher . . . I-I won't!" Her adolescent stutter staggered in her mouth.

"I—" he began, breath hard, but becoming softer, "I have been alone and not I for a long time. I must be alone for a little while longer."

"I s-see." Suspicion, very small and easily dealt with, came now. When he had backed away, it entered the space between them. But that was human, too. "Butcher? Can you read my mind?"

He looked surprised. "No. I don't even understand how you can read mine."

"All right. I thought maybe there was something in my head that you might be picking up that makes you afraid of me."

He shook his head.

"That's good. Hell, I wouldn't want somebody prying under my scalp. I think I understand."

"I tell you now," he said, coming toward her again. "I and you are one; but I and you are very different. I have seen a lot you will never know. You know of things that I will never see. You have made me not alone, a little. There is a lot in the brain, my brain, about hurting and running and fighting and, even though I was in Titin, a lot about winning. If you are ever in danger, but a real danger where someone might make a mistake with you, then go into the brain, see what is there. Use whatever you need. I ask you, only, to wait until you have done everything else first."

"I'll wait, Butcher," she said.

He held out his hand. "Come."

She took his hand, avoiding the cock spurs.

"No need to see the stasis currents about the alien ship if it is friendly to the Alliance. You and I will stay together awhile."

She walked with her shoulder against his arm. "Friend or enemy," she said as they passed through the twilight, heavy with ghosts. "This whole Invasion—sometimes it seems so stupid. That's something they don't allow you to think back where I come from. Here on Jebel Tarik you more or less avoid the question. I envy you that."

"You are going to Administrative Alliance Headquarters because of the Invasion, yes?"

"That's right. But after I go, don't be surprised if I come back." Steps later she looked up again. "That's another thing I wish I could get straight in my head. The Invaders killed my parents, and the second embargo almost killed me. Two of my Navigators lost their wife to the Invaders. Still, Ron could wonder about just how right the War Yards were. Nobody likes the Invasion, but it goes on. It's so big I never really thought about trying to get out of it before. It's funny to see a whole bunch of people in their odd, and perhaps destructive, way doing just that. Maybe I should simply not bother to go to Headquarters, tell Tarik to turn around and head toward the densest part of the Snap."

"The Invaders," the Butcher said, almost musingly, "they hurt lots of people, you, me. They hurt me too."

"They did?"

"The brain sick, I told you. Invaders did that."

"What did they do?"

The Butcher shrugged. "First thing I remember is escaping from Nueva-nueva York."

"That's the huge port terminal for the Cancer cluster."

"That's right."

"The Invaders had captured you?"

He nodded. "And did something. Maybe experiment, maybe torture." He shrugged. "It doesn't matter. I can't remember. But when I escaped, I escaped with nothing: no memory, voice, words, name."

"Perhaps you were a prisoner of war, or maybe even some-body important before they captured—"

He bent and put his cheek against her lips to stop her talking. When he rose, he smiled, sadly she saw. "There are some things the brain may not know, but it can guess: I was always a thief, a murderer, a criminal. And I was no I. The Invaders caught me once. I escaped. The Alliance caught me later at Titin. I escaped—"

"You *escaped* from Titin?"

He nodded. "I will probably be caught again, because that's what happens to criminals in this universe. And maybe I will escape once more." He shrugged. "Maybe I will not be caught again, though." He looked at her, surprised not at her but at something in himself. "I was no I before, but now there is a reason to stay free. I will not be caught again. There is a reason."

"What is it, Butcher?"

"Because I am," he said softly, "and you are."

5 "You finishing u' your dictionary?" Brass asked.

"Finished it yesterday. This is a poem." She closed the notebook. "We should be at the tip of the Tongue soon. Butcher just told me this morning that the Çiribians have been keeping us company for four days. Brass, do you have any idea what they—"

Magnified by the loudspeakers, Tarik's voice: "Ready Jebel for immediate defense. Repeat, immediate defense."

"What the hell is going on now?" Rydra asked. Around them the commons rose in unified activity. "Look, hunt up the crew and get them down to the ejection gates."

"That's where the s'ider-boats leave from?"

"Right." Rydra stood.

"We gonna mix it u' some, Ca'tain?"

"If we have to," Rydra said, and started across the floor.

She beat the crew by a minute and caught the Butcher at the ejection hatch. Jebel's fight crew hurried along the corridor in ordered confusion.

"What's going on? Did the Çiribians get hostile?"

He shook his head. "Invaders twelve degrees off galactic center."

"This close to Administrative Alliance?"

"Yes. And if Jebel Tarik doesn't attack first, Jebel's had it. They're bigger than Jebel, and Jebel's going to bump right into them.

"Tarik's going to attack them?"

"Yes."

"Then come on, let's attack."

"You are going with me?"

"I'm a master strategist, remember?"

"Jebel is in danger," the Butcher said. "This will be a greater battle than you saw before."

"The better to use my talents on. Is your boat equipped to hold a full crew?"

"Yes. But we use the Navigation and Sensory detail of Jebel by remote control."

"Let's take a crew, anyway, just in case we want to break strategy in a hurry. Is Tarik riding with you this time?"

"No."

Up the hall Slug turned the corner, followed by Brass, the Navigators, the insubstantial figures of the discorporate trio, and the platoon.

The Butcher looked from them to Rydra. "All right. Come inside. Get in, gang!"

She kissed his shoulder because she couldn't reach his cheek; the Butcher opened the ejection hatch, and motioned them on.

Allegra, as she started up the ladder, caught Rydra's arm. "Are we gonna fight this time, Captain?" There was an excited smile on her freckled face.

"There's a good chance. Scared?"

"Yep," Allegra said, still grinning, and scurried into the dark tunnel. Rydra and the Butcher brought up the rear.

"They won't have any trouble with this equipment if they have to take over from remote control, will they?"

"This spider-boat is ten feet shorter than the *Rimbaud*. Things are more cramped in discorporate quarters, but everything else is the same."

Rydra thought: We've worked the sensory details on a forty-foot one-generator sloop; this is a breeze, Captain—Basque.

"The captain's cabin is different," he added. "That's where the weapon controls are. We're going to make some mistakes."

"Moralize later," she said. "We'll fight like hell for Jebel Tarik. But on the chance fighting like hell won't do any good, I want to be able to get out of here. No matter what happens, I've got to get back to Administrative Alliance Headquarters."

"Tarik wanted to know if the Çiribian ship will fight beside us. They're still hanging T-ward."

"They'll probably watch the whole business and not understand what's gong on, unless they're directly attacked. If they are, they can pretty well take care of themselves. But I doubt they'll join us in an offensive."

"That's bad," the Butcher said. "Because we'll need help."

"Strategy Workshop. Strategy Workshop," Tarik's voice came over the speaker. "Repeat, Strategy Workshop."

Where language charts had hung in her cabin, a viewing screen—smaller replica of the hundred-foot projection in Jebel's gallery—spread over the wall. Where her console had been were ranged and banked assortments of bomb and vibra-blast controls. "Gross, uncivilized weapons," she commented as she sat down on one of the curved shock-boards where her bubble seat had been. "But effective as hell, I would imagine, if you know what you're doing."

"What?" The Butcher strapped himself beside her.

"I was misquoting the late Weapons Master of Armsedge."

The Butcher nodded. "You see to your crew. I'll go over the check list up here."

She switched on the intercom. "Brass, you wired in place?"

"Right."

"Eye, Ear, Nose?"

"It's dusty down here, Captain. When's the last time they swept out this graveyard?"

"I don't care about the dust. Does everything work?"

"Oh, everything works all right . . ." The sentence ended with a ghostly sneeze.

"*Gesundheit.* Slug, what's happening?"

"All in place, Captain." Then muffled: "Will you put those marbles away, Lilly!"

"Navigation?"

"We're fine. Mollya is teaching Calli judo. But I'm right here and'll call them soon as something happens."

"Keep alert."

The Butcher bent toward her, stroked her hair, and laughed.

"I like them too," she told him. "I just hope we don't have to use them. One of them is a traitor who's tried to get me twice now. I'd rather not give him a third chance—though if I have to, I think I can handle him this time."

Tarik's voice over the speaker: "Carpenters gather to face thirty-two degrees off galactic center. Hacksaws at the K-ward gate. Ripsaws make ready at the R-ward gate. Crosscut blades ready at T-ward gate."

The ejectors clicked open. The cabin went black and the view-screen flickered with stars and distant gases. Controls gleamed with red and yellow signal lights along the weapon board. Through the underspeakers the chatter of the crews, back with the Navigation department of Jebel, began.

This is gonna be a rough one. Can you see her, Jehosaphat?

She's right in front of me. A big mother.

I just hope she ain't seen us yet. Keep cool, Kippi.

"Drill presses, Bandsaws, and Lathes: make sure your components are oiled and your power lines plugged in."

"That's us," the Butcher said. His hands leapt in the half-dark among the weapon controls.

What's the three ping-pong balls in the mosquito netting?

Tarik says it's a Çiribian ship.

Long as it's on our side, baby, it's fine with me.

"Power tools commence operations. Hand tools mark out for finishing work."

"Zero," the Butcher whispered. Rydra felt the ship jump. The stars began to move. Ten seconds later she saw the snub-snouted Invader rooting toward them.

"Ugly, isn't it," Rydra said.

"Jebel looks about the same size, only smaller. And when we come home, it will be beautiful. There's no way to enlist the Çiribians' help? Tarik will have to attack the Invader directly at her ports and smash as many as he can, which won't be a lot. Then they'll attack, and if they still outnumber Jebel's spider-boats, and surprise doesn't play heavily on Tarik's side, then that's—" she heard fist strike palm in the darkness—"it."

"Can't you just lob a gross, uncivilized atom bomb at them?"

"They have deflectors that would explode it in Tarik's hands."

"I'm glad I brought the crew then. We may have to make a quick exit to Administrative Alliance Headquarters."

"If they let us," the Butcher said, grimly. "What strategies then to win?"

"Tell you soon as the attack starts. I have a method, but if I use it too much I pay high." She recalled the illness after the incident with Geoffry Cord.

While Tarik continued to set up formations, the men chatted with Jebel and the spider-boats slipped ahead in the night.

It started so fast she nearly missed it. Five hacksaws had

slipped within six hundred yards of the Invader. Simultaneously they blasted at the ejector ports, and red beetles scurried from the sides of the black hog. It took four and a half seconds for the remaining twenty-seven ejectors to open and shoot their first barrage of cruisers. But Rydra was already thinking in Babel-17.

Through her distended time sense she saw they did need help. And the articulation of their need was also the answer.

"Break strategy, Butcher. Follow me with ten ships. My crew is taking over."

The maddening feeling that her English words took so long on her tongue! The Butcher's request—"Kippi, put hacksaws on trail and leave them there!"—seemed like a tape played at quarter speed. But her crew was already in control of the spider-boat. She hissed their trajectory into the mike.

Brass flung them at right angles to the tide, and for a moment she saw the hacksaws behind her. Now a hairpin turn and they drove behind the first sheet of Invader cruisers.

"Warm their backsides!"

The Butcher's hand hesitated at a weapon. "Drive them toward Jebel?"

"The hell I will. Fire, sweetheart!"

He fired, and the hacksaws followed suit.

In ten seconds it was clear she was right. Tarik lay R-ward. Ahead were the poached eggs, the mosquito netting, the flimsy, feathery vessel of Çiribia. Çiribia was Alliance, and at least one of the Invaders knew it because he fired at the weird contraption hung up on the sky. Rydra saw the Invader's gun-port cough green fire, but the fire never reached the Çiribians. The Invader cruiser turned into white-hot smoke that blackened and dispersed. Then another cruiser went, then three more, then three more.

"Out of here, Brass!" and they swung up and away.

"What was—" the Butcher started.

"A Çiribian heat ray. But they won't use it unless they're attacked. Part of the treaty signed at the Court in '47. So we make the Invaders attack. Want to do it again?"

Brass's voice over the speaker: "We already are, Ca'tain."

She was thinking in English again, waiting for the nausea to hit, but excitement held it back.

"Butcher," came from Tarik now, "what are you doing?"

"It's working, isn't it?"

"Yes. But you've left a hole in our defenses ten miles across."

"Tell him we'll plug it up in a minute as soon as we drive the next batch through."

Tarik must have heard her. "And what do we do for the next sixty seconds, young lady?"

"Fight like hell." And the next batch of herded cruisers disappeared before the Çiribian heat ray. Then from the underspeakers:

Hey, Butcher, they're out for you.

They got the idea you're spearheading this thing.

Butcher, six on your tail. Shake 'em fast.

"I can dodge them easy, Ca'tain," Brass called up. "They're all on remote control. I've got more freedom."

"One more and we can really put the odds on Tarik's side."

"Tarik outnumbers them already," the Butcher said. "This spider-boat has got to shake those burrs." He called into the mike, "Hacksaws disperse and break up the cruisers behind."

Will do. Hold onto your heads, fellows.

Hey, Butcher, one of them's not giving up.

Tarik said: "I thank you for my hacksaws back, but there's something following you that may be out for a hand-to-hand."

Rydra questioned him with a look.

"Heroes," the Butcher grunted disgustedly. "They'll try to grapple, board, and fight."

"Not with these kids on this ship! Brass, turn around and ram them, or come close enough to make them think we're crazy."

"May break a cou'le ribs . . ." The ship swung and they were flung hard against the straps of the shock-boards.

A youngster's voice through the intercom: "Wheeeee . . . !"

On the view-screen the Invader cruiser swerved to the side.

"Good chance if they grapple," the Butcher said. "They don't know there's a full crew aboard. They have no more than two—"

"Watch out, Ca'tain!"

The Invader cruiser filled the screen. *Clunnggg* sang the bones of the spider-boat.

The Butcher yanked at the straps of the shock-board and grinned. "Now to fighting hand-to-hand. Where are *you* going?"

"With you."

"You have a vibra-gun?" He tightened the holster on his stomach.

"Sure do." She pushed aside a panel of her loose blouse. "And this, too. Vanadium wire, six inches. Wicked thing."

"Come." He slapped the lever on a gravity inductor down to full field.

"What's that for?"

They were already in the corridor.

"To fight in a space suit out there is no good. False gravity field released around both ships will keep a breatheable atmosphere to about twenty feet from the surface and keep some heat in . . . more or less."

"What's less?" She swung behind him into the lift.

"It's about ten degrees below zero out there."

He had abandoned even his breech since the evening they had met in Jebel's graveyard. All he wore was the holster. "I guess we won't be out there long enough to need overcoats."

"I guarantee you, whoever is out there more than a minute will be dead, and not from overexposure." His voice suddenly deepened as they ducked into the hatchway. "If you don't know what you're doing, stay back." Then he bent to brush her cheek with amber hair. "But you know, and I know. We must do it well."

At the same time he raised his head, he released the hatch. Cold came in for them. She didn't feel it. The increased metabolic rate that accompanied Babel-17 wrapped her in a shield of physical indifference. Something went flying overhead. They knew what to do and both did it: they ducked. Whatever it was exploded—it was a grenade that had just missed coming into the hatch—and light bleached the Butcher's face. He leaped, and the fading glow slid down his body.

She followed him, reassured by the slow motion effect of Babel-17. She spun as she jumped. Someone ducked behind the ten-foot bulge of an outrigger. She fired at him, the slow motion giving her time to take careful aim. She didn't wait to see if she hit, but kept turning. The Butcher was making for the ten-foot wide column of the Invader's grapple.

Like a triple-clawed crab, the enemy boat angled away into the night. K-ward rose the flattened spiral of the home galaxy. Shadows were carbon-paper black on the smooth hulls. From the K-ward side nobody could see her, unless her movement blotted a fugitive star or passed into the direct light of the Specelli arm itself.

She jumped again—at the surface of the Invader cruiser now. For a moment it got much colder. Then she struck, near the grappler base, and rolled to her knees as, below, someone heaved another grenade at the hatch. They hadn't realized she and the Butcher were out yet. Good. She fired. And another hiss sounded from where the Butcher must be.

In the darkness below, figures moved. Then a vibra-blast stung the metal hatch beneath her hand. It came for her own ship's hatch and she wasted a quarter of a second analyzing and disregarding the idea that the spy she had been afraid of from her own crew had joined the Invaders. Rather, the Invader's tactic had been to keep them from leaving their ship and blow them up in the hatch. It had failed, so now they had taken cover in the hatch itself for safety and were firing from there. She fired, fired again. From his hiding place behind the other grapple, the Butcher was doing the same.

A section of the hatch rim began to glow from the repeated blasts. Then a familiar voice was calling, "All right, all right already, Butcher! You got them, Ca'tain!"

Rydra monkeyed down the grapple, as Brass turned the hatch light on and stood up in the glow that fanned across the bulkhead. The Butcher, gun down, came from his hiding place.

The underlighting distorted Brass's demon features still further. He held a limp figure in each claw.

"Actually this one's mine." He shook the right one. "He was trying to crawl back into the shi', so I ste"ed on his head." The pilot heaved the limp bodies onto the hullplates. "I don't know about you folks, but I'm cold. Reason I came up here in the first 'lace was Diavalo told me to tell you when you were ready for a coffee break, he'd fixed u' some Irish whiskey. Or maybe you'd 'refer hot buttered rum? Come on, come on! You're blue!"

At the lift her mind got back to English and she began to shiver. The frost on the Butcher's hair had started to melt to shiny droplets along his hairline. Her hand stung where she had just missed a burning.

"Hey," she said, as they stepped into the corridor, "if you're up here, Brass, who's watching the store?"

"Ki"i. We went back on remote control."

"Rum," the Butcher said. "No butter and not hot. Just rum."

"Man after my own heart." Brass nodded. He dropped one arm around Rydra's shoulder, the other around the Butcher's. Friendly, but also, she realized, he was half-carrying both of them.

Something went *clang* through the ship.

The pilot glanced at the ceiling. "Maintenance just cut those grapples loose." He edged them into the captain's cabin. As they collapsed on the shock-boards, he called into the intercom: "Hey, Diavalo, come u' here and get these 'eo'le drunk, huh? They need them."

"Brass?" She caught his arm as he started back out. "Can you get us from here to Administrative Alliance Headquarters?"

He scratched his ear. "We're right at the ti' of the Tongue. I only know the inside of the Sna' by chart. But Sensory tells me we're in something that must be the beginning of Natal-beta Current. It flows out of the Sna' and we can take it down to Atlas-run and then into Administrative Alliance's front door. We're about eighteen, twenty hours away."

"Let's go." She looked at the Butcher. He made no objection.

"Good idea," Brass said. "About half of Tarik is . . . eh, discor'orate."

"The Invaders won?"

"No'e. The Çiribians finally got the idea, roasted that big 'ig, and took off. But only after Jebel got a hole in its side large enough to 'ut three s'ider-boats through, sideways. Ki''i tells me everyone who's still alive is sealed off in one quarter of the shi', but they have no running 'ower."

"What about Tarik?" the Butcher asked.

"Dead," Brass said.

Diavalo poked his head down the entrance hatch. "Here you go."

Brass took the bottle and the glasses.

Then static on the speaker: "Butcher, we just saw you cast off the Invaders' cruiser. So, *you* got out alive."

Butcher leaned forward and picked up the mike. "Butcher alive, Tarik."

"Some people have all the luck. Captain Wong, I expect you to write me an elegy."

"Tarik?" She sat down next to the Butcher. "We're going to Administrative Alliance Headquarters now. We'll come back with help."

"At your convenience, Captain. We're just a trifle crowded, though."

"We're leaving now."

Brass was already out the door.

"Slug, are the kids all right?"

"Present and accounted for. Captain, you didn't give anyone permission to bring firecrackers aboard, did you?"

"Not that I remember."

"That's all I wanted to know. Ratt, come *back* here . . ."

Rydra laughed. "Navigation?"

"Ready when you are," Ron said. In the background she heard Mollya's voice: *"Nilitake kulala, nilale milele—"*

"You can't go to sleep forever," Rydra said. "We're taking off!"

"Mollya's teaching us a poem in Swahili," Ron explained.

"Oh. Sensory?"

"Ka*chuuu!* I always said, Captain, keep your graveyard clean. You might need it some day. Tarik's a case in point. We're ready."

"Get Slug to send one of the kids down with a dust mop. All wired in, Brass?"

"Checked out and ready, Ca'tain."

The stasis generators cut in and she leaned back on the shock-couch. Inside something at last relaxed. "I didn't think we were going to get out of there." She turned to the Butcher, who sat on the edge of his couch watching her. "You know I'm nervous as a cat. And I don't feel too well. Oh, hell, it's . . . starting." With the relaxation the sickness which she had put off for so long began to climb her body. "This whole thing makes me feel like I'm about to fly apart. You know when you doubt everything, mistrust all your feelings, I begin to think I'm not me anymore . . ." Her breath got painful in her throat.

"I am," he said softly, "and you are."

"Don't ever let me doubt it, Butcher. But I even have to wonder about that. There's a spy among my crew. I told you that, didn't I? Maybe it's Brass and he's going to hurl us into another nova!" Within the sickness was a blister of hysteria. The blister broke, and she smacked the bottle from the Butcher's hand. "Don't drink that! D-D-Diavalo, he might poison us!" She rose unsteadily. There was a red haze over everything. ". . . Or one of the d-d-dead. How . . . how can I f-f-f . . . fight a ghost?" Then pain hit her stomach, and she staggered back as away from a blow. Fear came with the pain. The emotions were moving behind his face, and even they blurred in her attempt to see them clearly. ". . . to kill . . . k-k-kill *us!*" she whispered, ". . . s-s-something to kill . . . s-s-so no y-*you,* n-n-no *I* . . ."

It was to get away from the pain which meant danger and the danger which meant silence that she did it. He had said, *If you are ever in danger . . . then go into my brain, see what is there, and use what you need.*

An image in her mind without words: once she, Muels, and Fobo had been in a barroom brawl on Tantur. She had caught a punch in the jaw and staggered back, shocked and turning, just as somebody pulled the bar mirror from behind the counter and flung it at her. Her own terrified face had come screaming toward her, smashed over her outstretched hand. As she stared at the Butcher's face, through pain and Babel-17, it happened all over—

part four

The Butcher

... *turning in the brain to wake*
with wires behind his eyes, forking the joints
akimbo. He wakes, wired,
forked fingers crackling, gagging on his tongue.
We wake, turning.
                    Spined against the floor,
his spine turning, chest hollowed,
air in the wires, sparks
glint from the wired ceiling, tapping
his sparkling fingernails. Coughs, cries.
The twin behind the eyes coughs, cries.
The dark twin doubles on the floor, swallows his tongue.
Splashed to the dark pole circuited behind
the eyes, the dark twin snaps his spine free, slaps
his palms against the ceiling. Charged beads fly.
The ceiling, polarized, batters his cheek with metal.
Tears free sink. Tears ribs,
torn pectorals off metal curved away
black, behind the cracks, dried,
that are his torn lips. More.
Buttocks and shoulderblades grind on the floor
gritty and green with brine.
                    They wake.
We wake, turning.
                He, gargling blood, turns,
born, on the wet floor . . .
                        —from *The Dark Twin*

1   "We just left the Sna', Ca'tain. You two drunk yet?"
Rydra's voice: "No."

"How do you like that. I guess you're all right, though."
Rydra's voice: "The brain fine. The body fine."

"Huh? Hey, Butcher, she didn't have one of her s'ells again?"
The Butcher's voice: "No."

"Both of you sound funny as hell. Shall I send the Slug u'
there to take a look at you?"
The Butcher's voice: "No."

"All right. It's clear sailing now, and I can 'ut a cou'le of hours
off. What do you say?"
The Butcher's voice: "What is to say?"

"Try 'thanks.' You know, I'm flying my tail off down here."
Rydra's voice: "Thanks."

"You're welcome, I guess. I'll leave you two alone. Hey, I'm
sorry if I interru'ted something."

2   Butcher, I didn't know! I couldn't have known!
And in the echo their minds fused a cry, Couldn't have—
couldn't. This light—

I told Brass, told him you must speak a language without the word "I" and I said I didn't know of one; but there was one, the obvious one—Babel-17 . . . !

Congruent synapses quivered sympathetically till images locked, and out of herself she created, saw him—

—in the solitary confinement box of Titin, he scratched a map on the green wall paint with his spur over the palimpsestic obscenities of two centuries' prisoners, a map that they would follow on his escape and that would take them in the wrong direction. She watched him pace that four-foot space for three months till his six-and-a-half-foot frame was starved to a hundred and one pounds and he collapsed in the chains of starvation.

On a triple rope of words she climbed from the pit: starve, stave, stake; collapse, collate, collect; chains, change, chance.

He collected his winnings from the cashier and was about to stride across the maroon carpet of *Casino Cosmica* to the door when the black croupier blocked his way, smiling at the thick money case. "Would you like to take one more chance, sir? Something to challenge a player of your skill?" He was taken to a magnificent 3-D chessboard with glazed ceramic pieces. "You play against the house computer. Against each piece you lose, you stake a thousand credits. Each piece you win gains you the same. Checks win or lose you five hundred. Checkmate gains the winner one hundred times the rest of the game's earnings, for either you or the house." It was a game to even out his exorbitant winnings—and he had been winning exorbitantly. "Going home and take this money now," he said to the croupier. The croupier smiled and said, "The house insists you play." She watched, fascinated, while the Butcher shrugged, turned to the board—and checkmated the computer in a seven-move fool's mate. They gave him his million credits—and tried to kill him three times before he got to the mouth of the casino. They did not succeed, but the sport was even better than the gambling.

Watching him function and react in these situations, her mind shook inside his, curving to his pain or pleasure, strange emotions because they were egoless and inarticulate, magic, seductive, mythical. *Butcher*—

She managed to interrupt the headlong circling.

—*if you understood Babel-17 all along,* her questions hurled in her own storming brain, *why did you only use it gratuitously for yourself, an evening of gambling, a bank robbery, when a day later you would lose everything and make no attempt to keep things for yourself?*

What "self"? There was no "I."

She had entered him in some bewildering reversed sexuality. Enclosing her, he was in agony. *The light—you make! You make!* his crying in terror.

Butcher, she asked, more familiar in patterning words about emotional turbulences than he, *what does my mind in yours look like?*

Bright, bright moving, he howled, the analytical precision of Babel-17, crude as stone to articulate their melding, making so many patterns, re-forming them.

That's just being a poet, she explained, the oblique connection momentarily cutting the flood through. Poet *in Greek means* maker *or* builder.

There's one! There's a pattern now. Ahhhh!—so bright, bright!

Just that simple semantic connection? She was astounded.

But the Greeks were poets three thousand years ago and you are a poet now. You snatch words together over such distance and their wakes blind me. Your thoughts are all fire, over shapes I cannot catch. They sound like music too deep, that shakes me.

That's because you were never shaken before. But I'm flattered.

*You are so big inside me I will break. I see the pattern named

The criminal and the artistic consciousness meet in the same head with one language between them . . .

Yes, I had started to think something like—

Flanking it, shapes called Baudelaire—*Ahhh!—and* Villon.

They were ancient French po—

Too bright! Too bright! The "I" in me is not strong enough to hold them. Rydra, when I look at the night and stars, it is only a passive act, but you are active even watching, and halo the stars with more luminous flame.

What you perceive you change, Butcher. But you must perceive it.

I must—the light; central in you I see mirror and motion fused, and the pictures are meshed, rotating, and everything is choice.

My poems! It was the embarrassment of nakedness.

Definitions of "I," each great and precise.

She thought: I/Aye/Eye, the self, a sailor's *yes,* the organ of visual perception.

He began, *You—*

You/Ewe/Yew, the other self, a female sheep, the Celtic vegetative symbol for death.

—you ignite my words with meanings I can only glimpse. What am I surrounding? What am I, surrounding you?

Still watching, she saw him commit robbery, murder, mayhem, because the semantic validity of *mine* and *thine* were ruined in a snarl of frayed synapses. *Butcher, I heard it ringing in your muscles, that loneliness, that made you make Tarik hook up the* Rimbaud *just to have someone near you who could speak this analytical tongue, the same reason you tried to save the baby,* she whispered.

Images locked on her brain.

Long grass whispered by the weir. Alleppo's moons fogged the evening. The plainsmobile hummed, and with measured impatience he flicked the ruby emblem on the steering wheel with the tip of his left spur. Lill twisted against him, laughing. "You know, Butcher, if Mr. Big thought you'd driven out here with me on such a romantic night he'd get very hostile. You're really gonna take me to Paris when you finish here?" Unnamed warmth mixed in him with unnamed impatience. Her shoulder was damp under his hand, her lips red. She had coiled her champagne-colored hair high over one ear. Her body beside his moved in a rippling motion that had the excuse of her turning to face him. "If you're kidding me, about Paris, I'll tell Mr. Big. If I were a smart girl, I'd wait till after you took me there before I let us get . . . friendly." Her breath was perfumed in the sweltering night. He moved his other hand up her arm. "Butcher, get me off this hot, dead world. Swamps, caves, rain! Mr. Big scares me, Butcher! Take me away from him, to Paris. Don't just be pretending. I want to go with you so bad." She made another laughing sound with only her lips. "I guess I'm . . . I'm not a smart girl after all." He placed his mouth against her mouth— and broke her neck with one thrust of his hands. Her eyes still open, she sagged backwards. The hypodermic ampule she had been about to plunge into his shoulder fell from her hand, rolled across the dashboard, and dropped among the foot pedals. He carried her into the weir, and came back muddy to mid-thigh. In the seat he flipped on the radio. "It's finished, Mr. Big."

"Very good. I was listening. You can pick up your money in the morning. It was very silly of her to try and double-cross me out of that fifty thousand."

The plainsmobile was rolling, the warm breeze drying the mud on his arms, the long grass hissing against the runners.

Butcher . . . !

But that's me, Rydra.

I know. But I . . .

I had to do the same thing to Mr. Big himself two weeks later.

Where did you promise to take him?

The gambling caves of Minos. And once I had to crouch—

—though it was his body crouching under the green light of Kreto, breathing with wide open mouth to stop all sound, it was her anticipation, her fear controlled to calm. The loader in his red uniform halts and wipes his forehead with a bandanna. Step out quickly, taps his shoulder. The loader turns, surprised, and the hands come up leading with the heel, cock spurs opening the loader's belly, which spills all over the platform, then running, while the alarms start, vaulting the sandbags, snatching up the hawser chain and swinging it down on the amazed face of the guard standing on the other side who turned to see him with arms surprised open—

—*broke into the open and got away,* he told her. *The trail disguise worked and the Tracers couldn't follow me past the lava pits.*

Opening you up. Butcher. All the running, opening me?

Does it hurt, does it help? I didn't know.

But there were no words in your mind. Even Babel-17 was like the brain noise of a computer engaged in a purely synaptical analysis.

Yes. Now do you begin to understand—

—standing, shivering in the roaring caves of Dis where he had been wombed nine months, eaten all the food, Lonny's pet dog, then Lonny, who had frozen to death trying to climb over the mounded ice—till suddenly the planetoid swung out from the shadow of Cyclops and blazing Ceres flared in the sky so that in forty minutes the cave was flooded with ice water to his waist. When he finally freed his hop-sled, the water was warm and he was slimy with sweat. He ran at top speed for the two-mile twilight strip, setting the automatic pilot a moment before he collapsed, dizzy with heat. He fainted two minutes before he pulled into Gotterdammerung.

Faint in the darkness of your lost memory, Butcher, I must find you. Who were you before Nueva-nueva York?

And he turned to her in gentleness. *You're afraid, Rydra? Like before . . .*

No, *not like before. You're teaching me something, and it's shaking my whole picture of the world and myself. I thought I was afraid before because I couldn't do what you could do, Butcher.* The white flame went blue, protective, and trembled. *But I was afraid because I* could *do all those things, and for my own reasons, not your lack of reasons, because I am, and you are. I'm a lot bigger than I thought I was, Butcher, and I don't know whether to thank you or to damn you for showing me.* And something inside was crying, stuttering, was still. She turned in the silences she had taken from him, fearfully, and in the silences something waited for her to speak, alone, for the first time.

Look at yourself, Rydra.

Mirrored in him, she saw growing in the light of her, a darkness without words, only noise—growing! And cried out at its name and shape. *The broken circuit boards! Butcher, those tapes that could only have been made on my console when I was there! Of course—!*

Rydra, we can control them if we can name them.

How can we, now? We have to name ourselves first. And you don't know who you are.

Your words, Rydra, can we somehow use your words to find out who I am?

Not my words, Butcher. But maybe yours. Maybe Babel-17.

No . . .

I am, she whispered, *believe me, Butcher, and you are.*

3 "Headquarters, Captain. Take a look through the sensory helmet. Those radio nets look like fireworks, and corporate souls tell me it smells like corned beef hash and fried eggs. Hey, thanks for getting us dusted out. Had a tendency toward hay fever when I was alive that I never did shake."

Rydra's voice: "The crew will debark with the Captain and the Butcher. The crew will take them to General Forester, together, and not let them be separated."

The Butcher's voice: "There is a tape recording in the Captain's cabin on the console containing a grammar of Babel-17. The slug will send that tape immediately to Dr. Markus T'mwarba on Earth by special delivery. Then inform Dr. T'mwarba by stellarphone that the tape was sent, at what time, and its contents."

"Brass, Slug! Something's wrong up there!" Ron's voice overcut the Captain's signal. "You ever heard them talk like that? Hey, Captain Wong, what's the matter . . . ?"

part five

Markus T'mwarba

Growing older I descend November.
The asymptotic cycle of the year
plummets to now. In crystal reveries
I pass beneath a fixed white line of trees
where dry leaves lie for footsteps to dismember.
They crackle with a muted sound like fear.
That and the wind is all that I can hear.
I ask cold air, "What is the word that frees?"
The wind says, "Change," and the white sun,
  "Remember."
        —from *Electra*

1 The spool of tape, the imperative directive from General Forester, and the infuriated Dr. T'mwarba reached Danil D. Appleby's office within thirty seconds of each other.

He was opening the flat box when the noise outside the partition made him look up. "Michael," he asked the intercom. "What's that?"

"Some madman who says he's a psychiatrist!"

"I am not mad!" Dr. T'mwarba said loudly. "But I know how long it takes a package to get from Administrative Alliance Headquarters to Earth, and it should have reached my door with this morning's mail. It didn't, which means it's been held up, and this is where you do things like that. Let me in."

Then the door crashed back against the wall and he was.

Michael craned around T'mwarba's hip: "Hey, Dan, I'm sorry. I'll call the—"

Dr. T'mwarba pointed to the desk and said, "That's mine. Gimme."

"Don't bother, Michael," the Customs Officer said before the door was slammed again. "Good afternoon, Dr. T'mwarba. Won't you sit down. This *is* addressed to you, isn't it? Don't look so surprised that I know you. I also handle security psyche-index integration, and all of us in the department know your brilliant work in schizoid-differentiation. I'm so glad to meet you."

"Why can't I have my package?"

"One moment and I'll find out." As he picked up the directive, Dr. T'mwarba picked up the box and stuck it in his pocket:

"Now, you can explain."

The Customs Officer opened the letter. "It seems," he said,

pressing his knee against the desk to release some of the hostility that had built up in very little time, "that you may have . . . eh, keep the tape on condition you leave for Administrative Alliance Headquarters this evening on the *Midnight Falcon* and bring the tape with you. Passage has been booked, thanking you in advance for your cooperation, sincerely, General X. J. Forester."

"Why?"

"He doesn't say. I'm afraid, doctor, that unless you agree to go, I won't be able to let you keep that. And we *can* get it back."

"That's what you think. Have you any idea what they want?"

The officer shrugged. "You were expecting it. Who's it from?"

"Rydra Wong."

"Wong?" The Customs Officer had put both knees against the desk. He dropped them. "The poet, Rydra Wong? You know Rydra, too?"

"I've been her psychiatric advisor since she was twelve. Who are you?"

"I'm Danil D. Appleby. Had I known you were Rydra's friend, I would have ushered you up here myself!" The hostility had acted as a takeoff from which to spring into ebullient camaraderie. "If you're leaving on the *Falcon,* you've got time to step out a little while with me, haven't you? I was going to leave work early anyway. I have to stop off at . . . well, someplace in Transport Town. Why didn't you *say* you knew her before? There's a delightfully ethnic place right near where I'm going. Get a reasonable meal and a good drink there; do you follow the wrestling? Most people think it's illegal, but you can watch it there. Ruby and Python are on display this evening. If you'll just make that one stop with me first, I know you'll find it fascinating. And I'll get you to the *Falcon* on time."

"I think I know the place."

"You go downstairs and they have this big bubble on the ceiling, where they fight . . . ?" Effervescent, he leaned forward. "As a matter of fact, Rydra first took me there."

Dr. T'mwarba began to smile.

The Customs Officer slapped the desktop. "We had a wild time that night! Simply wild!" He narrowed his eyes. "Ever been picked up by one of those . . ." He snapped his fingers three times. ". . . in the discorporate sector? Now that still *is* illegal. But take a walk out there some evening."

"Come," laughed the doctor. "Dinner and a drink; best idea I've heard all day. I'm starved and I haven't seen a good match in a month."

"I've never been inside *this* place before," the Officer said, as they stepped from the monorail. "I called to make an appointment but they told me I didn't need one, just to come in; they were open till six. I figured what the hell, I'd take off from work." They crossed the street and passed the newsstand where frayed, unshaven loaders were picking up schedule sheets for incoming flights. Three stellarman in green uniforms lurched along the sidewalk, arms about each other's shoulders. "You know," the Customs Officer was saying, "I've had quite a battle with myself; I've wanted to do it ever since I first came down here—hell, ever since I first went to the movies and saw pictures. But anything really bizarre just wouldn't go at the office. Then I said to myself, it could be something simple, covered up when I was wearing clothes. Here we are."

The Officer pushed open the door of Plastiplasms Plus ("Addendums, Superscripts, and Footnotes to the Beautiful Body").

"You know I always meant to ask someone who was an

authority; do you think there's anything psychologically off about wanting something like this?"

"Not at all."

A young lady with blue eyes, lips, hair, and wings said, "You can go right in. Unless you want to check our catalog first."

"Oh, I know exactly what I want," the Customs Officer assured her. "This way?"

"That's right."

"Actually," Dr. T'mwarba went on, "it's psychologically important to feel in control of your body, that you can change it, shape it. Going on a six-month diet or a successful muscle building program can give quite a sense of satisfaction. So can a new nose, chin, or set of scales and feathers."

They were in a room with white operating tables. "Can I help you?" asked a smiling Polynesian cosmetisurgeon in a blue smock. "Why don't you lie down here?"

"I'm just watching," Dr. T'mwarba said.

"It's listed in your catalog as #5463," the Customs Officer declared. "I want it . . . there." He clapped his left hand to his right shoulder.

"Oh, yes. I rather like that one myself. Just a moment." He opened the top of a stand by the table. Instruments glittered.

The surgeon went off to the glass-faced refrigeration unit at the far wall where behind the glass doors intricate plastiplasm shapes were blurred by frost. He returned with a tray full of various fragments. The only recognizable one was the front half of a miniature dragon with jeweled eyes, glittering scales, and opalescent wings: it was less than two inches long.

"When he's connected up to your nervous system, you'll be able to make him whistle, hiss, roar, flap his wings, and spit sparks, though it may take a few days to assimilate him into your body picture. Don't be surprised if at first he just burps and looks seasick. Take your shirt off, please."

The Officer opened his collar.

"We'll just block off all sensation from your shoulder on . . . there, that didn't really hurt. This? Oh, it's a local venal and arterial constrictant; we want to keep things clean. Now, we'll just cut you along the—well, if it upsets you, don't look. Talk to your friend there. It'll just take a few minutes. Oh, that must have tickled all down in your tummy! Never mind. Just once more. Fine. That's your shoulder joint. I know; your arm does look sort of funny hanging there without it. We'll just stick in this transparent plastiplasm cage now. Exact same articulation as your shoulder joint, and it holds your muscles out of the way. See, it's got grooves for your arteries. Move your chin, please. If you want to watch, look in the mirror. Now we'll just crimp it around the edges. Keep this vivatape around the rim of the cage for a couple of days until things grow together. There's not much chance of its pulling apart unless you strain your arm suddenly, but you ought to be safe. Now I'll just connect the little fellow in there to the nerve. This will hurt—"

"*Gnnnnn!*" The Customs Officer half rose.

"—Sit! Sit! All right, the little catch here—look in the mirror—is to open the cage. You'll learn how to make him come out and do tricks, but don't be impatient. It takes a bit of time. Let me turn the feeling back on in your arm."

The surgeon removed the electrodes and the Officer whistled.

"Stings a little. It will for about an hour. If there's any redness or inflammation, please don't hesitate to come back. Everything that comes through that doorway gets perfectly sterilized, but every five or six years somebody comes down with an infection. You can put your shirt on now."

As they walked into the street, the Customs Officer flexed his shoulder. "You know they claim it should make absolutely no difference." He made a face. "My fingers feel funny. Do you think he might have bruised a nerve?"

"I doubt it," Dr. T'mwarba said, "but *you* will if you keep twisting like that. You'll pull the vivatape loose. Let's go eat."

The officer fingered his shoulder. "It feels odd to have a three-inch hole there and your arm still working."

"So," Dr. T'mwarba said over his mug, "Rydra first brought you to Transport Town."

"Yes. Actually—well, I only met her that once. She was getting a crew together for a government sponsored trip. I was just along to approve indices. But something happened that evening."

"What was it?"

"I saw a bunch of the weirdest, oddest people I had ever met in my life, who thought different, and acted different, and even made love different. And they made me laugh, and get angry, and be happy, and be sad, and excited, and even fall in love a little myself." He glanced up at the sphere of the wrestling arena aloft in the bar. "And they didn't seem so weird or strange anymore."

"Communication was working that night?"

"I guess so. It's presumptuous my calling her by her first name. But I feel like she's my . . . friend. I'm a lonely man, in a city of lonely men. And when you find some place where . . . communications are working, you come back to see if they'll work again."

"Have they?"

Danil D. Appleby looked down from the ceiling and began to unbutton his shirt. "Let's have dinner." He shrugged his shirt over the back of the chair and glanced down at the dragon caged in his shoulder. "You . . . come back anyway." Turning in his seat, he picked his shirt up, folded it neatly, and put it down again.

"Dr. T'mwarba, have you any idea why they want you to come to Administrative Alliance Headquarters?"

"I assume it concerns Rydra and this tape."

"Because you said you were her doctor. I just hope it isn't a medical reason. If anything happened to her, it would be terrible. For me, I mean. She managed to say so much to me in that one evening—say it so very simply." He laughed and ran his finger around the rim of the cage. The beast inside gurgled. "And half the time she wasn't even looking in my direction when she said it."

"I hope she's all right," Dr. T'mwarba said. "She'd better be."

---

2   Before the *Midnight Falcon* landed, he inveigled the captain into letting him speak with Flight Control. "I want to know when the *Rimbaud* came in."

"Just a moment, sir. I don't believe it has. Certainly not within the past six months. It would take a little time to check back further than—"

"No. It would be more like the past few days. Are you sure the *Rimbaud* did not land here recently under Captain Rydra Wong?"

"Wong? I believe she did land yesterday, but not in the *Rimbaud*. It was an unmarked fighter ship. There was some mixup because the serial numbers had been filed off the tubes and there was a possibility it might have been stolen."

"Was Captain Wong all right when she disembarked?"

"She'd apparently relinquished command to her—" The voice stopped.

"Well?"

"Excuse me, sir. This has been all marked classified. I didn't see the sticker, and it was accidentally put back in the regular file. I can't give you any more information. It's only cleared to authorized persons."

"I'm Dr. Markus T'mwarba," the doctor said, with authority and no idea whether it would do any good.

"Oh, there is a notation concerning you, sir. But you're not on the cleared list."

"Then what the hell does it say, young lady?"

"Just that if you requested information, to refer you directly to General Forester."

An hour later he walked into General Forester's office. "All right, what's the matter with Rydra?"

"Where's the tape?"

"If Rydra wanted me to have it, she had good reason. If she'd wanted you to have it, she would have given it to you. Believe me, you won't get your hands on it unless I give it to you."

"I'd expected more cooperation, Doctor."

"I am cooperating. I'm here, General. But you must want me to do something, and unless I know exactly what's going on, I can't."

"It's a very unmilitary attitude," General Forester said, coming around the desk. "It's one I'm having to deal with more and more, recently. I don't know whether I like it. But I don't know whether I dislike it either." The green-suited stellarman sat on the desk's edge, touched the stars on his collar, looked pensive. "Miss Wong was the first person I've met in a long time to whom I could not say: Do this, do that, and be damned if you inquire about the consequences. The first time I spoke to her about Babel-17, I thought I could just hand her the transcription, and she would hand it back to me in English. She told me flatly: No; I would have to tell her more. That's the first time anyone's told me I *had* to do anything in fourteen years. I may not like it; I sure as hell respect it." His hands dropped protectively to his lap. (Protective? Was it Rydra who had taught him to interpret that movement, T'mwarba wondered briefly.) "It's so easy to get caught in your fragment of the world. When a voice comes cutting through, it's important. Rydra Wong . . ." and the General stopped, an expression settling on his features that made T'mwarba chill as he looked at it with what Rydra had taught him.

"Is she all right, General Forester? Is this something medical?"

"I don't know," the General said. "There's a woman in my inner office—and a man. I can't tell you whether the woman is Rydra Wong or not. It certainly isn't the same woman I talked to that evening on Earth about Babel-17."

But T'mwarba, already at the door, shoved it open.

A man and a woman looked up. The man was massively graceful, amber-haired—a convict, the doctor realized from the mark on his arm. The woman—

He put both fists on his hips: "All right, what am I about to say to you?"

She said: "Noncomprehension."

Breathing pattern, curl of hands in lap, carriage of shoulders, the details whose import she had demonstrated to him a thousand times: he learned in the horrifying length of a breath just how much they identified. For a moment he wished she had never taught him, because they were all gone, and their absence in her familiar body were worse than scars and disfigurements. He began in a voice that was habitually for her, the one he had praised or chastened her with. "I was going to say—if this is a joke, sweetheart, I'll . . . paddle you." It ended with the voice for strangers, for salesmen and wrong numbers, and he felt unsteadied. "If you're not Rydra, who are you?"

She said: "Noncomprehension of the question. General Forester, is the man Dr. Markus T'mwarba?"

"Yes, he is."

"Look." Dr. T'mwarba turned to the General. "I'm sure you've gone over fingerprints, metabolic rates, retina patterns, that sort of identification."

"That's Rydra Wong's body, Doctor."

"All right: hypnotics, experiential imprinting, graft of presyn-apsed cortical matter—can you think of any other way to get one mind into another head?"

"Yes. Seventeen. There's no evidence of any of them." The General stepped back through the door. "She's made it clear she wants to speak to you alone. I'll be right outside." He closed it.

"I'm pretty sure who you're not," Dr. T'mwarba said after a moment.

The woman blinked and said: "Message from Rydra Wong, delivered verbatim, noncomprehension of its significance." Suddenly the face took on its familiar animation. Her hands grasped each other, and she leaned slightly forward: "Mocky, am I glad you got here. I can't sustain this very long, so here goes. Babel-17 is more or less like Onoff, Algol, Fortran. I am telepathic after all, only I've just learned how to control it. I . . . we've taken care of the Babel-17 sabotage attempts. Only we're prisoners, and if you want to get us out, forget about who I am. Use what's on the end of the tape, and find out who *he* is!" She pointed to the Butcher.

The animation left, and the rigidity returned to her face. The whole transformation left T'mwarba holding his breath. He shook his head, started breathing again.

After a moment he went back into the General's office. "Who's the jailbird?" he asked matter-of-factly.

"We're tracking that down now. I hoped to have the report this morning." Something on the desk flashed. "Here it is now." He flipped up a slot in the desktop and pulled out a folder. As he slit the seal, he paused. "Would you like to tell me what Onoff, Algol, and Fortran are?"

"To be sure, listening at keyholes." T'mwarba sighed and sat down in a bubble chair in front of the desk. "They're ancient, twentieth-century languages—artificial languages that were used to program computers, designed especially for machines. Onoff was the simplest. It reduced everything to a combination of two words, *on* and *off*, or the binary number system. The others were more complicated."

The General nodded, and finished opening the folder. "That guy came from the swiped spider-boat with her. The crew got very upset when we wanted to put them in separate quarters." He shrugged. "It's something psychic. Why take chances? We leave them together."

"Where is the crew? Were they able to help you?"

"Them? It's like trying to talk to something out of your bad dreams. Transport. Who can talk to people like that?"

"Rydra could," Dr. T'mwarba said. "I'd like to see if I might."

"If you wish. We're keeping them at Headquarters." He opened the folder, then made a face. "Odd. There's a fairly detailed account of his history for a five-year period that started with some petty thievery, strong-arm work, then graduates to a couple of rub-outs. A bank robbery—" The General pursed his lips and nodded appreciatively. "He served two years in the penal caves of Titin, escaped—this boy *is* something. Disappeared into the Specelli Snap where he either died, or perhaps got into a shadow-ship . . . Well, he certainly didn't die. But before December '61—" the General frowned—"he doesn't seem to have existed. He's usually called the Butcher."

Suddenly the General dived into a drawer and came up with another folder. "Kreto, Earth, Minos, Callisto," he read, then slapped the folder with the back of his hand. "Aleppo, Rhea, Olympia, Paradise, Dis!"

"What's that, the Butcher's itinerary until he went into Titin?"

"It just so happens it is. But it's also the locations of a series of accidents that began in December '61. We'd just gotten around to connecting them up with Babel-17. We'd only been working with recent 'accidents,' but then this pattern from a few years ago turned up. Reports of the same sort of radio exchange. Do you think Miss Wong has brought home our saboteur?"

"Could be. Only that isn't Rydra in there."

"Well, yes. I guess you could say that."

"For similar reasons I would gather that the gentleman with her is not the Butcher."

"Who do you think he is?"

"Right now I don't know. I'd say it's fairly important we found out." He stood up. "Where can I get hold of Rydra's crew?"

---

3   "A pretty snazzy place!" Calli said as they stepped from the lift at the top floor of Alliance Towers.

"Nice now," said Mollya, "to be able to walk about."

A headwaiter in white formal wear came across the civet rug, looked just a trifle askance at Brass, then said, "This is your party, Dr. T'mwarba?"

"That's right. We have an alcove by the window. You can bring us a round of drinks right away. I've ordered already."

The waiter nodded, turned, and led them toward a high, arched window that looked over Alliance Plaza. A few people turned to watch them.

"Administrative Headquarters can be a very pleasant place." Dr. T'mwarba smiled.

"If you got the money," Ron said. He craned to look at the blue-black ceiling, where the lights were arranged to simulate the constellations seen from Rymik, and whistled softly. "I read about places like this but I never thought I'd be in one."

"Wish I could have brought the kids," the Slug mused. "They thought the Baron's was something."

At the alcove the waiter held Mollya's chair.

"Was that Baron Ver Dorco of the War Yards?"

"Yeah," said Calli. "Barbecued lamb, plum wine, the best-looking peacocks I've seen in two years. Never got to eat 'em." He shook his head.

"One of the annoying habits of aristocracy," T'mwarba laughed, "they'll go ethnic at the slightest provocation. But there're only a few of us left, and most of us have the good manners to drop our titles."

"Late weapons master of Armsedge," the Slug corrected.

"I read the report of his death. Rydra was there?"

"We all were. It was a 'retty wild evening."

"What exactly happened?"

Brass shook his head. "Well, Ca'tain went early . . ." When he had finished recounting the incidents, with the others adding details, Dr. T'mwarba sat back in his chair.

"The papers didn't give it that way. But they wouldn't. What was this TW-55 anyway?"

Brass shrugged.

There was a click as the discorporaphone in the doctor's ear went on: "It's a human being who's been worked over and over from birth till it isn't human anymore," the Eye said. "I was with Captain Wong when the Baron first showed it to her."

Dr. T'mwarba nodded. "Is there anything else you can tell me?"

Slug, who had been trying to get comfortable in the hard-backed chair, now leaned his stomach against the table edge. "Why?"

The others got still, quickly.

The fat man looked at the rest of the crew. "Why are we telling him all this? He's going back and give it to the stellarmen."

"That's right," Dr. T'mwarba said. "Any of it that might help Rydra."

Ron put down his glass of iced cola. "The stellarmen haven't been what you'd call nice to us, Doc," he explained.

"They don't take us to no fancy restaurants." Calli tucked his napkin into the zircon necklace he'd worn for the occasion. A waiter placed a bowl of french-fried potatoes on the table, turned away, and came back with a platter of hamburgers.

Across the table Mollya picked up the tall, red flask and looked at it questioningly.

"Ketchup," Dr. T'mwarba said.

"*Ohhh . . . !*" Mollya breathed and returned it to the damask tablecloth.

"Diavalo should be here now." The Slug sat back slowly and stopped looking at the doctor. "He's an artist with a carbo-synth, and he's got a feel for a protein-dispenser that's fine for good solid meals like nut-stuffed pheasant, fillet of snapper-mayonnaise, and good stick-to-your-ribs food for a hungry spaceship crew. But this fancy stuff . . . ?" He spread mustard carefully across his bun. "Give him a pound of real chopped meat, and I bet he'd run out of the galley 'cause it might bite him."

Brass said: "What's wrong with Ca'tain Wong? That's what nobody wants to ask."

"I don't know. But if you'll tell me all you can, I'll have a lot better chance of doing something about it."

"The other thing nobody wants to say," Brass went on, "is that *one* of us don't want you to do anything for her. But we don't know who."

The others silenced again.

"There was a s'y on the shi'. We all knew about it. It tried to destroy the shi' twice. I think it's res'onsible for whatever ha''ened to Ca'tain Wong and the Butcher."

"We all think so," the Slug said.

"This is what you didn't want to tell the stellarmen?"

Brass nodded.

"Tell him about the circuit boards and the phony takeoff before we got to Tarik," Ron said.

Brass explained.

"If it hadn't been for the Butcher," the discorporaphone clicked again, "we would have reentered normal space in the Cygnus Nova. The Butcher convinced Tarik to hook us out and take us aboard."

"So." Dr. T'mwarba looked around the table. "One of you is a spy."

"It could be one of the kids," the Slug said. "It doesn't have to be someone at this table."

"If it is," Dr. T'mwarba said, "I'm talking to the rest of you. General Forester couldn't get anything out of you. Rydra needs somebody's help. It's that simple."

Brass broke the lengthening silence. "I'd just lost a shi' to the Invaders, Doc; a whole 'latoon of kids, more than half the officers. Even though I could wrestle well and was a good 'ilot, to any other trans'ort ca'tain, that run-in with the Invaders made me a stiff jinx. Ca'tain Wong's not from our world. But wherever she came from, she brought a set of values with her that said, 'I like your work and I want to hire you.' I'm grateful."

"She knows about so much," Calli said. "This is the wildest trip I've ever been on. Worlds. That's it, Doc. She cuts through worlds and don't mind taking you along. When's the last time somebody took me to a Baron's for dinner and espionage? Next day I'm eating with pirates. And here I am now. Sure I want to help."

"Calli's too mixed up with his stomach," Ron interrupted. "What it is, is she gets you thinking, Doc. She made me think about Mollya and Calli. You know, she was tripled with Muels Aranlyde, the guy who wrote *Empire Star*. But I guess you must, if you're her doctor. Anyway, you start thinking that maybe those people who live in other worlds—like Calli says—where people write books or make weapons, are real. If you believe in them, you're a little more ready to believe in yourself. And when somebody who can do that needs help, you help."

"Doctor," Mollya said, "I was dead. She made me alive. What can I do?"

"You can tell me everything you know—" he leaned across the table and locked his fingers—"about the Butcher."

"The Butcher?" Brass asked. The others were surprised. "What about him? We don't know anything exce't that Ca'tain and him got to be real close."

"You were on the same ship with him for three weeks. Tell me everything you saw him do."

They looked at one another, silence questioning.

"Was there anything that might have indicated where he was from?"

"Titin," Calli said. "The mark on his arm."

"Before Titin—at least five years before. You see, the problem is that the Butcher doesn't know either."

They looked even more perplexed. Then Brass said, "His language. Ca'tain said he originally had s'oken a language where there was no word for 'I.' "

Dr. T'mwarba frowned more deeply as the discorporaphone clicked again: "She taught him how to say *I* and *you*. They wandered through the graveyard in the evening, and we hovered over them while they taught each other who they were."

"The 'I,' " T'mwarba said, "that's something to go on." He sat back. "It's funny. I suppose I know everything about Rydra there is to know. And I know just that little about—"

The discorporaphone clicked a third time. "You don't know about the myna bird."

T'mwarba was surprised. "Of course I do. I was there."

The discorporate crew laughed softly. "But she never told you *why* she was so frightened."

"It was a hysterical onset brought about by her previous condition—"

Ghostly laughter again. "The worm, Dr. T'mwarba. She wasn't afraid of the bird at all. She was afraid of the telepathic impression of a huge worm crawling toward her, the worm that the bird was picturing."

"She told you this—?" and never told me, was the ending of what had begun in minor outrage and ceased in wonder.

"Worlds," the ghost reiterated. "Sometimes worlds exist under your eyes, and you never see them. This room might be filled with phantoms—you never know. Even the rest of the crew can't be sure what we're saying now. But Captain Wong, she never used a discorporaphone. She found a way to talk with us without one. She cut through worlds, and joined them—that's the important part—so that both became bigger."

"Then somebody's got to figure out where in the world,

yours, or mine, or hers, the Butcher came from." A memory resolved like a cadence closing, and he laughed. The others looked puzzled. "A worm. *Somewhere in Eden now, a worm, a worm* . . . That was one of her earliest poems. And it never occurred to me."

---

4 "Am I supposed to be happy?" Dr. T'mwarba asked. "You're supposed to be interested," said General Forester.

"You've looked at a hyperstatic map and discovered that though the sabotage attempts over the last year and a half lie all over a galaxy in regular space, they're within cruiser distance of the Specelli Snap across the jump. Also, you've discovered that during the time the Butcher was in Titin, there were no 'accidents' at all. In other words, you have discovered that the Butcher *could* be responsible for the whole business, just from physical proximity. No, I am not happy at all."

"Why not?"

"Because he's an important person."

"Important?"

"I know he's . . . important to Rydra. The crew told me that."

"Him?" Then comprehension struck. "*Him?* Oh, no. Anything else. He's the lowest form of . . . Not that. Treason, sabotage, how many murders . . . I mean he's—"

"You don't know what he is. And if he's responsible for the Babel-17 attacks, in his own right he's as extraordinary as

Rydra." The doctor stood from his bubble seat. "Now will you give me a chance to try out my idea? I've been listening to yours all morning. Mine will probably work."

"I still don't understand what you want, though."

Dr. T'mwarba sighed. "First I want to get Rydra and the Butcher and us in the most heavily guarded, deepest, darkest, most impenetrable dungeon Administrative Alliance Headquarters has—"

"But we don't have a dun—"

"Don't put me on," Dr. T'mwarba said evenly. "You're fighting a war, remember?"

The General made a face. "Why all this security?"

"Because of the mayhem this guy has caused up till now. He's not going to enjoy what I plan to do. I'd just be happier if there was something like, say, the entire military force of the Alliance, on my side. Then I'd feel I had a chance."

Rydra sat on one side of the cell, the Butcher on the other. Both were strapped to plastic-coated chair forms that were part of the walls. Dr. T'mwarba looked after the equipment that was being rolled from the room. "No dungeons and torture chambers, eh, General?" He glanced at a spot of red-brown that had dried on the stone floor by his foot, and shook his head. "I'd be happier if the place was swabbed out with acid and disinfected first. But, I suppose on short order—"

"Do you have all your equipment here, Doctor?" the General asked, ignoring the doctor's goad. "If you change your mind I can have a barrage of specialists here inside of fifteen minutes."

"The place isn't really big enough," Dr. T'mwarba said. "But I've got nine specialists right here." He rested his hand on a medium-sized computer that had been wheeled into the corner beside the rest. "I'd just as soon you weren't here, either. But since you won't go, just watch quietly."

"You say," General Forester said, "you want maximum security. I can have a few two-hundred-and-fifty-pound aikido masters in here also."

"I have a black belt in aikido, General. I think the two of us will do."

The General raised his eyebrows. "I'm karate myself. Aikido is one martial art I've never really understood. And you have a black belt?"

Dr. T'mwarba adjusted a larger piece of equipment and nodded. "So does Rydra. I don't know what the Butcher can do, so I'm keeping everybody strapped down good and tight."

"Very well." The General touched something at the corner of the door jamb. The metal slab lowered slowly. "We'll be in here five minutes." The slab reached the floor and the line along the edge of the door disappeared. "We're welded in now. We're at the center of twelve layers of defense, all impregnable. Nobody even knows the location of the place—including myself."

"After those labyrinths we came through, I certainly don't," T'mwarba said.

"Just in case somebody managed to map it, we're moved automatically every fifty seconds. He's not going to get out." The General gestured toward the Butcher.

"I'm just assuming no one can get in." T'mwarba pressed a switch.

"Go over this once more."

"The Butcher has amnesia, say the doctors on Titin. That means his consciousness is restricted to the section of his brain with synapse connections dating from '61. His consciousness is, in effect, restricted to one segment of his cortex. What this does"—the doctor lifted a metal helmet and put it on the Butcher's head, glancing at Rydra—"is create a series of 'unpleasantnesses' in that segment until he is, so to speak, driven out of that part of the brain back into the rest."

"What if there simply are no connections from one part of the cortex to the other?"

"If it gets unpleasant enough, he'll make some new ones."

"With the sort of life he's led," commented the General, "I wonder what would be unpleasant enough to drive him out of his head."

"Onoff, Algol, Fortran," said Dr. T'mwarba.

The General watched the doctor make further adjustments.

"Ordinarily this would create a snake pit situation in the brain. However, with a mind that doesn't know the word 'I,' or hasn't known it for long, fear tactics won't work."

"What will?"

"Algol, Onoff, and Fortran, with the help of a barber and the fact that it's Wednesday."

"Dr. T'mwarba, I didn't bother with more than a precursory check on your psyche-index—"

"I know what I'm doing. None of those computer languages have the word for 'I' either. This prevents such statements as 'I can't solve the problem.' Or, 'I'm really not interested.' Or 'I've got better things to waste my time with.' General, in a little town on the Spanish side of the Pyrenees there is only one barber. This barber shaves all the men in the town who do not shave themselves. Does the barber shave himself or not?"

The General frowned.

"You don't believe me? But General, I always tell the truth. Except Wednesdays; on Wednesday every statement I make is a lie."

"But today's Wednesday!" the General exclaimed, beginning to fluster.

"How convenient. Now, now, General, don't hold your breath until you're blue in the face."

"I'm not holding my breath!"

"I didn't say you were. But just answer yes or no: have you stopped beating your wife?"

"Damn it, I can't answer a question like—"

"Well, while you think about your wife, decide whether to hold your breath, bearing in mind that it's Wednesday, tell me: who shaves the barber?"

The General's confusion broke open into laughter. "Paradoxes! You mean you're going to feed him paradoxes he's got to contend with."

"When you do it to a computer, they burn out unless they've been programmed to turn off when confronted with them."

"Suppose he decides to discorporate?"

"Let a little thing like discorporation stop me?" He pointed to another machine. "That's what this is for."

"Just one more thing. How do you know what paradoxes to give him? Surely the ones you told me wouldn't—"

"They wouldn't. Besides, they only exist in English and a few other analytically clumsy languages. Paradoxes break down into linguistic manifestations of the language in which they're expressed. For the Spanish barber, and Wednesday, it's the words 'every' and 'all' that hold contradictory meanings. The construction 'don't until' has a similar ambiguity. The same with the word 'stop.' The tape Rydra sent me was a grammar and vocabulary of Babel-17. Fascinating. It's the most analytically exact language imaginable. But that's because everything is flexible, and ideas come in huge numbers of congruent sets, governed by the same words. This just means that the number of paradoxes you can come up with is staggering. Rydra had filled the whole last half of the tape up with some of the more ingenious. If a mind limited to Babel-17 got caught up in them, it would burn itself out, or break down—"

"Or escape to the other side of the brain. I see. Well, go ahead. Start."

"I did two minutes ago."

The General looked at the Butcher. "I don't see anything."

"You won't for another minute." He made a further adjustment. "The paradoxical system I've set up has to worm itself through the entire conscious part of his brain. There are a lot of synapses to start clicking on and off."

Suddenly the lips of the hard muscled face pulled back from the teeth.

"Here we go," Dr. T'mwarba said.

"What's happening to Miss Wong?"

Rydra's face underwent the same contortion.

"I'd hoped that wouldn't happen," Dr. T'mwarba sighed, "but I suspected it would. They're in telepathic union."

A *crack* from the Butcher's chair. The headstrap had been slightly loose and his skull struck the back of his chair.

A sound from Rydra, opening into a full-throated wail that suddenly choked off. Her startled eyes blinked twice, and she cried, "Oh, Mocky, it hurts!"

One of the armstraps gave on the Butcher's chair, and the fist flew up.

Then a light by Dr. T'mwarba's thumb went from white to amber, and the thumb jammed down on the switch. Something happened in the Butcher's body; he relaxed.

General Forester started, "He discor—"

But the Butcher was panting.

"Let me out of here, Mocky," came from Rydra.

Dr. T'mwarba brushed his hand across a microswitch and the bands that had bound her forehead, calves, wrists, and arms came loose with popping sounds. She rushed across the cell to the Butcher.

"Him too?"

She nodded.

He pushed the second microswitch and the Butcher fell forward into her arms. She went down to the floor with his weight, at the same time began working her knuckles along the stiffened muscles on his back.

General Forester was holding a vibra-gun on them. "Now who the hell is he and where is he from?" he demanded.

The Butcher started to collapse again, but his hands slapped the floor and he held himself up. "My . . ." he began. "I . . . I'm Nyles Ver Dorco." His voice had lost the grating mineral quality. The pitch was nearly a fourth higher and a slight aristocratic drawl suffused his words. "Armsedge. I was born at Armsedge. And I've . . . I've killed my father!"

The door slab raised into the wall. There was an inrush of smoke and the odor of hot metal. "Now what the devil is that smell?" General Forester said. "That's not supposed to happen."

"I would guess," Dr. T'mwarba said, "the first half dozen layers of defenses for this security chamber have been broken through. Had it taken a few minutes longer, chances are we wouldn't be here."

A rush of footsteps. A soot-streaked stellarman staggered through the door. "General Forester, are you all right? The outer wall exploded, and somehow the radio-locks on the double-gates were shorted out. Something cut halfway through the ceramic walls. It looks like lasers or something."

The General got very pale. "What was trying to get in here?"

Dr. T'mwarba looked at Rydra.

The Butcher got to his feet, holding on to her shoulder. "A couple of my father's more ingenious models, first cousins to TW-55. There are maybe six in inconspicuous, but effective, positions through the staff here at Administrative Alliance

Headquarters. But you don't have to worry about them any-more."

"Then I'd appreciate it," General Forester said measuredly, "if you would all get the hell up to my office and explain what's going on."

"No. My father wasn't a traitor, General. He simply wanted to make me into the Alliance's most powerful secret agent. But the tool is not the weapon; rather the knowledge of how to use it. And the Invaders had that; and that knowledge is Babel-17."

"All right. You could be Nyles Ver Dorco. But that just makes a few things I thought I understood an hour ago more confusing."

"I don't want him to talk too much," Dr. T'mwarba said. "The strain his whole nervous system has just been through—"

"I'm all right, Doctor. I've got a complete spare set. My reflexes are quite above normal and I've got control of my whole autonomic layout, down to how fast my toenails grow. My father was a very thorough man."

General Forester swung his boot heel against the front of his desk. "Better let him go on. Because if I don't understand this whole business in five minutes, I'll put you all away."

"My father had just begun his work on custom-tailored spies when he got the idea. He had me doctored up into the most perfect human he could devise. Then he sent me into Invader territory with the hope I would wreak as much confusion among them as I could. And I did a lot of damage too, before they captured me. Another thing Dad realized was that he would be making rapid progress with the new spies, and eventually they would far outstrip me—which was quite true. I didn't hold a candle to TW-55 for example. But because of—I guess it was family pride, he wanted to keep control of their operations in the family. Every spy from Armsedge can receive radio commands through a preestablished key. Grafted under my medulla is a hyperstasis transmitter most of whose parts are electroplastiplasms. No matter how complexed the future spies became, I was still in primary control of the whole fleet of them. Over the past years, several thousand have been released into Invader territory. Up until the time I was captured, we made a very effective force."

"Why weren't you killed?" the General asked. "Or did they find out and manage to turn that entire army of spies back on us?"

"They did discover that I was an Alliance weapon. But that hyperstasis transmitter breaks down under certain conditions and flushes out with my body's waste matter. It takes me about three weeks to grow a new one. So they never learned I was in control of the rest. But they had just come up with their own secret weapon: Babel-17. They gave me a thorough case of amnesia, left me with no communication facilities save Babel-17, then let me escape from Nueva-nueva York back into Alliance territory. I didn't get any instructions to sabotage you. The powers I had, the contact with the other spies dawned on me very painfully and very slowly. And my whole life as a saboteur masquerading as a criminal just grew up. How, or why, I still don't yet know."

"I think I can explain that, General," Rydra said. "You can program a computer to make mistakes, and you do it not by crossing wires, but by manipulating the 'language' you teach it to 'think' in. The lack of an 'I' precludes any self-critical process. In fact it cuts out any awareness of the symbolic process at all— which is the way we distinguish between reality and our expression of reality."

"Come again?"

"Chimpanzees," Dr. T'mwarba interrupted, "are physically quite coordinated enough to learn to drive cars, and smart enough to distinguish between red and green lights. But once they learn, they still can't be turned loose, because when the light goes green, they will drive through a brick wall if it's in front of them, and if the light turns red, they will stop in the middle of an intersection even if a truck is bearing down on top of them. They don't have the symbolic process. For them, red *is* stop, and green *is* go."

"Anyway," Rydra went on. "Babel-17 as a language contains a preset program for the Butcher to become a criminal and saboteur. If you turn somebody with no memory loose in a foreign country with only the words for tools and machine parts, don't be surprised if he ends up a mechanic. By manipulating his vocabulary properly you can just as easily make him a sailor, or an artist. Also, Babel-17 is such an exact analytical language, it almost assures you technical mastery of any situation you look at. And the lack of an 'I' blinds you to the fact that though it's a highly useful way to look at things, it isn't the only way."

"But you mean that this language could even turn you against the Alliance?" the General asked.

"Well," said Rydra, "to start off with, the word for Alliance in Babel-17 translates literally into English as: one-who-has-invaded. You take from there. It has all sorts of little diabolisms programmed into it. While thinking in Babel-17 it becomes perfectly logical to try and destroy your own ship and then blot out the fact with self-hypnosis so you won't discover what you're doing and try and stop yourself."

"That's your spy . . . !" Dr. T'mwarba interrupted.

Rydra nodded. "It 'programs' a self-contained schizoid personality into the mind of whoever learns it, reinforced by self-hypnosis—which seems the sensible thing to do since everything else in the language is 'right,' whereas any other tongue seems so clumsy. This 'personality' has the general desire to destroy the Alliance at any cost, and at the same time remain hidden from the rest of the consciousness until it's strong enough to take over. That's what happened to us. Without the Butcher's pre-capture experience, we weren't strong enough to keep complete control, although we could stop them from doing anything destructive."

"Why didn't they completely dominate you?" Dr. T'mwarba asked.

"They didn't count on my 'talent,' Mocky," Rydra said. "I analyzed it with Babel-17 and it's very simple. The human nervous system puts out radio noise. But you'd have to have an antenna of several thousand miles surface area to tune in anything fine enough to make sense out of that noise. In fact, the only thing with that sort of area is another human nervous system. It happens to an extent in everybody. A few people like me just happen to have better control of it. The schizoid personalities aren't all that strong, and I've also got some control of the noise I send out. I've just been jamming them."

"And what am I supposed to do with these schizy espionage agents each of you is housing in your head? Lobotomize you?"

"No," Rydra said. "The way you fix your computer isn't to hack out half the wires. You correct the language, introduce the missing elements and compensate for ambiguities."

"We introduced the main elements," the Butcher said, "back in Tarik's graveyard. We're well on the way to the rest."

The General stood up slowly. "It won't do." He shook his head. "T'mwarba, where's that tape?"

"Right in my pocket where it's been since this afternoon," Dr. T'mwarba said, pulling out the spool.

"I'm taking this right down to cryptography, then we're going to start all over again." He walked to the door. "Oh, yes—and I'm locking you in!" He left, and the three looked at each other.

5 ". . . yes, of course I should have known that somebody who could get halfway through to our maximum security room and sabotage the war effort over one whole arm of the galaxy could escape from my locked office! . . . I am *not* a nitwit, but I thought—I know you don't care what I think, but they—No, it didn't occur to me that they were going to steal a ship. Well, yes, I—I—No. Of course I didn't assume—Yes, it was one of our largest battleships. But they left a—No, they're not going to attack our—I have *no* way of knowing except that they left a note saying—Yes, on my desk, they left a note . . . Well, of course I'll read it to you. That's what I've been trying to do for the last . . ."

6 Rydra stepped into the spacious cabin of the battleship *Chronos*. Ratt was riding her piggyback.

As she lowered him to the floor, the Butcher turned from the control panel. "How's everybody doing down there?"

"Anybody really confused with the new controls?" Rydra asked.

The platoon boy pulled his ear. "I don't know, Captain. This here is a lot of ship for us to run."

"We just have to get back to the Snap and give this ship to

Tarik and the others on Jebel. Brass says he can get us there if you kids keep everything moving smooth."

"We're trying. But there're so many orders all coming through from all over the place at once. I should be down there now."

"You can get down there in a minute," Rydra said. "Suppose I make you honorary quipucamayocuna?"

"Who?"

"That's the guy who reads all the orders as they come through and interprets them and hands them out. Your great grandparents were Indian, weren't they?"

"Yeah. Seminoles."

Rydra shrugged. "Quipucamayocuna is Mayan. Same difference. They gave orders by tying knots in rope; we use punch cards. Scoot—and just keep us flying."

Ratt touched his forehead and scooted.

"What do you think the General made of our note?" the Butcher asked her.

"It doesn't really matter. It will make its round of all the top officials; and they'll ponder over it and the possibility will be semantically imprinted in their minds, which is a good bit of the job. And we have Babel-17 corrected—perhaps I should call it Babel-18—which is the best tool conceivable to build it toward truth."

"Plus my battery of assistants," the Butcher said. "I think six months should do it. You're lucky those sickness attacks weren't from the speeded-up metabolic rates after all. That sounded a little odd to me. You should have collapsed before you came out of Babel-17, if that was the case."

"It was the schiz-configuration trying to force its way into dominance. Well, as soon as we finish with Tarik, we have a message to leave on the desk of Invader Commander Meihlow at Nueva-nueva York."

"*This war will end within six months,*" she quoted. "Best prose sentence I ever wrote. But now we have to work."

"We have the tools to do it no one else has," the Butcher said. He moved over as she sat beside him. "And with the right tools it shouldn't be too difficult. What are we going to do with our spare time?"

"I'm going to write a poem, I think. But it may be a novel. I have a lot to say."

"But I'm still a criminal. Canceling out bad deeds with good is a linguistic fallacy that's gotten people in trouble more than once. Especially if the good deed is in the offing. I'm still responsible for a lot of murders. To end this war I may have to use Dad's spies to make a lot more . . . mistakes. I'll just try to keep them down."

"The whole mechanism of guilt as a deterrent to right action is just as much a linguistic fault. If it bothers you, go back, get tried, be acquitted, then go on about your business. Let me be your business for awhile."

"Sure. But who says I get acquitted at this trial?"

Rydra began to laugh. She stopped before him, took his hands, and laid her face against them, still laughing. "But I'll be your defense! And even without Babel-17, you should know by now, I can pretty much talk my way out of anything."

—*New York City,*
Dec 1964–Sept 1965

one

He had:

    a waist-length braid of blond hair;

    a body that was brown and slim and looked like a cat's, they said, when he curled up, half-asleep, in the flicker of the Field Keeper's fire at New Cycle;

    an ocarina;

    a pair of black boots and a pair of black gloves with which he could climb walls and across ceilings;

    gray eyes too large for his small, feral face;

    brass claws on his left hand with which he had killed, to date, three wild kepards that had crept through a break in the power fence during his watch at New Cycle (and in a fight once with Billy James—a friendly scuffle where a blow had suddenly come too fast and too hard and turned it into for real—he had killed the other boy; but that had been two years ago when he had been sixteen, and he didn't like to think about it);

    eighteen years of rough life in the caves of the satellite Rhys attending the underground fields while Rhys cycloided about the red giant Tau Ceti;

    a propensity for wandering away from the Home Caves to look at the stars, which had gotten him in trouble at least four times in the past month, and in the past fourteen years had earned him the sobriquet, Comet Jo;

    an uncle named Clemence whom he disliked.

    Later, when he had lost all but, miraculously, the ocarina, he thought about these things and what they had meant to him, and how much they defined his youth, and how poorly they had prepared him for maturity.

Before he began to lose, however, he gained: two things, which, along with the ocarina, he kept until the end. One was a devil kitten named Di'k. The other was me. I'm Jewel.

I have a multiplex consciousness, which means I see things from different points of view. It's a function of the overtone series in the harmonic pattern of my internal structuring. So I'll tell a good deal of the story from the point of view called, in literary circles, the omniscient observer.

Crimson Ceti bruised the western crags. Tyre, giant as solar Jupiter, was a black curve across a quarter of the sky, and the white dwarf Eye silvered the eastern rocks. Comet Jo, with hair the hue of wheat, walked behind his two shadows, one long and gray, one squat and rusty. His head was back, and in the rush of wine-colored evening he stared at the first stars. In his long-fingered right hand, with the nails gnawed like any boy might, he held his ocarina. He should go back, he knew; he should crawl from under the night and into the luminous cocoon of the Home Cave. He should be respectful to his Uncle Clemence; he should not get into fights with the other boys on Field Watch. There were so many things he should do—

A sound:

Rock and non-rock in conflict.

He crouched, and his clawed left hand, deadly on the lean arm, jumped to protect his face. Kepards struck for the eyes. But it was not a kepard. He lowered his claw.

The devil-kitten came scrambling from the crevice, balancing on five of its eight legs, and hissed. It was a foot long, had three horns, and large gray eyes the color of Jo's own. It giggled, which devil-kittens do when upset, usually because they have lost their devil-cat parents—which are fifty feet long and perfectly harmless, unless they step on you accidentally.

"Wha' madda?" Comet Jo asked. "Ya ma and pa run off?"
The devil-kitten giggled again.

"Sum' wrong?" Jo persisted.

The kitten looked over its left shoulder and hissed.

"Le' ta' look." Comet Jo nodded. "Com'n, kitty." Frowning, he started forward, the motion of his naked body over the rocks as graceful as his speech was rude. He dropped from a ledge to crumbling red earth, yellow hair clouding his shoulders in mid-leap, then falling in his eyes. He shook it back. The kitten rubbed his ankle, giggled again, and darted around the boulder.

Jo followed—then threw himself back against the rock. The claws of his left hand and the nubs of his right ground on the granite. He sweated. The large vein along the side of his throat pulsed furiously, while his scrotum tightened like a prune.

Green slop frothed and flamed in a geyser two feet taller than Jo was. There were things in that fuming mess he couldn't see, but he could sense them—writhing, shrieking silently, dying in great pain. One of the things was trying hard to struggle free.

Oblivious to the agony within, the devil-kitten pranced to the base, spat haughtily, and pranced back.

As Jo chanced a breath, the thing inside broke out. It staggered forward, smoking. It raised gray eyes. Long wheat-colored hair caught on a breeze and blew back from its shoulders, as, for a moment, it moved with a certain catlike grace. Then it fell forward.

Something under fear made Comet Jo reach out and catch its extended arms. Hand caught claw. Claw caught hand. It was only when Comet Jo was kneeling and the figure was panting in his arms that he realized it was his double.

Surprise exploded in his head, and his tongue was one of the things jarred loose. "Who you?"

"You've got to take . . ." the figure began, coughed, and for a moment its features lost clarity: ". . . to take . . ." it repeated.

"Wha'? *Wha'*?" Jo was baffled and scared.

". . . take a message to Empire Star." The accent was the clean, precise tone of off-worlders' Interling. "You have to take a message to Empire Star!"

"Wha' I say?"

"Just get there and tell them . . ." It coughed again. "Just get there . . . no matter how long it . . . "

"Wha' hell I say when I ge' there?" Jo demanded. Then he thought of all the things he should have already asked. "Whe' ya fum? Whe' ya go? Wha' happen?"

Struck by a spasm, the figure arched its back and flipped from Jo's arms. Comet Jo reached out to pry the mouth open and keep it from swallowing its tongue, but before he touched it, it . . . melted.

It bubbled and steamed, frothed and smoked.

The larger phenomenon had quieted down, was only a puddle now, sloshing the weeds. The devil-kitten went to the edge, sniffed, then pawed something out. The puddle stilled, then began to evaporate—fast. The kitten picked the thing up in its mouth and, blinking rapidly, came and laid it between Jo's knees, then sat back to wash its fluffy pink chest.

Jo looked down.

The thing was multicolored, multifaceted, multiplexed, and me.

I'm Jewel.

two

Oh, we had traveled so long, Norn, Ki, Marbika, and myself, to have it end so suddenly and disastrously. I had warned them, of course, when our original ship had broken down and we had taken the organiform cruiser from S. Doradus. Things went beautifully as long as we stayed in the comparatively dusty region of the Magellanic Cloud, but when we reached the emptier space of the Home Spiral, there was nothing for the encysting mechanism to catalyze against.

We were going to swing around Ceti and head for Empire Star with our burden of good news and bad, our chronicle of success and defeat. But we lost our crust, and the organiform, like a wild amoeba, plopped onto the satellite Rhys. The strain was fatal. Ki was dead when we landed. Marbika had broken up into a hundred idiot components, which were struggling and dying in the nutrient jelly, where we were suspended.

Norn and I had a quick consultation. We put a rather faulty perceptor scan over a hundred-mile radius from the crash. The organiform had already started to destroy itself. Its primitive intelligence blamed us for the accident, and it wanted to kill. The perceptor scan showed a small colony of Terrans, who worked producing plyasil, which grew in the vast underground caves. There was a small Transport Station about twenty miles south where the plyasil was shipped to Galactic-Center to be distributed among the stars. But the satellite itself was incredibly backward. "This is about as simplex a community as I've ever run into that you could still call intelligent," Norn commented. "I can't detect more than ten minds in the whole place that have ever been to another star-system; and *they* all work at the Transport Station."

"Where they have nonorganic, reliable ships that won't get hostile and crack up," I said. "Because of this one we've both got to die, and we'll never get to Empire Star now. That's the sort of ship we should have been on. This thing—bah!" The temperature of the proto-photoplasm was getting uncomfortable.

"There's a child somewhere around here," Norn said. "And a . . . what the hell is that, anyway?"

"The Terrans call it a devil-kitten," I said, picking up the information.

"That certainly isn't a simplex mind."

"It's not exactly multiplex either," I said. "But it's something. Maybe it could get the message through."

"But its intelligence is sub-moronic," Norn said. "The Terrans at least have a fair amount of gray matter. If we could only get the both of them cooperating. That child is rather bright—but *so* simplex! The kitten is complex, at least—so at least it could carry the message. Well, let's try. See if you can get them over here. If you crystallize, you can put off dying for a while, can't you?"

"Yes," I said, uncomfortably, "but I don't know if I want to. I don't think I can take being that passive, being just a point of view."

"Even passive," Norn said, "you can be very useful, especially to that simplex boy. He's going to have a hard time, if he agrees."

"Oh, all right," I said. "I'll crystallize. But I won't like it. You go on out and see what you can do."

"Damn," Norn said, "I don't like dying. I don't want to die. I want to live, and go to Empire Star and tell them."

"Hurry up," I said. "You're wasting time."

"All right, all right. What form do you think I should take?"

"Remember, you're dealing with a simplex mind. There's only one form you can take that he's likely to pay much attention to and not chalk up to a bad dream tomorrow morning."

"All right," Norn repeated. "Here goes. Good-bye, Jewel."

"Good-bye," I said and began to crystallize.

Norn struggled forward, and the boiling jelly sagged as he broke through onto the rocks where the child was waiting. *Here, kitty, kitty, kitty,* I projected toward the devil-kitten. It was very cooperative.

three

Comet Jo walked back to the caves, playing slow tunes on the ocarina, and thinking. The gem (which was Jewel, which was me) hung in the pouch at his waist. The devil-kitten was snapping at fireflies, then stopping to pick bristles out of its foot cups. Once it rolled on its back and hissed at a star; then it scurried after Comet. It was not a simplex mind at all.

Comet reached the ledge of Toothsome. Glancing over the rock, he saw Uncle Clemence at the door of the cave, looking very annoyed. Comet stuck his tongue in his cheek and hunted for leftover lunch, because he knew he wasn't going to get any dinner.

Above him someone said, "Hey, stupid! Unca' Clem is mad on y', an' how!"

He looked up. His fourth cousin Lilly was hanging onto the edge of a higher precipice, staring down.

He motioned, and she came down to stand beside him. Her

hair was cut in a short brush, which he always envied girls. "Tha' ya' devil-kitty? Wha's's name?"

"It ain't none o' mine," he said. "Hey, who says ya can use my boots and gloves, huh?"

She was wearing the knee-high black boots and the elbow-length gloves that Charona had given him for his twelfth birthday.

"I wanted to wait for ya an' tell ya how mad Unca' Clem is. An' I had to hang up there whe' I could see ya comin' in."

"Jhup, ya did! Gimme. Ya jus' wan'ed to use 'em. Now gimme. I di'n' say ya could use 'em."

Reluctantly Lilly shucked the gloves. "Jhup ya," she said. "Ya won' lemme use 'em?" She stepped out of the boots.

"No," Comet said.

"All right," Lilly said. She turned around and called, "*Unca' Clem!*"

"Hey . . . !" Jo said.

"Unca' Clem, Comet's back!"

"Shedup!" Comet hissed, then turned and ran back across the ledge.

"Unca' Clem, he's runnin' away again—" Just then the devil-kitty stuck two of its horns into Lilly's ankles, picked up the gloves and boots in his mouth, and ran after Comet—which was a very multiplex thing to do, considering no one had said anything to him at all.

Fifteen minutes later Comet was crouching in the starlit rocks, scared and mad. Which was when the devil-kitty walked up and dropped the boots and gloves in front of him.

"Huh?" said Comet, as he recognized them in the maroon half-dark. "Hey, thanks!" And he picked them up and put them on. "Charona," he said, standing up. "I'm gonna go see Charona." Because Charona had given him the boots, and because Charona was never mad at him, and because Charona would be likely to know what Empire Star was.

He started off, then turned back and frowned at the devil-kitten. Devil-kittens are notoriously independent, and do not fetch and carry for human beings like dogs. "Devil-kitty," he said. "D'kitty. Di'k; that's a name. Di'k, you wanna come wi' me?" which was a surprisingly un-simplex thing to do—anyway, it surprised me.

Comet Jo started off. Di'k followed.

It rained toward dawn. The spray drooled his face and jeweled his eyelashes as he hung from the underside of the cliff, looking down at the gate of the Transport Area. He hung like a sloth. Di'k sat in the cradle of his belly.

Between the rocks in the reddening light, two plyasil trucks crept forward. In a minute Charona would come to let them in. Leaning his head back until the world was upside down, he could see across the rocky valley, spanned by the double cusp of Brooklyn Bridge, to the loading platforms where the star ships balanced in the dawn's red rain.

As the trucks came out of the thicket of chupper vines that at one point arbored the road, he saw Charona marching toward the gate. 3-Dog ran ahead of her, barking through the mesh at the vehicles as they halted. The devil-kitten shifted nervously from one foot to another. One way in which it resembled its namesake was its dislike for dogs.

Charona pulled the gate lever, and the bars rolled back. As the truck trundled through, Jo hollered down from the cliff, "Hey, Charona, hol' 'em up f'me!"

She lifted her bald head and twisted her wrinkled face. "Who art thou aloft?"

3-Dog barked.

"Watch it," Jo called, then let go of the rocks and twisted in the air. He and Di'k both took the fall rolling. He sprang open before her, light on his booted feet.

"Well!" she laughed, putting her fists in the pouch of her silver skin suit that glistened with rain. "Thou art an agile elf. Where has thou been a-hiding for the best part of the month?"

"The New Cycle watch," he said, grinning. "See, I'm wearin' ya' present."

"And it's good to see thee with them. Come in, come in, so I can close the gate."

Comet ducked under the half-lowered bars. "Hey, Charona," he said as they started down the wet road together, "wh' Empire Star? An' whe' it? An' how I ge' 'ere?" By unspoken consent they turned off the road to make their way over the rougher earth of the valley below the tongue of metal called Brooklyn Bridge.

" 'Tis a great, great star, lad, that thy great-great-great-grand-fathers on Earth called Aurigae. It is seventy-two degrees around the hub of the galaxy from here at a hyperstatic distance of fifty-five point nine, and—to quote the ancient maxim—thou canst not get there from here."

"Why?"

Charona laughed. 3-Dog ran ahead and barked at Di'k, who arched, started to say something back in kittenish, thought better of it, and pranced away. "One could hitch a ride on a transport and get started; but *thou* couldst not. Which is the important part."

Comet Jo frowned.

"Why cou'nt I?" He swiped at a weed and tore off the head. "I gonna ge' off this planet—now!"

Charona raised the bare flesh where her eyebrows would have been. "Thou seemst a mite determined. Thou art the first person born here to tell me that in four hundred years. Return thou, Comet Jo, to thine uncle and make peace in the Home Cave."

"Jhup," said Comet Jo and kicked a small stone. "I wanna go. Why can' I go?"

"Simplex, complex, and multiplex," Charona said. And I woke up in the pouch. Perhaps there was hope, after all. If there was someone to explain it to him, the journey would be easier. "This is a simplex society here, Comet. Space travel is not a part of it. Save for trucking the plyasil here, and a few curious children like thyself, nobody ever comes inside the gates. And in a year, thou wilt cease to come, and all thy visits will eventually mean to thee is that thou wilt be a bit more lenient with thine own when they will wander to the gates or come back to the Home Caves with magic trinkets from the stars. To travel between worlds, one must deal with at least complex beings, and often multiplex. Thou wouldst be lost as how to conduct thyself. After half an hour in a spaceship, thou wouldst turn around and decide to go back, dismissing the whole idea as foolish. The fact that thou hast a simplex mind is good, in a way, because thou remainest safe at Rhys. And even though thou comest through the gates, thou are not likely to be 'corrupted,' as it were, even by visits to the Transport Area, nor by an occasional exposure to something from the stars, like those boots and gloves I gave thee."

She seemed to have finished, and I felt sad, for that certainly was no explanation. And by now I knew that Jo would journey.

But Comet reached for his pouch, pushed aside the ocarina, and lifted me out into the palm of his hand. "Charona, ya ever see wonna these?"

Together they loomed above me. Beyond the tines of Comet's claws, beyond their shadowed faces, the black ribbon of Brooklyn Bridge scribed the mauve sky. His palm was warm beneath my dorsal facet. A cool droplet splashed my frontal faces, distorting theirs.

"Why . . . I think . . . No, it cannot be. Where didst thou retrieve it?"

He shrugged. "Jus' foun' it. Wha'cha think it is?"

"It looks for all the light of the seven suns to be a crystallized Tritovian."

She was right, of course, and I knew immediately that here was a well-traveled spacewoman. Crystallized, we Tritovians are not that common.

"Gotta take him to Empire Star."

Charona thought quietly behind the wrinkled mask of her face, and I could tell from the overtones that they were multiplex thoughts, with images of space and the stars seen in the blackness of galactic night, weird landscapes that were unfamiliar even to me. The four hundred years as gate guardian to the Transport Area of Rhys had leveled her mind to something nearly simplex. But multiplexity had awakened.

"I shall try and explain something to thee, Comet. Tell me, what's the most important thing there is?"

"Jhup," he answered promptly, then saw her frowning. He got embarrassed. "I mean plyasil. I din' mean to use no dirty words." And I was dropped back in his pouch.

"Words don't bother me, Comet. In fact, I always found it a little funny that thy people had such a thing as a 'dirty word' for plyasil. Though I suppose 'tis not so funny when I recall the 'dirty words' on the world I came from. Water was the taboo term where I grew up—there was very little of it, and thou dared not refer to it by other than its chemical formula in a technological discussion, and never in front of your teacher. And on Earth, in our great-great-grandfather's time, food once eaten and passed from the body could not be spoken of by its common name in polite company."

"But wha' dirty about food an' water?"

"What's dirty about jhup?"

He was surprised at her use of the common slang. But she was always dealing with truckers and loaders who had notoriously filthy mouths and lacked respect for everything—said Uncle Clemence.

"I dunno."

"It's an organic plastic that grows in the flower of a mutant strain of grain that only blooms with the radiation that comes from the heart of Rhys in the darkness of the caves. It's of no use to anyone on this planet, except as an alloy strengthener for other plastics, and yet it is Rhys' only purpose in the Universal plan—to supply the rest of the galaxy. For there are places where it is needed. All men and women on Rhys work to produce or process or transport it. That is all it is. Nowhere in my definition have I mentioned anything about dirt."

"Well, if a bag of it breaks open and spills, it's sort of . . . well not dirty, but messy."

"Spilled water or spilled food is messy too. But none of them by nature so."

"You just don' talk about certain things in front o' nice people. That's what Unca' Clem says." Jo finally took refuge in his training. "An' like ya say, jhup is the most important thing there is, so that's why you have to . . . well, be a little respectful."

"I didn't say it. You did. And that is why thou hast a simplex mind. If thou passeth through the second gate and asketh a ride of a Transport captain—and thou wilt probably get it, for they are a good lot—thou wilt be in a different world, where plyasil means only forty credits a ton and is a good deal less important than derny, kibblepobs, clapper boxes, or boysh, all of which bring above fifty. And thou might shout the name of any of them, and be thought nothing more than noisy."

"I ain't gonna go shoutin' nothing aroun'," Comet Jo assured her. "An' all I can get from ya' jabber about 'simplex' is that I know how to be polite, even if a lotta other people don'—I know I'm not as polite as I should be, but I do know how."

Charona laughed. 3-Dog ran back and rubbed her hip with his head.

"Perhaps I can explain it in purely metaphorical terms, though painfully I know that thou wilt not understand until thou hast seen for thyself. Stop and look above."

They paused in the broken stone and looked up.

"See the holes?" she asked.

In the plating that floored the bridge, here and there were pinpricks of light.

"They just look like random dots, do they not?"

He nodded.

"That's the simplex view. Now start walking and keep looking."

Comet started to walk, steadily, staring upward. The dots of light winked out, and here and there others appeared, then winked out again, and more, or perhaps the original ones, returned.

"There's a superstructure of girders above the bridge that gets in the way of some of the holes and keeps thee from perceiving all at once. But thou art now receiving the complex view, for thou art aware that there is more than what is seen from any one spot. Now, start to run, and keep thy head up."

Jo began to run along the rocks. The rate of flickering increased, and suddenly he realized that the holes were in a pattern, six-pointed stars crossed by diagonals of seven holes each. It was only with the flickering coming so fast that the entire pattern could be perceived—

He stumbled, and skidded onto his hands and knees.

"Didst thou see the pattern?"

"Eh . . . yeah." Jo shook his head. His palms stung through the gloves, and one knee was raw.

"That was the multiplex view."

3-Dog bent down and licked his face.

Di'k watched a little scornfully from the fork of a trident bush.

"Thou hast also encountered one of the major difficulties of the simplex mind attempting to encompass the multiplex view. Thou art very likely to fall flat on thy face. I really do not know if thou wilt make the transition, though thou art young, and older people than thou have had to harken. Certainly I wish thee luck. Though for the first few legs of thy journey, thou canst always turn around and come back, and even with a short hop to Ratshole thou wilt have seen a good deal more of the universe than most of the people of Rhys. But the farther thou goest, the harder it will be to return."

Comet Jo pushed 3-Dog aside and stood up. His next question came both from fear of his endeavor and the pain in his hands. "Brooklyn Bridge," he said, still looking up. "Why they call it Brooklyn Bridge?" He asked it as one asks a question without an answer, and had his mind been precise enough to articulate its true meaning, he would have asked, "Why is that structure there to trip me up at all?"

But Charona was saying, "On Earth, there is a structure similar to this that spans between two islands—though it is a little smaller than this one here. 'Bridge' is the name for this sort of structure, and Brooklyn is the name of the place it leads to, so it was called Brooklyn Bridge. The first colonists brought the name with them and gave it to what thou seest here."

"Ya mean there's a reason?"

Charona nodded.

Suddenly an idea caught in his head, swerved around a corner, and came up banging and clanging behind his ears. "Will I get to see Earth?"

"'Twill not take thee too far afield," Charona said.

"And c'n I see Brooklyn Bridge?" His feet had started to move in the boots.

"I saw it four hundred years ago, and 'twas still standing then."

Comet Jo suddenly jumped up and tried to beat his fists against the sky, which was a beautifully complex action that gave me more hope; then he ran forward, leaped against one of the stanchions of the bridge and, from sheer exuberance, scurried up a hundred feet of thermoplast.

Stopping at two girders' groin, he looked down. "Hey, Charona! I'm gonna go Earth! Me, Comet Jo, I'm gonna go Earth an' see Brooklyn Bridge!"

Below us the gatekeeper smiled and stroked 3-Dog's head.

four

They came up from beneath the balustrade as the rain ceased. Climbing over the railing, they strolled across the water-blackened tarmac toward the second gate. "Thou art sure?" Charona asked him once more.

A little warily, he nodded.

"And what should I say to thy Uncle when he comes inquiring, which he will."

At the thought of Uncle Clemence, the wariness increased. "Jus' say I gone away."

Charona nodded, pulled the second lever, and the gate rose.

"And wilt thou be taking that?" Charona pointed to Di'k.

"Sure. Why not?" And at that he strode bravely forward.

Di'k looked right, left, then ran after him. Charona would have gone through herself to accompany the boy, but suddenly there was a signal light flashing, which said her presence was required at the first gate again. So only her gaze went with him, as the gate lowered. Then she turned back across the bridge.

He had never done more than look through the second gate at the bulbous forms of the ships, at the loading buildings, at the mechanical loaders and sledges that plied the pathways of the Transport Area. When he stepped through, he looked around, waiting for the world to be very different, as Charona had warned. But his conception of *different* was rather simplex, so that twenty feet along he was disappointed.

Another twenty feet and disappointment was replaced by ordinary curiosity. A saucer-sled was sliding toward him, and a tall figure guided it austerely down the slip. There was a small explosion of fear and surprise when he realized the saucer was coming directly at him. A moment later it stopped.

The woman standing there—and it took him a minute to figure it out, for her hair was long like a man's and elaborately coiffed like no one's he'd ever seen—wore a glittering red dress, where panels of different textures (though the color was all the same) wrapped her or swung away in the damp dawn breeze. Her hair and lips and nails were red, he realized. That *was* odd. She looked down at him, and said, "You are a beautiful boy."

"Wha'?" asked Comet.

"I said you are a beautiful boy."

"Well, jhup, I mean . . . well . . ." Then he stopped looking at his feet and stared back up at her.

"But your hair is a mess."

He frowned. "Whaddya mean it's a mess?"

"I mean exactly what I say. And *where* did you learn to speak Interling? Or am I just getting a foggy telepathic equivalent of your oral utterance?"

"Wha'?"

"Never mind. You are still a beautiful boy. I will give you a comb, and I will give you diction lessons. Come to me on the ship—you *will* be taking my ship, since there is no other one leaving soon. Ask for San Severina."

The saucer-disk turned to slide away.

"Hey, whe'ya goin'?" Comet Jo called.

"Comb your hair first, and we shall discuss it at lessons." She removed something from a panel of her dress and tossed it to him.

He caught it, looked at it. It was a red comb.

He pulled his mass of hair across his shoulder for inspection. It was snarled from the night's journey to the Transport Area. He struck at it a few times, hoping that perhaps the comb was some special type that would make unsnarling easier. It wasn't. So it took him about ten minutes, and then, to avoid repeating the ordeal as long as possible, he braided it deftly down one shoulder. Then he put the comb to his pouch and took out the ocarina.

He was passing a pile of cargo when he saw a young man a few years his senior perched on top of the boxes, hugging his knees and staring down at him. He was barefooted, shirtless, and his frayed pants were held on by rope. His hair was of some indiscriminately sexless length and a good deal more snarled than Jo's had been. He was very dirty, but he was grinning.

"Hey!" Jo said. "Know where I can getta ride outta here?"

"T'chapubna," the boy said, pointing across the field, "f'd jhup n' Lll."

Jo felt a little lost that the only thing he understood in the sentence was a swear word.

"I wanna get a ride," Jo repeated.

"T'chapubna," the boy said, and pointed again. Then he put

his hands to his mouth as though he too were playing an ocarina.

"You wanna try?" Jo asked and then wished he hadn't, because the boy was so dirty.

But the boy shook his head, smiling. "Jus' a shuttle-bum. Can' make no music."

Which half made sense, maybe. "Where ya from?" Jo asked.

"Jus' a shuttle-bum," the boy repeated. Now he pointed to the pink moon-moon above the horizon. "Dere n' back, dere n' back, 'sall I ever been." He smiled again.

"Oh," Jo said, and smiled because he couldn't think of anything else to do. He wasn't sure if he'd gotten any information from the conversation or not. He started playing the ocarina again and kept walking.

He headed directly for a ship this time; one was being loaded.

Jo crossed what seemed acres of tarmac.

A beefy man was supervising the robo-loaders, checking things off against a list. His greasy shirt was still damp from the rain, and he had tied it across his hairy stomach, which bulged below and above the knot.

Another boy, this one closer to Jo's age, was leaning against a guy cable that ran from the ship. Like the first, he was dirty, shoeless, and shirtless. One pant leg was torn off at the knee, and two belt loops were held together with a twist of wire. The weatherburned face even lacked the readiness to smile that the other's held. The boy leaned out from the guy and swung his body slowly around, to watch Jo as he came past.

Jo started to approach the big man checking the loading, but the man had gotten very busy reorganizing the pile that one of the loaders had done incorrectly, so Jo stepped back. He looked at the boy again, gave a half-smile and nodded. Comet didn't feel much like getting into a conversation, but the boy nodded shortly back, and the man looked like he was going to be busy for a while.

"Ya a shuttle-bum?" Jo asked.

The boy nodded.

"Ya go from there n' back?" he asked, pointing toward the disk of the moon-moon.

The boy nodded again.

"Any chance my hoppin' a ride out toward . . . well, anywhere?"

"There is if you want to take a job," the boy said.

The accent surprised Jo.

"Sure," Jo said. "If I gotta work, I don't mind."

The boy pulled himself upright on the wire. "Hey, Elmer," he called. The man looked back, then flipped a switch on his wrist-console, and the robo-loaders all halted. *That was simple,* Jo thought.

"What dost thou wish?" Elmer asked, turning around and wiping his forehead.

"We have that second shuttle-bum. The kid wants a job."

"Well and good," Elmer said. "Thou wilt take care of him, then. He looks a likely lad, but feed him well and he'll work, I warrant." He grinned and turned back to the robo-loaders.

"You're hired," the boy said. "My name's Ron."

"I'm Jo," Jo said. "They call me Comet Jo."

Ron laughed out loud and shook Jo's hand. "I'll never figure it. I've been running the stasiscurrents for six months now, and every tried and true spaceman you meet is Bob or Hank or Elmer. Then, the minute you hit some darkside planet or one-product simplex culture, everybody's Starman, or Cosmic Smith, or Comet Jo." He clapped Jo on the shoulder. "Don't take offense, but thou wilt lose thy 'comet' soon enough."

Jo took no offense, mainly because he wasn't sure what Ron was talking about, but he smiled. "Whe' ya from?"

"I'm taking a year off from Centauri University to bounce around the stars, work a little when I have to. I've been shuttle-bumming across this quarter of the spiral for a couple of months. You notice Elmer here's got me talking like a real space-man?"

"That guy sittin' back there? He from the . . . University too?"

"Hank? That darkside, noplex kid who was sitting on the cargo?" Ron laughed.

"Noplex?" Jo asked. He connected the word to the others he had learned that morning. "Like simplex, complex, and that stuff."

Ron apparently realized that the query was serious. "There's no such thing as noplex, really. But sometimes you wonder. Hank just bums between Rhys and moon-moon. His folks are h-poor, and I don't even think he can read and write his name. Most shuttle-bums come from similar situations, thou wilt discover. They just have their one run, usually between two planets, and that's all they'll ever see. But I star hop too. I want to make mate's position before the Half Spin is over, so I can go back to school with some money, but thou must begin somewhere. How far are you going?"

"Empire Star," Jo said. "Do ya . . . I mean doest thou know whe' it is?"

"Trying to pick up a spaceman's accent already?" Ron asked. "Don't worry, it'll rub off on you before you know. Empire Star? I guess it's about seventy, seventy-five degrees around galactic center."

"Seventy-two degrees, at a distance of 55.9," Jo said.

"Then why did you ask me?" Ron said.

"'Cause that don' tell me nothin'."

Ron laughed again. "Oh. I see. Thou hast never been in space before?"

Jo shook his head.

"I see," repeated Ron, and the laugh got louder. "Well, it will mean something shortly. Believe thou me, it will!" Then Ron saw Di'k. "Is that yours?"

Jo nodded. "I can take him wi' me, can' I?"

"Elmer's the Captain. Ask him."

Jo looked at the Captain, who was furiously rearranging a cargo pile to balance on the loader. "All right," he said, and started toward him. "Elm—"

Ron grabbed his shoulder. Jo swung around. "Wha'? Jhup—"

"Not *now*, noplex! Wait till he's finished."

"But *you* just—"

"You're not me," Ron explained, "and he wasn't trying to balance the load when I stopped him. If you call him by his name, he has to stop, and you might have killed him if that load fell over."

"Oh. Wha' should I call him?"

"Try 'Captain,'" Ron said. "That's what he is, and when you call him that, he doesn't have to stop what he's doing unless it's convenient. Only call him Elmer if it's an emergency." He looked sideways at Jo. "On second thought, let somebody else decide if it's an emergency or not. To you he's 'Captain' until he tells you otherwise."

"Was it an emergency when you called him?"

"He wanted another shuttle-bum for this trip, but I also saw that he wasn't doing anything he couldn't stop, and . . . well, you've just got a lot to learn."

Jo looked crestfallen.

"Cheer up," Ron said. "You do nice things on the sweet potato there. I have a guitar inside—I'll get it out, and we can play together, hey?" He grabbed hold of the guy line and started to climb hand over hand. He disappeared into the overhanging hatch. Jo watched, wide-eyed. Ron wasn't even wearing gloves.

Just then Captain Elmer said, "Hey, thou canst take thy kitten, but thou must leave those gloves and boots."

"Huh? Why?"

"Because I say so. Ron?"

The shuttle-bum looked out of the hatch. "What?" He was holding a guitar.

"Explain to him about culture-banned artifacts."

"Okay," Ron said, and slid down the guy wire again with his feet and one hand. "You better chuck those now."

Reluctantly Jo began to peel them from his hands and feet.

"You see, we're going to be running to some complex cultures, with a technology a lot below the technology that made those boots. If they got out, it might disrupt their whole culture."

"We couldn't make them boots," Jo said, "and Charona gave . . . 'em to me."

"That's because you're simplex here. Nothing could disrupt *your* culture, short of moving it to another environment. And even then, you'd probably come up with the same one. But complex cultures are touchy. We're taking a load of jhup to Genesis. Then the Lll will go on to Ratshole. You can probably pick up a ride there to Earth if you want. I guess you want to see Earth. Everybody does."

Jo nodded.

"From Earth you can go anywhere. Maybe you'll even get a ride straight on to Empire Star. What do you have to go there for?"

"Gotta take a message."

"Yeah?" Ron began to tune the guitar.

Jo opened his pouch and took me out—I rather wished he wouldn't go showing me around to everyone. There were some people who would get rather upset if I showed up, crystallized or not.

"This," Jo said. "I gotta take this there."

Ron peered at me. "Oh, I see." He put the guitar down. "I guess it's good you're going with the shipment of Lll then."

I smiled to myself. Ron was a multiplexually educated young man. I shuddered to think what would have happened had Jo shown me to Hank; the other shuttle-bum would just as likely have tried to make Jo trade me for something or other, and that would have been disastrous.

"What's Lll?" Jo asked. "Is that one of the things more important than jhup?"

"Good lord, yes," Ron said. "You've never seen any, have you?"

Jo shook his head.

"Come on, then," said Ron. "We can play later. Up into the hatch with you, and throw your boots and gloves away."

Jo left them on the tarmac and began to climb the cable. It was easier than he'd anticipated, but he was sweating at the top. Di'k simply climbed up the ship's hull with his cupped feet and was waiting for him in the hatch.

Jo followed Ron down a hallway, down through another hatchway, down a short ladder. "The Lll are in here," Ron said before a circular door. He was still holding the guitar by the neck. He pushed open the door, and something grabbed Jo by the stomach and twisted. Tears mounted in his eyes, and his mouth opened. His breath began to come very slowly.

"Really hit you, didn't it?" Ron said, his voice soft. "Let's go inside."

Jo was scared, and when he stepped into the half-darkness, his gut fell twenty feet with each step. He blinked to clear his vision, but the tears came again.

"Those are the Lll," Ron said.

Jo saw tears on Ron's weathered face. He looked forward again.

They were chained by the wrists and ankles to the floor; seven of them, Jo counted. Their great green eyes blinked in the blue cargo light. Their backs were humped, their heads shaggy. Their bodies seemed immensely strong.

"What am I . . ." Jo tried to say, but something caught in his throat, and the sound rasped. "What am I feelin'?" he whispered, for it was as loud as he could speak.

"Sadness," Ron said.

Once named, the emotion grew recognizable—a vast, overpowering sadness that drained all movement from his muscles, all joy from his eyes.

"They make me feel . . . sad?" Jo asked. "Why?"

"They're slaves," Ron said. "They build—build beautifully, wonderfully. They're extremely valuable. They built over half the Empire. And the Empire protects them, this way."

"Protects . . . ?" Jo asked.

"You can't get near them without feeling like this."

"Then who would buy them?"

"Not many people. But enough so that they are incredibly valuable slaves."

"Why don't they turn 'em *loose?*" Jo asked, and the sentence became a cry halfway through.

"Economics," Ron said.

"How can ya think 'bout economics feelin' like . . . this?"

"Not many people can," Ron said. "That's the Lll's protection."

Jo knuckled his eyes. "Let's get outta here."

"Let's stay awhile," Ron countered. "We'll play for them now." He sat down on a crate, put his guitar on his lap, and pulled from it a modal chord. "Play," Ron said. "I'll follow you."

Jo began to blow, but his breath was so weak that the note quavered and died half-sung. "I ... I don' wanna," Jo protested.

"It's your job, shuttle-bum," Ron said, simply. "You have to take care of the cargo once it's aboard. They like music, and it will make them happy."

"Will it ... make me happier too?" Jo asked.

Ron shook his head. "No."

Jo raised the ocarina to his mouth, filled his lungs, and blew. The long notes filled the hold of the ship, and as Jo closed his eyes, the tears melted the darkness behind his lids. Ron's obligato wove around the melody Jo coaxed from his ocarina. Each note took on a pungency like perfume and called up before Jo, as he played with eyes shut and streaming, the New Cycle when the plyasil had failed, the funeral of Billy James, the day that Lilly laughed at him when he had tried to kiss her behind the generator of the power fence, the time when the slaughtered kepards had been weighed and he had learned that his weighed ten pounds less than Yl Odic's—and Yl was three years his junior and everybody was always saying how wonderful she was—in short, every sad and painful memory of his simplex existence.

When they left the hold half an hour later and, as Ron secured the hatch, the feeling rolled from him like a receding wave, Jo felt exhausted; and he was quivering.

"Hard work, huh?" Ron said, smiling. Tears had streaked the dust on his face.

Jo didn't say anything, only tried to keep from sobbing in earnest with homesickness that still constricted his throat. *You can always turn around and go home,* Charona had said. He almost started to. But a voice over the loudspeaker said, "Will the Beautiful Boy please come for his Interling lesson."

"That's San Severina," Ron said. "She's our only passenger. The Lll belong to her."

An entire matrix of emotions broke open in Jo's head at once, among them outrage, fear, and curiosity. Curiosity won out.

"Her cabin's just up that way and around the corner," Ron said.

Jo started forward. How, he wondered, could she possibly bring herself to own those incredible creatures?

five

"A vast improvement," San Severina said when he opened her door. "I'm sure you're wondering how I could possibly bring myself to own those incredible creatures."

She sat in an opulent bubble chair, sheathed in blue from neck to ankles. Her hair, her lips, her nails were blue.

"It isn't easy."

Jo stepped inside. One wall was covered with crowded bookshelves.

"You, at least," San Severina went on, "only have to feel it when you are in their presence. I, as owner, am subjected to that feeling throughout the entire duration of my ownership. It is part of the contract."

"You feel that way . . . now?"

"Rather more intensely than you did just then. My sensitivity band is a good deal wider than yours."

"But . . . why?"

"It cannot be helped. I have eight worlds, fifty-two civilizations, and thirty-two thousand three hundred and fifty-seven complete and distinct ethical systems to rebuild. I cannot do it without Lll. Three of those worlds are charred black, without a drop of water on their surfaces. One is half-volcanic and must be completely recrusted. Another has lost a good deal of its atmosphere. The other three are at least habitable."

"Wha' happened?" Jo asked incredulously.

"War," said San Severina. "And it is so much more disastrous today than it was a thousand years back. Sixty-eight billion, five hundred thousand, two hundred and five people, reduced to twenty-seven. There was nothing to do but pool our remaining wealth and agree to purchase the Lll. I am bringing them back now, by way of Earth."

"Lll," Jo repeated. "Wha' *are* they?"

"Didn't you ask that other young man?"

"Yeah, but—"

San Severina's smile stopped him. "Ah, the seeds of complexity. When you receive one answer, you ask for a second. Very good. I will give you a second. They are the shame and tragedy of the multiplex universe. No man can be free until they are free. While they are bought and sold, any man may be bought and sold—if the price is high enough. Now come, it's time for your Interling lesson. Would you get me that book?"

Obedient but bewildered, Jo fetched the book from the desk.

"Why I gotta learn speakin'?" he asked as he handed it to her.

"So people can understand you. You have a long journey, at the end of which you must deliver a message, quite precisely, quite accurately. It would be disastrous if you were misheard."

"I don' even know wha' is it!" Jo said.

"You will by the time you deliver it," San Severina said. "But you'd best get to work now."

Jo looked at the book apprehensively. "You got somethin' I

can maybe learn it real quick wi', in my sleep or sompin'—like hypnotizin'?" He recalled his disappointment with her comb.

"I have nothing like that with me now," San Severina said sadly. "I thought the other young man explained. We're passing through some rather primitive complex societies. No culture-banned artifacts allowed. I'm afraid you'll have to do it the hard way."

"Jhup," Jo said. "I wanna go home."

"Very well. But you'll have to hitch a ride back from Rats-hole. We're a hundred and fifty-three thousand miles away from Rhys already."

"Huh?"

San Severina rose and raised a set of Venetian blinds that covered one wall. Beyond the glass: darkness, the stars, and the red rim of Ceti.

Comet Jo stood with his mouth open.

"While you're waiting, we might get some studying done."

The rim of Ceti grew smaller.

six

The actual work on the ship was certainly as easy as tending the underground fields of plyasil. Save for the Lll, it was comparatively pleasant, once it became routine. San Severina's wit and charm made the language lessons a peak of pleasure in an otherwise enjoyable day. Once she rather surprised both Jo and me by saying during one lesson when he seemed particularly recalcitrant and demanded another reason for why he had to improve his Interling: "Besides, think how tiring your clumsy speech will be to your readers."

"My what?" He had already, with difficulty, mastered his final consonants.

"You have undertaken an enterprise of great pith and moment, and I am sure someday somebody will set it down. If you don't improve your diction, you will lose your entire audience before page forty. I suggest you seriously apply yourself, because you are in for quite an exciting time, and it would be rather sad if everyone abandoned you halfway through because of your atrocious grammar and pronunciation."

Her Multiplexedness San Severina certainly had *my* number down.

Four days out, Jo was watching Elmer carefully while he sat whistling at the T-ward viewport. When he had (definitely) decided that the Captain was not engaged in anything it would be fatal to interrupt, he put his hands behind his back and said, "Elmer?"

Elmer looked around. "Yeah. What is it?"

"Elmer, how come everybody knows more about what I'm doing on this boat than I do?"

"Because they've been doing it longer than thou hast."

"I don't mean about my work. I mean about my trip and the message and everything."

"Oh." Elmer shrugged. "Simplex, complex, and multiplex."

Jo was used to having the three words shoved at him in answer to just about anything he didn't comprehend, but this time he said, "I want another answer."

The Captain leaned forward on his knees, thumbed the side of his nose, and frowned. "Look, thou hast come on board, telling us that thou must take a message to Empire Star about the Lll, so we—"

"Elmer, wait a minute. How do you know the message concerns the Lll?"

Elmer looked surprised. "Doesn't it?"

"I don't know," Jo said.

"Oh," Elmer said. "Well, I do. It does concern the Lll. How it concerns the Lll thou wilt have to find out later, but I can assure thee that it does. That's why Ron showed them to thee first off, and why San Severina is so interested in thee."

"But how does everybody know when I don't?" He felt exasperation growing again in the back of his throat.

"Thou art going to Empire Star," Elmer began again, patiently, "and it is the Empire that protects the Lll."

Comet Jo nodded.

"They are extremely concerned about them, as they should be, as we all are. Thou hast with thee a crystallized Tritovian, and the Tritovians have spearheaded the movement for the emancipation of the Lll. They have worked for it for nearly a thousand years. Therefore, the probability is very high that thy message concerns the Lll."

"Oh . . . that makes sense. But San Severina seems to know things she couldn't even see or figure out."

Elmer gestured for Jo to come closer. "For a person to survive a war that reduces sixty-eight billion people to twenty-seven individuals, that person must know a great deal. And it's a little silly to be surprised that such a person knows a trifle more than thou or I. It's not only silly, it is *unbelievably* simplex. Now get back to work, shuttle-bum."

Having to admit that it was pretty simplex after all, Jo went down in the hole to turn over the boysh and rennedox the kibblepobs. He would not have to play for the Lll again until after supper.

Two days after that, they landed in Ratshole. San Severina took him shopping in the open market and bought him a black velvet contour-cloak with silver embroidery whose patterns changed with the pressure of the light under which it was viewed. Next she took him to a body salon. During the trip he had gotten as grimy as any of the other shuttle-bums. Holding him gently by the ear, she extended him to the white-smocked proprietor. "Groom this," she said.

"For what?" the proprietor asked.

"First for Earth, then for a long journey."

When they were finished, his braid was gone, his claws had been clipped, and he had been cleaned from teeth to toenails. "How do you like yourself?" she asked, placing the cloak over his shoulders.

Jo ran his hand over his short, yellow hair. "I look like a girl." He frowned. Then he looked at his fingernails. "I just hope I don't run into any kepards on the way." Now he looked at the mirror again. "The cloak's great, though."

When they went outside again, Di'k looked once at Jo, blinked, and got so upset that he giggled himself into the hiccups and had to be carried back to the Transport Area while his belly was scratched and he pulled himself together.

"It's a shame I'm going to have to get dirty again," he told San Severina. "But it's dirty work."

San Severina laughed. "Most delightfully simplex child! You will travel the rest of the way to Earth as my protégé."

"But what about Ron and Elmer?"

"They have already taken off. The Lll have been transferred to another ship."

Jo was surprised, sad, then curious.

"San Severina?"

"Yes?"

"Why have you been doing all this for me?"

She kissed his cheek, then danced back from a halfhearted swipe Di'k made with his horns. Jo was still scratching his tummy. "Because you are a very beautiful boy, and very important."

"Oh," he said.

"Do you understand?"

"No." They continued to the ship.

A week later they stood together on a rocky rise, watching the comparatively tiny disk of the sun set behind the Brooklyn Bridge. A thin worm of water crawled along the dried, black mud ditch still referred to in their guidebook as the East River. The jungle whispered behind them. Across the "river" the webbed cables lowered the bridge itself to the white sands of Brooklyn. "It's smaller than the one at home," Jo said. "But it's very nice."

"You sound disappointed."

"Oh, not with the bridge," Jo said.

"Is it because I have to leave you here?"

"Well . . ." He stopped. "I'd like to say yes. Because I think it would make you feel better. But I don't want to lie."

"The truth is always multiplex," San Severina said, "and you must get in the habit of dealing with multiplexity. What's on your mind?"

"Remember I was saying how nice everybody has been up till now? And you said I could stop expecting people to be nice once I got to Earth? That scares me."

"I also said there would be things other than people that would be nice."

"But people means any sapient being from any life-system. You taught me that. What else, if it's not people?" Suddenly he caught her hand. "You're going to leave me all alone, and I may never see you again!"

"That's right," she said. "But I wouldn't just throw you out into the universe with nothing. So I will give you a piece of advice: find the Lump."

"Eh . . . where do you suggest I find it?" He was bewildered again.

"It's too big to come to Earth. I last saw it on the Moon. It was waiting to have an adventure. You might be just what it's waiting for. I'm sure it will be nice to you; it was always very nice to me."

"It's not a people?"

"No. There, I've given you your advice. I'm going now. I have a lot to do, and you have some idea of the pain I am in till it's accomplished."

"San Severina!"

She stopped.

"That day on Ratshole, when we went shopping, and you laughed and called me a delightfully simplex child—when you laughed, were you happy?"

Smiling, she shook her head. "The Lll are always with me. I must go now."

She backed away, till the leaves brushed across her silver lips, dress, and fingertips. Then she turned, carrying with her the incredible sadness of Lll ownership. Jo watched her, then turned back to see the last points of sunlight melt from the sand.

It was night when he got back to the Transport Terminal. Earth was a large enough tourist area so that there were always people beneath the glittering ceiling. He had not even begun to think about how he was going to get to the Moon, and was walking around expending his curiosity, when a portly, well-dressed gentleman began a conversation. "I say there, young fellow, but you've been here for some time, haven't you? Waiting for a ship?"

"No," Jo said.

"I saw you here this afternoon with that charming young lady, and I couldn't help seeing you this evening. My name's Oscar." He extended his hand.

"Comet Jo," Jo said, and shook it.

"Where you off to?"

"I'd like to get to the Moon. I hitchhiked in from Rhys."

"My, my! That's a long way. What ship are you taking?"

"I don't know. I guess you can't hitch from the terminal very well, can you? I suppose I'd do better to try a commercial stop."

"Certainly, if you wanted to hitch. Of course, if Alfred doesn't show up, maybe you can use his ticket. He's missed two ships already; I don't know why I stick around here waiting for him. Except that we *did* make plans to go together."

"To the Moon?"

"That's right."

"Oh, great," Jo said, brightening. "I hope he doesn't get here—" He caught himself. "That came out all simplex, didn't it?"

"The truth is always multiplex," intoned Oscar.

"Yeah. That's what *she* said."

"The young lady you were with this afternoon?"

Jo nodded.

"Who was she, anyway?"

"San Severina."

"I've heard the name. What was she doing in this arm of the galaxy?"

"She just bought some Lll. She had some work to do."

"Bought *some* Lll, eh? And she didn't leave you with any money for a ticket? You'd think she could spare you the hundred and five credits for Moon fare."

"Oh, she's a very generous person," Jo said. "And you mustn't think badly of her because she bought the Lll. It's awfully sad to own them."

"If I had enough money to buy Lll," said Oscar, "nothing, but *nothing* could make me sad. *Some* Lll? How many did she buy?"

"Seven."

Oscar put his hand on his forehead and whistled. "And the price goes up geometrically! It costs four times as much to buy two as it does to buy one, you know. She didn't give you *any* fare?"

Jo shook his head.

"That's incredible. I never heard of such a thing. Have you any idea how fabulously wealthy that woman must be?"

Jo shook his head again.

"You're not very bright, are you?"

"I never asked how much they cost, and she never told me. I was just a shuttle-bum on her ship."

"Shuttle-bum? That sounds exciting. I always wanted to do something like that when I was your age. Never had the nerve, though." The portly man suddenly looked around the terminal with a perturbed expression. "Look, Alfred isn't going to show up. Use his ticket. Just go up to the desk and ask for it."

"But I don't have any of Alfred's identification," Jo said.

"Alfred never has his identification with him. Always losing his wallet and things like that. Whenever I make reservations for him, I always stipulate that he will probably not have any identification with him. Just tell them you're Alfred A. Douglas. They'll give it to you. Hurry up now."

"Well, okay." He made his way through the people to one of the desk clerks.

"Excuse me," he said. "You've got a ticket for A. Douglas?"

The desk clerk looked through his clipboard. "Yeah. It's right here." He grinned at Jo. "You must have had a pretty good time while you were on Earth."

"Huh?"

"This ticket's been waiting for you for three days."

"Oh," Jo said. "Well, I was sort of in bad shape, and I didn't want my parents to see me till I got myself together."

The desk clerk nodded and winked. "Here's your ticket."

"Thanks," Jo said, and went back to Oscar.

"The next ship's boarding right now," Oscar said. "Come along, come along. He'll just have to figure out some other way to get there."

On the ship, Jo asked, "Do you know if the Lump is still on the Moon?"

"I would expect so. He never goes anywhere, that I've heard of."

"Do you think I'll have trouble finding him?"

"I doubt it. Isn't that a beautiful view out the window?"

Oscar was recounting still another off-color story when they walked from the terminal on Luna. A bright crescent of sunlight lined the plastidome that arched a mile above their heads. The lunar mountains curved away on their right, and Earth hung like a greenish poker chip behind them.

Suddenly someone cried, "*There* they are!"

A woman screamed and moved backward.

"Get them!" someone else called.

"What in the . . . ?" Oscar began to splutter.

Jo looked around. Habit made him raise his left hand. But the claws were gone. Four men—one behind, one in front, one on either side . . . He ducked and bumped into Oscar, who . . . fell apart! Pieces went whirling and skittering about and under his feet.

He looked around, as the four men also exploded. The buzzing, humming fragments whirled through the air, circling him, drawing closer, blurring the bewildered faces of the other debarkees. Then suddenly all the pieces coalesced, and Jo was in shaking darkness. A light came on, just as he collapsed.

"Bosie!" someone shrieked. "Bosie . . . !"

Jo landed in a bubble chair in a very small room which seemed to be moving, but he couldn't be sure. A voice that was Oscar's said, "April fool. Surprise."

"Jhup!" Jo exclaimed, and stood up. "Wha' the jhup is goin'—what's going on?"

"April fool," the voice repeated. "It's my birthday. You look a mess; you haven't let all this upset you?"

"I'm scared to death. What is this? Who are you?"

"I'm the Lump," the Lump said. "I thought you knew."

"Knew what?"

"All that business with Oscar and Alfred and Bosie. I thought you were just playing along."

"Playing along with what? Where am I?"

"On the Moon, of course. I just thought it would be a clever way of getting you here. San Severina *didn't* pay your fare, you know. I suppose she just assumed I would. Well, since I'm footing the bill, you have to allow me a little fun. You didn't get it?"

"Get what?"

"It was a literary allusion. I make them all the time."

"Well, watch it, next time. What are you, anyway?"

"A linguistic ubiquitous multiplex. Lump to you."

"Some sort of computer?"

"*Um-hum.* More or less."

"Well, what's supposed to happen now?"

"You're supposed to tell *me*," the Lump said. "I just help."

"Oh," Jo said.

There was a giggle from behind the bubble chair, and Di'k marched out, sat down in front of Jo, and looked at him reproachfully.

"Where are you taking me?"

"To my home console. You can rest up and make plans there. Sit back and relax. We'll be there in three or four minutes."

Jo sat back. He didn't relax, but he took out his ocarina and played on it until a door opened in the front wall.

"Home again, home again, back the same day," said the Lump. "Won't you come in?"

seven

"I"—he flung his cape at the console—"have got"—he hurled the pouch against the glass wall—"to get outta here!" His final gesture was a flying kick at Di'k. Di'k dodged; Jo stumbled, and regained his balance shaking.

"Who's stopping you?" the Lump asked.

"Jhup ya," Jo grunted. "Look, I've been here for three weeks, and every time I get ready to go, we end up in one of those ridiculous conversations that last for nine hours, and then I'm too tired." He walked down the hall and picked up his cloak. "All right, so I'm stupid. But why do you take such delight in rubbing it in? I can't help it if I'm a dark-sided noplex—"

"You're not noplex," the Lump said. "Your view of things is quite complex by now—though there is a good deal of understandable nostalgia for your old simplex perceptions. Sometimes you try to support them just for the sake of argument. Like the time we were discussing the limiting psychological factors in the apprehension of the specious present, and you insisted on maintaining that—"

"Oh, no you don't!" Jo said. "I'm not getting into another one." By now he'd reached his pouch at the other end of the hall. "I'm leaving. Di'k, let's go."

"You," said the Lump, a lot more authoritatively than it usually spoke, "are being silly."

"So I'm simplex. I'm still going."

"Intelligence and plexity have nothing to do with each other."

"There's the spaceship you just spent four days teaching me how to use," Jo said, pointing off through the glass wall. "You put a hypno implant of the route in my head the first night I was here. What under the light of seven suns is stopping me?"

"Nothing is *stopping* you," replied the Lump. "And if you would get it out of your head that something was, you could relax and do this thing sensibly."

Exasperated, Jo turned to face the sixty-foot wall of microlinks and logic-blocks, with their glitter of check lights and reprogram keyboards. "Lump, I *like* it here. You're great to have for a friend, you really are. But I get all my food, all my exercise, everything; and I'm going crazy. Do you think it's easy just to walk out and leave you like this?"

"Don't be so emotional," the Lump said. "I'm not set up to deal with that sort of thing."

"Do you know that since I've stopped being a shuttle-bum, I've done less work than I ever have in my life during any comparable period?"

"You have also changed more than you have during any comparable period."

"Look, Lump, try and understand." Jo dropped his cloak and walked back over to the console. It was a large mahogany desk. He pulled out the chair, crawled in under it, and hugged his knees. "Lump, I don't think you *do* understand. So listen. Here you are, in touch with all the libraries and museums of this arm of the galaxy. You've got lots of friends, people like San Severina and the other people who're always stopping by to see you. You write books, make music, paint pictures. Do you think you could be happy in a little one-product culture where there was nothing to do on Saturday night except get drunk, with just one teletheater, and no library, where maybe four people had been to the University, and you never saw them anyway because they were making too much money, and everybody knew everybody else's business?"

"No."

"Well, I could, Lump."

"Why did you leave, then?"

"Well . . . because of the message. And because there were a lot of things I don't think I really appreciated. I don't think I was ready to leave. *You* couldn't be happy there. *I* could. It's as simple as that, and I don't really think you fully comprehend that."

"I do," Lump said. "I hope you can be happy in someplace like that. Because that's what most of the universe is composed of. You're slated to spend a great deal of time in places like that, and if you *couldn't* appreciate them, it would be rather sad."

Di'k looked under the desk and then jumped into Jo's lap. It was always ten degrees warmer under the desk, and the two warmblooded creatures, Di'k and Jo, independently or together, sought the spot out again and again.

"Now *you* listen," Lump said.

Jo leaned his head against the side of the desk. Di'k jumped down from his lap, went out, and came back a moment later dragging the plastic pouch. Jo opened it and took out the ocarina.

"There are things I can tell you, most of which I have already told you. There are things you have to ask me. Very few of them have you asked. I know much more about you than you know about me. And if we are to be friends—which is very important for you and for me—that situation must be changed."

Jo put his ocarina down. "That's right—I don't know that much about you, Lump. Where do you come from?"

"I was built by a dying Lll to house its disassociating consciousness."

"Lll?" Jo asked.

"You'd almost forgotten about them, hadn't you?"

"No I didn't."

"You see, my mind is a Lll mind."

"But you don't make me sad."

"I'm half Lll and half machine. So I forfeit the protection."

"You're a Lll?" Jo asked again, incredulously. "It never occurred to me. Now that you've told me, do you think it will make any difference?"

"I doubt it," the Lump said. "But if you say anything about some of your best friends, I will lose a great deal of respect for you."

"What about my best friends?" Jo asked.

"Another allusion. It's all just as well you didn't get it."

"Lump, why don't we go on together?" Jo said suddenly. "I am leaving—that I've made up my mind to. Why don't you come with me?"

"Delightful idea. I thought you'd never ask. That's the only way you could get out of here anyway. Of course, the area in which we're going is very hostile to free Lll. It's right into Empire territory. They protect Lll, and they get rather upset if one shrugs off their protection and decides to stay free on her or his own. Some of the things they have been known to do are atrocious."

"Well, if anybody asks, just say you're a computer. Like I said, I wouldn't have known if you hadn't said anything."

"I do *not* intend to pass," the Lump said sternly.

"Then *I'll* say you're a computer. But let's get going. We'll be here for hours if this keeps up. I can feel another one of those discussions starting." He stood up from under the desk and started for the door.

"Comet?"

Jo stopped and looked back over his shoulder. "What? Don't change your mind on me now."

"Oh, no. I'm definitely going. But . . . well, if I were—now be honest—just lumping along the street, do you really think people would just say, 'Oh, there goes a linguistic ubiquitous multiplex,' and not think about Lll?"

"That's what I'd say if I said anything at all."

"All right. Take the tube to Journal Square, and I'll meet you in forty minutes."

Di'k octopeded after Jo as he ran across the cracked, dusty plain of the Moon toward the egg-shaped spaceship.

The tube was an artificial stasis current that took ships quickly beyond Pluto, where they could leave the system without fear of heavy solar-dust damage.

The great slab of plastic, some ten miles on either side— Journal Square—supported buildings, its own atmosphere, and several amusement areas. Jo parked his ship on a side street and stepped into the chill air.

Soldiers were practicing drill formation in the square.

"What are they doing that for?" he asked one uniformed man resting on the side.

"It's the field brigade of the Empire Army. They'll be heading out of there in a few days; they won't be here long."

"I wasn't objecting," Jo said. "Just curious."

"Oh," the soldier said, and offered no further explanation.

"Where are they going?" Jo asked after a moment.

"Look," the soldier said, turning to Jo as he would to a persistent child, "everything about the Empire Army that you can't see immediately is secret. If where they're going doesn't concern you, forget it. If it does, go see if you can get clearance from Prince Nactor."

"Nactor?" Jo asked.

"That one." The soldier pointed to a dark man with a goatee who was leading one platoon.

"I don't think it does," Jo said.

The soldier gave him a disgusted look, got up, and moved away. Together black capes swung out as the men snapped briskly around a turn.

Then there was a commotion among the spectators. People looked up and began to point and talk excitedly.

It caught the sun, spinning toward the square, getting larger and larger. It was roughly cubical and—huge! As one face turned toward the light, another disappeared, till Jo suddenly regained his sense of proportion: it was nearly a quarter of a mile long on each side.

It struck the square, and Jo and all the soldiers—and one of the taller buildings—fell down. There was mass confusion, sirens sounded, and people ran to and from the object.

Jo started running toward it. Low gravity got him there fairly quickly. There were a couple of large cracks in the square that jagged out across the area. He leaped across one and saw stars below him.

Catching his breath, he landed on the other side and proceeded a little more slowly. The object, he realized, was covered with some sort of boiling jelly; the jelly looked surprisingly familiar, but he could not place it. The face of the object that was turned toward him, he could make out through the mildly smoking slop, was glass. And beyond the glass, dim in the interior transplutonian night: microlinks, logic-blocks, and the faint glitter of check-lights.

"Lump!" Jo cried, running forward.

"*Shhhh*," a familiar voice said, muffled by jelly. "I'm trying not to attract attention."

Soldiers were marching by now. "What the hell *is* that thing, anyway?" said one.

"It's a linguistic ubiquitous multiplex," said the other.

The first scratched his head and looked up and down the length of the wall. "Ubiquitous as hell, isn't it?"

A third was examining the edge of a crack in the square. "Think they're gonna have to get a damned Lll in here to rebuild this?"

Lump whispered, "Just let one of them say anything to my face. Just one—"

"Oh, shut up," Jo said, "or I won't let you marry my daughter."

"What's that supposed to mean?"

"It's an allusion," Jo explained. "I did some reading while you were taking a nap last week."

"Very funny, very funny," the Lump said.

The soldiers started to walk away. "They won't get no Lll in," one of the soldiers said, scratching his ear. "This is soldier work. We do all the real building around here anyway. Wish there *was* a damned Lll around, though."

Several of Lump's check-lights changed color behind the jelly.

"What's that jhup all over you?" Jo asked, stepping back now.

"My spaceship," the Lump said. "I'm using an organiform. They're much more comfortable for inanimate objects like me. Haven't you ever seen one before?"

"No—yes! Back on Rhys. That's what the Tritovian and those other things came in."

"Odd," said Lump. "They don't usually use organiforms. They're not particularly inanimate."

More people were gathering around the computer. The sirens were getting close.

"Let's just get out of here," Jo said. "Are you all right?"

"I'm fine," Lump said. "I just wonder about the square."

"Bloody but unbowed," Jo said. "That's another allusion. Get going and we'll reconnoiter at Tantamount."

"Fine," Lump said. "Step back. I'm taking off."

There was a bubbling, a tremendous *suck,* and Jo staggered in the wind. People started screaming again.

Back at Jo's ship, Di'k was hiding under the dashboard with forepaws over his head. Jo pushed the takeoff button, and the robo-crew took over. The confusion of the square dropped beneath them. He ran over his hyperstasis checkout, then signaled for the jump.

The stasis generators surged, and the ship began to slip into hyperstasis. He hadn't finished slipping when the ship lurched and he smashed forward into the dashboard. His wrists took the shock, and he bounced away with both of them aching. Di'k screeched.

eight

Jo pried his canines out of his lower lip.

"You're not playing chess," the voice went on. "If you occupy my square, I will not be removed from the board. Look out, next time."

"*Gnnnnnnng,*" Jo said, rubbing his mouth.

"Same to you and many more."

Jo shook his head and put on his sensory helmet. It smelled like old jhup. It sounded like scrap metal being crushed under a hydraulic press. But it looked beautiful.

Ramps curved away into structures that blossomed like flowers. Thin spires erupted at their tips in shapes of metal, and fragile observation domes were supported on slender pylons.

"You might come out of there and see if you've done any damage to us."

"Oh," Jo said. "Yeah. Sure."

He started to the lock and was about to release it when he realized the warning light was still on. "Hey," he called back toward the intercom, "there's no air out there."

"I thought you were going to take care of that," the voice answered. "Just a second." The light went off.

"Thanks," Jo said. He pulled the release. "What are you, anyway?"

Outside the lock a balding man in a white smock was coming down one of the ramps. "This is the Geodesic Survey Station that you almost ran down, youngster." His voice was much diminished, in person. "You better get on inside the force-field, before this atmosphere escapes. I don't know what you thought you were doing anyway."

"I was finishing up a stasis jump, on my way to Tantamount. Simplex of me, wasn't it?" Jo started back up the ramp with the man, who shrugged.

"I never pass judgments like that," the man said. "Now tell me your specialty."

"I don't have one, I don't think."

The man frowned. "I don't think we need a synthesizer right now. They tend to be extremely long-lived."

"I know just about everything there is to know about raising and storing plyasil," Jo said.

The man smiled. "I'm afraid that wouldn't do much good.

We're only up to volume one hundred and sixty-seven: *Bba* to *Bbaab*."

"Its common term is jhup," Jo said.

The man smiled benignly at him. "*Jh* is still a long way away. But if you're alive in five or six hundred years, we'll take your application."

"Thanks," Jo said. "But I'll just forget it."

"Very well," the man said, turning to him. "Good-bye."

"Well, what about the damage to *my* ship? Aren't you going to check me over? You're not supposed to be here, in the first place. I've got through clearance on this path."

"Young man," the gentleman said, "first of all, we have priority. Second of all, if you don't want a job, you are abusing our hospitality by using up our air. Third of all, there is advance work being done in *biology, human*—and if you bother me anymore, I'll ship you off for a specimen and have you cut up in little pieces. And don't think I won't."

"What about my message?" Jo demanded. "I've got to get a message through concerning the Lll, to Empire Star. And it's important. That's why I rammed into you in the first place."

The man's face had become hostile.

"Eventually," he said, evenly, "we will finish our project, and there will be enough knowledge so that Lll will be economically unfeasible, because building will be able to proceed without them. If you want to benefit the Lll, I'll order you sliced up immediately. Father is working on the adenoids now. There is a raft of work to be done on the bicuspids. We've just started the colon, and the duodenum is a complete mystery. If you want to deliver your message, deliver it here."

"But I don't know what it is!" Jo said, backing out toward the edge of the force-field. "I think I'll be going."

"We have a computer for just such problems as yours," the

man said. "Not with a lungful of *our* air, you're not," he added, and lunged toward Jo.

Jo saw where he was lunging and simply wasn't there.

The force-field was permeable, and he ducked through, sprang to the lock of his ship, and slammed it behind him. The warning light blinked on less than a second afterward.

He threw her into reverse and prayed that the automatic pilot could still negotiate the currents and move to a deeper stasis level. It did, if a little jerkily. The Geodesic Survey Station faded from the viewplates of the sensory helmet that was lying face-up on the dashboard.

He reconnoitered easily with Lump in an orbit around Tantamount. It was a planet of iced methane with so much volcanic activity that the surface was constantly being broken and exploded. It was the single daughter of an intensely hot white dwarf, so that from here they looked like two eyes, one jeweled and glittering, one of silver-gray, spying on the night.

"Lump, I want to go home. Back to Rhys. Give up the whole thing."

"What in the world for?" came the computer's incredulous voice over the intercom.

Jo leaned on his elbows, looking morosely at his ocarina. "The multiplex universe doesn't appeal to me. I don't like it. I want to get away from it. If I'm complex now, it's too bad, it's a mistake, and if I ever get back to Rhys, I'll try as hard as I can to be simplex. I really will."

"What's got into you?"

"I just don't like the people. I think it's that simple. You ever heard of the Geodesic Survey Station?"

"Certainly have. You run into them?"

"Yeah."

"That *is* unfortunate. Well, there are certain sad things in the multiplex universe that must be dealt with. And one of the things is simplexity."

"Simplexity?" Jo asked. "What do you mean?"

"And you better be thankful that you have acquired as much multiplexity of vision as you have, or you never would have gotten away from them alive. I've heard tell of other simplex creatures encountering them. They don't come back."

"They're simplex?"

"Good God, yes. Couldn't you tell?"

"But they're compiling all that information. And the place they live—it's beautiful. They couldn't be stupid and have built that."

"First of all, most of the Geodesic Survey Station was built by Lll. Second of all, as I have said many times before, intelligence and plexity do not necessarily go together."

"But how was I supposed to know?"

"I suppose it won't hurt to outline the symptoms. Did they ask you a single question?"

"No."

"That's the first sign, though not conclusive. Did they judge you correctly, as you could tell from their statements about you?"

"No. They thought I was looking for a job."

"Which implies that they should have asked questions. A multiplex consciousness always asks questions when it has to."

"I remember," Jo said, putting down the ocarina, "when Charona was trying to explain it to me, she asked me what was the most important thing there was. If I asked them that, I know what they would have said: their blasted dictionary, or encyclopedia, or whatever it is."

"Very good. Anyone who can give a nonrelative answer to that question is simplex."

"I said jhup," Jo recalled wistfully.

"They're in the process of cataloging all the knowledge in the Universe."

"That's more important than jhup, I suppose," Jo said.

"From a complex point of view, perhaps. But from a multiplex view, they're about the same. First of all, it's a rather difficult task. When last I heard, they were already up to the B's, but I'm sure they don't have a thing on *Aaaaaaaaaaaaaaaaaavdqx.*"

"What's . . . well, what you just said?"

"It's the name for a rather involved set of deterministic moral evaluations taken through a relativistic view of the dynamic moment. I was studying it some years back."

"I wasn't familiar with the term."

"I just made it up. But what it stands for is quite real, and well worth an article. I don't think they could even comprehend it. But from now on, I shall refer to it as *Aaaaaaaaaaaaaaaaaavdqx,* and there are two of us who know the word now—so it's valid."

"I guess I get the point."

"Besides, cataloging all knowledge, even all available knowledge, while admirable, is . . . well, the only word is simplex."

"Why?"

"One can learn all one needs to know; or one can learn what one wants to know. But to need to learn all one wants to know, which is what the Geodesic Survey Station is doing, even falls apart semantically. What's the matter with your ship?"

"The Geodesic Survey Station again. We collided."

"I don't like the looks of it."

"My takeoff was sort of jerky."

"Don't like the looks of it at all. Especially considering how far we have to go. Why don't you hop on over here and travel with me? This organiform is a beauty, and I think I've got my landings and takeoffs a little more under control."

"If you promise not to break my back when we land."

"Promise," the Lump said. "I'll open up. Swing around to your left and you can leave that jalopy right where it is."

They made contact.

"Jo," Lump said, as the flexible tube attached to his air lock, "if you really want to, you can go back. But there comes a point where going back is harder than going on. You've received a great deal of very specialized education. Not only what San Severina and I have tried to teach you, but even back on Rhys you were learning."

Jo started through the tube. "I still wanna go home." He slowed his pace as he moved toward the console room. "Lump, sometimes, even if you're simplex, you ask yourself, who am I? All right, you say the Geodesic Survey Station was simplex. That makes me feel a little better. But I'm still a very ordinary kid who would like to get back to a jhup field, and maybe fight off some wild kepards. That's who I am. That's what I know."

"If you went back, you would find the people around you very much like you found the Geodesic Survey. You left your home, Jo, because you weren't happy. Remember why?"

Jo reached the console room but stopped, his hands on either jamb. "Jhup, yeah. Sure I remember. Because I thought I was different. Then the message came along, and I thought that was proof I was special. Else they wouldn't have given it to me. Don't you see, Lump"—he leaned forward on his hands—"if I really knew I was something special—I mean if I was *sure*—then I wouldn't get so upset by things like the Survey Station! But most of the time I just feel lost and unhappy and ordinary."

"You're you, Jo. You're you and everything that went into you, from the way you sit for hours and watch Di'k when you want to think, to the way you turn a tenth of a second faster in response to something blue than to something red. You're all you ever thought, all you ever hoped, and all you ever hated, too. And all you've learned. You've been learning a lot, Jo."

"But if I knew that it was mine, Lump. That's what I want to be sure of: that the message was really important and that I was the only one who could deliver it. If I really knew that this education I'd gotten had made me—well, like I say, something special—then I wouldn't mind going on. Jhup, I'd be happy to do it."

"Jo, you're you. And that's as important as you want to make it."

"Maybe that is the most important thing there is, Lump. If there is an answer to that question, Lump, that's what it is, to know you're yourself and nobody else."

Just as Jo stepped inside the console room, the speakers from the communications unit began to whisper. As Jo looked around, the whisper increased. "What's that, Lump?"

"I'm not sure."

The door closed, the tube fell away, and the wrecked cruiser drifted back. Jo watched it through the glass wall covered with vaguely distorting organiform.

The speaker was laughing now.

Di'k scratched his ear with one foot.

"It's coming from over there," Lump said. "It's coming awfully fast, too."

Laughter got louder, reached hysteria, filled the high chamber. Something hurtled by the Lump's glass wall, then suddenly swung around and came up short, twenty feet away.

The laughing stopped and was replaced by exhausted gasps.

The thing outside looked like a huge chunk of rock, only the front face had been polished. As they drifted slightly in the glare of Tantamount, the white light slipped from the surface; Jo saw it was a transparent plate. Behind it a figure leaned forward, hands over his head, feet wide apart. Even from here Jo could see the chest heave in time to the panting that stormed through the console room. "Lump, turn down the volume, will you?"

"Oh, I'm sorry." The panting ceased to be something happening inside his ear and settled to a reasonable sound a respectable number of feet away. "Do you want to speak to him, or shall I?"

"You go ahead."

"Who are you?" Lump asked.

"Ni Ty Lee. Who are you, blast it, to be so interesting?"

"I'm the Lump. I've heard of you, Ni Ty Lee."

"I've never heard of you, Lump. But I should have, I know. Why are you so interesting?"

Jo whispered, "Who is he?"

"Shhh," the Lump said. "Tell you later. What were you doing, Ni Ty Lee?"

"I was running toward that sun there, and staring at it, and thinking how beautiful it was, and laughing because it was so beautiful, and laughing because it was going to destroy me, and still be beautiful, and I was writing a poem about how beautiful that sun was and how beautiful the planet that circled it was: and I was doing all that until I saw something more interesting to do, and that was find out who *you* were."

"Then come aboard and find out some more."

"I already know you're a linguistic ubiquitous multiplex with a Lll-based consciousness," Ni Ty Lee answered. "Is there any more I should find out before I sail into the fires?"

"I have a boy on board your own age that you know nothing about at all."

"Then I'm coming over. Get your tube out." He started forward.

"How did he know you were Lll?" Jo asked as the chunk of rock approached.

"I don't know," Lump said. "Some people can tell right off.

That's better than the ones who sit around and talk to you for an hour before they get around to asking. Only I bet he doesn't know *which* Lll I am."

The tube connected up with Ni's vessel. A moment later the door opened, and Ni Ty Lee stepped leisurely inside, his thumbs in his pants pockets, and looked around.

Jo was still wearing the black cape San Severina had bought him on Ratshole. Ni Ty Lee, however, looked like a shuttle-bum. He was barefooted. He wore no shirt. His faded work pants had one frayed knee. His too-long hair was silver-blond and clutched at his ears and forehead; his face was high-cheeked, with sloping Oriental eyes the color of slate chips.

The face fixed on Jo and grinned. "Hello," he said, and came forward.

He extended his hand, and Jo started to shake it. There were claws on the fingers of his right hand.

Ni's head leaned to the side. "I'm going to write a poem about the expressions that just went over your face. You're from Rhys, and you used to work in the jhup fields, and curl up by the fires at New Cycle, and kill kepards when they broke through." He made a small, sad, amused sound without opening his mouth. "Hey, Lump. I know all about him now, and I'll be on my way." He began to turn.

"Were you on Rhys? You were really on Rhys?" Jo said.

Ni turned back. "Yes. I was. Three years ago. Hitched there as a shuttle-bum and worked for awhile down in field seven. That's where I got these." He held up his claws.

A pulsing ache had begun in the back of Jo's throat that he had not felt since first he had played for the Lll. "I worked field seven just before New Cycle."

"Did Keeper James ever knock some sense into that brat son of his? I get along with most people, but I got into a fight four times with that pesky know-it-all. And once I nearly killed him."

"I . . . I did," Jo whispered.

"Oh," Ni said. He blinked. "Well, I guess I can't really say I'm surprised." But he looked taken aback nevertheless.

"You really were there?" Jo asked. "You're not just . . . reading my mind?"

"I was there. In the flesh. For three and a half weeks."

"That's not very long," Jo said.

"I didn't say I was there a *long* time."

"But you *were* really there," Jo repeated.

"It's not that big a universe, friend. It's too bad your culture was so simplex, or there'd be more to know about you and I'd stay longer." He turned once more to leave.

"Wait a minute!" Jo called. "I want . . . I *need* to talk to you."

"You do?"

Jo nodded.

Ni Ty put his hands back in his pockets. "Nobody's needed me for a long time. That should be interesting enough to write a poem about." He swaggered over to the console and sat down on top of the desk. "I'll hang around awhile, then. What do you need to talk about?"

Jo was silent, while his mind darted. "Well, what's your spaceship made of?" he asked at last.

Ni Ty looked up at the ceiling. "Hey, Lump," he called, "is this guy putting me on? He doesn't really need to know what my ship is made of, does he? If he's putting me on, I'm going to go. People put me on all the time, and I know all about that, and it doesn't interest me a bit."

"He needs to warm up to what's important," Lump said. "And you need to be patient."

Ni Ty looked back at Jo. "You know, he's right. I'm always leaving words and paragraphs out of my poems because I write too fast. Then nobody understands them. I don't know too much about being patient, either. This might be very interesting after all. This your ocarina?"

Jo nodded.

"I used to play one of these things." He put it to his lips and ran through a bright melody that slowed suddenly at the end.

The knot in Jo's throat tightened further. The tune was the first song he had ever learned on the instrument.

"That's the only tune I ever learned. I should have stuck with it longer. Here, you play. Maybe that'll warm you up."

Jo just shook his head.

Ni Ty shrugged, turned the ocarina over in his hands, then said, "Does it hurt?"

"Yeah," Jo said, after a while.

"I can't help it," Ni Ty said. "I've just done a lot of things."

"May I interject?" the Lump said.

Ni shrugged again. "Sure."

Jo nodded.

"You will find, during your reading, Jo, that certain authors seem to have discovered all the things you have discovered, done all you've done. There was one ancient science fiction writer, Theodore Sturgeon, who would break me up every time I read him. He seemed to have seen every flash of light on a window, every leaf shadow on a screen door, that I have ever seen; done everything I had ever done from playing the guitar to laying over for a couple of weeks on a boat in Arransas Pass, Texas. And he was supposedly writing fiction, and that four thousand years ago. Then you learn that lots of other people find the same things in the same writer, who have done none of the things you've done and seen none of the things you've seen. That's a rare sort of writer. But Ni Ty Lee is that sort. I have read many of your poems, Ni Ty. My appreciation, were I to express it, I'm sure would only prove embarrassing."

"Gee," Ni Ty said. "Thanks." And he got a grin on his face

that was too big to hide even by looking at his lap. "I lose most of the best ones. Or don't write them down. I wish I could show you some of them. They're really nice."

"I wish you could too," said the Lump.

"Hey." Ni Ty looked up. "But you need me. I can't even remember what you asked."

"About your ship," Jo said.

"I just hollowed out a chunk of nonporous meteor and bolted in a Kayzon Drive in the back, and ran my controls for igneous permeability."

"Yes, yes!" cried the Lump. "That's exactly how it's done! Bolted the Kayzon in with a left-handed ratchet. The threads run backwards, don't they? It was years ago, but it was such a beautiful little ship!"

"You're right about the threads," Ni Ty said. "Only I used a pliers."

"It doesn't matter. Just that you really did it. I told you, Jo, with some writers, it's just uncanny."

"There's a problem, though," Ni Ty said. "I never do anything long enough to really get to know it—just long enough to identify it in a line or a sentence, then I'm on to something else. I think I'm afraid. And I write to make up for all the things I really can't do."

At which point I began to twinge a little. I had said the same thing to Norn an hour before we'd cracked up on Rhys, when we had been discussing my last book. Remember me? I'm Jewel.

"But you're only my age," Jo said at last. "How could you do all this and write all this so early?"

"Well, I . . . I mean, it's . . . I guess I don't really know. I just do. I suppose there's a lot I never will do because I'm too busy writing."

"Another interjection," the Lump said. "Would it embarrass you if I told him the story?"

Ni Ty shook his head.

"It's like Oscar and Alfred," Lump said.

Ni Ty looked surprisingly relieved. "Or Paul V. and Arthur R.," he added.

"Like Jean C. and Raymond R.," said Lump, in rhythm.

"Or Willy and Colette."

"It's a recurrent literary pattern," the Lump explained. "An older writer, a younger writer—often a mere child—and something tragic. And something wonderful is given to the world. It's been happening every twenty-five or fifty years since Romanticism."

"Who was the older writer?" Jo asked.

Ni Ty looked down. "Muels Aranlyde."

"I've never heard of him," Jo said.

Ni Ty blinked. "Oh. I thought everybody knew about the whole, unpleasant mess."

"I'd like to meet him," Jo offered.

"I doubt you ever will," said the Lump. "What happened was very, very tragic."

"Aranlyde was Lll." Ni Ty took a breath and began to explain. "We made a long trip together, and . . ."

"You made a long trip with a Lll?"

"Well, he was really only part—" Then he stopped. "I can't help it," he said. "It's what I've done. I swear I can't help it."

"You know about the sadness of the Lll, then," Jo said.

Ni Ty nodded. "Yes. You see, I sold him. I was desperate, I needed the money, and he told me to go ahead."

"You sold him? But why—"

"Economics."

"Oh."

"And with it I bought a less expensive Lll to rebuild the world we had destroyed; so I know about the sadness of Lll, and the sadness of Lll ownership—though it was a small world, and only took a little while. I was explaining that to San Severina only days ago, and she got very upset—she too has bought and sold Lll and used them to rebuild a—"

"You know San Severina?"

"Yes. She gave me Interling lessons when I was a shuttle-bum—"

"No!" Jo cried.

Ni Ty shook his head and whispered, "I swear I can't help it! I swear!"

"No!" He turned and put his hands over his ears, crouched down and staggered.

Behind him, Ni Ty cried out, "Lump, you said he needed me?"

"You are fulfilling his need very well."

Jo whirled. "Get out of here!"

Ni Ty looked frightened and stood up from the desktop. "It's my life, damn it, not yours. It's mine!" He grabbed Ni's clawed hand. "Mine. I gave it up—but that doesn't mean you can have it."

Ni sucked a quick breath. "It's not interesting now," he said quickly, edging from the desk. "I've been through this too many times before."

"But *I* haven't!" Jo cried. He felt as if something in him had been raped and outraged. "You can't steal my life!"

Suddenly Ni pushed him. Jo slipped to the deck, and the poet stood over him, shaking now. "What the hell makes you think it's yours? Maybe you stole it from *me*. How come I never get to finish anything out? How come any time I get a job, fall in love, have a child, suddenly I'm jerked away and flung into another dung heap where I have to start the same mess all over again? Are you doing that to me? Are you jerking me away from what's mine, picking up for yourself the thousand beautiful lives I've started?" Suddenly he closed his eyes and flung his left hand against his right shoulder. With his head back he hissed to the ceiling, "God, I've said this so many times before! And it bores me, damn it! It bores me!" He'd raked the claws across his shoulder, and five lines of blood trickled to his chest—and for one horrid instant the scene came flashing into Jo's mind when he'd run from Lilly's laughter and stood with his eyes clenched and his head back, and pulled his talons across his shoulder. He shook the memory from his head and blinked his eyes. There was a lot of old scar tissue banding Ni Ty's shoulder under the path the fresh welts cut.

"Always returning, always coming back, always the same things over and over and *over!*" Ni Ty cried.

He lurched toward the door.

"Wait!"

Jo flipped to his belly and scrabbled to his knees after him.

"What are you going to do?" He threw himself around Ni Ty and put his arm across the door.

Ni Ty put his clawed hand around Jo's forearm. Jo shook his head—Billy James had blocked his way from the corral, and he had put his claws on the boy's arm so, and that's how it all started . . .

"I'm going to get in my ship," Ni Ty said evenly, "and I'm going to face that sun and jam the throttle all the way. I've done it once laughing. This time I'll probably cry. And that damn well better be interesting."

"But *why?*"

"Because someday—"and Ni Ty's face twisted with the strain of words—"somebody else is going to come plunging toward a silver sun, first laughing, then crying, and they'll have read about this, and they'll remember, and suddenly they'll know, don't you see? They'll know that they're not the only ones—"

"But nobody will ever read what you have to say about—"

Ni Ty slapped his arm away and ran down the tube, just missing Di'k, who was stepping down with a sheaf of paper in his mouth.

The tube popped free, and the organifoam swarmed together as the door closed in the console room. Jo saw Ni Ty bending at the controls; then he stood and pressed his face and hands against the viewport as the automatic pilot took the hollow meteor into the glare of the sun. Jo squinted after it till his lids ached. The sobbing that came over the intercom lasted for perhaps a minute after the ship was out of sight.

Jo rubbed his hand across his forehead and turned from the wall.

Di'k was sitting on the sheaf of papers, chewing on a dog-eared corner. "What are those?"

"Ni Ty's poems," the Lump said. "The last batch he was working on."

"Di'k, did you steal them out of his ship?" Jo demanded.

"With somebody like that, the only thing you can do is get their work away from them before they destroy it. That's how everything of his we have has been obtained. This has all happened before," Lump said wearily.

"But Di'k didn't know that," Jo said. "You were just stealing, weren't you?" He tried to sound reproving.

"You underestimate your devil-kitten," the Lump said. "He does not have a simplex mind."

Jo bent over and tugged the papers from under Di'k, who finally rolled over and slapped at his hands a couple of times. Then he took them to the desk and crawled underneath.

Three hours later, when he emerged, Jo walked slowly over to the glass wall and squinted once more at the white dwarf. He turned, blew three notes on his ocarina, then dropped his hand. "I think that's the most multiplex consciousness I've encountered so far."

"He may be," Lump said. "But then, so are you, now."

"I hope he doesn't plunge into the sun," Jo said.

"He won't if he finds something more interesting between here and there."

"There's not much out there."

"It doesn't take much to interest a mind like Lee's."

"The thing you were saying about multiplexity and understanding points of view. He completely took over my point of view, and you were right; it was uncanny."

"It takes a multiplex consciousness to perceive the multiplexity of another consciousness, you know."

"I can see why," Jo said. "He was using all his experiences to understand mine. It made me feel funny."

"You know he wrote those poems before he even knew you existed."

"That's right. But that just makes it stranger."

"I'm afraid," Lump said, "you've set up your syllogism backwards. You were using your experiences to understand his."

"I was?"

"You've had a lot of experiences recently. Order them multiplexually and they will be much clearer. And when they are clear enough, enough confusion will remain so that you ask the proper questions."

Jo was silent for a moment, ordering. Then he said, "What was the name of the Lll your mind is based on?"

"Muels Aranlyde," the Lump said.

Jo turned back to the window. "Then this has all happened before."

After another minute of silence, the Lump said, "You know you will have to make the last leg of the trip without me."

"I'd just begun to order that out," Joe said. "Multiplexually."

"Good."

"I'll be scared as hell."

"You needn't be," Lump said.

"Why not?"

"You've got a crystallized Tritovian in your pouch."

He was referring to me, of course. I hope you haven't forgotten me, because the rest of the story is going to be incomprehensible if you have.

nine

"What am I supposed to do with it?" Jo asked.

He laid me on a velvet cloth on the desk. The lights in the high ceiling of the console room were dim and had haloes in the faint fog from the humidifiers.

"What's the most multiplex thing you can do when you are not sure what to do?"

"Ask questions."

"Then ask."

"Will it answer?"

"There's an easier way to find that out than by asking me," Lump said.

"Just a second," Jo said. "I have to order my perceptions multiplexually, and it may take a little time. I'm not used to it." After a moment he said, "Why will I have to join the Empire Army and serve Prince Nactor?"

"Excellent," Lump said. "I've been wondering about that one myself."

Because, I broadcast, *the army is going your way.* It was a relief to be able to speak. But that's one of the hardships of crystallization: you can only answer when asked directly.

Incidentally, between the time that Jo said, "I'm not used to it," and the time he asked his question, the radio had come blaring on, and Prince Nactor's voice had announced that all humans in the area were up for immediate conscription, to which Lump had said, "I guess that takes care of your problem." So there's nothing mysterious about Jo's question at all. I want to stress, for those who have followed the argument to this point, that multiplexity is perfectly within the laws of logic. I left the incident out because I thought it was distracting and assumed it was perfectly deducible from Jo's question what had happened, sure that the multiplex reader would supply it for himself. I have done this several times throughout the story.

"Why can't I just deliver my message and go on about my business?" Jo asked.

In crystallization one has the seeming activity of being able to ask rhetorical questions. *Are you ready to deliver the message?* I broadcast.

Jo pounded both fists on the desk. The room seemed to shake as I rocked back and forth.

"Jhup! What *is* the message? That's what I have to find out now. What *is* it?"

Someone has come to free the Lll.

Jo stood up, and concern deepened the young lines of his face. "That's a very important message." The concern turned to a frown. "When will I be ready to deliver it?"

Whenever someone has come to free them.

"But I've come all this way . . ." Jo stopped. "Me? Me free

them? But . . . I may be ready to deliver the message, but how will I know when I'm ready to free them?"

If you don't know, I broadcast, *obviously that's not the message.*

Jo felt confused and ashamed. "But it ought to be."

He'd asked no questions, so I could broadcast nothing. But Lump said it for me: "That's the message, but you have misunderstood it. Try and think of another interpretation that contains no contradictions."

Jo turned from the table. "I don't see enough," he said, discouraged.

"Sometimes one must see through someone else's eyes," Lump said. "At this point, I would say if you could use Jewel's, you would be doing yourself a great service."

"Why?"

"You are becoming more and more intimately concerned with the Lll, and our struggle for release. The Tritovians are the most active of the non-Lll species in this struggle. It's that simple. Besides, it would greatly facilitate your military career."

"Can it be done?" Jo asked.

"A very simple operation," Lump said. "You can perform it yourself. Go get the Tritovian."

Jo went back to the desk and lifted me from the velvet.

"Now pull up your right eyelid."

Jo did. And did other things at Lump's instruction. A minute later he screamed in pain, whirled from the desk, and fell to his knees, with his hands over his face.

"The pain will go away in a little while," the Lump said calmly. "I can give you some eyewash if the stinging is too bad."

Jo shook his head. "It's not the pain, Lump," he whispered. "I see. I see you and me and Di'k and Jewel, only all at the same time. And I see the military ship waiting for me, and even Prince Nactor. But the ship is a hundred and seventy miles away, and

Di'k is behind me, and you're all around me, and Jewel's inside me, and I'm . . . not me anymore."

"You better practice walking for a little while," Lump said. "Spiral staircases are particularly difficult at first. On second thought, you'd better get used just to sitting still and thinking. Then we'll go on to more complicated things."

"I'm not me anymore," Jo repeated softly.

"Play your ocarina," Lump suggested.

Jo watched himself remove the instrument from his pouch and place it on his own lips, saw his lids close, one over his left eye, one over the glittering presence that had replaced his right. He heard himself begin a long, slow tune, and with his eyes shut he watched Di'k come tentatively over, then nuzzle his lap.

A little later Jo said, "You know, Lump, I don't think talking to Jewel got me anything."

"Certainly not as much as looking through him."

"I'm still awfully foggy about that message."

"You've got to make allowances. When people become as militant as he is, the most multiplex minds get downright linear. But his heart's in the right place. Actually, he said a great deal to you if you can view it multiplexually."

Jo watched his own face become concentrated. It was rather runny, he thought in passing—like an overanxious, towheaded squirrel wearing a diamond monocle. "The message must be the words: *Someone has come to free the Lll.* And I have to be ready to free the Lll. Only it's not me that's going to free them." He waited for Lump to approve his reasoning. There was only silence, however. So he went on: "I wish it were me. But I guess there're reasons why it can't be. I have to be ready to deliver the message, too. The only way I can really be ready is if I make sure whoever is going to free the Lll is ready."

"Very good," the Lump said.

"Where am I going to find this person, and how can I make sure he's ready to free the Lll?"

"You may have to get him ready yourself."

"Me?"

"You've received quite an education in the past few months. You are going to have to impart a good deal of that education to somebody as simplex as you were when you began this journey."

"And lose whatever uniqueness Ni Ty left me with?"

"Yes."

"Then I won't do it," Jo said.

"Oh, come on."

"Look, my old life was stolen from me. Now you want me to give my new life to somebody else. I won't do it."

"That's a very selfish way of—"

"Besides, I know enough about simplex cultures to know that the only thing you could do to them with an army that might shake loose one or two people is destroy it. And I won't."

"Oh," said the Lump. "You've figured that out."

"Yes, I did. And it would be very painful."

"The destruction will happen whether you go or not. The only difference will be that you won't be able to deliver your message."

"Won't he be ready without me?"

"The point is you will have no way to know."

"I'll take the chance," Jo said. "I'm going someplace else. I'll take the gamble that everything will work out for the best, whether I'm there or not."

"You have no idea how risky that is. Look, we have some time. Let's take a little side trip. I want to show you something that will change your mind."

"Lump, I don't think I could take any exposure to slave-driven, exploited, long-suffering Lll right now. That's where you want to take me, isn't it?"

"Lll suffering is something that happens to you, not to Lll," the Lump said. "It is impossible to understand the suffering of the Lll from the point of view of the Lll itself unless you are one. Understanding is one of the things the Empire protects them from. Even the Lll can't agree on what's so awful about their situation. But there is enough concurrence so you must take our word. There are certain walls that multiplexity cannot scale. Occasionally it can blow them up, but it is very difficult and leaves scars in the earth. And admitting their impermeability is the first step in their destruction. I am going to show you something that you can appreciate in any plex you like. We are going to talk to San Severina."

ten

"Is this one of the worlds she rebuilt with the Lll?" Jo asked, looking through the silver streets of the empty city, then back to the rolling woody hills that crept to the edge of the breeze-brushed lake behind them.

"This is one of them," said Oscar. "It's the first one finished and will be the last to be repopulated."

"Why?" Jo asked, stepping over the new cast-iron gutter grating on the curb. The bluish sun flamed in the spiral window that circled the great tower to their left. A magnificent fountain sat empty on their right. Jo ran his fingers over the dry, granite rim of the forty-foot pool as they turned past.

"Because she is here."

"How much work remains to be done?"

"All the worlds have been rebuilt. Forty-six of the civilizations have been reestablished. But it's those ethical systems that take time. They'll be in the works for another six months or more." Oscar gestured toward a black metal door, studded with brass. "Right through there."

Jo looked around at the tremendous spires. "It's beautiful," he said. "It really is. I think I understand a little more why she wanted to rebuild it."

"In here," Oscar said.

Jo stepped inside.

"Down these steps."

Their feet echoed in the dim, wide stairwell.

"Right through here." Oscar pushed open a smaller door in the gray stone wall.

As Jo stepped through, he wrinkled his nose. "Smells funn—"

She was naked.

Here wrists and ankles were chained to the floor.

When the gray blade of light fell across her humped back, she reared against the shackles and howled. Her lips pulled back from teeth he hadn't realized were so long. The howl stopped in a grinding rasp.

He watched her.

He watched himself watching her and watched himself back into the door and the door swing to and clank closed behind him.

Strain had caused the muscles of her shoulders to grow hard and defined. Her neck was corded, her shaggy, matted hair hung half across her face. *A comb!* he thought nonsensically. *Oh lord, a red comb!* And watched tears start in his real eye. The other grew crusty dry.

"They keep her here, now," Oscar said. "The chains are just short enough so she can't kill herself."

"Who—"

"There were twenty-six others, remember. Oh, she passed the point a long time ago where if she could release them, she would. But the others keep her here now, like this. And her Lll go on working."

"That's not fair!" Jo cried. "Why doesn't somebody turn her loose!"

"She knew what she was getting into. She told them before that they would have to do this. She knew her limitations." Oscar made a pained face. "Seven of them. That's more than any one person's ever owned at one time. It really *is* too much. And the sadness increases the more the Lll build. Geometrically. Like the price."

Jo stared at her, appalled, fascinated, torn.

"You came here to talk to her," Oscar said. "Go ahead."

Jo walked forward gingerly and watched himself do so. There were scabs on her wrists and ankles.

"San Severina?"

She pulled back, a constrained choking in her throat.

"San Severina, I've got to talk to you."

A thin trickle of blood wormed across the ligaments on the back of her left hand.

"Can't you talk to me? San Severina—"

With rattling links, she lunged for him, her teeth snapping on what would have been his leg had he not dodged back. She bit into her tongue and collapsed shrieking on the stone, her mouth awash with blood.

Jo only saw that he was beating on the door and Oscar was holding him. Oscar got the handle opened, and they stumbled into the bottom of the stairwell. Oscar was breathing hard too as they started up the steps. "I almost felt sorry for her," he said, halfway up.

Shocked, Jo turned to him on the stairway. "You don't . . ."

"I feel sorry for the Lll," Oscar said. "I am one, remember."

Jo watched himself begin to climb the steps again, carrying his own confusion. "I feel sorry for her," Jo said.

"Enough to join the army?" Oscar said.

"Jhup," Jo said. "Yes."

"I had hoped so."

As they stepped out of the upper door and onto the street again, Jo squinted in the light. "Ni Ty," he said after a moment. "He said he'd come to speak to San Severina a few days ago."

Oscar nodded.

"Here? He saw her like this?"

Oscar nodded again.

"Then he's done this too," Jo said. He started down the street. "I hope he made the sun."

"They couldn't put her to sleep with something or maybe hypnotize her?" Jo mused, staring through the glass wall back in the console room.

"When she goes to sleep, the Lll cease building," the Lump explained. "It's part of the contract. Ownership must be conscious ownership at all times, for the Lll to function."

"That's what I'd more or less figured. How can you even be sure she's conscious inside that . . . beast? Can anybody get through to her?"

"That beast is *her* protection," Lump explained. "Are you ready to leave?"

"As much as I'll ever be."

"Then I want you to take a complex statement with you that is further in need of multiplex evaluation: The only important elements in any society are the artistic and the criminal, because they alone, by questioning the society's values, can force it to change."

"Is that true?"

"I don't know. I haven't evaluated it multiplexually. But let me say, further, that you are going to change a society. You haven't got the training that, say, Ni Ty has to do it artistically."

"I'm already with you, Lump," Jo said. "Lump, where's the army going, anyway?"

"Empire Star," Lump told him. "Have you any idea what your first criminal action is going to be?"

Jo paused a moment. "Well, up until you told me what our destination was, it was going to be going AWOL. Now I'm not so sure."

"Good," Lump said. "Good-bye, Jo."

"Good-bye."

eleven

Almost immediately Jo decided he did not like the army. He had been on the ten-mile spaceship for three minutes, milling around with the other recruits, when Prince Nactor strode by. As the recruits stepped back, Prince Nactor saw Di'k. The devil-kitten was kicking his legs in the air and chirping. As Jo went to pick him up, Prince Nactor said, "Is that yours?"

"Yes, sir," Jo said.

"Well, you can't bring that aboard."

"Of course, sir," Jo said. "I'll take care of it right away."

With his expanded vision, there was no problem locating someplace on that battleship where he could hide Di'k. It had been reconverted a few years back, and a lot of the old equipment had been removed, to be replaced by more compact components. The old view-chamber which had housed the direct-contact photo-regenerator had been done away with, and the compartment on the glass-walled hull had been first used as storage for things that would never be needed, then sealed up.

Jo slipped away, swiped a croten-wrench from the maintenance cabinet, and found the sealed hatchway. He wrenched off the stripping, shooed Di'k through into the darkness, started to close the door, but got an idea. He went back up to maintenance, took an alphabetic stencil, a can of yellow paint, and a brush. Back at the hatch he lettered onto the door:

AUTHORIZED ENTRANCE
FOR J-O PERSONS
ONLY

He got back upstairs in time to be issued uniform and equipment. The quartermaster demanded his allowance card. Jo explained that he didn't have one. The quartermaster went to chew out the control computer. Jo went back down to the hatch and walked in. There was a small hallway, and the top of his yellow head brushed the ceiling and got dusty. Then he heard music.

He'd heard an instrument like that, a long time ago, back when he'd been a shuttle-bum. Ron's guitar. Only this was a guitar played differently, much faster. And the voice—he'd never heard a voice like that. It was slow, and rich as his ocarina.

He waited, tempted to look and see, but resisted. He heard the song through once, and the melody repeated, so he took his instrument and began to play with the singing. The singing stopped; the guitar stopped. Jo played to the end of the melody, then stepped out.

She was sitting on the floor in front of a pile of crystal blocks. The glass wall of the spaceship let in the white light of Tantamount. She looked up from her guitar, and the face—it was a beautiful face, fine-featured, dark, with heavy brown hair that fell to one shoulder—twisted in silent terror.

"What are you doing?" Jo asked.

She backed against the wall of crystal blocks, her hand flat on the blond face of the guitar, fingers sliding across the wood and leaving paths of glimmer on the varnish.

"Have you seen Di'k?" Jo asked. "A devil-kitten about so big, eight legs, horns? Came in about fifteen minutes ago?"

She shook her head hard, a violence in the motion that told him the negation was general and not connected with his particular question.

"Who are you?" he asked.

Just then Di'k stepped out from behind the crystal blocks, pranced in front of the girl, lay on his back, kicked his legs in the air, meowed, stuck his tongue out, and was, in short, perfectly engaging. Jo reached out and scratched Di'k's belly with his bare toe. He was still naked from the induction physical, and his uniform was over his arm.

The girl was wearing a white blouse that came up around her neck, and a dark skirt that came just below her knees. Whatever frightened her about him seemed to be behind his uniform, because she stared at it as though she were trying to see through it. He could see in the shifting muscles of her face the thoughts becoming more confused.

"I like your singing," Jo said. "You shouldn't be afraid. My name's Jo. What are you doing here?"

Suddenly she clamped her eyes, let the guitar fall face down in her lap, and clapped her hands on her ears. "Singing," she said quickly. "I'm just singing. Singing's the most important thing there is, you know. I'm not hurting anybody. No, don't say anything more to me. I refuse to answer any questions."

"You look pretty confused," Jo said. "Do you want to ask any?"

She shook her head, then hunched it down between her shoulders as if to avoid a blow.

Jo frowned, moved his mouth to one side of his face, then the other. He chewed the inside of his lip and said at last, "I don't believe you're really that simplex." She just crouched farther back against the crystal blocks. "You know, I'm not really a soldier."

She looked up. "Then why do you have the uniform?"

"See! You just asked one."

"Oh!" She sat up and put her hand over her mouth.

"I have the uniform because I came very close to being a soldier. I only have to wear it when I go outside. If it frightens you, I'll put it away." He tossed it over the crystal pile. The girl lowered her shoulders and visibly relaxed. "You're hiding from the soldiers," Jo said slowly. "If they find you, you'd prefer they thought you were simplex. Are you going to Empire Star too?"

She nodded.

"Who are you?"

She picked up the guitar. "I'd rather not say. It's not that I don't trust you. But the fewer people on this battleship who know, the better."

"All right. But would you answer another one, then?"

"Yes. All these soldiers under Prince Nactor are going to Empire Star to kill me, unless I get there first."

"That's not the answer to the question I was going to ask."

She looked dreadfully embarrassed.

"But I guess it's a pretty good one." Jo smiled.

She reached out to scratch Di'k's belly. "Someday I'll learn how to do that answer-before-you're-asked bit. It's so impressive when it comes off. I thought you were going to ask what this was all about."

Jo looked puzzled. Then he laughed. "You're hiding from the soldiers by staying under their noses! Very multiplex! Very multiplex!" He lowered himself cross-legged to the floor on the other side of Di'k.

"Also, if I go with them, it's fairly certain I won't get there *after* they do. At worst we'll arrive at the same time." She pursed her mouth. "But I've got to contrive some way to get there first."

Jo scratched Di'k too, and their fingers touched knuckles. He grinned. "Only I was going to ask you where you were coming from. I know where you're going and where you are now."

"Oh," she said. "Do you know Miss Perrypicker's?"

"Who?"

"Where. Miss Perrypicker's Finishing Academy for Young Ladies."

"What's that?"

"That's where I come from. It's a perfectly dreadful place where basically nice girls are taken from the best families and taught how to appear so simplex you wouldn't believe it."

"I didn't believe *you*," Jo said.

She laughed. "I'm one of Miss Perrypicker's failures. I suppose there's a lot there to enjoy—tennis, antigrav volleyball, water polo, four-walled handball—which is my favorite—and three-D chess. A few teachers did slip in who actually knew something. But singing and playing the guitar, which is what I really like to do, I picked up on my own."

"You do it very well."

"Thanks." She pulled from the strings a descending run of chords, opened her lips, and ejected a melody that rose on slow, surprising intervals that plucked sympathetic strings of pleasure, nostalgia, and joy that Jo had not felt since he had sung for the Lll.

She stopped. "That's a song the Lll made. It's one of my favorites."

"It's beautiful," Jo said blinking. "Go on, please. Sing the rest."

"That's all there is," she said. "Very short. Just those six notes. It does what it has to do, then stops. Everything that Lll make is very economical."

"Oh," Jo said. The melody was like a rainbow slick over his mind, calming, spreading.

"I'll sing anoth—"

"No," Jo said. "Let me just think about that one awhile."

She smiled and dropped her hand, silent, over the strings.

Jo's hand meandered over Di'k's stomach. The devil-kitten was snoring softly. "Tell me," Jo said, "why does Prince Nactor want to kill you at Empire Star?"

"My father is very ill," she explained. "I was called home suddenly from Miss Perrypicker's because it looks like he's going to die any day. When he does, I shall inherit the reins of the Empire—if I'm there. If not, Prince Nactor will seize them. We've been racing each other all the way."

"You're a princess of the Empire?"

She nodded.

"You must be pretty important," Jo said wonderingly.

"I won't be anything if I don't beat Nactor. He's been waiting for this for years."

"Why should you have them and not Nactor?"

"For one thing, I'm going to free the Lll. Prince Nactor wants to keep them under his protection."

"I see." He nodded and hugged his knees. "How are you going to do this, and why won't Nactor?"

"Economic," the girl said. "I have the support of the twenty-six richest men in the Empire. They trust me to deal with the matter multiplexually. They are waiting at Empire Star to hear what the outcome between myself and Nactor will be. They refuse to support Nactor, and all he's left with is the army. Although he is quite a multiplex man, he only has the one tool of force to pry with. If you only have one direction in which you can push, you might as well be simplex, whether you want to be or not. So they await me, assembled in the brass-columned council chamber, while the tessellations of the stained-glass windows cast their many shadows on the blue tiles, and somewhere in a crystal bed, my father lies dying . . ."

"Jhup," said Jo, impressed.

"I've never been there. I read about it in a novel by Muels Aranlyde. We all read his political trilogy at Miss Perrypicker's. Do you know his work?"

Jo shook his head. "Only . . ."

"Yes?"

"I think I have a message for them, there in the council chamber."

"You do?"

"That's why I'm going to Empire Star. I have a message to deliver, and I think I must be fairly close to delivering it."

"What is it?"

Jo let go of his knees now. "You're not anxious to tell me who you are; I think I'd best keep my message to myself until I get to the council chamber."

"Oh." She tried to look content, but curiosity kept struggling to the surface of her face.

"I'll tell you this," Jo said, half-smiling. "It concerns the Lll."

"Oh," she repeated, more slowly. Suddenly she rose up on her knees, leaning over her guitar. "Look, I'll make a deal with you! You can't get into the council chamber without my help—"

"Why not?"

"Nobody can. The great iris of energy that guards the chamber only opens to twenty-eight mind patterns—you better read up on it in your Aranlyde. Twenty-six of them are inside already. My father's dying, and I doubt if his is still recognizable. So there's just me left. I'll help you get into the council chamber if you help me beat Prince Nactor."

"All right," Jo said. "All right. That's fair. What sort of help do you need?"

"Well," she said, sitting back down. "You've got that uniform, so you can sneak in and out of here."

Jo nodded and waited for her to go on.

But she shrugged. Then looked questioningly. "That's something, isn't it?"

"You mean I have to figure out the rest," Jo said. "I'll try. What sort of help have you had already?"

"I've got a small computer running interference for me."

"I may be small," a voice said from beneath Jo's uniform where it lay over the piled blocks, "but I haven't reached my full growth yet."

"Huh?" Jo said.

"That's a Lump," the girl said. "He's a linguistic—"

"—ubiquitous multiplex," Jo finished. "Yeah. I've met one before." For the first time he realized that the haphazard crystals were logic-blocks. But there were surprisingly few. He'd been used to seeing them organized over the sixty-foot wall in the console room.

"It was his idea to hide out in the battleship."

Jo nodded, then stood. "Maybe," Jo said, "if everybody works together, we can muddle through this thing. Though I have a feeling it's going to be a little confusing. Say, one thing I've been meaning to ask. What planet around Empire Star are we going to?"

The girl looked very surprised.

"Well, we're not going inside the star itself, are we?"

Lump said, "I don't think he knows. You really should read Aranlyde."

"I guess he doesn't know," she said, and bit at a knuckle. "Should I tell him?"

"Let me."

"You mean people *do* live in the star?"

"People could," Lump said. "The surface temperature of Aurigae is less than two thousand degrees Fahrenheit. It's a very dim star, and it shouldn't be difficult to devise a refrigeration plant to bring that down to a reasonable—"

"They don't live inside," the girl said. "But there are no planets around Aurigae."

"Then where—"

"Let me. Please," the Lump repeated. "Aurigae is not only the largest star in the galaxy—hundreds of times the mass of Sol, thousands of times as big. But it is not just simply a star—"

"It's more complicated—" the girl began.

"Multiplicated," Lump said. "Aurigae has been known to be an eclipsing binary for ages. But there are at least seven giant stars—giant compared to Sol—doing a rather difficult, but beautiful, dance around one another out there."

"All around one point," the girl said. "That point is the center of Empire."

"The still point," said Lump, "in the turning world. That's an allusion. It's the gravitational center of that vast multiplex of matter. It's also the center of the Empire's power."

"It's the origin of the reins of Empire," the girl said.

"Can you imagine the incredible strain both space and time are subjected to at that point? The fibers of reality are parted there. The temporal present joins the spatial past there with the possible future, and they get totally mixed up. Only the most multiplex of minds can go there and find their way out again the same way they went in. One is always arriving on Wednesday and coming out again on Thursday a hundred years ago and a thousand light years away."

"It's a temporal and spatial gap," the girl explained. "The council controls it, and that's how it keeps its power. I mean, if you can go into the future to see what's going to happen, then go into the past to make sure it happens like you want it, then you've just about got the universe in your pocket, more or less."

"More or less," Jo said. "How old are you?"

"Sixteen," the girl said.

"Two years younger than I am," said Jo. "And how many times have you been through the gap at Empire Star?"

"Never," she said, surprised. "This is the first time I've ever been away from Miss Perrypicker's. I've only read about it."

Jo nodded. "Tell me—" he pointed toward the pile of logic-blocks—"is Lump there based on a Lll consciousness?"

"I say—" began the Lump.

"You know, you're really very gauche," the girl announced, straightening. "What possible difference could that make to you—"

"It doesn't," Jo said. He sighed. "Only I think this has all happened before. I also think I have a lot of things to tell you."

"What things?"

"What's he talking about?" Lump asked.

"Listen," Jo said. "It's going to take a bit longer to free the Lll than you think right now. You're going to have to undergo the unbearable sadness of Lll ownership yourself—"

"Oh, I would never own a—"

"You will," Jo said sadly. "You'll own more than anyone else has ever owned. That's probably the only way you will be able to free them." Jo shook his head. "There will be a war, and a lot of what you hold most beautiful and important will be destroyed."

"Oh, a war! With who?"

Jo shrugged. "Perhaps Prince Nactor."

"Oh, but even with war, I wouldn't—Oh, Lump, you know I wouldn't ever—"

"Many people will be killed. The economics will be such, I imagine, that the council and you will decide that purchasing the Lll is the only way to rebuild. And you will. You will have a great deal of sadness and worse to carry, both of you. But a long time from now, while what I am telling you about now is happening, you will run into a boy." Jo glanced at his reflection on the glass. "I was going to say that he looks like me. But he doesn't, not that much. His eyes—well, he doesn't have this glass thing in place of his right eye. His hands—he'll have claws on his left. He'll be a lot browner than I am because he's spent more time outside than I have recently. His speech will be almost unintelligible. Though his hair will be about the color of mine, it will be much longer and a mess—" Suddenly Jo reached for his pouch and dug inside. "Here. Keep this, until you meet him. Then give it to him." He handed her the red comb.

"I'll keep it," she said, puzzled. She turned it around to look at it. "If he speaks all that poorly, I can give him diction lessons in Interling. Miss Perrypicker was a real fanatic about diction."

"I know you can," Jo said. "Both of you, remember me, and when he comes to you, try and make him as much like me as you can. Here, you'll recognize him this way." He pointed to Di'k. "He'll have one of these for a pet. He'll be going to Empire Star like we are now, only by then you'll be going someplace else. He'll have a message to deliver, but he won't know what it is. He's very unsure of himself, and he won't understand how you can bring yourself to own such incredible creatures as the Lll."

"But *I* don't understand how—"

"By then you will," Jo said. "Reassure him. Tell him he'll

learn what his message is by the time he has to deliver it. He's a very insecure little boy."

"You don't make him sound very attractive."

Jo shrugged. "Perhaps by then your band of sensitivity will be broader. There'll be something about him—"

"You know," she said suddenly, looking up from the comb, "I think *you're* a very beautiful boy!" Then self-surprise and modesty contended for possession of her smile.

Jo broke out laughing.

"I didn't mean to . . . Oh, I'm sorry if I said any—"

"No!" Jo rolled back on the floor. "No, that's all right!" He kicked his feet in the air. "No, everything's perfectly all right." He rolled back to a sitting position. Then his laughter stopped.

She had twined her hands together, catching a fold of her skirt.

"I didn't mean to laugh at you," Jo said.

"It's not that."

He leaned forward. "Then tell me what it is."

"It's just that—well, since I left Miss Perrypicker's the weirdest things have been happening to me. And everybody I run into seems to know a bleb of a lot more about what's going on than I do."

". . . bleb?"

"Oh, dear. I didn't mean to say that either. Miss Perrypicker would have a fit."

"Eh . . . what exactly is *bleb*?"

She giggled and involuntarily hushed her voice as she leaned toward him. "It's what all the girls at Miss Perrypicker's *pick!*"

Jo nodded. "I get the general idea. You haven't been multiplex very long, have you?"

"I haven't. And up until a few weeks ago"—she pointed to Lump—"he was called Lusp."

"Really," Lump said, "you don't have to tell him *everything*."

"That's all right," Jo said. "I understand."

"I've been having so many adventures since I got started. And they all come out so weird."

"What sort of adventures?" Jo asked. "Tell me about them."

"The last thing was on the ship I was on before that one—I didn't have to hide there—there was a shuttle-bum who I was giving Interling lessons to. It turned out he had written the most marvelous poems. They completely changed my life, I think—sounds rather melodramatic, I know, and I suppose you wouldn't understand how. But anyway, he introduced me to Lump. Lump was a friend of his before he was a Lump. Lump says he got the idea of hiding in the battleship from him. Apparently an army had been after *this* boy, too, once, and—"

"Ni Ty had done it before?"

"How did you know his name?"

"I'm familiar with his poems," Jo said. "I understand how they changed your life. He lets you know how much of your life is yours and how much belongs to history."

"Yes. Yes, that's exactly how it struck me!" She looked into her lap. "And if you're a princess of the Empire, so much belongs to history there's hardly any left for you."

"Sometimes—" he reached into his pouch and took out his ocarina—"even if you're not. Play with me."

"All right," she said, and picked up her guitar.

They made a soft, climbing melody. Beyond the glass wall night sped by. It might as well have been still and listening, as the youngsters made their music and their ship hove forward.

"You look at me," she said at last, "as though you know so much about me. Are you reading my mind?"

Jo shook his head. "Just simplex, complex, and multiplex."

"You speak as though you know, too."

"I know that Lump there was based on Muels Aranlyde's consciousness."

She turned "Lump . . . you didn't tell me!"

"I didn't know. Ni Ty didn't tell me. He just told me I was Lll-based. He didn't say *which* Lll."

"And you're San Severina."

She whirled back. "But you said before that you didn't know—"

"And now I say I do."

"As time progresses," Lump stated, "people learn. That's the only hope."

Through the battleship wall the dark and flaming masses of the multiplex system of Empire Star were just visible.

San Severina went to the wall and leaned her cheek against the glass. "Jo, have you ever been through the time gap at Empire Star? Maybe that's why you know so much about the future."

"No. But you're going to."

She raised her head, and her eyes widened. "Oh, you'll come with me, won't you? I'd be scared to go alone!"

She touched his shoulder.

"Jo, do you know whether we'll win or not?"

"I only know that, win or lose, it will take longer than we think."

Her hand slipped down his arm and seized his. "But you will help me! You *will* help!"

He raised his hands and placed both of them on her shoulders. Her hand came up with his. "I'll help you," he said. Empire Star drew nearer. "Of course I'll help you, San Severina. How could I refuse after what you've done for me?"

"What have I done?" she asked, puzzled again.

"*Shhh*," he said and touched her lips with a finger. "If you ask questions that nobody can answer, you just have to wait and see."

Di'k hiccuped in his sleep, and Lump coughed discreetly. They turned to look at Empire Star again, and, from the protective socket of bone and flesh, I too looked, and saw much further.

I'm Jewel.

twelve

The multiplex reader has by now discovered that the story is much longer than she thinks, cyclic and self-illuminating. I must leave out a great deal; only order your perceptions multiplexually, and you will not miss the lacunae.

No end at all! I hear from one complex voice.

Unfair. Look at the second page. There I told you that there was an end and that Di'k, myself, and the ocarina were with him till then.

A tile for the mosaic?

Here's a piece. The end came sometime after San Severina (after many trips through the gap), bald, wrinkled, injured, healed, and aged a hundred years, was allowed to give up her sovereignty and with it her name and a good many of her more painful memories. She took a great 3-Dog for her companion and the name Charona and retired to a satellite called Rhys, where for five hundred years she had nothing more taxing to do than guard the gate of the Transport Area and be kind to children, which suited her old age.

Another tile? *Bleb* is water, picked drop by drop from the

leaves of lile-ferns at dawn by the girls of Miss Perrypicker's Finishing Academy for Young Ladies.

Oh, I could tell you good news and bad, of successes and defeats. Prince Nactor waged a war that charred eight worlds, destroyed fifty-two civilizations and thirty-two thousand three hundred and fifty-seven complete and distinct ethical systems, a small defeat. A great victory, now: Prince Nactor, through a chain of circumstances I leave you to deduce, fear-crazed, clammy with sweat, fled at midnight through the jungles of Central Park on Earth when Di'k yawned, emerged from behind a clump of trees, and stepped on him, quite by accident—Di'k having gained by then his adult size of fifty feet.

I have told you how San Severina, aged and bald and called Charona, first taught the child, Comet Jo, about simplex, complex, and multiplex under a place called Brooklyn Bridge on a satellite called Rhys. As well I could tell you how Jo, as old and as wrinkled and then called Norn, first taught the child San Severina the song they played together in the abandoned chamber of a battleship, on a world unnamed in this story so far—under a place called Brooklyn Bridge.

I could tell you how, at the final emancipation of the Lll, when the crowds silenced before the glorious music, a man named Ron, who as a boy had himself sung for the Lll while a shuttle-bum, tears quivering in the corners of his eyes, his throat half-blocked with emotion, both then and now, turned to the Lll standing next to him in the tremendous crush of people and whispered (indicating not only the straining attentions around him, and the incredible effect of the brief song, but as well the shattering culmination the emancipation represented) "Have you ever seen anything like it before?"

The Lll was silent, but the Oriental youngster standing by him shot back with shocking, subdued rage, "Yeah. *I* have!" and then to the Lll, "Come *on,* Muels, let's get *out* of here, huh?"

and the Lll and the boy began to push their way toward the edge of the crowd, to begin a journey as incredible as the one I have recounted, while Ron stayed there, open-mouthed, incredulous at the sacrilege.

A joyous defeat: When Prince Nactor burned Jo's body on the ice, blasted plains of the planet that circled Tantamount— joyous, because it freed Jo to be able to use many other bodies, many other names.

A tragic victory: When the Lump destroyed Prince Nactor's mind, only a few hours before the incident with Di'k in Central Park, by crashing his full growth—several times as big as we have seen him to date—into the Geodesic Survey Station, where Nactor had secreted his brain in an ivory egg flushed with nutrient fluid deep within the station—tragic, because the Lump too was finally destroyed in the collision.

Or I can tell you the very end, happening at the same time as the very beginning, when at last someone *had* come to free the Lll, and Comet Jo—still called Norn, then—Ki, Marbika, and myself were bringing the message from S. Doradus to Empire Star in an organiform, when suddenly the encycsting mechanism broke down and we went out of control. As the rest of us fought to save the ship, I turned for a moment and saw Norn standing at the front, staring out at the glittering sun at which we hurtled. He had begun to laugh.

Struggling to pull us back on course, I demanded, "And just what's so funny?"

He shook his head slowly, without looking away. "Did you ever read any of the poems of Ni Ty Lee, Jewel?"

As I said, this was at the beginning, and I hadn't yet. I wasn't crystallized then, either. "This is no time to discuss literature!" I shouted—even though a moment before the breakdown, he'd been patiently listening for hours as I had detailed a book I was intending to write.

Ki came swimming through the proto-photoplasm. "I don't think there's anything we can do." The light through the greenish jelly gleamed on his fear-stained face.

I looked back at Norn, who still hadn't moved, as the blot of illumination spread over the darkness. The laughter had stopped, and tears glistened on his face.

"There's a satellite," Marbika cried from the interior darkness. "Maybe we can crash-land—"

We did.

On a place called Rhys where there was nothing but a one-product simplex society with a Transport Area.

They died. I was the only one able to go on, though Norn gave the message over to someone else to carry, and I went with them to see that it was delivered—

Or have I told you this part of the story before?

I doubt it.

In this vast multiplex universe there are almost as many satellites called Rhys as there are places called Brooklyn Bridge. It's a beginning. It's an end. I leave to you the problem of ordering your perceptions and making the journey from one to the other.

—*New York City,*
Sept 1965